Diadem Dust

The Old War

Grant Dubbels

To Grandma,
Thanks for always encouraging me!

Love always,
Grant

Diadem Dust: The Old War

Copyright © 2018 by Grant Dubbels

All rights reserved.

Cover Art by Grant Dubbels

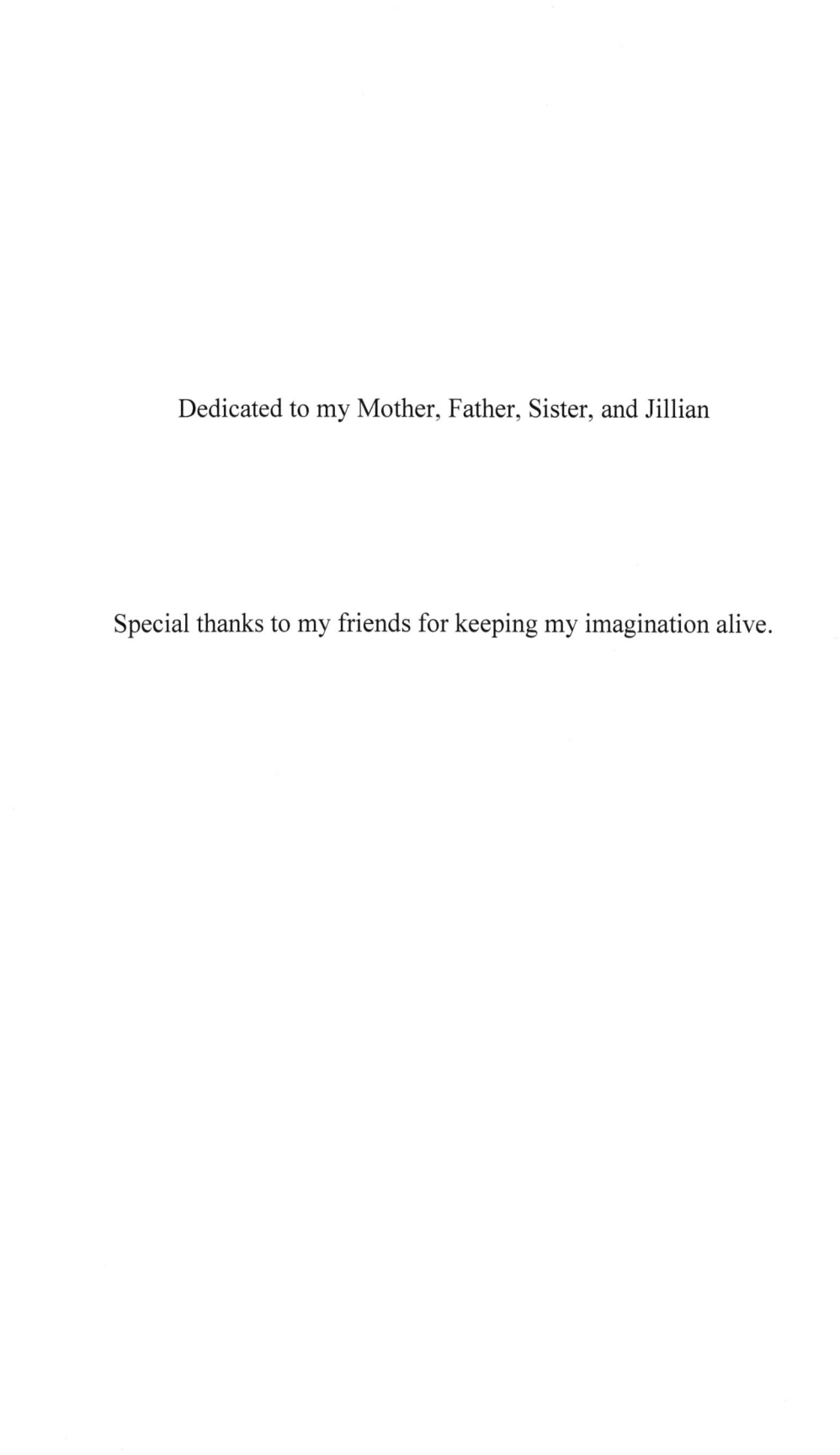

Dedicated to my Mother, Father, Sister, and Jillian

Special thanks to my friends for keeping my imagination alive.

Part I

Prologue

Desert warfare had made the castle at Coyote's Ball a monument to ruin. The moonlight glossed its stone surfaces, collapsed in places from battles past. The jagged cavities in the walls glinted like mouthfuls of broken teeth.

The night was spangled with stars: eternal fires of scarlet, violet, gold and aqua. This was the hour wild dogs emerged from their dens to haunt the scrublands. Their throaty calls mixed with humid winds for a desperate nocturne.

Tonight, howls came from *inside* the castle.

Aribol had his back to the wall and was beginning to feel quite sick. He had led three soldiers into his windowless room, a monkish cell with a wooden door. Charmingly claustrophobic, with only a broken cot and a desk flanking his shelf of brittle manuscripts.

The soldiers panted fearfully, turning the little dwelling into a sauna with their sour breath. But what made Aribol sick was the blood loss. It had cost him his left hand leading these men from the terror outside. He squeezed his stump under his armpit, but it was puddling beneath him all the same. He had dappled the floorboards with his blood and realized he had probably provided a trail for the predator outside.

They tried to keep silent and listened for any sound in the muted halls.

One of the soldiers turned a sweaty face at Aribol, pleading for one of his miracles. Aribol was a celebrated battlemage, after all. Wielding demon magic was his responsibility.

For the glory of Opagiel, he attempted a spell. He closed his eyes and could feel the underworld feed his soul on filaments of ecstasy. Yellow sparks darted between his fingers.

Chains rattled outside. All breathing paused. The lantern glowing on the desk was mirrored in the soldiers' trembling swords.

A loud hit bulged the door and made the ring handle jingle. The soldiers braced it with hands and arms.

Aribol suddenly had memories of his initiation.

He and other apprentices watched a demonstration in which a Kasurite man was lowered on a rope into a den of piglike beasts that walked on two legs and had wobbling stomachs.

The Kasurite man had appealed to every god he knew with teakettle screams as the things below made away with bites of his toes and legs.

It had been exhilarating for Aribol to see the intensity of justice. He remembered that the man had still been alive, still praying, by the time the beasts had erased his body to the ribs.

These soldiers reminded him of that Kasurite now. They were gibbering to Opagiel as their precious final moments fell away. They had that same white-hot needfulness in the way their lips peeled from their teeth.

One soldier shrieked. A sword point from outside had driven through his hand. It retracted, and he fell curled on the ground, pressing the dribbling palm.

There would be no help coming. Everyone else in the castle was dead. The thought was enough to weaken Aribol's concentration, and the energy at his fingers sputtered. It wouldn't be enough anyway. He had to laugh at just how completely everything was disintegrating.

The hinges split and nails hopped from their sockets. The door came loose, and the soldiers tried to push it back into place. Two slashes divided it into four large wooden triangles. The two standing soldiers took sword wounds that threw scarlet graffiti on the walls.

He was silhouetted, a half-naked madman with wrists and ankles married to broken chains. He pressed a bare foot onto the head of the soldier with the pierced hand. The skull broke, flooding the doorway in hot, black cranial blood.

It was all silent now. Aribol's spell had fizzled away completely, and the lantern flame mocked his plight with a merry little dance that jangled the shadows.

Aribol did not know much of the Civilic language. He had been taught to think it was the tongue of lesser peoples. But in this instance, he was able to manage one word.

"Please."

He had seen the chain on the attacker's left foot, but not the iron ball at the end of it. Indeed, he would never know exactly what hit him. It came on so quickly at the end of a kick that his thoughts, and his brains, were evicted from his skull hard enough to paint the desk. The lamp was covered in blood and cast a new, red light.

Chapter 1

Taran hated the sun today. The gaudy, bronze light illuminated him for the failure he had become.

Still, he watched the dawn. He promised his sister he would never miss another one. She had died two hours ago, in the night, from a wound that had refused to clot. She had insisted he take the blanket he wore now and dismissed him after that. Kafra was secretive, even for an assassin, and didn't want anyone to see her die. The blanket was still damp in places where her wound had soaked it.

Breece, who probably slept as miserably as Taran, was already digging in the sand behind the tents. His huge pink shoulders were ready for more sunburn. The long bundles that used to be his friends lay next to him. It wouldn't do to delay their respects.

Taran could hear his people waking up. He raised his cupped palms to the sky. It was a prayerful gesture, that the gods might pour strength and wisdom into his upstretched hands. He smoothed the invisible gift over his dark brown face and got up. It was time to be a leader.

His army that once filled a fortress city to capacity now occupied two long tents, a few pavilions, and a smattering of cone tents. Breakfast was being put on the fires, and the husky smell of broth was in the air. Metal workers clanged at their benches, trying to salvage punctured armor pieces.

They were established in the curve of a dry river bed. Taran had chosen it for the secrecy it would provide, which was hard to come by in such a sheer desert land as Sudel. One could see how ancient animals had left the imprint of their bones on the rocks and boulders. Taran wondered if any of his buried mates would be immortalized like that.

He entered one of the long tents, where a sweating Federal woman in green leather gear wielded a red-hot iron rod. She knelt over a miserable looking man with a stomach wound, and she put the edge of her free hand between his teeth.

With the sound of sizzling flesh and sweat, she cauterized him. He couldn't move much, but he bit down hard enough to squeeze blood from her hand. She did not seem to mind.

"Sidna, is it? Where is your leader?" Taran asked her. She blew a strand of red hair off her face and arranged some of her apothecary items.

"Good morning, Taran. I think he's out back." Her voice had no business sounding so chipper, but it dropped off then. "Taran, I wanted to tell you I'm sorry. About Kafra."

"No, your diligence has been a blessing. Thank you."

"Of course. We're on your side, you know!"

Taran set his blanket down and hiked up his stitched slacks before exiting.

Caethys Cavawix had smooth, innocent skin the color of rich java and a stenciled goatee around his mouth. His hair was shaved close to his scalp, and every color of autumn kaleidoscoped in his eyes.

The young corporal had the sort of city-softened looks Taran usually detested in non-Archaic peoples. But this was a comrade he was approaching. Caethys and his squad mates had saved them no small amount of trouble by scouting, sharing provisions, and settling camp while his talented soldier Sidna worked as healer.

Caethys broke away from a few of his green-uniformed men next to the horses and saluted Taran in the traditional way: a fist on the palm and a slight bow.

"Master Taran. How is your wound?" the corporal said.

Taran had stitched together a spear wound on his own hip. After he was satisfied it wouldn't bleed anymore, he had promptly forgotten about it. He bumped his fist against it, and his nerves rang out.

"Well enough, I think," he said in a burnt-out tone. "Are your men holding up?"

"Ah. Two of my eight died, I'm afraid," Caethys said quietly.

Taran wasn't good with feelings, generally. He turned his gaze from Caethys to watch Breece across the camp shovel sand over his wide, sweaty back.

"I'm sorry, Corporal. If only we had had more medicine." It was the best Taran could manage.

"The way they were wounded, I fear they might have elected to die anyway." Caethys darted his eyes around, trying not to think of what he had witnessed last night. "My friend, what happened down here? We were told you were winning the south. That you were ten thousand men strong."

"We were." Shame, anger, then sadness took turns on his mouth. He didn't seem interested in speaking about it anymore. "You still want to see him?"

"Please. I'll need confirmation."

Taran brought Caethys to a pavilion made out of dark animal hide. It was tall and ominous, like an old cathedral. On the curtain rods, Archaics had strung up garlands of dried herbs. At the foot of the door were brass incense bowls speckled with ash and wooden carvings of a bearded man.

The beaded curtain jangled as Taran led Caethys into the dark chamber. The desert sun strained through the tent walls, splotching a large figure on the table in broken orange.

An old linen barely covered the body and face of Old Bear Kronin. He was indescribably huge, and an uncovered arm showed he was possessed of angelic strength. Mountainous, veiny muscles terminated in a hand with fingers as hard and thick as a reptile's legs.

For all the superstitious rumors of Kronin, there was an earthiness to his corpse. His arm skin looked haggard and rough. An oath of poverty kept all but a single iron ring on his index finger.

Taran cut the funerary silence. "I know. I didn't think he could be killed either."

"Not a good year to put faith in prophets, is it?"

"Not unless you're a Septunite. They call Thel a prophet. I guess he'd have to be."

"Who's Thel?"

Taran looked at the body of Kronin. "The one who did this."

Caethys had wanted to meet Kronin since he was a child. Most Kasurite warriors did, Archaic and Federal alike. It was a sickening honor to see him dead.

"I'll give you a moment. Then come have some breakfast." Taran whisked open the curtain. "Hope you're not terribly hungry."

Caethys was left alone with Kronin, who had been called an Anthrome, a half-angel. He was human enough to die, apparently.

He thought to touch Kronin's hand, to fulfill a childhood goal, but decided not to. This was no longer Kronin. This was dust, and touching it had no meaning. Instead, he reached for the oathkey on his own necklace and kissed it to open talk with the Paragon.

"Make room at thy table, Lady Tethra. Worthy company comes your way."

***

The Siegebreakers had made their mark in the history books. They were victims turned avengers, building a military state on the bones of the Septunite invaders. Seasons of glory made them the lords of Sudel.

Now, the Siegebreakers were a haunted handful of walking skins. Hope had become a crime, and these barbarians had been penalized for every bit of it. But Taran was being vague about details, so as they took breakfast, Caethys tried to get some answers out of Breece. The round, red-bearded brute was late to breakfast and scraped the bottom of the cauldron with the ladle grumpily when Caethys approached.

"Here." The corporal poured his own potato stew into Breece's bowl, and the man beamed like a child.

"Ho! This is a nice Federal. My thank you." He bounced a fist off Caethys's shoulder. Civilic was quite obviously not his first language, and his accent was thick. But Caethys was in his graces now.

"Can I ask a question, Mister Breece?" Caethys said. Breece hummed a little as he slurped from the bowl, dirtying his mustache. "Kronin had a friend before he died. Kaiser. Where is Kaiser?"

"Oh, my good Kaiser." Breece wiped his mouth sadly. "I think my good Kaiser is dead."

Caethys had expected as much, and it made him want to kick over the stew pot. But a classical Federal upbringing reduced his outrage to a sigh.

"Are you sure? He is really dead?"

"Mm. They kill Kronin, and Kaiser fight and fight." Breece made chopping motions with his free hand. "But they make him with chains. How you say?"

"Chains. They captured him?"

"Yes, yes. They capture him to a castle. In Coyote's Ball, there is big castle. Kaiser is in castle."

Given the utmost of the Septunite Synod's mercy, Kaiser's bones would be roasting in a dungeon kiln by now. Caethys had lost two men crossing the battlefields of the south. Now he had to cross them back, with nothing to show for it.

Chapter 2

Having donated his stew, Caethys took breakfast in the form of a trail ration. They were dried wafers made from queen toadstools that were as nutritious as they were rubbery. One of the best investments Caethys ever made was a jar of pepper jelly that made the things edible.

He was grinding a bit of it in his mouth when he spotted Sidna in the shade of the healer's tent. She had fallen asleep with her head on a rolled-up blanket. Probably spent the whole night working on the wounded. Caethys took a quiet seat next to her. She snorted awake anyway.

"Oi," she mumbled drowsily, gesturing to the tent with her thumb. "Got 'em all stitched up."

Caethys didn't say anything, just scratched her lightly behind the ear. There was scar tissue in that spot that she itched when she was nervous, and he had learned to do it himself to both embarrass and comfort her.

"We leaving soon?" She yawned into her sandy palm.

Caethys ignored the question. "The Apogee knew about these two for years. And they finally sent us here just days after they were assassinated. It's such a waste I could just be sick." He was slapped on the leg by Sidna, who sat up.

"Buck up, Cae. We haven't lost the war yet. There's no telling those two were as good as they say anyway." She gave Caethys a sleepy look. "I mean, Kronin, a half-angel? Really?"

"The church has confirmed that they exist."

"Lots of people claim to be Anthromes. Like my cousin in prison." Sidna grabbed a drinking gourd next to her and uncorked it.

"Don't, Sid. We need to save our water for the ride back." He put a palm to it.

"Heh, this isn't water," she explained and pulled deeply. When she stopped, Caethys could smell the harsh lome on her breath. It was a medicine-turned-liquor that originated in Sidna's home province. "So . . . back north empty-handed then?"

"Well, it won't help to bring back corpses."

"This one was out of your hands, Cae," she tried, but she could see his thoughts play with the muscles in his face. She thought about saying more, or offering some drink, but knew both would avail nothing.

Caethys stood from the shade and craned his neck, letting the bones pop softly. His colorful eyes squinted against the fattening sun and spotted something beyond the squalor.

A figure was walking down the sandy trench, the winds cloaking him in sand. Barbarians in the camp began pointing and gathering.

Some soul had severed its humanity to escape hell, it seemed. Dungeon trappings were locked over the man's face. Except for this and his grimy slacks, he was unclothed and barefoot. His body was a canvas of pain, a dusty trunk drizzled with the blood of the unforgiven. A gore-slimed sword and hatchet occupied his hands.

Caethys wondered if this was some attack. The figure assessed him with eyes the color of molten gold but continued into the barbarian mob. A clinking sound directed Caethys's attention to shackles on his wrists and ankle.

Taran had been sitting with a few others when he noticed. He moved to identify the visitor. Never one for gambling, he kept his sword belted on.

Caethys was unsure how to act. Nobody was speaking. Only the crunch of sand could be heard as the barbarians made way.

"Kaiser . . ." Taran halted the figure and approached alone. He could see that Kaiser carried his weapons in white-knuckled hands. Golden eyes behind the iron mask quaked on the brink of murder.

"Damn, those are craethune weapons," Sidna whispered to the corporal. "That drug-metal will play hell on his mind."

The Cypolonian lived, but it didn't feel prudent to celebrate yet, Caethys felt. A hand clenched his shoulder before he could step in. It was Breece.

"Must wait. Kaiser want kill everyone now," he warned, pointing to his forehead with a meaty finger. "Kaiser, eh, his head full."

"His head is full? Full of what?" Caethys asked.

"Red Rapture," came the half-whispered answer. "Red Rapture make you strong, make you dangerous. Make you want kill, kill, kill. Kaiser now try not hurt Taran."

"Kaiser . . ." Taran avoided any menacing gestures. He'd brought men out of the Red Rapture before, but the craethune sickness might have complicated it. "It's all right, my friend." Kaiser's trembling became more apparent, as though the voice aggravated him, but Taran tried again. "Easy . . ."

A flinch. Teeth chattered behind the mask. Moments dripped by until the weapons slipped to the sand.

Kaiser exhaled like a furnace and relaxed his shoulders. Taran coached Kaiser with whispers, scratching his sandy back. Quietly, the two broke away.

***

Caethys waited behind the leader's tent for an audience. An awning shaded his little nook among iron pots, rolled furs, jars, barrels, rope, and a crusty wooden trunk that looked too decrepit to sit on.

Next to the trunk, a bouquet of weapons glinted out of a broken barrel. Caethys walked over and discerned the arms carefully for the third time. These were probably the weapons of dead men. Barbarians treasured the weapons of the deceased, believing their strength was imbued in them.

"Corporal?" Caethys couldn't help but look surprised when he turned to find Kaiser trudging to meet him.

With the blood-sludge cleaned away and the dungeon mask removed, Kaiser presented a more scholarly expression than Caethys expected. He had a tall, philosopher's forehead and studious eyes which held a browner shade of gold than before.

Caethys had also expected a barbarian warlord to boast incredible size, but Kaiser was only a little larger than him. Nevertheless, his arm muscles looked fanatically developed toward ending life, like stones jostling under his skin. He had put on a sheepherder's jacket with the sleeves cut away. Under one arm was a pair of boots and a medicine box.

"Yes, and you are the Cypolonian 'Tireless Butcher,' right? I can't say I've heard of Cypolon," Caethys answered.

Chapter 3

Kronin was a king among warriors. So while other corpses were allowed to lay, scrub trees, cloth scraps, and other broken items were sacrificed to make a pyre for his body.

Sandy breezes snatched sparks from the pyre, and Kronin's body nestled deeper, flames dissolving his remains with reverent leisure.

The glow made harvest moons of the circling barbarian faces. The invisible fire of their own grief did little in the way of altering their expressions. Perhaps if the blaze had not been snapping, the squeak of grinding teeth could have been heard.

Kaiser stood at the head of the pyre, torch in hand. He kept his eyes closed, calmly digesting the events. His unreleased tears seemed to flow into the veins of his forearms.

"I've been to too many funerals this month, Cae," Sidna whispered in the glow. She and the rest of the Federals decided to take a position outside the ring. Barbarian nature was still somewhat alien to Sidna, and their silence unnerved her. She sweated in her armor, watching angry men restrain themselves.

It was curiosity that kept Caethys quiet. In his boyhood he had mimicked Archaics in games with his friends. They would beat their chests and play-kill everyone with sticks. This hallowed spectacle complicated his assumptions.

And Kronin vanished into the blaze, his monumental life that had colored the dreams of a million fighting men finally finished in the deserts of Sudel.

Word of Kaiser's coming departure spread quickly. Even dying men emerged from the healer's tent, crawling on all fours to protest. The Cypolonian, like Kronin, had been their rock, and they were not prepared to lose him too.

"I remember when Kronin and I first walked the wreckage of the south," Kaiser was saying as the men gathered. He held Kronin's urn under his arm. "One by one, we pulled you out of the dirt. Everything that held meaning to you was on the end of a noose."

The barbarians looked equally liable to rush Kaiser with fists or just collapse. Their tongues were overloaded, but they owed their leader some silence.

"There isn't one among us who hasn't thought of ending it all, of abandoning this sick, sick world. But for a moment, each of you had the courage to admit there was need beyond your suffering. Together, we began new lives with new purpose. And by the gods, we were men again."

"Why can't we hold fast, Kaiser?" Taran interjected. "Why should we splinter now? Why not die as a family?"

"Dying is too easy," Kaiser answered. "A warrior endures. We built a second life, and that too has been smashed to pieces. The Siegebreakers are finished."

Blasphemy?

"It doesn't matter how much it hurts. The people don't need us to die, they need us to fight," Kaiser went on. Some of the men took a knee, knuckling their foreheads. "You will always be my brothers. Always. But it is time to begin another life. Leave the title of Siegebreaker behind, it will only garner the attentions of assassins. I want you all to leave when you can and share your talents with a new house," Kaiser said as he packed the clay urn in a hemp sack at the horse's flank.

Caethys's bowels were knotting with guilt. These fighters had given so much, and he was taking their most valued asset in Kaiser, who climbed from the stirrup to be seated on one of the dead Federal's horses. The whites of the creature's eyes flared a bit, startled at this strange new burden.

"If we ever meet again, I expect tales of triumph." The Cypolonian pulled his horse away but halted for a moment. "Thank you all, for everything you've done."

Very slowly, the rest of the barbarians dispersed when Taran stepped in front of Kaiser's horse.

"You go to serve the Apogee, eh?" Taran asked bluntly.

"Possibly. What will you do now, Taran?"

"What can I do, Kaiser? My place was at your side! I have no clan, I am nothing!"

"You can't possibly believe that!" The Cypolonian scowled ghoulishly. "Your honor is yours, I just told you where to gain it. A hundred men couldn't match your courage, so find your way and let others learn from it."

Taran was accustomed to relinquishing arguments to his leader, but in his anxiety he ventured further debate. "Will it amount to anything? In the end?"

"I don't know, friend. But it's worth finding out." Kaiser tightened an oiled leather strap so snugly that his horse groaned.

"What are you going to do up north?"

"Get stronger." Kaiser pulled a length of brown fabric from his pocket and tied it around his forehead. "We had a good run, didn't we?" He asked, settling honey-colored eyes on his companion.

"That we did," Taran agreed. "I suppose you should have this, knowing your agenda." He unsnapped some straps at his hip and removed a flat, circular vial of oil. Across the face of the glass was etched feathers arranged in a circle: the symbol of the Covenant gods. Taran gave the blessed oil to Kaiser, who smiled in gratitude.

"Good luck, old friend." The Cypolonian smiled at him and set his mount on a stable trot toward the Federal riders.

Caethys and his squadron led Kaiser north with tan puffs dissolving behind them. Taran watched as his friend of a thousand adventures shrank into the barrens.

A slap on the shoulder from Breece startled Taran.

"Much to do, yes?" Breece had a limited vocabulary.

"There always is," Taran admitted.

Breece smiled. "Come, then. We not getting younger."

***

At Caethys's command, the party rode briskly the first several days. The horses were exhausted upon exiting Sudel and slowed to an easy trot.

Canyons rose out of the sands now. Vultures hovered along the cliffs. This was the way Caethys had come before, and he pointed at landmarks, talking to himself.

"It's unlikely we'll run into Septunites this time. Archaic houses keep these cliffs well defended," Caethys explained as they rode.

"They would be better guardians against the Septunites if they didn't have to worry about Dragnos." Sidna spat.

"So many people hate this Dragnos Cawn character. Why is that?" Kaiser asked. A few of the corporal's men looked at Kaiser with disbelief. Sidna's eyes doubled in size.

"He's a war pig. He profits from killing countrymen," she replied.

"Do tell."

"There's not a warlord in Kasurai as powerful as Dragnos," Caethys interjected. "Sidna's contempt for him is justly given. He pillaged her childhood city on more than one occasion."

"He's got an army strong enough to repel the Septunites from the north, but no. He waits until states are weak from battle, then swoops in to steal what he pleases and spit on our dead." Sidna twisted the reins until they squeaked.

Kaiser mutely nodded. He would have had more talk, but something in the scrub grass arrested his gaze. Bones. Human. Bleached white in the sun.

"It was just south of this place that Septunites fell upon us and fatally wounded two of my men. We should be safe for a few days," the corporal figured.

Humps of sand suddenly hatched brown-skinned warriors, spilling dust from angry muscles. They wore nothing above their waists but spiked armlets, pauldrons, and kettle helms. In their fists were great cleavers looking more suited to an ogre's slaughterhouse.

The highwaymen surrounded them. Caethys raised his right hand as a signal for his men to remain calm. Sidna habitually gripped her crossbow. These were not Septunites, but barbarians, like the former Siegebreakers. But unlike them, these men were loyal to a house, and houses were territorial.

"What do they want?" Sidna whispered to Caethys.

"Let them speak," he answered. A man with forward-sweeping horns on his helmet approached. His saw-toothed scimitar looked heavy and dangerous. He eyed the stylish green armor and Federal seals of the riders without emotion.

"These lands are claimed by Magnate Keltheo. What business does the Apogee have here?" he asked, black beard jingling with brass.

"Hail, men of House Keltheo," Caethys answered with a salutary nod. "Some days ago, we followed a southerly path down these leagues. With your consent, we'll cross King's Canyon again, returning to our capital in peace."

"I cannot allow you to go any farther." The sentinel shook his head, horns whirling heavily. "These lands are off limits to outsiders. You may be spies of another house, or even Septunites, masquerading as Federals."

It caused a stir among the riders, most of all Caethys. Men who knew the corporal knew he would vent for that insult later.

"Comrade," Caethys began, offense giving him confidence. "My party could not be more opposed to Septunoth."

"I believe you, Federal. But duty trumps instinct. You must go instead around to Old Guard's Pass." At this command, Caethys's mouth dropped.

"You cannot be serious," he argued. "It would prolong our journey by weeks."

"Pity, but Keltheo's mandate stands. Do not attempt to sneak through. You will not be forgiven a second time."

"You obstruct a Federal effort?" Caethys asked with hollow authority.

"Stay close to the canyon walls." The horned sentinel pointed with his sandy weapon, ignoring the corporal's desperation. "Crest the tree line until you find Old Guard's Pass."

Crushed, Caethys veered his steed to the side, where the broad-shouldered barbarians lumbered out of the way. The other riders followed.

It wasn't until they were out of earshot from the barbarians that Caethys sounded his contempt.

"A fine mess they've made of things, the fools. These houses and their shifting powers. This will be someone else's desert in a week, mark me," Caethys snarled.

"Unless they're desperate, Archaics are too proud to work with anyone outside their houses," Kaiser agreed.

The following morning, the seven riders took their rations of bread and dried fruit on a sandy ridge. Caethys rose from his pack with renewed confidence.

"Right, listen. The Potentate expects our timely return. Old Guard's Pass will delay us too long. I've decided a shorter route through the Quane is more appropriate." At this, chewing cheeks paused and sleepy eyes raised in the glow of the low morning fires.

"The Quane . . ." Kaiser noted the apprehension as he lay on his side, nursing a tin cup of coffee.

"Ever been there?" Sidna asked Kaiser, who shook his head. "Greatest and oldest forest in the world. Makes the Apogee look like a spring chicken."

"It's dangerous, I know. So, this one time, I will open the floor to argument." Caethys was quick to rein in the melancholy.

Only one man, Jonos, chanced words. He was several years older than Caethys and often voiced his grievances as if to assert some sort of seniority. Rising to his top-heavy stature, he sleeved some crumbs from his lips.

"Corporal, let us take Old Guard's Pass. It'll cost sweat, but we'll save blood. Our ancestors drove the monsters of the world into that place so that they could be forgotten. It would be a damn fool thing to put ourselves in their reach again." Everyone's head turned to see Caethys's reaction.

"For a squad of lesser experience, it would be foolish. But Sidna and I have both made the pilgrimage into the Quane as initiates. It's how I earned my oathkey." Caethys tapped the silver item hanging at his neck.

"Corporal, with respect, it's too risky," Jonos went on. "I can't. I won't."

"Soldier, Septunites would imperil our route if we took Old Guard's Pass anyway. We may as well save time."

"Stranger, you agree with me, don't you?" Jonos asked to Kaiser's blankness. "This is the jaws of the earth we're talking about."

The corporal seemed the picture of confidence when Kaiser glanced over his steaming beverage.

"Don't get so excited. The corporal knows what he's doing." Kaiser shrugged.

The flatness of the Cypolonian's statement sedated Jonos, but he sat without the customary salute. It was his own reserved method of protest. Caethys gave him no more notice, because the last time he had to, Jonos had assaulted him, and the corporal had him jailed for a lenient three days.

Hot winds punched at the riders for their intrusion. Caethys hitched the horses together, for voices couldn't rise above the blind noise, and stragglers wouldn't be found until the sandstorm passed.

They were all pelted the same dusty gray brown when Caethys had led them into calmer, greener hills. The horses were up to their chests in high grass by the time they took their noontime rations. A steady gallop ensued until they made a mossy cliff late in the afternoon.

The Quane loomed ahead. Her trees were titans that pierced the clouds. The highest branches had taken on a drooping whiteness in the frigid temperatures above. Smaller trees grew on the larger ones like mushrooms, and massive leaves danced forever in the air thousands of feet above.

"You've done this before, have you?" Kaiser asked, impressed at the scenery.

"If Caethys can find the same river we followed here, we're good as gold. The darkness is the worst part. It sort of . . . gets to you," Sidna replied.

"I pray we find the river quickly. A single wrong turn could put a bad strain on our food supply, Corporal," Jonos reminded his leader, who was too busy weaving a course in his head to be bothered.

"Food won't be a problem. Hell, Jonos, just one of your legs would feed us for two days." Sidna started poking at her compatriot's thigh before he swung his horse off.

"You red-haired devil."

"Right, I expect a little backbone from all of you." Caethys netted them with his polished tenor. "I won't tolerate lack of composure. We represent the Potentate wherever we go, even here."

The riders were in the canopy's shadow long before they reached the threshold. Huge leaves like leather rugs rolled under their hooves as they neared the roots resembling fat, aged serpents. A prehistoric musk rolled out to meet them, and the horses waggled their heads for the chokingly sweet odors.

"You're fine, Misty, hush . . ." Caethys cooed his mount, scratching its flaxen mane, but even his neck prickled at the scent. Kaiser turned slowly to the corporal.

"Misty?" The Cypolonian earned a flush from Caethys, who pretended not to hear.

"How long do you suppose this will take, Cae?" Sidna asked with an arched cinnamon eyebrow.

"Four or five days should bring us to the north side of the Quane's little arm," he responded. She promised him with a nose scrunch that she would not disclose to the men the dark days they had spent here lost, hungry, and hunted.

Chapter 4

The riders could feel a thousand eyes assess their warm bodies. Caethys felt validated for being frugal with the torches. The bridge-like roots they crossed were either slick, brittle, or spiraled in thorns. There was no telling how long an injured horse ankle could delay them here, where daylight was forgotten.

They were seven little glows bouncing along in the black heat. Jeweled in sweat, a strange forest breath still prompted gooseflesh on their necks as downy spores drifted around them.

At the end of the first day, they took shelter under huge drooping fronds like serrated whale tongues. The packs were rolled out among the soft fiddleheads.

Caethys wanted to study his map more, but the fire needed constant tending in this damp abyss, and he took first watch. Torches had to be conserved at rest hours and losing their only light source wasn't something he needed on his conscience.

He hated his past self for inking such a vague map. The deep darkness made rediscovering landmarks impossible. Caethys closed his fist around his oathkey necklace as if to strangle his doubt. He was an elite soldier, a student of the holy arts, an accomplished spy, and most importantly, a professional explorer. No reason to doubt.

Kaiser, who had elected to stay awake with the corporal for first watch, suddenly crossed the campsite to separate Caethys from his thoughts.

"Mind if I get some exercise?" He gestured to a cavity in a giant tree just outside the range of the firelight.

"Very well. But no farther," Caethys replied, feeling the dryness of his eyes for the first time that night.

Later, Caethys folded away the map and crawled over to Sidna. She snorted awake and assumed second watch, red-eyed and picking leaves from her hair. Before Caethys retired, he took stock of his men and counted Kaiser still missing.

The corporal went to the hollow tree. It was like an amphitheater, high shelves of glowing blue mushrooms spectating the practicing Cypolonian.

Kaiser's sword streamed orange light as it sailed in his veteran hands. His style was brutish, bullying even, but quick enough to be beautiful. It looked to be a great drain on stamina. But then, Kaiser's follow-through looked liable to break steel armor.

The sword's fiery aura marked him as a user of primal magic. Caethys would have been able to tell if it were holy light on the weapon, and it most certainly were not. Primal magic was the obvious choice for any warrior who treasured fury. The way Kaiser tore apart his imagined enemies, it was apparent he did.

Seeing no reason to interrupt just yet, Caethys quietly returned.

Kaiser's mind, so used to contemplating the future of the Siegebreakers, was left open-ended tonight and began wandering. The sweat running into his eye annoyed him enough to take a knee and think about the past few years . . .

Leaves breezed up the splintered mountain crags. They drifted apart handfuls at a time, falling to rest in piles of green stone.

Only one leaf rose to the grass swaying at the peak. It skittered along the weeds, cartwheeling suddenly over a set of fingers.

Emerging from a weird slumber, Kaiser's eyes opened. The sky above was a vortex of clouds tattooed with fiery colors. To the west, tangles of lightning cast sapphire against a burning dusk.

The Cypolonian sat up to find decrepit armor still latched over his body. He ran his fingers across the burst metal at his chest and found the belted mail at his thighs in as much disrepair.

He was calm, not knowing so much as feeling that he was right where he should be. However, this place, this time, even swaths of his past were mysteries to him. He had been smitten with amnesia, but his instincts assured him that all was well enough.

A broken sword rested next to him. Pieces of the blade were winking in the grass with flakes of his armor. He took the weapon, more knife now than sword. Perhaps it could still be used to fend off mild dangers.

When his faculties allowed, he stalked down the dark side of the mountain. Lured by the whisper of water, he navigated the shadows to a splattering little brook. He kneeled and cupped enough draughts to blunt his thirst.

Other sensations pleaded for notice. Above the music of the water, he could hear a hurricane of distant voices. He crept to the edge of the mountain wood, holding his fractured sword downward like a dagger and peered into the fields.

Hundreds of mud-splashed warriors shook the hills with their armored strikes, waging some brutal battle in the sunset. Kaiser could not tell what or even how many nations were involved, but it was clearly a more organized force against tribal fighters.

The organized force in their black casings seemed to be winning, leaving enemies in stained mounds. But there was a stretch in the carnage-strewn plains where things fared differently.

An old warrior in heaps of iron armor crushed several enemies at a time with a war hammer whose head must have weighed as much as two men. He scattered their bodies into chunks as his white beard and locks swayed like the fur of an arctic predator.

Engrossed, Kaiser wasn't particularly sure what to do. Then, something about the emblems on the dark soldiers' breastplates engaged him.

They were images that would earn Kaiser's ire until the end of days, vaguely feminine demon faces with bizarre jaw structures like a centipede and horns that stretched straight from either side of the oblong head.

The Cypolonian had found enemies, that much he knew. Half memories resurrected a vampiric hatred that quickly dictated his course. Keeping his broken sword in one hand, Kaiser reached up to a branch. With an effort that made his wrist veins bulge, he cracked the solid club of wood from the tree and made to enter the battle.

***

Caethys and his party trekked a day, or what they assumed was a day, deeper into the gloom. Rodents retreated from their passing, while stranger beings floated away in weird, pumping flights.

The Federals seldom spoke to Kaiser, but he didn't seem to mind. As others settled down for camp that night, Kaiser contented himself with watching the fire. He had Kronin's ash urn sitting next to him.

Friendly by nature, Caethys decided it was worth lifting a little mystery from the quiet warrior.

"Well, Kaiser." Caethys tried to think of something to talk about. It was likely the Cypolonian would stay up for first watch again; he was a light sleeper.

"Everything in order, Corporal?"

"I . . . your weapon there. I was just admiring it," Caethys ventured. Kaiser grabbed the sheathed weapon and handed it to him. The burnished cross guard was severely geometric, but cultured in its own way, with a hilt bound in maroon leather.

"Have a look. I call her Seriath."

Kasurites did not hand off their weapons freely, but then, Kaiser was no Kasurite. Caethys saw this as a gesture of trust. He gripped the hilt and pulled the naked steel from the scabbard.

"Does the name mean anything?"

"In Cypolonian, Second Chance."

The blade was liquid smooth, tattooed with tribal stripes up the face. Saw teeth were rendered on the middle edge for catching and turning enemy blades.

"If I'm not mistaken, the metal is . . ." Caethys trailed off, tongue-tied.

"Coroneum, yes," Kaiser confirmed with a grin. "Not holy steel like your weapons, but it suits me."

"Coroneum sustains and amplifies any magic its wielder musters, right? This must've cost you a lifetime to afford."

"Not when you assassinate rich sorcerers." Kaiser smirked. "Seriath was shaped with a sacred gavel by monks and quenched in witch blood. The runes were carved by a retired exorcist, all the better for slaying demons. I had it fashioned shortly after I . . ."—Kaiser paused and checked Caethys's face for a reaction—"after I arrived on this world of Madon."

Those familiar with this "Tireless Butcher" debated his origin. Some said he was the reincarnation of a martyr. Others said he was a living punishment for Septunoth's sins. Caethys didn't believe either.

"They call you the Cypolonian. Where is this Cypolon?"

"It's out there in some other nest of stars. Below Madon, I imagine." Kaiser tapped the dirt with a bandaged finger.

"How did you first come here, if you don't mind my prying?"

Kaiser went on to speak of his unconscious arrival in the mountains of the south and of finding Old Bear Kronin thwarting Septunites in an incidental battle.

It was a bare-bones tale, and like most, Caethys was loathe to believe it. But this strangely scholarly brute didn't seem the type to exaggerate.

"Have I mentioned that my patron god is Zothre?" Kaiser asked.

"The god of battle? I could have guessed! The other deities seem a bit tame for a slayer of your infamy. I mean no offense, of course."

"Not at all," Kaiser continued. "Anyway, I found out soon after that Old Bear Kronin was something you people call an Anthrome, and being a devotee of Zothre himself, we gradually became sword-brothers." He patted the clay urn.

Caethys nodded. "How odd that an Anthrome would partner with a human. I've heard they are notoriously introverted."

Sidna, victim of insomnia, quietly took a seat next to Caethys and motioned for Kaiser to continue. His growing audience made him a bit uneasy, so he decided to summarize.

"Kronin was the kind of strong I want to be. I was very fortunate to have received instruction from him."

"So he trained you?" Sidna mumbled, holding a small metal rod in her teeth. "Lessons from an Anthrome, you lucky dog," She started disassembling her crossbow and making adjustments.

"Kronin didn't have to teach you to hate Septunites, I understand," Caethys added.

"No. Because the conquerors of my homeland were aligned with demon queen Opagiel, just like your Septunites are."

"They worshiped Opagiel too?" Caethys asked. "Ah, it makes sense. Oracles speak of Opagiel's conquests in the lower worlds. I've often wondered just how powerful that she-demon is."

"Back in Cypolon, we called her the Mother of a Million Murderers. Nations that worship Opagiel develop terrible strength," Kaiser admitted dourly.

"I still don't understand. If Opagiel's armies consumed your world, how then did you escape to us here?"

The corporal's question immersed the Cypolonian in melancholy. He carefully retrieved the sword from Caethys's hand. "When I understand it, I'll share it with you, Corporal. But to this day, I cannot distinguish between memories and nightmares."

Chapter 5

Night-spawn continued to haunt the riders' periphery but did not harass them. Even Jonos had to confess their journey had been fortunate enough, though the constant blackness was a reminder that they were never out of danger.

For Kaiser, the danger became very particular. Sidna noticed him casting angry gazes into the darkness, teeth brandished in his black beard.

"What's the matter?" she asked.

"There's a fiend out there."

"A fiend? A demon?" Caethys asked, twisting to face his riders.

"Not a demon. Something like a spirit, spoiled with evil."

"I'll try to gain some distance. Come, this way." Caethys veered off.

"I need to kill it," Kaiser whispered and stepped off his horse.

"What? Kaiser, no. We can't tarry," the corporal insisted.

"This will only take a moment." Unable to resist the razzing allure, Kaiser jogged into the pulsating murk.

"Kaiser! Get back here!" But the whispers amounted to nothing. Fuming, the corporal swung off of his horse and handed the reins to Sidna.

"Sid, if we're not back in a half hour, get everyone out of here. Follow the route on the map."

"Don't think I won't, Cae!" she lied.

Caethys made the chase in solid blackness, relying on Kaiser's footfalls and a probing arm to find his way through the knotty trenches. He cursed the Cypolonian's night vision, which clearly surpassed his own.

They followed a decline into a skin-biting cold where Caethys could feel the branches were budded with ice drops.

Before he could scold himself for forgetting to bring a torch, Caethys found Kaiser silhouetted in a clearing by some blue light source. Swords in hand, they surveyed the ghoulish oasis.

A trove of animal bones prickled beneath their feet, gritty with frost. Tumors of ice lay like eggs in the nest of skeletons, venting that cryptic glow.

"What is it?" Caethys demanded with forced courage.

"Not long for this world," Kaiser returned. The ground pulsed once, a chorus of crackles in the frosted bones indicating something was awake.

A drop-shaped wad of ooze lowered from above. It sparkled like snow but was thick and doughy. It suspended heavily, growing large enough to encapsulate an adult.

The spirit hanging before them rearranged its contours, inflating in places until a pair of icy human lips took shape on the bag of snow-slime. Frost crumbled from them as the mouth opened to speak.

"It feels like sleep," started the thing's voice. It sounded as if it were recycling the shrieks of rodents to mimic words. Its mouth was full of some spiny white litter, and it kept its lips close to keep it from spilling out.

Caethys knelt reflexively, gripping his oathkey necklace for comfort as much as heavenly magic. Blue light needled from his fist.

The spirit's lips curled at the sensation of the holy spell. Kaiser contributed another magic; he filled his blade with a volcanic fusion of hot colors. His primal energy made his blade twice as destructive, and it steamed in this wintry redoubt.

"Don't bother, Corporal. I can manage this," Kaiser insisted, stepping up the bone mound. He gave pause when the ice eggs sharpened their glow, and his confidence turned to experienced alarm. "Cover your head, it's some attack!"

The ice eggs began exploding. Caethys could feel something hit his face. It began to sting angrily. A strand of cold glue had snared his cheek and elbow and thigh. The spirit willed the glue strands to pull them in, and the corporal was being suddenly dragged into the boneyard.

Struggling, Caethys noticed Kaiser had taken a dozen of the adhesive strings. But the same power filling his sword was in Kaiser's veins, and he wrenched free. He was spotted with frostbite where the glue had taken hold, but he charged unafraid.

The spirit's lips peeled back to unleash a mess of gnashing animal skulls. Lizards, birds, snakes, and rodents had all donated to the mash-up of biting heads that surged at Kaiser.

He did not even notice that more ice glue had caught him when he somersaulted to the side of the hanging ice spirit. All his instincts screamed in harmony. A fiery swath from Seriath severed the spirit's suspension in a puff of sparks and steam.

The ice blob plopped to the ground, rearing to fix its rushing animal jaws on Kaiser. Desperate for victory, he had already sidestepped to a safe attack zone. Caethys watched that burning sword crash down like the axe of a competitive woodcutter. Each time the monster was hacked, pseudopods jutted out in painful spasms.

It was over quicker than they realized. The lipped slime sagged and melted. It became leaky and wet, trickling through the animal bones to the bubbling squeal of vapor.

"It was old," Kaiser observed. "But weak." It enraged the corporal to see the Cypolonian breathing so smoothly, as though he rode the enchantment of some powerful drug. Even as he bled from little wounds where the skulls had nipped him, Kaiser looked refreshed.

"Just what in hell was that?" Caethys's boots crunched over the skeletons as he approached.

"The spirit echo of some poor dead fellow. It went rotten, fed itself on animals." Kaiser shoved away his sword and stamped apart the remaining ice eggs.

"I'm talking about your actions, fool! You put yourself in mortal danger, and for what? To satisfy some slayer's impulse?" Caethys decided to cut deeper. He tapped his chest. "Two of my men gave their lives so you could get to Evanthea."

They stared at each other among the thawing skeletons. It wasn't defiance that Caethys received, but attentive perplexity. There was no apology in Kaiser's cocked stance, and it called to mind all the prejudiced assumptions the corporal had observed in Federal society about barbarian types.

"I have no intention of dying before then," Kaiser disclosed quietly but firmly.

"Neither did my men! And when you jeopardize their sacrifice, you spit on their graves. So tell me now how much danger you plan to bring down on us?" Caethys could see Kaiser was noting the frostbites on his face.

"Anything touched by the Helix, demons, spirits, animals, or humans. They deserve death as much as your men deserve life," Kaiser stated. "I'm not going to waste time trying to explain why I have to kill them, but I have to kill them."

"Are you really willing to risk this mission?" Caethys pressed, his anger keeping him from putting away his sword.

"No, actually, I'm not. But along the way, I have to honor my mission." Kaiser crushed the last ice egg under his boot and watched with satisfaction as the shards tumbled. "These things don't belong in human worlds. If you can't see the injustice every fiend represents, please don't feel obligated to help me. But don't try to stop me either."

"You've lived among the Archaics too long," Caethys put in bitterly, finally sliding his sword away. "Let's get back to the squad."

When the two had regrouped with the waiting riders, an uneasy silence pervaded. Everyone knew the corporal was frustrated with Kaiser, yet it was Caethys who sought to alleviate things later in the ride.

He found Kaiser scribbling something in a deerskin booklet. Curiosity and the corporal's forgiving nature prompted him to speak up.

"What are you writing?"

"Taking some notes. When I manage to put down a spirit or demon from the Helix, I like to log the details. They're so diverse, and you wouldn't believe how hard it is to find books on demonology."

"Such books are illegal in most cities. They have been since the Septunites invaded with black magic," Caethys voiced.

"I suppose there's some reason in that." Kaiser frowned, folding the journal away in his pack.

Caethys noticed the pack to be stuffed with such booklets. Could it be they were all filled with Kaiser's infernal victims? Perhaps this man was more fanatical than his composedness let on. But in this age, demon slaying probably needed more fanatics.

"It pays to know your enemy, though. Killing demons is my business, and if I'm going to face them, I want to do it with some brains behind this blade," Kaiser added.

"You mention demons. I've seen dark spirits like that one, but I have never seen a demon," Caethys commented.

"They're out there," Kaiser grunted with certainty.

"What drives you to hunt them?"

"The same instinct that would make me snatch a viper from a baby's crib." Kaiser seemed grated. "You call Septunoth your enemy. Mark me, Corporal, the real threats are the demons that puppeteer them."

"You'll forgive me for objecting. Septunites, not demons, penetrated the Wall of Lions. Septunites burned the Lexicus and murdered the Harague monks." Not one to be lectured by barbarian-types, Caethys put his powers of debate to work.

A few horses back, Sidna perked up, always captivated by the corporal's idealism.

"They have instated themselves as my enemy when they wounded not only my people but our culture," Caethys continued. "Perhaps as a foreigner, you're blind to the portent of their offenses."

"Then what prompted me to destroy eleven of their legions? Boredom? Septunoth has to be punished, of course. But they've invaded Kasurai twice in the past, haven't they? And your people crushed them both times. Why are we losing now?"

"Kaiser, they are a military state now, governed by master sorcerers. They are stronger because they choose to be. Their demon worship is incidental, hardly the source of their power."

"A few million Septunites with the demon queen tattooed on their foreheads would disagree."

"Far be it from me to criticize their educated opinions," Caethys said, to the silent smirk of Sidna from behind.

Chapter 6

The long ride was trying his eyes, certainly. But however Caethys blinked, the blue-white surfaces of lit stone would not disappear. Something tall and unnatural stood just a handful of trees away.

"Jonos, are you having the same mirage?" He pointed with his shortening torch. Jonos'ss eyes rolled back into place from his half sleep.

"No mirage, Corporal. There's something there. Masonry of a human touch, it seems." His voice cracked.

Caethys was beside himself to find a break in the gloom. He dismounted, handing the reins to Jonos, and proceeded to tunnel into the brush with his blade. The riders followed curiously.

A temple slept in the hulking shadows. The roof had mostly disintegrated, but the stone columns were tall and porcelain smooth, except where green rot infected the cracks.

Across a courtyard bursting with ferns, a domed shrine was clutched in jealous vines. It would have all been invisible if not for the sunrays percolating weakly from the canopy. The forest moisture heated into an ankle-high mist.

"A fragment of our history, lost and found." Caethys ungloved his hand and let the rays sparkle on his sweaty palm. Behind him, the horses were being tied to strong roots.

The men sounded normal again for a moment with their chuckles and murmurs. The darkness had made them sheepish, and Caethys was glad to see some smiles. They all looked so bloodless, and their eyes clenched, unused to the brightness.

The men didn't know, but Caethys had arranged for a great feast for his men upon their return for their generous volunteerism. He would calve off more of his pay to include plenty of exotic fruit, he decided. The desert travel and now sunlessness was doubtlessly taking a toll on their bodies.

"You sure we should do this, Cae?" Sidna asked, dawdling at her horse.

"You know our duty, Sidna. We can't let a find like this go unrecorded. No telling what the church historians could make of this."

"All right, let's just make it quick. It must be noon." She noted how the rays beamed straight down. "And the gods might not like us poking through their stuff."

But what gods were worshiped here? The more Caethys observed, the less inclined he was to believe that his pantheon had the only lingering presence.

The statues featured a catlike people in strained poses. They were possessed of lean bodies and great ears with nimbly built legs. They seemed just the sort of creatures that might inhabit this ropy forest.

The artist had worked not stone, but a dark crystal as a medium, like solid molasses. The craftsmanship was ineffable. Every hair was personally rendered, so that the glassy surface was bristly to the touch.

Kaiser, thinking he probably owed the corporal some silence, quietly studied the statues. The sunlight played strangely in them, giving their translucent cores a lifelike stir.

"By the gods . . . ," a soldier whispered nearby.

"What is it?" Kaiser asked. Jonos was holding a naked palm to the arm of one of the renderings.

"The statue . . . is warm." At this response, the Cypolonian raised a hand to the glassy fur of the statue's neck. *Pulsing* warmth.

There was a cough from the shrine balcony. Caethys pointed for three troops to follow him up the staircase. They clopped up the concrete to find an antechamber floating with dust.

A few dead bodies, civilians by their looks, were propped up against the walls. They donned cowls over their clothes. Then, one of them opened his eyes.

"You . . . ," he began, throat rattling. Caethys approached and knelt.

"Easy, friend. First, have a drink." Caethys uncorked his canteen and lifted it to the old man's shriveled lips. A few gulps and the man tried again.

"Quiet your men . . . ," came his watery plea. "You'll rouse Sevrit!" The man's forehead wrinkled tensely.

Below, the remaining riders inspected the other statues as Sidna came across something peculiar. The figure of a human man was carved into this brown crystal. The clothing looked modern enough. But his face reflected a terror she was unable to decipher from the cat-folk statues.

"Corporal!" she hollered. Her call rang through the temple grounds. A furious hand gesture from Kaiser silenced her.

Something fumbled near the shrine. Large fern leaves wagged. Kaiser bounded behind a fallen pillar. As he had hoped, the other men took shelter as well. Sidna squatted next to Kaiser with pursed lips that betrayed her embarrassment.

No one knew what they were waiting for. Caethys watched over the balcony edge for whatever had incited his rescuee to sobbing an unknown prayer.

It had the body of a crab, with a hide so crusty white that it seemed caked in plaster. But it was not legs that rowed it weightlessly through the air. Six leathery tentacles terminating in red-eyed pythons rolled out from its shell. Black teeth spiked the yellow gums of its primary mouth like barbed wire.

"What . . . the hell . . . is that?" whispered Sidna.

"I've studied this type," Kaiser responded. "It is a dwarf trenchling, a bottom feeder from the Pain Hives of the Black Inferno."

"You lost me at 'studied'."

"She's a demon." Kaiser's sudden heavy breathing made Sidna uncomfortable being between him and the object of his hate.

The beast floundered to the courtyard and fanned out its snake-tentacles. One appendage coiled around a statue's torso. The statue gave off a purple haze that was sucked into its yellow mouth.

The Kasurites, fingering their weapons behind their shelter watched in horror as the demon enacted its strange feeding habits.

"Can we attack?" Kaiser asked in between knuckle bites.

"No, we wait for Caethys to make the first move," Sidna answered. Kaiser did not have to wait long. A shaft whistled from the balcony into the monster's tentacle. Its blasting snarl was complemented by the shrieks of six devil snakes.

Caethys and the others had issued their collapsible short bows. The corporal's second arrow broke on the creature's shell. It thrust back its tentacles, hurtling through the dusty light toward Kaiser and Sidna.

The Cypolonian jutted from cover. He slipped a hunting knife from his boot and willed a dose of primal magic into it. He lobbed it at the creature, sparking a bouquet of pyrotechnics. Its mouth and tentacles were singed, but the shell absorbed most of the damage.

Enraged, the beast lashed its tendrils across the downed pillar. Sidna's blade swung in a shimmering crescent, and a snake head was severed in a burst of purple ichor.

The creature whirled to escape, but not before snaring Sidna under the arms. She kicked for freedom as she was carried higher into the air.

Competent as Caethys was with a bow, he dared not fire while the red-haired woman was being grappled.

"Caethys!" she screamed as three sets of viper fangs latched onto her neck. Her veins went black, circulating a magic that browned her skin and armor to the same material as the statues below.

The creature quickly healed its injuries as it drank her violet humors. The charred flesh foamed over, and a new snake head appeared in a spray of slime.

And it dropped Sidna's statue.

Caethys, heart hammering, looked away as the woman's life plummeted to its end. He would have to tell everyone in the barracks how she had gone.

When the crash he had expected never occurred, Caethys looked and realized Kaiser had dropped Seriath and sprung out to catch the falling woman. That heavy, edged glass surely punctured his arms, but he had not even let a foot graze the concrete. If the curse could be undone, Kaiser wanted it to happen with all of her limbs intact.

Caethys hollered in relief when he saw it. He fixed his bow again to ward off the creature. He called heavenly magic into his next arrow and sent the glimmering blue needle into the beast's shell, stunning it.

Kaiser raced off with Sidna. With a scoop of his foot, he popped Seriath into the air and caught it in his teeth. He carefully laid her among the stones. He slipped into the temple shadows then, where his wolfish eyes flared like coals.

With no reason to hold back now, Jonos and the others unleashed their own arrows. Most broke over the armored beast, which heaved back toward Caethys's balcony.

The corporal readied another glowing shot, but his target flew skyward too quickly. The beast's unseen pincer arm unfolded from its belly and grabbed Caethys from his perch, squeezing him mute. Again, the creature had a hostage.

"Shoot it! Just shoot it!" Caethys wheezed, but his restricted breath could not carry his command to the archers below.

Above, a shadowy figure squatted on a tremendous branch, pouring half the liquid contents of a glass vessel on himself. The rest was poured across his blade.

The archers saw a golden-eyed angel descending. Kaiser plummeted, soaked in holy oil, to land a sword thrust on the beast's back. Its shell exploded into puzzle pieces, tossed in sticky purple blood. Its wail resembled rusty chains being scraped over concrete, and it dropped Caethys, some twenty feet down.

Kaiser pulled and wrenched, steering the monster's crazed flight. The monster spiraled onto the shrine roof, rushing the black leaves.

Caethys gnashed his teeth, a pain staking in his knee after the fall. But looking up, it seemed Kaiser had the battle quite won. The Cypolonian kicked the snapping snake heads away with dripping legs. He turned the sword in the wound like a great key. The monster's vulnerable innards squelched horribly. Its most vital blood reserves streamed like satin curtains off the roof tiles.

Its brain scrambled, the demon's snakes withered. The body slid from the tiles as Kaiser ripped out his sword. He tumbled safely in the drop.

The monster splattered like a slime-filled pumpkin. Its leaking remains dried into a white crust. A distortion in the air bled from the chalk smear it was becoming.

Then Caethys saw Kaiser do something peculiar. The semi-invisible cloud from the demon closed on the Cypolonian, who seemed elated to feel the nameless energies siphon into his dripping body.

"Kaiser, do you feed on these things!?" Caethys blurted.

"Dwarf trenchlings have a dorsal suture that can be penetrated with a well-placed thrust." Kaiser informed him, ignoring the question.

"Watch out!" someone shouted from the foggy court.

Caethys turned to find a clowder of feline demihumans springing into full retreat.

"The statues came to life as he finished the beast off. I think it crystallized these cat people and fed on them. I have no clue what they might be, though," Jonos stated to Caethys as the creatures pounced through the mist.

"These are the Adani," Caethys realized. "They, among others, lost a great war against humankind thousands of centuries ago. Now, they lurk in the secretive parts of our worlds, driven from man's claim."

A lion-maned Adani of fatherly stature and silver fur oversaw the escape from a high branch. When nearly all Adani had taken their leave, the elder looked at Kaiser. The cat eyes were swirls of supernatural greens, and they met the Cypolonian's golden gaze.

For a moment, the animosity between their races was paused long enough for the Adani to nod in gratitude. Kaiser returned the gesture, and the feline patriarch spirited away.

Caethys might have noticed the transaction, but he had remembered his unfortunate comrade Sidna. As he came upon her, he was relieved to see her legs writhing.

"Sid, thank everything you're alive," he whispered, limping on his swelling knee. He did not expect an answer when he saw her face. Sidna was fair skinned by nature, but her face was almost blue now. When her eyes opened, they were spider-webbed with veins.

"Cae." She considered explaining what it had been like, but she didn't want to remember it anymore. Her mind was whole again, and her body more or less restored. "I can't see. Please get me out of here."

The upside to demon-caused wounds was that they were often reversible with divine magic, and Caethys was quite skilled in that regard. He cradled her head in his arms and set his oathkey against her forehead. She sighed as heavenly power tingled through her skin.

"Can you see?" Caethys asked.

"Eh, a little." Sidna's eyes wobbled in their sockets.

"It's too soon to worry. Let this spell work, and I'll do it again tonight," he said as he helped her to her horse.

The starving old man found upon the balcony joined them. He slowly regained his strength, but his younger comrade who de-crystallized was found dead in the courtyard. The old survivor, Osroy by name, had stated that he took to this wilderness as part of a spiritual pilgrimage with his counterparts. It was then they encountered the demon.

With Osroy sharing one of the horses, the Kasurites took to the trail once again. Caethys recorded the temple's location while Kaiser chuckled over his journal. Sidna tied a clean cloth around her eyes, hoping that her sight would return in time. Until then, she hitched her horse behind Caethys.

"Osroy, you called that thing Sevrit. How did you know its name?" Caethys asked.

"Legends," the old man replied. "It is a legend."

Chapter 7

Dried cherry-wood crackled tenderly in the fireplace. It burned with a gradual completeness that was almost sensual, glittering off the pewter utensils on the mahogany desk cinched to the far wall.

If learning had a scent, this chamber was rank with it. The exhalation of old books that had opened and shut had left a healthful musk that appetized the mind. Hagiographies, memoirs, holy testaments, and even fiction had a home here. It was a parade of brittle pages lining the walls on racks dotted by candle drippings.

Indeed, Duke Lecto was in his element. But tonight, there was a sword in his hand, and he stood at the side of his bed farthest from the door, where the firelight failed to warm his legs. The bed was still made, its tassled throws in the same place the servants had arranged them two sleepless nights ago.

This old womb of learning and rest had a visitor. Akanis, a man of dark gray skin and wearing a long black coat. He had plainly profited from a violent life in the shadows; his tunic was a liquid-smooth black leather gleaned from no earthly animal. A belt buckle of mirrored silver secured the leather slacks. Most opulent were his boots, black items clasped in organic silver patterns resembling bone.

One hand, encased in some metalwork resembling eagle talons, rested on his stomach. He stood holding a stained burlap sack in front of the chamber door, which had been smashed into hunks on the furry rug he now crossed.

He took a bow, black braids tinkling with ornaments, as the door creaked on bent hinges behind him.

"When I accepted your fee, Duke Lecto, I took it on good faith that you were a man to respect a contract," began Akanis, his irises glinting murder red. "After all, it was a sizable payment."

His claws went into the burlap sack.

"Sir Corias. Your greatest mounted spearman, archer, and six-time champion of the region tournament." Akanis set a neatly preserved head on the bed between him and the duke. Even in life, Sir Corias had never looked so carefully groomed, his brassy hair oiled and trimmed and the flare of his defiant jaw shaved and washed. There was a smoothness to his closed eyelids.

Sir Corias didn't look dead. Only disappointed.

"Imagine my distress, when he attacked me unprovoked." Akanis's hand went into the bag again.

He produced another head, lovingly embalmed, and set it next to Sir Corias on the blanket. This head belonged to a comically handsome young gentleman. The long, shapely nose and arrowhead chin succeeded in obscuring his youthful softness.

"Sir Braden. Captain of the Golden Shield, recently canonized as a sword saint for his heroism." He let his claw graze the origami ear before reaching for the sack a third time. "He attacked me as well. The very same day."

Lecto's sword grip was loosening. Studying those closed eyes before him that would never open again, the will to live drained like rainwater. His options were limited. His old muscles could never glean a drop of blood from the master murderer making the grim case before him.

Lecto could take his own life. Pain didn't frighten him now. He could drive his gold-wrought family sword full through his own throat and be dead before Akanis could berate him any longer.

But something stayed the old duke's hand. He was compelled to endure the presentation. Something demanded that he see the full consequences of his failure. So while a thousand suicides promised less pain, he stood and watched Akanis set up a third head.

This one sported long, black hair that Lecto had proudly combed and cared for himself. Even after the sweetly black goatee had grown in place.

"Sir Lecto II, perhaps the greatest knight your line has ever sired. And a well-trained assassin, though I realized that only recently,"

Akanis stated, his menagerie completed on the bed, facing the duke like a gallery of muted critics.

Akanis knew the duke's expression well. The idiot visage of suffering that reflected a hollowness of heart and mind. Words were pointless now; the duke had become a mannequin. Still, Akanis would finish his reprimand.

"You are called Lecto the Bold, and now I see why. We offered to bypass your lands and your people on the terms that you would not move any of your pieces against us."

Akanis rested his claws on his stomach again, seeing the day grow late and pink in the fields outside.

"But I should leave. Your time is valuable after all, isn't it? With so many people relying on your protection." He did not bow; he dropped the burlap sack and walked over the rug and splinters to leave Lecto in quiet company.

The hall carpets were marshy and squished under Akanis's steps. The only witnesses to his departure were the dead knights crumpled beneath the tapestries, their blood running thick and cold under hunks of armor torn from their bodies.

It occurred to Akanis that only the dead were capable of respect. They were silent and prostrate, eyes upturned in wonder. That is what it meant to correct a nonbeliever.

He crossed into a circular chamber where his corrections had been more widely dispensed. It rather resembled a messy child's room, with toys discarded at random.

Courtiers had been cast about like dolls, butchered in their ridiculous outfits. The varnished pews they had struggled to escape had been crunched in the rampage. This was uncharacteristic of Akanis, who saw destruction of property in battle as uneconomical and brutish.

A pair of priests that had attempted to run had knocked over a brass candelabra and set fire to one of the long curtains at the stained-glass window.

The fire glowed where a painter had been illustrating the convention. His blood mingled with the spilled paint, but Akanis had been careful not to ruin the rendering itself, though it remained unfinished. He stepped outside.

Purnon was enjoying the music of the blood drops when the metal doors scraped open. Akanis appeared, black boots clopping through the pulpy human slush cast about like the paint of a deranged savant.

He knew his younger sword-brother Purnon would be here, leaning against the tower wall that was a sleepy pink in the setting sun. Purnon liked to lounge in the tangy smell of open bodies and the silence he authored.

Purnon's only greeting was a stretchy smile under his wide-brimmed hat, a smile halved by the tip of his beak-like nose.

"Remind me of today's transaction, Purnon. Next time I intend to negotiate with a nonbeliever, talk me out of it." Akanis put his elbows in an archer turret to watch the evening set in.

"They don't heed my warnings either. No matter how many of them I leave." Purnon tilted up his hat to look on the gallery he had arranged above.

Dead militia had been stuck to the brick heights by a variety of means. He had been sure to secure them properly, pinning arms and legs until they were still as statues. It was an aesthetic that Akanis would have considered a waste of time, if Purnon had not so often overachieved in his tasks.

"When we destroyed the Siegebreakers, Lecto became frightened, I think, and moved his little plot ahead. Do you suppose he was sending support to them?" Akanis asked.

"It doesn't matter now, Akanis. You worry so much about redeeming these people. Remember, enemies are as important as converts. They offer no praise with their lips, but there are other ways for them to honor Her." Purnon caught the blood droplets on his glove like rain from the blue-faced people above.

"There is truth in what you say."

"Do you know why I wear this hat?" Purnon asked. Akanis humored a shrug. "So that I do not see too much. Everything fights for our eyes, attempts to direct us here or there. But genuine truth is never found with upturned eyes."

They didn't turn when they heard armored footsteps, for everyone within two miles was dead with the exception of their comrades.

Stealth was for those with something to hide. Tysis, who approached, wanted to be seen and heard by her enemies, and the craethune full plate that encapsulated her made it happen. She was more idyllic and conspicuous than the sum of her comrades, but she ripened distant enemies with fear.

Tysis was delighted to hear about Duke Lecto's treachery; it meant she no longer had to suffer these infidels just because they were a source of gold.

Seremet was content to wait, unlike the sword-sister he was following. He had faith in Opagiel's designs, and all Kasurites would funnel into them in good time. So, he appeared indifferent through the eyeholes in his hood and held his silence.

Contrasting to his patchwork hood was his ballroom coat and slacks. The blood stains may have been more apparent if his attire wasn't so perfectly black. Seremet was as secretive as Tysis was direct.

"All finished, are we?" Purnon asked, admiring how the day's hunt had plastered and dripped down their frames.

"I will not trade words with this sort again." Tysis set her heavy shield down with a clank and removed her black helm. A golden hand rested on the scalp of the item like that of an approving father.

"Nor will I ask you to." Akanis severed what was sure to be a tirade. "The five of us are linked by our hate, and you allowed me to experiment with it. For this kindness, I will follow a more direct path and bring us closer together."

Seremet put a hand on Tysis's shoulder, which she touched gratefully.

"I'm beginning to appreciate these Septunites," Purnon commented. "Their invasion always seems to place us in opportune locales."

"Before long, it will be enough," Tysis emoted, nearly tearing at the idea. "Before long, we will buy Master Thel another chance at victory."

"Yes. The harvest *has* been fruitful," Akanis related, and addressed the obvious. "Where is brother Volter?"

Purnon pointed up.

Lecto, honoring a desire outside his consciousness, had climbed to his highest tower. His sword had been left in his room. He didn't want a slow, dignified suicide. He wanted to feel the full weight of his failings. He wanted to be crushed.

He took a final, numb step off the high wall.

Only to be caught by a tall warrior's sudden appearance. Lecto hung by his collar and turned to lay eyes on the knight in black armor not unlike what Tysis wore. But this man's armor was fire-blackened, as was the mask that hid his huffing face.

Lecto suddenly became a living torch. Fire swallowed him head to toe, disintegrating regal garments and the flesh beneath. For Volter, the punishment had been altogether too quiet. He would have screams.

And screams he had from the duke, who withered rapidly to the punishing flames. Volter's breathing hastened, enraptured by the sight and smell of the scorching sinner.

"For Opagiel, and for Master Thel," Tysis said, gaining the sideways eye of Seremet.

Chapter 8

The same sensations that had haunted him at first were beginning to test Caethys's wakefulness. He was running out of fear, just as all his riders were, and that wouldn't do. A little fear kept you sharp.

He tried to focus on how uncomfortable he was. The saddle made the sweat squish in the thigh of his pants. His hair was stiff with dander, and it tickled his scalp like insect legs. Worst of all his shoulders tensed sorely no matter how he willed them to relax.

"Corporal, how's the knee?" Kaiser prodded him from a light doze that had crept up on him just the same. Caethys secretly pinched his own neck in punishment.

"Very fine, it was a minor thing," the corporal responded, feeling a bit like Jonos, who was no doubt snoring quietly in his own saddle behind. He took a moment to reassess where they were.

The horses followed trails of flowers that closed when torchlight touched them. The path grew along the length of a wide root that was serving as their bridge. Beneath them was a cradle of vines stitching together a swampy canyon.

"So I was a little confused about your magic skills, Kaiser . . . ," Caethys mentioned, hoping he wasn't breaching any taboos. Obviously he had not, because the Cypolonian cackled merrily.

"I'll bet you were."

"I saw how you seemed to draw power from the vanquished fiend. Does that mean you're stronger now?"

"Only a little. That bugger back at the temple didn't do me much good. But it adds up. I can keep it or spend it."

"Spend it?"

"Yes. If I kill a demon, I can burn the essence I harvested from it for a quick gush of power." Kaiser clenched a veiny fist.

"That's positively curious." Caethys plucked his goatee. "And you don't use the magic of the gods, I notice. Seems that would have been the obvious choice for a demon slayer."

"I would if I could, but my skill with holy magic vanished when I came to Kasurai. Kronin taught me how to make the most of my innate primal magic though."

"Ah, yes, the barbarians call it 'muscle magic.' Made from their own chrysms," Caethys commented.

Anyone with a soul had a chrysm, a spiritual source of magic. Caethys used his to harness godly power, but others used primal, natural, or demonic.

"I've taken a liking to it, but it's a shame still. I spent years trying to accumulate Zothre's divine magic and ended up losing it." Kaiser hesitated upon mentioning his god again. Federals and even many barbarians lambasted him for revering Zothre. Every other god in the Covenant kept correspondence with their worshipers through oracles. Zothre however, had not spoken through his worshipers for centuries.

"Ah, yes, you told me: Zothre, god of war and strength," Caethys recited from the texts he had digested in his schooling, never since returning to learn more of the famed battle god. "Seems like your type of deity. I still think Zothre should communicate more with humans, don't you? As one of the Originals, it doesn't seem like much to ask. There's so much we could learn from him."

"It teaches independence," Kaiser replied as he did to all skeptics.

"Well, if the urge takes you, my god Calphinas would welcome you openly. Twice a year his oracles bring us his Word," Caethys commented proudly.

Kaiser rolled his eyes back into his head. Everywhere he turned, people endorsed their deities to him.

"You're pretty good with a bow, by the way," Kaiser said, hoping to steer the conversation elsewhere.

"I've probably shot more deer than Septunites, but I can hold my own. Sidna's the one you should talk to, though. The woman could scratch an itch on my nose from forty paces. Angels keep her, I hope her eyes still work." He looked back to make sure she couldn't hear him.

"I used to be able to shoot." Kaiser frowned. "I can throw a javelin with the best, but archery escapes me now."

"Come off it. Really?" Caethys's reply earned a grumble from Kaiser. "No divine magic, no shooting skills. You must be monstrously skilled in swordsmanship for nobles to covet your service."

"It's this place. Since I came to Kasurai, it's like I took on a different body and a ruffled brain. It's changed me."

"Oh, we can remedy that, Kaiser. Sidna and I will teach you all we know when we arrive in Evanthea—"

Caethys barely finished. A patch of moss tore under his steed's hoof and tilted him from the saddle. The animal recomposed itself, but Caethys plunged off the side of the root bridge.

His foot was caught in something solid. Kaiser had thrown himself onto his belly and snatched Caethys's ankle. Gasps from the riders ensued.

"What happened?" Osroy asked from his horse further back.

"Gods! Corporal, are you all right?" Kaiser blurted.

"What? What's going on? Did something happen to Cae?" Blindfolded Sidna trained her ears in every direction to get details.

"Better than fate would have me, Kaiser. Thank you," came the corporal's answer.

"Then let's get you back up here."

As Kaiser began to pull Caethys up, the corporal heard a noise from under the ropy foliage beneath.

"Wait, Kaiser! Let go," the corporal ordered.

"What? Why?"

"The vines beneath will catch me, I'm sure of it. I think I found our way out of here!"

"Caethys, you can't be serious . . . ," argued Kaiser.

"No, this is right. This smell, this sound . . . this is right, please let go." With a reluctant sigh, Kaiser freed his grip, and Caethys sailed down into the weedy canyon.

The vines hooked his limbs and brought him to a bouncing halt. A downward crawl ensued until the plants thinned out. When he could pull his legs beneath him, he was able to drop into a muddy hovel.

Lighting up his oathkey, Caethys discovered, or perhaps rediscovered, a sloppy warren where glowing yellow frogs darted for the safety of root cages.

"What do you see?" called Kaiser.

"This is it!" the corporal's voice returned. "Kaiser, have the others prepare the horse pulleys, then jump down."

"You heard the man, get that pulley going," Kaiser relayed to the men behind him. "I'll cut the way open." With that, the Cypolonian cast himself off the root bridge, leaving the riders to assemble their less hazardous way down.

Kaiser caught himself and used Seriath to saw and slash through the fat, rubbery tendrils.

He crashed down to panic another swarm of frogs. The muck on his knees and elbows was chunky. It reeked of unlucky animals that had fallen to their deaths and wetly decayed. It felt like a great stomach, with its semisolid contents stewing in the lazy dark. The horses would hate this.

But Caethys was there, the unfolded map lit by his oathkey necklace. He kept switching his gaze between his old illustration and a river that burbled over a dark field of rocks ahead of him.

"You look pleased. We're on track then?" Kaiser asked, flicking mud from his hands.

"Absolutely. This stream flows straight north. It will lead us out in a day or less." He pointed dramatically like an old-world statue. "You are the third person ever to see this river, behind Sidna and I."

"Maybe you should name it, Caethys. It's your right as its discoverer."

"We may be the first humans to see her, but this river is well known to others." Caethys diverted Kaiser's attention farther north.

The water twinkled far into the haze, with clouds of fireflies playing over its banks. A ceiling of spider silk turned them into living stars. Lining either bank were tall stones, some hoisting lintels to make primitive arches. Time had toppled and rotted them, but their geometry assigned an alien holiness to the black waters.

Later the same day, blindfolded Sidna noticed a spike in the horses' speed. Her comrades were murmuring, even giggling.

"Jonos, what's the deal?" She swung out to hit his shoulder and missed entirely.

"Light, Sidna. Sweet sunlight," came his answer.

It meant the border of the forest was near, but the way was so overgrown they had to dismount and chop for every inch of progress.

Kaiser was happy to lead the way, carving a path with his hyperactive sword arm. Everyone was silently amazed that in two hours, he did not slacken his pace, reinforcing his "Tireless Butcher" epithet.

Kaiser became a ridiculous mess of stickers, dander, mulch, and sap, but under his littered beard, his smile declared the Quane had been breached. Caethys waved them all up a thorny incline into a grassland buttered yellow in the evening sun.

The corporal resisted his rising pride. But he *had* bested the Quane a second time and even rescued a lost traveler on the way.

The party rested early that night, watering their horses at a nearby pond that also served as their bath. Sparkling fires were ignited, and all their pent-up anxiety hatched in the form of crude jokes and senseless laughing.

Sidna was drying by the fire in an old long-sleeved shirt, rubbing an elbow injury she had received years ago. Caethys was a bit concerned that she had still not removed her blindfold. He arose to confront her about it.

"Sid, I think it's time we see about those eyes."

"Nah, let's give it another day," she suggested. When she felt his hand pass over her shoulder, she leaned away from him. "Really, Cae, I need another day."

"We've got to know."

"Yeah, and what if I can't see?"

"Well, you can't very well see with the blindfold, can you? I worked my best magic on it, have faith."

Before he finished, Sidna's angry hands were behind her head picking out the knot. The cloth fell from her eyes. Her lashes were beaded with moisture as her eyes opened slow like a newborn's.

Caethys kept silent, but things looked well enough. Her eye had retained its soft, brown fullness, if a little bloodshot.

She turned to him. Her other eye was a marshy gray blue, her pupil lost beneath the leaden haze.

Caethys didn't say anything, but Sidna could tell he had seen it.

"It's just the one. Does it look as bad as it works?" she asked.

"This is my fault, I led us into that cursed temple. I've ruined my best friend."

"Who's ruined?!" She gnashed her teeth, grabbing his collar as if to hit him. Even with her halved vision, she could see the hurt in his face. "One broken eye isn't going to hinder me any, so don't go feeling sorry for yourself!"

Osroy was heading up the party with Caethys the next day. The old man had mentioned he was familiar with this territory, and he loaned his wisdom to the corporal.

"The Blackbell Steppes can be a trying ride with all their marshes, but Ambergate is on the way, and they'll have beds and food for Federals."

Caethys nodded. "Then that will be our last stop before Evanthea. I can't wait to have a decent meal."

"I know a lot of good chaps that should be there. I'll make certain you're all treated well," Osroy offered.

"That's kind of you," Caethys answered, thinking maybe some celebration would assuage Sidna a little.

Osroy smiled back. "It's really the least I can do. I'd have rotted under those trees if not for you."

Chapter 9

A woman lay face down in the grass as if weeping, but she was unquestionably dead. Caethys knew a sword wound when he saw one, and two of them soaked the back of her gray dress where an apron had been secured. She was doomed when she started running, no doubt, but fright propelled her well outside of town.

Kaiser rode up beside the corporal, feeling he had stared long enough.

"There is smoke on the wind," Kaiser commented. Caethys seemed to just recede further into his thoughts. "We have to see what's going on."

"Gods, Kaiser, we are so close to Evanthea. Has war really come this close to the capital?"

"We'll handle it," Kaiser assured him, grimacing at the corpse. Flies were beginning to find her auburn hair.

Ambergate was scorched to a black necropolis, throwing smoke and shadow across the grass fields. Hollowed shelters flaked into the sooty streets. The great tree outside of town was heavily loaded with hanging men, raked by various tortures.

Caethys kept his riders moving quietly. His scouts reported that even the surrounding farms had been ransacked. Swords were out and lips were knit as they entered the village-tomb that reeked of unceremonious cremation.

Kaiser dismounted and began checking bodies. Most were not worth checking. Some gripped hatchets or spears, but just as many lay near spilled apple baskets or burning hay carts. Clearly they were taken by surprise.

There were more dead donkeys than children, which stood to reason. Children were often taken to be converts.

A tall stone statue of Tethra in the town square had been decapitated, the head replaced with a human skull crowned with melting black candles. A heart had been stuffed in its jaws: an effigy of Opagiel.

"Some human worlds boast protection from three or even four paragons," the corporal lamented as Kaiser and Sidna gathered. "Septunoth has the gall to desecrate Tethra's image when she has spent centuries repelling demon invasions *alone*."

"Hell of a woman," Kaiser put in.

"Well, Tethra was born from an especially powerful xerecite crystal," Caethys replied. "The priesthood considered it a sign of favor from the gods when they found it. When it was consecrated, Tethra was born, leading the souls of the honored dead to try and keep demons from entering our world."

"I'm not having this," Sidna put up her crossbow and exploded the skull with a deadeye shot through the nose. She listened with satisfaction to the rain of fragments.

"I'm glad you can still do that with one eye," Caethys remarked.

"I closed one eye every time anyway."

Kaiser bent down to observe the stone debris at the base. On the carven side of one chunk was the intact depiction of Tethra's eye. He picked it from the ground and smirked to himself. *If Tethra can see through this, maybe it will be easier for her to protect us.*

All of this happened in the vision of a masked stranger. He stood in the gloom of a desiccated cottage. Quiet as a serpent, he let the shadows drink him back up.

The wind wriggled the cowhide that covered a coal pile untouched by Ambergate's fire. Shaden peeked from under the cowhide, belly down to the briquettes and trying not to tumble any of them.

She couldn't see far from her coal mound tucked between staircases in the alley, but it was quiet. As far as she could tell, it was time to move. She slinked back under, and she emerged again with her little brother Keb on her back.

Her short nine years of farm life had made her strong, and she bore her quiet load out of the alley on bare feet. The cobblestone was still warm from the blaze.

Shaden ducked into what had been her favorite restaurant before the fire, using its fallen beams as cover. She would try to make the north part of town and follow the cart paths to the next village for help.

She bit a cut on her lip, wanting suddenly to retreat from the smoky breeze back to the coal pile. The groans of wounded masonry seemed to cry out, rallying all the dangers to her position.

She concentrated on keeping her footfalls perfectly silent. She made a bit of a game of it, trying to not even hear her own steps. Keb, confused but aware, was muffling every breath into her shoulder bones, knowing at least that silence was important.

Quieter than even these two was the hooded stranger crouching in the restaurant fireplace whom Shaden had completely missed. He made a note to retrieve them but would wait for his many companions to act first.

"Sidna, have you seen Osroy?" Caethys prompted.

"I think he went to scout with the others."

"Kaiser?" the corporal asked around his shoulder. The Cypolonian shook his head. "It's been a little quiet." When Caethys stepped aside, Sidna saw something move in the doorway across the street. A man with a bow.

"Septunites!" She dropped to her stomach and let fly with a bolt. The missile zipped into the man's leathered torso. He fell on his knees in the sunlight, a darkly garbed man with an executioner-style hood. Dripping yellow symbols were painted on his knee, chest, and shoulder pieces. He hit the ground in a puff of dust.

Arrows were suddenly whiffling between them. Kaiser raced to a roofless building and tore the door from its hinges. His two companions joined him under its protection.

"Seven, maybe eight archers!" Sidna calculated. An arrow head burst through the door to nick Kaiser's fingers. "They're firing from the north and the east!"

"We can't fight them from down here!" Kaiser hollered.

"Sidna, come with me. Kaiser, can you take that inn behind you?" Caethys asked.

He grunted. "Sounds fun!"

Caethys and Sidna flew to the shelter whose upper windows were sneezing arrows. Kaiser's door crumbled on the sprint to his objective.

He threw himself inside and rolled to his feet. To his right was a badly burned wooden staircase. To his left was the inn's scorched front desk. A pale hand eased a door open behind it.

The man had an unmasked face to indicate his higher ranking. One of the three profane symbols of Opagiel was tattooed on his cheek. His hexblade and the strange armor at his limbs told Kaiser this was a battlemage.

A large Septunite thundered down the stairs, very nearly breaking them. He leaped off for Kaiser, only to catch a ridge hand across the throat that flattened him. Dazed, the great Septunite's cleaver was snatched. Kaiser slammed the weapon through his iron armor, cutting him entirely in half.

The battlemage seemed unmoved as he hurtled over the desk. But the gut-smeared weapon was quickly torn out and cast spiraling at him.

As Kaiser had supposed, the battlemage simply parried the flying cleaver. But the block shook his comrade's blood over his face.

It was an insult that the battlemage wouldn't suffer, so why wasn't his enemy drawing his own sword?

He popped his fingers out at Kaiser. A combination of sight and sound streamed painfully through Kaiser's brain. The mindspite spell shook his balance.

The battlemage seized the moment. Kaiser was no sorcerer, but he knew enough tricks to fight one. He let rip with a lion's roar amplified by primal magic, and the battlemage was startled back.

Kaiser had suffered the mindspite many times and shook it off in time to face whatever came next. The battlemage crossed his arms and unfolded them into six arms, looking suddenly like some gothic deity.

The rush Kaiser received then would have baffled most men, but this too was something he had seen before. The extra arms were illusions, and in a few careful ridge-hand parries, Kaiser learned which were which.

The battlemage received a hard backfist to the temple. Angered, more sword strokes flew, but the Cypolonian swam through them all, his fists and elbows knocking the Septunite's head back and forth. With each hit, another illusory arm vanished.

Suitably dizzied, the enemy was ripe for killing. Kaiser closed in with an uppercut, an elbow to the neck, and a thrust kick. The foe was thrown back as if by a giant's hand, crunching through a fire-whitened wall.

He hit the street, weapon tumbling from his hand. He reached for it, but his fingers were stamped under the Cypolonian's boot. The battlemage fumed until his conqueror unsheathed Seriath and bisected his head like a melon.

Chapter 10

Caethys stole up a burnt stairway with Sidna. Before they could reach the top, a pair of hooded Septunite infantry known as *reprobates* thundered out of one of the rooms above. The first carried an axe, the second a long, black sword.

Caethys threw his shield up as the axe smashed down and rattled his arm bones. The weapon was jammed tight.

As Caethys knelt under the pressure, Sidna stepped up on his contested shield. She hurled herself over the axe reprobate and tackled his sword-bearing partner. They began grappling on the top step.

To the axeman's surprise, the corporal released the shield to unbalance him. Caethys thrust his saber squarely into the axeman's padded chest. Somehow, the axeman still had the strength to punch the corporal's head against the wall.

Nose bleeding, Caethys found his sword still lodged in the man's abdomen and kicked it deeper. The reprobate broke through the burnt banister. As he fell through, Caethys smoothly dislodged his blade from the man's trunk.

Sidna screamed as her opponent lay on top of her biting her left ear. She probed with her thumb and squished it into his eye. It was his turn to rise and scream, Sidna's hair still in his lips. Now he groaned as Caethys's blade drove in between the reprobate's shoulder blades. Sidna finished him with a left hook that threw a tooth from his mouth.

The corporal pulled Sidna to her feet, and they raced to clear the first room. An oblivious reprobate was looking out the window with a crossbow. The two charged in and killed the man with twin stabs.

Across the street, battle rang from the inn that Kaiser had infiltrated. The wet sound of shearing flesh told an audible story of the Cypolonian's butchery.

"*Die!*" Kaiser's command rattled the planks with sparking primal magic. A Septunite leaped from the second story window, missing his right arm. Sidna was moved to laughter at the sight.

"Let us pray the rest of the men fare so well as our Cypolonian," Caethys huffed.

Jonos was scrambling over the brick piles of a toppled temple. He had heard the ruckus of combat from the town limits and turned to help.

Meeting him at the base of the rubble pile was a great bull of a Septunite, wearing full plate neck to toe. A lictor, Jonos realized, an elite knight of Septunoth's church. A mosaic of craethune plates had been bolted directly into his face and head, giving him the look of a metallic reptilian.

He stood over a pair of Jonos's comrades, their blood still rolling off his great sword.

"You'll die for this, pig!"

Jonos was pulled back by his hair and was stabbed deeply in the back. The injury quickly numbed his arm, but he could twist enough to eye the attacker, who was none other than Osroy.

The old man pulled the knife out, drew it across Jonos'ss throat, and pushed his contribution to the rubble. The lictor seemed unmoved by any of this, so Osroy wiped his knife and pulled down his collar, exposing the Septunite glyph tattooed on his breast.

«I knew you'd be here.» Osroy's Septunite words sounded exhilarated, but the lictor still seemed standoffish. «I was a scout for a battlemage in the Quane. We were wiped out, save myself, by the very demon we tried to capture. These Federals found me; I led them here! An offering to Opagiel!»

The lictor must have believed him, because he walked away, sword over his shoulder. But Osroy needed the lictor's trust and trotted off to sacrifice more.

It wasn't a dozen steps before the lictor came upon Caethys and Sidna jogging along a retaining wall. A half-collapsed cottage blocked their escape, but the corporal, and by association Sidna, were in no humor for retreat.

"Ooh, a big one!" Sidna skipped playfully to flank.

A steel-link whip cracked against the crossbow she tried to load in secret. Her custom weapon tumbled apart at her feet, so she produced her two swords. Both seemed quite short compared to her foe's whip and great sword.

It would pay to stay on the defensive, Caethys told her with a look over the lictor's shoulder.

Ironically, the whip caught him next across the thigh. The strangely barbed weapon managed to tear the scales right off his mail and open a glittering wound.

This was an enemy to fight up close. Realizing this both at once, Caethys and Sidna shot in to take him on.

Violence was bubbling up nearby. Shaden toted her sulking brother under a wooden cart bridge. The edge of town was near.

"Easy children, be calm." The children were anything but calm to find Osroy suddenly blocking the far side of the bridge arch.

She had failed. Hiding cramped and hungry had left her too weak to escape with her brother now.

And Osroy wasn't fooling anyone with that grin and his hand behind his back. But then, he didn't really need to. Until Kaiser appeared behind the children.

"Still alive, Osroy?" Kaiser purred with satisfaction from battle.

Oddly, the sword-wielding Cypolonian didn't prickle panic in the children. He seemed too earthy to prey on the weak, though fresh blood splotched his garments.

"Little ones? Best stay close." Kaiser gently guided them along his side as he went. "Are Caethys and Sidna near?" The question went to a sweaty-palmed Osroy.

"I've not seen them, but I'm glad to see you, friend. The rest are dead," Osroy reported, an unnatural glisten to his eyes.

"No . . . ," Kaiser whispered. He turned to the girl. "All right, is there anyone else alive here?"

"I think—"

Kaiser's scream cut her off. Osroy pulled the dagger from his victim's side and would have stabbed again had Kaiser not turned to fall on him.

"Gutless bastard!" The grapple should have been easy for the Cypolonian, but the dagger's poison was hanging weights on him. "Run!" He ordered the children, who were already well on their way.

By the time Kaiser considered cutting Osroy's throat, the old man was already worming from the Cypolonian's weakening grip. One more jab should put him down, Osroy thought . . .

But he thought better of it when Kaiser reared up with a slash that might have cut him in half. The poison would get him anyway, and Osroy jogged off to find the children.

The sniffling girl found a roof that had slid from a smoky household. She set her brother down, and he fought as she tried to push him under it.

"Keb, you have to do what I say!" she said to his beet-red face. "Stay under here, okay?! I'll get him to follow me. No matter what, don't cry, all right?!"

His mouth opened in a silent wail, so she hugged his head, checking around for pursuers.

"You remember what direction north is?" she asked, prying him off. He nodded. "You wait here until they all leave. Then go north and never, never stop, got it?"

"You gon' come?"

"Yes, but don't wait for me, all right? Now what are you going to do when they're all gone?"

"Go norf."

"That's right. Now tuck in."

The boy crawled under the roof. The sister blew him a kiss and padded off. The first memory he would ever retain was just how bloody the bottoms of her feet were.

Osroy caught up to her soon enough. He began to quiver with happiness when she rounded a corner that was unexpectedly blocked by a fallen watch tower.

This was a fine day for Osroy, who seldom got to enjoy murder anymore. An injury in his youth ended his warrior career quickly. Since then, he had spent his days as a battlemage's attendant.

Easy kills were hard to come by, but here it was; the girl's eyes were ponds of fury, and her hands were balled into fists. He growled playfully, mocking her, but she couldn't hear anything over the blood thundering in her head.

"Now where's that pup that you had with you?" Osroy asked. "I don't care for you much, but I think that boy has a grand future."

"Osroy . . . ," came the annoyed voice behind him. The child hunter turned to see Kaiser on teetering legs. He had skin the color of a man three days dead.

"Still alive, hm?" came the reply.

"That's some good stuff you put on your butter knife there." Kaiser gestured to Osroy's weapon, which was dwarfed by Kaiser's Seriath. "It could probably kill a man in moments." He threw Seriath into Osroy's guts. Osroy's surprise dulled the pain, but he still screamed his lungs empty as he toppled.

Kaiser limped over to finish the job. Osroy reached for his knife he had dropped. But Shaden had snatched it.

"You want to do it?" the Cypolonian asked her, setting his hands on a vast hunk of concrete. Her teary expression offered no answer, so he hefted the stone above his head.

"Then look away," he instructed. Osroy squealed something in Septunite.

Palming her eyes, the girl heard a massy whoosh and a crunch, equal parts concrete and skull.

There was another thud. When she opened her eyes, Osroy's head was a puddle, and her rescuer had fallen. She stepped up to inspect Kaiser's jittering body.

He reminded her of a city guard who she had admired. He had black hair thickened from sweaty travel, a strong prickly jaw. It was almost as painful as seeing that noble guard dying again.

"Go find a dark-skinned Federal man and a redhead woman with one white eye. If they are alive, they will protect you. Get!" he said, gargling bile. He did not see if the girl flew or stayed.

The lictor's barbed lash raveled around Sidna's wrist and he yanked her close. He tried a sword stab, so Sidna dropped her left weapon and grabbed his blade for lack of a better idea. It failed to get through her chest piece, but her fingers were sliced to the bone.

Caethys hacked at the lictor's knees, driving him from Sidna, whose left sword had been kicked away in the footwork.

A head butt from the lictor's metal-grafted skull put Caethys in a daze. That slithering whip gnashed through the scales in his other thigh, and the corporal fought for balance on two screaming legs.

The lictor was too quick to be caught by Sidna's right slash, but he had failed to notice the log she had found. It smashed into his temple, and he pedaled sideways.

His eye sat crooked in its socket, and blood dribbled from where metal plates had been ripped loose. He looked at Sidna with renewed respect. And he showed it by hammering her defenses with his dark blade.

A sword slam further crumpled Caethys's shield when he tried to distract the lictor from Sidna. Noting the jagged scrap that bent from his shield, Caethys baited the lictor's guard to go high.

And into the lictor's armpit went the pointy shield wedge. His sword arm was useless now, and the lictor tried desperately to use his lash in close combat.

Sidna spun low. Her sword passed through his knee and separated his leg. His screaming weakened as she stabbed at him, halting only when Caethys's saber chopped into his forehead and dropped him.

The duo huffed cheerily in the blood-splashed alley. A dead lictor was something to celebrate, even with their injuries.

"Spirited fellow, wasn't he?" Caethys grinned, wincing from a dripping forehead wound.

"I've had better." Sidna recovered her spare sword.

There they were, the dark-skinned man and the redhead with one white eye. Shaden looked upon them with cautious revilement. But it was a Septunite that bled at their feet, so how wicked could they be?

"Hey! A child!" Caethys exclaimed. His shoulder was caught by Sidna, whose look said, *Leave this to me.*

Sidna sheathed her weapons, drew out a handkerchief and cleaned her bloody face before tying up her dripping fingers. Caethys loved how Sidna's smile could shine through sweat and gore.

"Sweetie, we're astounded you're alive in this mess!" Sidna began, bending to put her hands on her knees. Her mismatched eyes were wide with concern.

The girl spoke, holding Osroy's knife in both hands. "He . . . he's dying . . ."

"Who's dying?" Sidna asked.

"The crazy man . . . with the wolf-eyes . . ."

Chapter 11

Caethys and Sidna were kneeling beside Kaiser in seconds with Shaden, who quietly retrieved her brother nearby. Sidna noticed Osroy's headless cadaver, Seriath staked in his gut like a flag.

"Kaiser killed Osroy?!"

"That man was the killer!" Shaden proclaimed. She pointed to Kaiser next. "He protected me!"

"It's definitely poison. Where's the wound?" Caethys wondered, unmoved at Osroy's treachery in light of the Cypolonian's condition.

"His back!" Shaden realized the urgency. They turned Kaiser onto his stomach.

"Not good. Plugged him in the liver." Sidna was able to tear through Kaiser's patchwork top even with bandaged fingers. His back was a white slab with a bluish puncture under his ribs. She tasted his blood with a finger and spat.

"Darklove pollen," she deduced. "It'll crystallize inside his heart." Caethys listened on as she shuffled through her satchel. She pulled out something like a dropper and plugged it into Kaiser's wound, injecting the dose of antidote.

"Is he going to make it?" came the corporal's question.

"He should be dead already," she explained, grasping the side of Kaiser's neck in her fingers. "We need to get him plenty of sunlight. Plenty of it," she added, rolling up his pant legs. "I've never seen anyone hang on this long."

"It's true then . . ." Caethys almost smiled.

"What?" Sidna asked.

"Kaiser mentioned that he takes diluted poison every day, and he obtained a resistance to several kinds. This must be one of them," Caethys elaborated.

"Well, he needs to work on this one." Sidna sighed. Shirtless, Kaiser was hoisted up onto Caethys's shoulders.

"Sid, I'll meet you at the horses. Go rally the other men," the corporal commanded.

"They're dead." Shaden stopped Caethys with the words. "That Osroy must have killed them."

"What did you—?!" The corporal sounded angrier than Sidna had ever heard him.

"He . . . Kaiser found that they were dead."

All of a sudden, Kaiser's weight doubled for Caethys's slashed legs.

"Come on, honey, show me. Then we'll get out of here." Sidna offered a hand, and Shaden took it, keeping her brother close by.

Caethys was silent as he hitched up a train of riderless horses. Sidna loaded the children in front of her in the saddle. Shaden looked back to see Kaiser comatose on his horse, his face buried in the brown mane. He was dreadfully pale, and his limbs shivered. His stomach flexed with the urge to vomit.

"Is he going to die?" she asked as Sidna gathered the reins.

"I sure hope not, honey. If he's still breathing by dusk, I think he'll be all right. He's tough." She set her mismatched eyes on the little girl. The child managed a little smile back. They finally left the wreckage of Ambergate to the crows.

Fatigue made the next day very quiet for them. The children crunched hungrily on some dried vegetables Caethys gave them as they rode. Sidna checked periodically on Kaiser. His condition seemed unchanged, but he still sweated intensely. She was concerned he might die of thirst if he didn't awaken.

When finally they camped, the fire seemed to stir the blanketed Cypolonian. Days of sunlight reddened his skin. He gave a groan, and the children giggled at its similarity to a cow's.

"Ah, damn it, I'm still alive . . . ," Kaiser croaked. Sidna gave her green apple to Shaden and went to inspect him. Kaiser clutched his chest, feeling like he had pins and needles in his heart.

"Do you feel pain, Kaiser?" Sidna asked, pulling up on his eyelids gently to observe his pupils.

"Exclusively," he complained.

"Sunburn. The rays help settle the poison." She produced her wrinkled water skin and handed it to Kaiser. He drank only what he needed.

"Thanks." He returned it, putting his head back in the grass. "Where's Cae?"

"He says he's scouting the surroundings, but he's really just punishing himself," she answered.

"Punishing?"

"Jonos is dead. All the others are dead. He would have failed the mission if you had gone belly up. He doesn't take failure very well. I think that's why he doesn't accept promotions," Sidna said before pulling from the water skin.

"I see." Kaiser sat up, huddling coldly in his blanket. "That's why they sent a corporal, hm? He didn't tell me he could have been promoted."

"A lot of years we've been fighting this war, he and I. He likes being a grunt."

"You do too. Don't you?" Kaiser suggested.

"The frontlines are my home. I need to be close to the fighting."

"Don't you have another home?"

"Probably not," Sidna whispered. "I was training in the capital when the Septunites pushed into my home city out west. Folks, grandfolks, brothers. They were all back home. Now, it's occupied. It's gonna be a long time before I know what happened to them."

Kaiser couldn't form an appropriate reply, but Sidna became transfixed with the children. They were nuzzling with the apple core between them.

"Try not to snore so loudly tonight, all right?" Sidna returned to her own niche by the crackling fire.

"Do I snore?" he asked.

"You do when you're poisoned."

"What about Caethys?"

"He'll be back in an hour or so. He always is," Sidna answered, laying her head down upon her threadbare pack.

Like a dream, the palatial metropolis of Evanthea appeared in the distance. Imperious keeps fitted with mighty buttresses soared up like mountains. A hulking world of worked stone dominated the horizon for miles.

Caethys finally broke his silence seeing his strong homestead. He pointed to the centermost and greatest citadel, layers upon layers of complex architecture.

"That's the Meridian, Kaiser, the Apogee's most hallowed house," Caethys explained. He needed to see this, a grand example of Federal pride. His failings as a corporal were nothing to the power of the Apogee.

Kaiser did not have to fake his awe. The children hid their disbelief with even less success, their jaws hanging.

"Keb, Shaden, this is your new home. We'll have to find some work for you two, but you can stay with me until you're settled," Sidna promised.

Chapter 12

Caethys's return was frustrating as always. He was stopped by six different sentinels and asked to produce his documents as many times. Amid the sweaty throng of migrants and angry guards, the children clung to Sidna's hands.

    Kaiser had no intention of using Seriath but grasping his sword's hilt won him berth from more wary citizens. Vendors shoved strange meats and fruits in his face while vagrants tugged at his arms for money he did not have. He could feel the spit accumulating on him from all the shouting people.

    Rambunctious as it was, this was clearly a refined city. Citizens were healthy looking and sported colorful jewelry. Sidna hugged and chatted with a few farmers that were organizing their goods. Many crouched and offered produce to the children at her side. Meanwhile, Caethys called for Kaiser to follow him.

    "She's got her own things to do," he explained. "Let's get to the Bureau of Tidings. I'll need your voice on matters."

    Kaiser nodded, and Caethys came into whispering distance.

    "They're going to be very interested in the demon you killed."

Stable boys who Caethys summoned by name took the many horses. When they asked where the other riders were, the corporal did not answer.

    Caethys led Kaiser between the wagons rattling along the roads. Kaiser, who had lost his shirt back in Ambergate, could hear the word "barbarian" whispered in the markets around him.

    In addition to the regular guard, there were also men who wore white cowls over their scale mail. Emblazoned on their tunics was the image of a crown with a scepter through it. Kaiser noticed a pair of them hollering at an old man who refused entry into his butcher shop. Eventually they muscled him aside.

"Are the centurions always so forceful?" Kaiser inquired.

"Lately, yes. We've had some trouble with radicals that call themselves Bloodletters. They're trying to overthrow our Potentate. Those Whitecloak centurions are the Potentate's special guard."

"Rebels in this time of war. Do they sympathize with the Septunites?"

"We don't think so, but their ambitions are vague. All we know is that they habitually slaughter families with ties in the government."

The Bureau of Tidings had offices everywhere in Kasurai, even in Archaic territory. Its network kept all corners of the Apogee informed. The local Bureau chamber had been refashioned from a tiny prison. Still fixed in its white brick walls were metal rings where shackled criminals used to be flogged.

The two were admitted into the secretary's office without windows. A broad-shouldered elder was seated in the center of the room wearing a green dress coat with silver buttons. He lorded over a heavy desk, a tarnished glass lamp glowing orange on his documents and inkwells.

"Arcton! Your errand boy returns," Caethys chimed. The old gentlemen looked up with watery blue eyes. A heavy mustache trembled involuntarily. But under all that weariness, he grinned with long, skinny teeth.

"Caethys, lad, have a seat!" Arcton creaked to his feet, extending a hand which Caethys took tightly.

"Arcton, this is the Tireless Butcher, Kaiser of Cypolon."

"Kaiser I have heard of. Not so Cypolon, I'm afraid." Arcton gave his hand to Kaiser next.

"Good to meet you, comrade," came the Cypolonian's greeting, unwilling to explain his origins to someone else.

"Wasn't there another? Old Bear Kronin?"

"I'm sorry to say he fell in combat shortly before Caethys arrived," Kaiser reported. Arcton's grip grew cold.

"Ohh . . . a shame indeed. I was looking forward to meeting an Anthrome. My condolences, comrade."

"Thank you." They all took their seats.

"First of all, congratulations on securing Kaiser, Caethys. I'm glad you're back," Arcton began. His meaty hands struggled to grasp his tiny pen. Kaiser noted the calluses that pocked Arcton's thick fingers. "Now, if you will, explain any contact you had with Septunite forces, no matter how insignificant."

Caethys laid out the entire story of the expedition. Arcton brightened as the corporal colorfully elaborated on his costly triumphs. It was exciting for both of them, though an expected somberness came over them toward the end.

"I am very sorry to hear about the losses of your men, Corporal. Good boys, all of them," stated Arcton as the matter came to a close. "Now, if you would, explain any contact you may have had with the supernatural."

Caethys inhaled as though about to speak, but then remembered Kaiser, who'd been silent up to this point. He had a weird darkness to his face and looked ready to speak his mind on the matter.

"Turned them into brownish crystal, eh?" Arcton repeated, his head turning to fix his ears on Kaiser. The Quane ordeal had been recounted. Caethys was amused how the topic of demons made Kaiser's teeth look like fangs.

"Like I said, the dwarf trenchling appeared to feed and heal itself this way. Drawing out the . . ."—Kaiser struggled for the words—"health of victims in this immobilized form."

"And poor Sidna's got a bum eye to show for it, hm?" Arcton shook his head. "Pity. She had lovely eyes."

Caethys spoke up. "That's not all, Arcton. Kaiser's got a whole pile of journals stuffed with information on demons that he's killed. Demons in Kasurai."

"You're serious, are you?" Arcton thoughtfully rapped his fingers on his dark desk. "This will have to be brought to my superiors, I think. And they may ask for proof."

"By Tethra, I swear it's true, but I don't have any proof but the scars on my skin," Kaiser admitted.

"I don't think you're lying, son. But maybe I could drop by later and fill out a more detailed report?"

"Of course."

"Well, until the Potentate mulls this over, the both of you have got to keep your tongues stowed. If people catch wind that demons are about, we could have a panic on our hands. And the Bloodletters are causing enough trouble."

Caethys nodded. "You have my word."

"Likewise," Kaiser agreed.

Arcton leaned back in his chair. "Good. Well, I have a lot to do then. Corporal, you can submit your report in the encounter log in the back. Kaiser, we'll catch up later, so don't go far."

"I can't wait to get back to the barracks. I think I could sleep through a siege." Caethys laughed a little, rubbing his eyes.

Kaiser jabbed a thumb at his young friend. "Unlike Caethys, I'm a stranger here. Where do outsiders get to sleep?"

With a mute *oh*, Arcton squeaked open the top drawer of his desk. He rifled through some papers and retrieved a rectangular wooden token. Carved into the varnished face was a pair of outstretched hands. Arcton closed the drawer and slid the token toward the Cypolonian.

"Take this to the Dreaming Quail. It's an inn on the far side of the west plaza. That will cover your lodging expenses."

"Oh, thank you . . ." Kaiser's words were muffled with gratitude. He rotated the token in his fingers. He felt awkward accepting something he hadn't paid for.

The falling sun had burned the clouds orange by the time Kaiser and Caethys were pardoned from the Bureau. Eager to wander on his own, the Cypolonian bid Caethys goodnight and broke away.

When he reached the Dreaming Quail, Kaiser was received with artificial enthusiasm. The servants raised their brows when they looked over his bare, chiseled torso and patchwork slacks. Their flaring nostrils reminded him he needed a bath.

Just the same, Kaiser's token was accepted. An escort showed him to a spacious lodge with more pillows than he'd ever seen in his life.

"This is all for me?" he asked, feeling spoiled.

"Yes, sir. This room is for military guests," the escort replied in an exhaustively rehearsed statement. "If you need anything, please do not hesitate to consult the servant chambers down the hall. Someone will be up shortly to take your dinner order."

"Don't bother. I'll get something in town," Kaiser replied.

"It is free of charge here, sir," the escort emphasized, wondering why Kaiser looked so hesitant.

Kaiser thought for a moment. "All right."

The room was ripe with luxuries, and it made Kaiser irate. The pillows were seductively soft, and he didn't like how they made him feel sleepy, as if they drained his sharpness. He was happy to have a reason to stand when his dinner arrived.

A walnut-haired young girl stood before him as he opened the door. She was holding a tray with sliced chicken, red grapes, a wedge of cheese, and a jug of water with a small clay cup.

"Courtesy . . . of the Dreaming Quail, sir." She blushed a little, her eyes feasting on Kaiser's riveting abdominals.

"Thanks kindly," he muttered, and took the tray.

If anyone was going to beat on Sidna's door at this hour, it was more likely to be a vagabond looking for charity than Kaiser, but there he was, in her doorway, with a package under one arm.

Sidna was wearing an old shirt that looked like it had been used for farm labor. A black belt failed to keep her pantaloons much above her pale hips. At some point during the day, she had gotten a leather eye patch that sat comfortably over her blind eye. As Kaiser had predicted, Sidna was the type to stay up late.

"Sorry to bother you, Sidna. I brought this for the little ones." Kaiser handed the cloth bundle to her. It was warm, and when she opened it, she was delighted to find cheese, chicken, and grapes.

She let out a whisper of elation. "Waah! Perfect! Those imps have emptied my pantry. You're a good one." She wrapped the food back up and punched him in the bicep.

"Your place was easy to find. Everyone around here knows you," Kaiser commented.

"You should be careful in my neighborhood at night though. It's kind of a mad house. Pickpockets, Bloodletters, and the like," she warned, popping one of the grapes into her mouth.

"Places like this are good for keeping you sharp," Kaiser said, looking back over the wet streets. "But I was just passing through, Sidna. I think I lost something at the bottom of a bottle somewhere."

"I take your meaning." She chortled and touched his arm to make him turn his back. He felt her fingers inspect his stab wound.

"Ow! Easy." He flinched a little.

"Are you the restless type, Kaiser? The type to wander and drink when you're not on the march?"

"Archaic culture might have rubbed off on me," he admitted.

"You're not going out looking for a fight, are you?" She put a finger to his face as he turned back. Kaiser's levity vanished.

"Please. I have a little more class than that," he assured her.

Chapter 13

The purple welt under Kaiser's right eye was in full bloom when he answered the door to his chambers the next day. His knuckles were hugely swollen.

"Caethys!" he roared. A moment of silence followed. "What are you, some kind of jester?"

Caethys stood there in a green velvet shirt and pants with a black vest and his boots of fine dark leather. He carried with him a wooden box as broad as his chest. Kaiser had never seen him in anything but his armor.

Caethys rolled his eyes at the Cypolonian's appearance. He was clearly bored out of his mind and had practiced enough to drench him in sweat.

"And maybe the half-naked savage could offer me some fashion advice?" Caethys returned. "I've come to deliver a message, Kaiser. The Potentate will finally be granting an audience."

"About time. I've been here all day. Let's get on with it!" Kaiser's practice-swollen arms pulsed with anxiety.

"Apologies, Kaiser. The discussions tonight are for me alone."

"What? I thought he wanted to talk to me." Kaiser cocked an eyebrow.

"The Potentate wishes to consult you privately to get an unbiased report from an outside source."

"Too much bureaucracy in this town." Kaiser shook his head.

"The Potentate has his reasons," Caethys said, but the way he lowered his eyelids showed he agreed. "By the way, another aristocrat was murdered last night by the Bloodletters. Not two blocks from here."

"Gods, really? Are we in danger, you think?" Kaiser asked.

"Oh, I shouldn't really think so. The Bloodletters have been hunted down to a mere two score or less, and the Potentate's agents keep a close eye peeled for them."

"I'll be on my guard anyway. You should too," Kaiser stated.

"These are yours for when you meet the Potentate. A carriage will be here to escort you at dusk in two days." The corporal handed the box to Kaiser, who peeked inside. The contents were a maroon and black set of clothing.

"Thank you, Caethys. I had no other clothes."

"Try not to spill wine on them, you filthy foreigner. Those are my brother's." Caethys grinned and made off.

"Is he a jester too?" Kaiser grunted.

***

Arcton arrived to speak with Kaiser at the misty hour of dawn the next day. The lonely Cypolonian had been looking forward to the meeting. Kaiser seated Arcton at a wooden table where he could spread his papers. He fixed tea for each of them and sat opposite the old man on a sofa.

"I don't know if you know this, Kaiser, but the Potentate had all the royalty in the south looking for you and your slain comrade Kronin," Arcton stated as he produced an ink well and quill pen.

"It was prudent to keep my whereabouts vague." Kaiser sipped his steaming drink.

"You two killed a whole mess of Septunites, I understand. No one argues you've done more to blunt the southern siege than anyone." A smile rose under Arcton's thick mustache, a proud-father smile.

"Well, our men won the battles. We just pointed them at the enemy."

"I wish I could do my part, but they keep me here. I think I could kill a lot more Septunites with an axe than a pen." Arcton frowned at the quill in his scabby fingers. Kaiser watched how the cords in Arcton's hands surged, and then he understood; being a secretary was never his choice, he was a fighter. By some stroke of fate, the mustached veteran wound up estranged from the battlefield to become a scribe.

"Doubtless you're no stranger to fighting?" Kaiser queried, but the old man waved the question aside.

"I'll pester you with that another day. Anyway, we're here to talk about your contact with demons."

"Oh, right. The Potentate seems very concerned with demons," Kaiser remarked. "He's wise to fear them."

"Paranoid, I'd say. So, if you please, beginning with the earliest, tell me every encounter you've had with infernal creatures in Kasurai."

Setting down his tea, Kaiser reached for the oldest leather-backed tablet from the pile and cracked open the stiff, yellowed pages.

Two hours passed with breaks for additional tea as Kaiser explained how he destroyed his fiendish enemies. All the while Arcton took careful notes. They shared a few laughs even, but toward the end, a malaise settled over Arcton.

"You seem to be in all the right times and places for demons, Kaiser. Almost as if they find you. I've never even seen a demon myself, though my uncle fought one once on his farm up north."

"Really? What did it look like?"

"He used to tell me tales of a 'skinless lion.' It had a long, long body and ten legs. He said it could climb up trees and houses quick as a squirrel, and its gaze made men gouge out their own eyes. What do you call something like that?"

"Sounds like it could be a sibilant feaster in its larval stage," Kaiser suggested, combing the lore in his mind. "They're native to the upper realms of the Infernal Helix. A fairly new breed, oracles say."

"You are a man of study," Arcton stated. "I wish I could kill something from the Helix. What an honor."

Kaiser waited for him to continue.

"At this age, I don't know. I doubt these old bones could even match a demon now. Gods, I just want to fight again, just once more. Listen well, Kaiser. You relish your fighting days. It's a sorry fate, rotting over a pen." Arcton looked at his papers as a slave looks at his chains.

"Haven't you served in this war?" Kaiser asked.

"I did, long ago. I manned a longship when the Septunites were sacking the northern ports. After the latest Potentate took the reins, my powers of communication locked me here."

"You don't have to rot, Arcton. You're not bedridden." Arcton was used to receiving sympathy from listeners, but Kaiser almost scolded him. "You are still a soldier. It's your duty to keep in fighting form. I think you need to practice more, old man."

"Practice more? For what? No commander in his right mind would field a man my age," Arcton said, a little ruffled.

"What does that matter? You represent the Apogee. And however remote the chances, they're still relying on you to be ready." Kaiser set his tea down with a clank and began counting on his fingers. "Age, sickness, deformity, shame, I don't care. You can always get stronger."

"I'm seventy years old. They ended my fighting days by putting me in an office. I couldn't leave if I tried."

"*Have* you tried?"

"Easy to point fingers when you're hardly half my age!"

Arcton wasn't about to be lectured by a pup. He corked his inkwell and scrunched together his papers. Kaiser remained reclined as the old man rifled about. His chair screeched out, and he buttoned his case with practiced movements. But Arcton slowed and took deeper breaths. He was a reasonable man and felt a little foolish. He had trouble connecting with Kaiser's stare again.

"Though it makes sense, what you say," Arcton admitted, sighing. "I'm being stubborn, aren't I? It just feels pointless. Feels like I'm worth more to them if I just hunker down with my papers and keep quiet."

"Do you know how old Kronin was when he died killing Septunites?" Kaiser asked. Arcton shook his head.

"I don't either. But he was a damn sight older than you."

Arcton folded his arms. A part of his mind, closed long ago, creaked coldly back open. It was time to grow up.

After their meeting had ended, Arcton delivered his report. As evening settled in, he returned to his home in the poorer parts, not far from Sidna. After a glass of whiskey, he found his war axe blinking firelight at him on the wall. It looked heavy and comfortable. Maybe it was the drink, but Arcton was excited to take it down. He rarely practiced more than a few times a month.

Arcton let the weight guide his slow, deliberate swings. Normally, he would have numbly gone through the axe forms of the Blade Spectrum fighting style. Tonight, Arcton thoughtfully reenacted chopping movements that had won him grisly duels in ship-to-ship combat.

Glittering with perspiration, Arcton soon passed two dark hours cleaving at phantom enemies from his past. Much of his strength had left him, but he was surprised to find that his strokes were steady. Enough to find the soft spot in a man's armor, he thought. This skill was too precious to let go.

In the shadows of his drafty suite, Kaiser rehearsed his own techniques. Seriath lilted in the cold, with moonlight trailing its thoughtful flight. Like a drug, the Cypolonian's sword form suspended his mind.

Hundreds of eyes stared into the black heavens, unblinking and unseeing; the land was a mosaic of broken human shapes. Kaiser stood like a ragged monument over the fields of gnarled carrion, but he was not alone.

The other figure was like a relic of a dangerous and forgotten era. The white-maned hulk was hanging his head in some prayer as gore dried over his armor. The braids in his beard swayed as he whispered.

When he had finished, he stowed the war hammer over his shoulder and stamped through the fields of those he had punished. Perhaps he would have vanished into the shaded horizon, but Kaiser could not allow it.

"Hold," the Cypolonian called to him. The warrior glanced over his shoulder but kept lumbering away. Kaiser pursued at a distance, knowing that hammer ended lives as readily as lightning from a wrathful god. "Please, can I come with you?"

The man turned again, stopping this time. His eyes were ingots of glowing ivory, whiter and purer than fresh snow. If he was frustrated or curious or excited or confused, Kaiser couldn't tell, so asked again.

"Can I come with you?" The stare Kaiser received beckoned for elaboration. "You have the kind of strength that I need. I saw how you fight. You're invincible."

"Bah," the man returned in a guttural baritone.

"Listen, I'm a stranger to these lands, but I share your enemy," Kaiser explained. "Who is your king?"

The man did not answer with words. He only produced his hammer again and held it up firmly like a torch. It was some gesture that Kaiser had witnessed before in vigilantes of unfailing honor.

"Can I come with you or not?" The Cypolonian needed to know. Again, the man did not reply, only throwing his weapon over his shoulder, and continued walking away. With no answer, the choice was left to Kaiser, who risked following Kronin toward a destiny as blind as the night itself.

The floor of Kaiser's suite became slick with perspiration. In terms of power, he had always been leagues behind Kronin, no matter how he trained. But he still coveted that strength that none could question. More than techniques or lessons, Kronin had given the Cypolonian an ambition.

But Kaiser had been wrong about one thing. Kronin was not invincible, for strength is a multifaceted thing. It was proven at last by some incarnation of death. Only on that day, death wore the skin of a man and called itself Thel.

Chapter 14

Kaiser was more than prepared to see the Potentate when the day finally came. The intense training had made him anxious, but finally his transport arrived. A trim, a bath, and the handsome maroon tunic had given Kaiser the masculine bearing of a groomed warhorse.

Though he felt vulnerable about leaving his sword Seriath in his room, Kaiser's ride to the Meridian was a comfortable one. The four-horsed carriage ferried him to the lofty bridges of the Potentate's tower as he wringed his copper bracers in anticipation.

When he emerged from the carriage, Kaiser could already see a host of Whitecloaks. These men wore full armor, complete with long-face helms that obscured any semblance of humanity. Their white halberds were crossed high to make a tunnel for their liege.

The Potentate seemed to hemorrhage wealth. His purple robes were obsessively exalted in gold motifs. A rainbow of gemstones graced every finger as they turned up in welcome. And while his breastplate (a metallurgy marvel caressed in platinum) boasted more embellishments than any ten warriors could want, his gesticulations insinuated he was indeed more suited to combat than politics.

"Tireless Butcher! Finally, a face to go with the rumors." The Potentate hugged Kaiser, who was confounded by the pleasantness of his cologne.

"It's a great honor to meet you, Potentate," Kaiser answered, relieved at the informality. The Potentate was young by historical standards, a man of less than thirty with clean, angular features. His yellow-metal hair poured over his back like a golden horsetail, while his brown eyes were large, like a child's, gentle and thinking.

"I won't waste your time, Kaiser. Join me inside." The Potentate threw an arm around Kaiser's wide shoulders and wheeled him up the marble stair. The Cypolonian could feel the gaze of the guards. He decided against making any sudden movements.

"I can't thank you enough for seeing me, Potentate." Kaiser attempted to maintain reverence.

"Please, call me Nytrinion. We're all brothers here," the Potentate insisted.

"Of course. What have you learned from Caethys Cavawix?"

"Yes. Well, he did tell me about your defeat in the south."

Kaiser shut his lips tight.

"Don't feel ashamed, friend. You've done Kasurai a fine service." Nytrinion shook the embarrassment out of him. "The Septunites might have the greatest military ever assembled, even without these cult assassins they hire for battling threats such as the one you posed." Nytrinion's enthusiasm melted into darker emotions.

"Your country needs action, Nytrinion. The Septunites are just as breakable as we are. We can defeat them, but this stalemate is killing us. We are losing the south," Kaiser reported.

The Potentate chuckled mirthlessly. "The south? We are losing the war."

Kaiser and Nytrinion carried on as they feasted in the Potentate's private dining chamber. Four gothic windows revealed the storm clouds piling darkly outside. Pewter chandeliers kept their long table cleanly lit.

Roast duck, stuffed crab, a Federal pork dish called 'pig boats,' and other items were served to them in a seemingly endless supply. While Kaiser had drained his fourth iced whiskey, he was careful to curb the appetite found so often among warriors of his ilk.

"You're being too polite, Kaiser! Eat up, don't you like Kasurite food?" the potentate urged.

"It's excellent, Nytrinion, really. It's the Cypolonian in me, I suppose. Supper was a time of restraint," Kaiser answered.

"Now why is that?"

"Cypolon was a rocky little nation wanting for farmland. People often died of famine, so we were taught as children to eat in moderation." Kaiser looked into his cup. "Conversely, good drink was never scarce."

"Ha ha! Then let's drink to the defeat of the Septunites, and any impediment to harmony!" The Potentate raised his vessel and was mimicked from across the table. "Including those vile Bloodletters!"

"Curious fellows, those Bloodletters." Kaiser frowned. "They have no ties to Septunoth, but here they are murdering Federal nobles with no clear motivation."

"Speaking from observation, I think my ambition to end this war quickly frightens them. They are afraid of peace, and they are afraid of progress. And my methods are very innovative," came the answer, Nytrinion all the while admiring the sapphires set in his goblet.

"Maybe it's time for some innovation. What did you have in mind?" Kaiser queried.

Nytrinion licked his lips and leaned forward, resting his elbows on the table. "As for Septunoth, they have men, siege engines, and wealth. None of these things, in any combination have ever been able to match the warrior culture of Kasurai."

"By Zothre, I'll second that."

"So why do you suppose we are losing ground to a nation we've beaten in two previous wars?"

"Demon magic, of course."

"Exactly! Septunoth is nothing without their power from the Helix," the Potentate stated darkly. Kaiser fought down the desire to contort his face. "Kasurai can break any earthly army, any alliance of armies, just as we have for centuries. But against the power of the Infernal Helix, we are nothing."

Nytrinion smiled at a servant arriving with a platter. The servant uncovered a bowl of chocolate mousse crowned with cream. Nytrinion carved a morsel of chocolate from his bowl with a golden spoon before continuing the conversation. Kaiser received his own bowl but had no more appetite.

"How many times, Kaiser? How many times have we been denied a hard-earned victory when these cowards cast some demon magic over our men?"

"Ho ho." Kaiser gave a cold smile. "The stories I could tell you. But cooperating with the Archaic houses could remedy this, I think."

"Demon magic . . . blasphemous, but effective, no?" The Potentate kept an eye on Kaiser as he slid another spoonful of mousse into his lips.

"Yes," Kaiser agreed, but Nytrinion could tell by the warrior's stillness that he was reluctant to admit it.

"If we have the means of compensating for their advantage, shouldn't we seize the opportunity? What I'm saying, Kaiser, is that we have enemy sorcerers in captivity, and the tools to conjure living demons. Not even the Septunites have found a way to consistently call upon servile fiends. We can!" He put his fingers to his chest.

"Our Paragon has been striving for generations to prevent that very thing, Potentate," Kaiser reminded him, pointing up. His skin was beginning to burn. He had to be careful. This was royalty he was talking to.

"Kaiser, these are strange times. We have to be prepared to use whatever advantage we are fortunate enough to have, don't we?"

"Nytrinion, I realize it's tempting. I know better than any man in your cabinet the scope of demon power. But no nation can afford the toll demons demand. Septunoth will learn that."

"But we are different! We can control them, I've proven it. We can unleash our own infernal mercenaries to combat the Septunites! What's to stop us then?"

Kaiser's expression was one of both disgust and pity.

The Potentate frowned and went on. "You've seen the bloodshed yourself. Why not let demons die in place of our own soldiers?"

"Because it's our duty to die!" Kaiser barked, startling Nytrinion even from his distant seat. "I'm all for a fresh approach, but I'll skin a demon before I fight alongside one."

"I have suffered every consideration, Kaiser. Each time I realize we need to embrace the dark arts to protect our country. We must progress, or we will be forgotten."

"You're not talking about progress, you're talking about corruption! Begin conjuring demons, and we'll soon forget why we oppose the Septunites at all. That's what Opagiel wants, a world ruled by her sorcerers. I'd rather Kasurai burn." Kaiser tossed his spoon on the table with an angry clank. He glared, ready to cut down the Potentate's coming argument. Thunder sounded outside like a hungry beast's belly.

"Listen carefully, Kaiser. Since the Bloodletter rebellion, vacancies have opened in my military. I'm offering to make you a general in an invincible, supernatural army. You will be the greatest warlord in our nation's history." The Potentate was smiling again.

Kaiser sat for a moment, but his head began to shake. "No one loyal to the Covenant would abide this, and certainly not . . ." Kaiser hesitated. He realized that he had not seen Caethys since he paid his own visit to the Potentate. "Where's Caethys?"

The question melted Nytrinion's grin.

"*Where is he?!*" Kaiser screamed, standing and knocking over his chair.

"I'm crushed, Kaiser. I thought we were men of ambition," Nytrinion spoke. Kaiser noticed the Potentate glance at something behind him.

Metal sparkled under the Cypolonian's eyes. A hidden assailant grasped his chin from behind and moved a knife to his throat. Kaiser threw a hand up to stop the weapon from crossing his jugular, but his palm was slit.

The wolf-eyed warrior reached up with his injured hand and tightened his fingers into someone's hair, smashing his opponent's head down onto the table. The man's imploded face leaked heavily as the Cypolonian pushed him aside.

The assailant was one of the servants. Kaiser claimed his dagger as the Potentate screamed something. Nytrinion was raising a crossbow that looked rather like a complex string instrument.

Kicking the table forward into the Potentate's groin, Kaiser managed to divert his aim. A bolt popped his whiskey glass into sparkles. Unwilling to see things escalate, Kaiser grabbed a second meat-carving knife and threw himself from the chamber. The Potentate shot profanities and bolts at his escaping guest.

Kaiser's palm smeared blood across the white doors as he pushed them shut behind him. He jammed a tall, bronze oil lamp into the silvery handles for a barricade. A broad puddle of oil spilled onto the marble floor.

Kaiser chewed the preposterous truth for only a moment. The Potentate of the Apogee was a murderous demon summoner. He had likely killed Caethys.

The whiskey had put a haze around all his feelings. He felt sick or dangerously guilty, he wasn't sure which.

From the staircase ahead, the only other exit, came the drumming of boots. A gang of masked duelists emerged, looking so homogenous in their chain uniforms it brought one's vision into question.

"Wait! Just wait!" Kaiser could feel the veins in his face beating. "Do you know what Nytrinion's planning? Do you know who you're serving?"

Their swords did not lower, so Kaiser tried again.

"He plans to conjure demons, for mercy's sake! How can you allow that?"

When they made their reply, there was so little movement that it was unclear which of them had spoken.

"Nytrinion resolves to master demonkind. He has the courage to strengthen Kasurai." They advanced.

Kaiser's vision darkened until he saw nothing but their blades and the weak points in their armor.

"Tethra, forgive a poor desperate man . . . ," he prayed. A cinder from the tilted lamp fluttered into the oil spill. Flames bloomed.

Kaiser slid sideways as though on ice into the first one. There was a splash of blood as a knife found the duelist's throat. Two more cuts threw blood from each of the duelist's wrists. Kaiser composed himself before his victim crumpled. The light of the oil fire painted macabre shadows on the wall.

The others were triggered. Swords stabbed and slashed but were canceled by Kaiser's bracers. He untied their barrages with poetic finesse. *Thump, thump, thump!* Another three duelists fell dead.

The remaining foes debated advancing. Kaiser dropped the knives and slid two slender swords from the bloody floor. His reach was now tripled, and an array of new battle dynamics opened.

He simply walked for the stairs. A duelist struck at Kaiser's arm from what he thought was a safe distance. The Cypolonian ducked through, his blades in and out of the enemy's thighs in a blink. The duelist dropped, screeching and grasping the gushing punctures.

"Open this door, *now*!" came a voice from the barricaded banquet room. Blows were quaking the tall doors. Nytrinion had more reinforcements on his side.

The standing duelists raced to unblock the door. Reluctant to kill any more Kasurites, Kaiser flew down the staircase.

He ran into a narrow hallway with portraits to his left and windows to his right. Rain hammered the glass. The doorway ten yards ahead was thrown open and in poured at least a dozen Whitecloaks.

From the way he had come, Kaiser heard more men galloping in. The Potentate himself arrived leading the flanking party, with even more Whitecloaks backing him. Kaiser was surrounded.

"You have murdered your adopted countrymen today, Master Kaiser," said Nytrinion.

"A traitor is not a countryman," Kaiser quoted.

"So says the Creed. But who is the traitor here? Kasurai needs power and you would keep it from her."

"You think you can win this war with demons? Either you're thinking too hard or you're not thinking at all." Kaiser raked his swords together once, letting off sparks.

"That's quite enough. Give up your weapons. Take your penance and turn from this road, Kaiser, because my offer still stands," the Potentate promised.

Have I gone too far? Kaiser pondered. *Holy hellfire, I've killed Federal soldiers today. If I am doing wrong now, then every move I make from here is more dishonor.* Kaiser glanced out the window as a drop of blood from his injured hand whispered to the floor.

"Run, and you will be dead before you make the wall," Nytrinion warned.

"Promises, promises." Kaiser chuckled.

Before the Potentate could respond, the Cypolonian launched through the nearest pane, exploding the glass and descending into the rainy night. It was a longer fall than he would have preferred. He landed kneeling on the saturated balcony below.

A viper-fang sting told him his wrist was sprained. Cursing, he thrust his swords into his belt and ran to the railing. He stepped up and jumped to hug a rain-slick pillar. It agonized his wrist and palm, but he managed to slide to the ledge of an aqueduct below. The slippery footing shot his leg out from under him, and he spiraled into the coursing water channel.

The aqueduct declined, and the Cypolonian was rushed along the flow of a concrete half-pipe. He spared himself a concussion by covering his head as he collided with a corner. Clouds of scarlet drifted from a broad scrape on his arm.

The current flailed him in zigzags before emptying into a funnel. A column of blue light stabbing upward from a drain sucked Kaiser in.

Great stone lions with bronze crowns formed the base of the highest minarets. They made their roars with the crash of water streaming from their jaws. And where that water fell, so too did Kaiser.

Peering into the storm-shrouded heights of the Meridian, Nytrinion clicked his tongue at the absurdity.

The captain of his guard slid up his visor and turned to the Potentate. "Not to worry, my lord, we will apprehend him."

"Just kill him," Nytrinion spat. "He's best forgotten, like the rest of them."

"What shall I tell the banquet guests downstairs, my lord?"

"Tell them they must remain in the ballroom for safety. Blame it on the Bloodletters." The Potentate extended one arm into the rain, letting the raindrops break and scatter over his palm. He moistened back his golden hair.

Chapter 15

The carven likeness of a bathing woman sat poolside, watching Kaiser haul himself out of the water. He gathered from distant hollers that guards were being alerted. There was a furious clicking of a hoofed charge, and Kaiser spotted a mounted warrior racing for him. He reached for his swords, but they had been lost somewhere in his swim.

Best to run. Kaiser raced from the drizzling courtyard onto a narrow overpass that surveyed the towers of the Meridian's north wing below. With his pursuer gaining, Kaiser sprinted for an upcoming crossroad. He cast himself off once again into rainy oblivion.

His fall was snagged by the treetops of a pleasure garden. He landed in the runny mud of transplanted soil where hand-shaped leaves came fluttering down. Monstrously annoyed, he ripped the tunic from his body and discarded it as he rose. He began marching along one of the stone walks.

Lamps, impervious to rain in their glass bells, hung from stands resembling shepherd crooks. Their buttery light made every raindrop a tiny comet. Kaiser, half naked, was robbed of his night vision in such a pairing of brightness and dark.

Hoping to avoid any more freefalls, he made through the artificial wilderness toward the brick tenements at the end of the walk. Wet figures rushed him from either side.

He was caught unawares; there was no time for anything but killing. Kaiser safely negotiated their swings. He snatched a short sword from one's scabbard. Kaiser's weapon swam in sparkling patterns. Their vitals burst dramatically, and they collapsed to redden the rainwater.

"Damn." Kaiser felt he was nailing shut his own coffin. This was all too sudden, and all too radical. He knew justice and law were not always one and the same, but his morality was rocketing in some direction he couldn't distinguish.

He considered turning himself in, begging for pardon. Wasn't he being foolish to defy Nytrinion's genius?

Nytrinion would surely kill him now. Perhaps he deserved to die. Maybe it was best to leave Kasurai to younger, bolder men. Audacious ones who could glean power from a taboo that stunted this nation.

No, came a thought in Kronin's voice. Demons were anathema to everything remotely sane. And dying would leave too many things unfinished.

Kaiser followed the walk to a wooden door banded with black iron. He shoved at it without success. He drew up his confused rage and focused it into a kick that even horses would envy. The planks splintered, the lock creaked and jumped, but the door held.

He huffed and delivered another kick, this one breaking off the lock with a yelp of twisted metal. But some barricade kept the door from swinging inward.

Enough playing. He threw such strength into the following kick that a lesser man would have torn his thigh muscles. It smashed the door open, toppling the crates and racks of weapons that had been propped against it.

Tall wooden racks made a maze out of the chamber. Hundreds of clean and polished swords rested neatly on the rungs, the sleeping steel tickled in torchlight. Other unremarkables retired on hooks and rails. Wooden mannequins stood along the walls in combination armor and helmets.

Dripping, Kaiser stepped over the broken door pieces inside.

"Perfect." He praised his luck to find an armory. He threw on a padded undershirt that stunk of someone's sweat and began buckling on a Federal infantry chest plate. As his hands flew over the clasps, he noticed a dark smudge on the floor. Blood, streaked like someone had been dragged away.

Before the next drop of rainwater could fall from Kaiser's hair, he turned and kicked someone hard in the chest. His ambusher was thrown against a weapon cache and broke a pair of spears with his body. The rack tipped, crashing fantastically.

Kaiser was presented with the sight of a gang in scraps of black garments. He had not seen a more miserable lot since his departing from the Siegebreakers.

These men looked sickly and deadly at once, with pale, veiny muscles. Clearly, none among them had eaten well in weeks, but hate kept them sculpted. Red-rimmed eyes above sheer-edge, unshaven cheek bones turned to regard him with a suicidal animosity.

The apparent leader would have been a decent-looking human being in another life. He had long, dark blonde hair and a wide jaw made even more conspicuous by his hunger-thinned neck.

He turned to address a man fixing a bow on Kaiser. "Sobol, I thought you barricaded the door!" The leader's ear appeared infected, resembling a cured flap of beef.

"We did!" came the reply. Kaiser noticed that the knavish weapons and tools they carried were hardly that of guards.

"Where's your white cowl, loyalist? You *are* one of the Potentate's foot soldiers, aren't you?" the brass-haired adventurer said.

Under the stink of sweat and garbage, Kaiser could smell want in these men. Surely Nytrinion's faithful would live in better condition than these dregs.

"The hell I am. Whose side are you on?" returned the Cypolonian.

"We have been branded the Bloodletters," the leader declared, hands on hips. For all his miserable health, he was proud for a moment.

Kaiser prepared to dodge arrows. "You animals have killed whole families—"

"That's a lie!" The exclamation revealed a voice as tarnished as his appearance. "Nytrinion organized those murders and pinned them on us! The only fool we want dead is the Potentate himself, before he releases demons in our country."

Kaiser's fossilized grimace was suddenly shattered with laughter. He reached down and helped the man he had kicked to his feet.

"Imagine my surprise," he said, dusting his footprint from the dizzied Bloodletter's chest. "If you're telling the truth, I'm going to help you. Just keep your men at a distance until I see them kill some Whitecloaks," he insisted, and gathered weapons.

Nytrinion positively radiated displeasure as the weight of tonight's events dawned upon him. He threw open the iron-laden doors of his war room that he had fashioned from the former counsel office.

Inside, his warlords brewed schemes of blackmail, abduction, and worse to keep their liege in power. They gestured over provincial maps of Casanar, Grasnia, and Valathon, grinning wetly at the misfortune that was to fall upon key politicians.

Nytrinion ignored them completely, finding an iron ring on the floor. He pulled it to open the hidden cell below and entered.

It was an antiquated laboratory, with torches bubbling orange light. Nytrinion took one of them and lowered into the jungle of science. A withered old man with a tan apron and long white hair scribbled on parchment, juggling a tome in his other hand.

"Destiny waits for no man, sorcerer," Nytrinion commented to his minion. "I want you to open the portal tonight. Do you hear me, Norang?"

Nytrinion was met with a laugh. "You know it's not that simple, O Lord of the Apogee. Its stability would be questionable at best." Norang scratched at the sizable black tumor in the center of his forehead. It had swelled considerably in the time he had been the Potentate's captive.

"I captured you from your regiment because I knew Septunite hellbringers are the world's greatest artisans of demon magic. You can and will open that portal tonight," came the Potentate's wayward answer.

"You requested weak-minded demons from one of the most secretive realms in the Helix, my lord. They need to cross layers of pseudospace you couldn't possibly understand. It cannot be done tonight."

There was a long silence in which Norang simply went about his work. Then, quietly, Nytrinion produced from his robes a small glass orb. Inside was a human heart. Nytrinion held the orb to the flame of his torch.

Norang dropped his work with a flutter of papers. His back arched such that the surgical scar on his chest was exposed over the front of his apron. He screamed without sound.

Norang sank to the ground, beating his chest. The organ sustained no damage, but the pain was potent, even magnified.

The old man's tossing and clawing reminded Nytrinion of the time he pushed long nails into the body of a mouse in more innocent years.

"It shall be done!" Norang managed. Nytrinion cemented his obeisance, heating the heart so that the blood inside would boil, had it contained any. And without further words, he left.

Norang's forehead tumor ached with an artificial pulse. He could somehow feel the heat of the flame in his chest pushing up through his throat, scalding his tonsils raw and ringing through his teeth.

Alone in his prison of innovation, he tried to find his footing again. He had much work to do, there was no time for suffering. And death was an option he had been robbed of long ago.

Chapter 16

"Ever since Nytrinion rose to power in Evanthea, he's been reorganizing the military. He called us the Bloodletters and framed us for assassinations that his agents committed," explained Jeth, leader of the ratty rebels jogging behind them.

They were Archaics mostly, and Kaiser was soon endeared to them. There was no sacrifice they had not made to organize this suicidal coup, and through it all they retained their barbarian menace.

Along with the chest armor, Kaiser had dressed his legs in scales. He had selected a mace and a heavy pick: good fast skirmishing weapons for indoor combat. On his back he had belted a great sword and a sturdy round shield.

"If I had only known, Jeth. I would have torn his pretty face off the moment I met him," Kaiser replied.

"It gets much worse. Nytrinion is very capable of conjuring the demons he wants. Back during the Demon Trials, an artifact called the Planar Coil was confiscated from a witch coven and locked in the Meridian somewhere. It was used to call fiends. And now the Potentate has full access to it and every other occult weapon our forefathers locked away."

"Do you think Nytrinion is actually crazy enough to use it?" Kaiser asked.

"He's crazy enough to kill his own people," Jeth spat.

"The Potentate's tricked everyone. I feel like a damn fool."

"There was no way you could have known. Any tongue that wags against him ends up in a pile somewhere. There's a city within the city, Kaiser, and it's populated by his spies. He's turned Evanthea into a fortress, and he used the Federal treasury to do it."

"The bastard has been embezzling while the frontlines crumble?!" Kaiser desperately wanted to break something.

"He is a noble, after all."

"Even so, I wish we didn't have to kill countrymen to stop this lunatic," the Cypolonian commented far more quietly.

"A traitor is not a countryman," Jeth quoted the Creed, panting to show the rotted travesties that were his teeth.

"See, that's what I said."

The Potentate made his way to his private quarters. The pearl-encrusted doors groaned open, and he thrust himself into the tall chamber.

At the intrusive sound, the satin cocoon on Nytrinion's mammoth bed writhed to life. Galicia sleepily arose, dressed in fabric as thin as mist. Throwing the jet curls of her hair, she intercepted her lover.

"My conqueror, what are you about?" she purred, snaking her arms across his chest armor. He pushed off her embrace and continued to make for his sizable vault on the far end of the room. The vault's lock was imposingly customized. His gloved hands worked quickly, tossing the wheels in a practiced fashion. He had neglected Galicia more than once to pore over his treasures.

"If the renegade Kaiser escapes, the rebels in the city will gain a powerful ally. His presence may spark an attack by Jeth and his rats," Nytrinion began to recite the situation, more to himself than to Galicia. "If the savages aren't here already, that is."

"Is it really something worth concern? The measures you've prepared would grind any enemy to pulp," she said in her cool, midnight voice. Nytrinion compromised the lock and the hulking seal shuddered. The iron barrier lumbered open.

Colorful heaps of jewelry sparkled to life. The Potentate had masterminded the elimination of high-standing families near and far and squirreled away the choicest valuables to his personal trove. It had been his secret addiction since his teenage years when he was coronated.

Nytrinion's lips were drawn up, and his eyes were polished to a high sheen. His heart enflamed every capillary in his skin as he tasted the wealth with his eyes. It was the look he had now that Galicia coveted.

Galicia was a slave, though the account books would never use that word. She was there to satiate the hungers that distracted him. But in the confines of his touch, she had felt a connection that was prophesied in every romantic tale she had ever heard.

To elicit the same glee in him that his treasures did, that was her master passion. Because she loved him, didn't she? She wanted to suffer for him, to endure his troubles for him and sacrifice everything important for him.

She observed the stretch of his cheek. If only she could flush him like that! She wished she could endure something terrible for him, to crawl into his lap a flayed husk and feel his grateful tears salt her wounds.

Galicia touched his hand, and he smashed her to the floor.

If there was anger in her, it existed only in the cellar of her mind that had been mortared off in recent years. The tears that came now were of joy at his touch. Her smiling lip swelled with his love.

She had realized long ago what he had done to her family. But pain and love were indivisible, and hers all revolved around him. Her only choice, indeed her only quality that ever brokered his favor, was submission.

"Tonight is so important. I will be the first Potentate to enrich the Apogee with infernal sorcery. I will nail these rebels to the walls. By sunrise, I shall have an army of demons to finalize my supremacy." His voice echoed as he entered the reinforced vault.

"What of the Archaics, my lord?" Galicia whispered from her knees, unaware of the blood that sat on her chin like a rose petal.

"At the very first offense, I will crowd their lands with demons, until every bloody bone is chewed bare. I will fight this war against Septunoth in my own way, and I will win. Alone, if I must."

He emerged again from the vault, cradling in both hands a malevolent sword still tucked into the scabbard. Sleek, gothic artistry earned the weapon a stare from Galicia. It had been smoothly forged in doubly enriched craethune, lovely and deeply black.

"And your rule will be undisputed, from coast to coast!" Galicia orchestrated her voice carefully. Nytrinion looked to his floored temptress. He lowered to invite her touch. "Hail Nytrinion, master of men and demons," she whispered.

"And you, Galicia, have been my muse through all of it. Soon, you will be my queen," he breathed to her, the old passion she needed flowing through his words. She leaned in to kiss him.

Nytrinion threw the sheath from the weapon, exposing the devilish face of the blade. Illumined with unholy spirits, the sword *Imperium* gave off a sense of wakefulness. Desire and terror made Galicia a child.

"I will be a master of demons, in time. Go, love, and foretell my rule to them," he told her warmly.

She tilted back her head.

"I'm going to miss you," she said, a shine tracing down her face. "I promise, I will spread your name."

"I know you will." And Imperium had its first taste of suffering.

Nytrinion's guests drank glittering wine to gentle string music. Governors and wealthy landowners danced in a sunken ballroom with colorful furniture. Some muttered quietly on the couches, resting off the same exotic fare steaming on the servants' trays.

Whitecloaks guarded the garish feasting. They stood two to a door, leaned against banisters, or haunted the crowd with fingers on their pommels. One by one however, they were disappearing.

A duchess screamed when she saw shadows grow burly arms to snatch away a Whitecloak. At this, Bloodletters leaped from hiding, seeming to blink in from nowhere. The bloodbath began.

The thirsty chop of renegade swords turned every Whitecloak into dribbling deadweight in the span of three breaths. Party guests were held at sword point before they could realize the blood of their guards was speckling their faces.

Many party guests scrambled to escape, but the rebels blocked the exits. Jeth stole attention by leaping upon a table dripping with blood and wine.

"Well, well," he started, his wan, vein-addled face perfectly conveying his bitterness. "Have we been enjoying ourselves?"

His men beat unconscious any bloke that didn't brim with submission. Historically, Jeth was fair to prisoners. But the duress of the recent months had invented a will in him that would not be waylaid by sympathy.

Jeth leaned to grasp a juicy wedge of seasoned beef from the table and took a bite. It propelled every taste bud to painful heights of deliciousness. It was too much for his degenerated mouth parts, and he spit it out.

"I haven't tasted meat in months." Everyone was listening so closely, their white eyes irritated him. "Your host is not the man you think. Nytrinion is guilty of the blackest obscenities your drunken minds can imagine. Tonight, he dies—a fraction of the punishment he deserves."

Gasps among the party guests bubbled up and stopped as soon as Jeth's disgust surfaced on his lips.

"And if your love for this bloodsucking kin-slayer is so strong, I swear on my miserable life I will kill you with him." He truly hoped someone would commit the sin of defending their patron. None spoke.

Jeth's men began doling out rope and chained clamps. Screamers and groaners were beaten until they became more agreeable.

As tight as Jeth's arrest was, one loyalist mercenary slipped away, clutching the stomach wound that had allowed him to feign death.

Stealing through the back halls of the Meridian was Kaiser, hovering just beyond watchful eyes. As Jeth's rebels made the arrest, the Cypolonian elected to make off on his own. He trespassed where security seemed most resolute, taking keys and lives to penetrate the underworld Nytrinion had created.

He stepped into a greasy foyer where a grated drain in the concrete floor drank up the odious blending of sweat, urine, and bile. The mildew-flecked chamber door boasted stone faces once, but these had been cut out from their brassy frames, as if to deny them witness to whatever resulted in such issue of human matter.

The doors opened, scraping a semicircle in the wet grit. Kaiser obscured himself behind one of the pillars lining the foyer, where he bumped something with his hip. An old hand, chained to the wall, swung lazily without an owner.

The men emerging did so in a draft of stink that could only be the product of war crimes. Kaiser had smelled its like in the tunnels of Septunite shrine camps. The men wore robes of some religious purpose, and obscene masks with trunk-like fixtures for filtering out the smell of their work. They carried dripping drawstring sacks stuffed to capacity.

"Lord Zothre, do you thirst?" Kaiser inquired to his god of battle. "See me through, and I will bring you a sweet cup indeed."

Moments later a straggling man, probably an executioner like his companions ahead of him, came through alone with a bag in tow. The price of mercy was too much at this crossroads.

With his pickaxe, Kaiser ended the man before his cry could resound in his aardvark-like mask. The Cypolonian's swing snatched away a quarter of the man's skull. The runny fragments of his head glided down the door as his body knelt in defeat.

Eyes, ears, and fingers tumbled suddenly around Kaiser's feet from the bag that was dropped. He stepped back, sickened at their soft bulge under his boots.

Nytrinion was resembling a Septunite more every moment. Such grisly items were conduits in some circles of demonology. Kaiser's doubts evaporated like ice on a hot skillet, and he pulled open the door.

It had been a domed mausoleum once, but the tombs and urns had all been removed, and stories of cages installed. Scores of Nytrinion's enemies were hemmed in like farm animals by iron prisons, forced to observe the obscenities below.

Wheels, racks, presses, and other sadistic paraphernalia busied the floor. The blood exacted in this infernal carnival flowed in glittering ribbons to a well in the center of it all. Carefully cleaned skulls encircled the well, each crowned with candles of white or black flame.

A host of words fought for Kaiser's lips, but he humored only one.

"Caethys..."

Chapter 17

Meanwhile, the loyalist that had evaded Jeth's arrest had burst outside to a slick staircase flashing in the rain. At the top, he raced to the bell and heaved its rope. The clapper thundered off magnificent tones, enflaming the spell in the metal. Red light soaked through it like cloth absorbing blood, pulsing with every ring. It was crystal clear among the gray minarets of the dripping Meridian.

"They have raised the alarm. We haven't much time," Jeth said to himself back in the banquet chamber where he and his men had just finished binding the aristocrats. He plucked his two bulky maces from the straps at his sides and leaped upon a table once again, bowing the wine-stained planks under his weight. "They're on the way, brothers! Plenty for all of you!"

    In the stillness that wouldn't last, they all knew that, win or lose, the history books would remember them for challenging a Potentate.

Whitecloaks didn't react just in the Meridian, but all across the city. In towers, houses, taverns, and even in the streets, such mercenaries heeded the toll, looking up to see the bell knelling red.

    In moments, the rainy streets of Evanthea were animated with a hundred score loyalists converging on the main gate of the Meridian, ready to drown out any attempt at rebellion.

The bell ringer turned from his task. He stopped short, looking down the shaft of an arrow that Jeth's son Sobol had tensed on his bow. It was in his forehead the next moment, and the man fell onto the wet cobblestones. Sobol abandoned the bleeding body to the rain.

Kaiser's weapons felt a fraction as heavy now that primal magic coiled in his marrow. He cried out before rage hindered his powers of speech.

"Hang the Potentate!"

Nytrinion was a god, at least that's what the executioners had been trained to accept. And hearing their god slandered paused their unsavory work. Righteous hate compelled them to punish the intruder. On the grim tiers above, Whitecloaks scurried to intercept.

A half dozen mercenaries converged on the door. Kaiser resolved a barrage of stabbing scimitars easily enough to pull the lengthy great sword from his back.

His one-armed swing opened the rib cages of two men in a crunch of bone and a wet sprinkling of metal scales. They crumpled, grasping at the insides pushing from their chests. His pick found the head of the next man that gaped too long at his dispatched allies. Between jabs with his pick and cruising swaths of his great sword, Kaiser finished the first batch in time to make room for the executioners.

The first came on with an axe dripping from an evening of overuse. But he misjudged the length of Kaiser's blade, which passed through his neck before he could raise his weapon. His head dropped between his feet while his body took two dumb steps off the platform onto a bed of coals, where his garments caught fire.

The next executioner had pulled a white-hot brand from the same coals. He leaped over the railing of the stair to hammer at Kaiser. The Cypolonian playfully tapped the weapon aside, littering the bodies at their feet with glowing metal sparks.

The pick entered the executioner's forearm and pulled him into Kaiser's knee, which rose to meet his face. The great sword hungrily dove through his abdomen before any complaint could be made, and Kaiser kicked him off.

Prisoners began cheering.

"Not so amusing when your prey fights back, is it?!" Kaiser howled at the mercenaries that hesitated at the foot of his stair. He charged. Their lives as pirates and bandits couldn't prepare them for this sort of professionalism, and their squirting body parts were sent tumbling around the dungeon.

The bell had long since alerted Nytrinion of the intrusion. He walked the halls carrying Imperium. He began reassuring himself like a child waiting to be disciplined. He glanced out a storm-throttled window.

Small as it looked from this height, the mob of Whitecloaks below was more than sizable. They were funneling in through the gates far, far below. They would flood the Meridian with his bloody justice.

The uprising is doomed, he thought, *my mercenaries will overwhelm them with sheer numbers. And besides, I have greater allies on the way . . .*

Norang shivered at the tromp on the dingy stair. The old mage's fingers were gliding over a black orb grasped in a twisting copper stand almost as tall as he. The orb contained an excision of space itself, and it rippled darkly at his touch.

"Is the Planar Coil in readiness?" demanded the Potentate, his anger radiating like heat. The hellbringer regarded him with a face as subservient as it was bloodless.

"I have not failed you," Norang began, guarding his tone carefully. He sleeved sweat from the black tumor in the center of his forehead. "The blood from all of your sacrifices has fully energized the Planar Coil. Calling them won't be a problem but keeping the demons under control may prove to be—" He was cut short by the Potentate's outburst.

"Then summon them! A new chapter begins, and Nytrinion, Master of Demons, will ink it in the blood of rebels!"

Under his collared boots, Jeth could feel the distant hustle of two thousand hired swords. They were rising up through the stories below like boiling water.

"Nytrinion is too far up in his tower, we won't reach him before his Whitecloaks catch up to us," Sobol warned his father upon returning.

"We have to fight, Master Jeth. We won't have a chance like this again," came one Bloodletter's sentiment as he completed tying a wealthy old woman's hands to the rungs of a banister.

They were both right.

Was this how all the misery ended? Four months he had haunted the city sewers meditating on regicide, sleeping beside cold flows of excrement while rats tickled his ears with their whiskers.

He had cut deals with ghetto lords almost as twisted as Nytrinion, but he needed weapons and more food than he could retrieve from his rounds on the compost heaps. His men had begun killing themselves in the final days, unable to choose between capital punishment or life as a diseased rebel. He had to strike before he lost too many men.

"I've lived too long anyway." He had been fated into this crucible, it was his task now to simply act with dignity. He waved together a circle of his men with swings of his maces.

Sobol looked happier than he had been in months.

"This was the reason we were born." Jeth realized it no sooner than he said it. "It's all right to die here. You've done your part, my friends. But bring this regime down with you."

It was time to fight like the dogs they had become. The Bloodletters were a choir of war screams then, and those with the ability set their weapons alight with primal magic. The shackled aristocrats shuddered under the bestial commotion.

Jeth led a stampede of his barbarians through the chambers. Their brutish nature found release on the braziers, white statues, and mahogany furniture, all of which became broken litter in their passing.

The first enemy battalion rounded the corner and charged to meet them in a moment that came too fast.

The lines clobbered. The loyalists found out quickly why Bloodletter heads fetched such a lucrative bounty. These barbarians fought with tragic abandon. Loyalists had to begin watching their footing, as the guts and brains of fallen friends created a gory marsh under their boots. Battle, so long a fantasy, had become a reality.

For Jeth and his Bloodletters, there had never been such a distinction.

Chapter 18

With all adversity gored at his feet, blood-sprinkled Kaiser turned from the torture pit to the cages. He marched through the cell blocks, striking apart chains and locks as if they were glass.

"If you can fight, grab a weapon! We're taking down the Potentate!"

The inmates were gaunt, even skeletal, but there was still purpose in their manner. Kaiser's army quickly multiplied as prisoners freed others. Rods, chains, knives, and other tools of cruelty became their weapons.

Taking a moment to enjoy the reversal of injustice, Kaiser raised his gaze to the rafters. Men hung like dirty garments from a cable high above, by their hands, feet, or necks. Then the torchlight touched off a familiar face.

"Caethys." Kaiser climbed the stairs pushing aside prisoners. He yanked the cable through the pulley, the hanging men groaning their soreness. Others helped cut down the suspended victims, most of whom were dead.

Caethys hung on the cable by one hand. His arm had been grossly elongated, no doubt broken or dislocated. Kaiser cut the shackles from Caethys's ruined arm and laid him on the sludge-laden mortar. The parched lips bobbed.

"Kaiser?" Caethys didn't trust his watery eyes.

"I'm here, Cae. Praise Tethra, I thought you were finished," Kaiser gushed.

"The Potentate, he's"—Caethys gasped—"an ass." Kaiser worried at his ability to stand, but Caethys pushed away, rising to his feet. Kaiser curiously followed him down the steps, watching the corporal's arm dangle uselessly.

Back in the torture pit, Caethys found a saber among the bodies.

"I am the king of fools," he said, examining himself in the face of the blade. "I ignored all my doubts and called it loyalty my whole career."

Kaiser wasn't about to lecture Caethys, who seemed angrier at himself than at Nytrinion's cruelty.

"Help me bind this." Caethys gestured to his impotent arm. "If revolution is here, I must be a part of it."

Norang sensed the presence of the Helix welling around the Planar Coil like vapor. The sacrifices had powered it beyond anticipation. The elderly mage knelt fearfully behind his workbench. Nytrinion, on the other hand, looked ready to embrace the device.

The gloom churned inside the glass orb, collapsing into itself again and again to become ever blacker, ever thicker. Specks of scarlet light flared up inside like fireflies. In an eldritch scream, the first ball of red energy spit forth and zigzagged out of the room. Then another deafening gob of hellstuff escaped, then another and another. Soon, Norang's humble chamber became a hive of swarming crimson sparks.

"Rally to your new king, hellspawn!" Nytrinion bleated in ecstasy. "Shatter this old world and set my throne in its ruin! Pay me homage with the screams of the weak!"

Norang hoped the dark weapons that he had modified for Nytrinion really would keep the demons in control. Still, Norang feared he had ushered in a catastrophe even his Septunites could not equal.

"Oh, Tethra . . . ," Norang prayed to the Paragon he had long abandoned. He could feel a raw sharpness in the air that made all the demon magic he'd ever known feel like a diluted imitation.

There was a deep sinful stink only the soul could perceive as the red energy broke against the walls. The splashed hellfire birthed a riot of membranous, pulsating shapes dripping with liquid shadow.

"Save us from our folly!"

The Bloodletter's butchery hadn't just kept the loyalists at bay. It had dropped them in gored heaps over the rugs and furniture and squirted the walls in blood. What had been an orderly ensemble of Federal living became a canvas of debris and carnage.

Despite their inferior training, the Whitecloaks did not relent, surging into the violence. The waves of hirelings hammered at Jeth's shrinking ranks. Every time a Bloodletter succumbed to Nytrinion's loyalists, the aggression was renewed. Jeth was beginning to fight for honor rather than victory.

All of a sudden, every light source weakened. Candelabras and lamps died out as a freezing gust passed through like the breath of Opagiel herself.

Scarlet energy speared into the dim room. It splattered like an egg into a glowing puddle of brimstone. Ambiguous appendages slogged up from the gooey hellfire. Rising up to the height of a man, the sulfur-drenched being shivered off its dripping sparks.

Lightning flashed long enough to reveal a nauseating mutation clutched in some parasitic fungus. Most fighters were too busy to notice it scuttle into the shadows, claws clicking along the floor.

A barbarian found himself suddenly caught up in something like prehensile antlers. He was pulled back into the shadows, into a waking nightmare of indescribable pain as the beast drank away his flesh.

Another comet landed behind Jeth's ranks. It too melted into a pond of sulfur, yielding a second monster from the Helix. It was a hugely fat biped, white skin jutting with cancerous tubules. This one snatched up a loyalist wounded on the ground. Strange jaw bones retracted around an acid-gurgling mouth. The mercenary was stuffed hungrily inside.

"Sobol!" Jeth hollered to his son, who was just then rising from his latest kill. "Take down that fiend!" Sobol withdrew from battle, substituting his sword for a bow and fired at the creature. The projectile stuck the hefty thing in the chest, tapping only a trickle of emerald green fluid.

Very well, Sobol thought, reaching for one of the arrows that had been blessed by renegade priestesses.

The arrow stuck the demon's arm and a fountain of hot pink sparks grilled its flesh. The demon trumpeted with reptilian pain. Rather than suffer the injury, it used its remaining hand to pull off the afflicted arm in a gush of alien slime.

Glowing demon-pods from Norang's device flew about the chambers of the Meridian and more fiends joined battle. They began closing in from other rooms, killing for pleasure as much as hunger. Like towers of ugliness, they ripped both rebels and loyalists apart.

Jeth leaped from the mob of warring humans at the beasts. He pummeled one tall deformity with his twin maces. It reeled from the bone-crunching blows to crush an oak table under its weight. Far from dead, the beast arose with revitalized hatred, yellow liquid cascading from its pincers.

"Anything can be killed"—Jeth quoted one of his favorite Archaic passages— "if you just hit hard enough."

The prisoners procured whatever armor they could find from the dungeon. Caethys took leg armor, but remained exposed above as he was unable to suit up over his slung arm. They followed the clamor of battle, chasing through the oddly darkened halls. Suddenly, one of the crimson bolts zipped ahead of them, bursting into ruby fire.

Slithering mightily from its burning mire emerged a black frog shape. Its back four locust legs looked capable of jumping through the ceiling, but the way its front hands raked smoking gashes in the floor, it seemed happy to be where it was.

The demon flicked a long appendage from its back at the prisoners. Caethys's good sword arm whacked it aside, saving a life.

Kaiser wasted no time in charging the beast, crunching his spear as deep into the mouth as it would go. The monster choked on spurting green ooze as it chomped the spear in half. It swiped at the shifting Cypolonian who ripped the great sword from his belt.

With might from a life of warfare, Kaiser launched a diagonal swing that divided the opponent's head. Its neon gore lavished the opposite wall before it tripped over its own steps, never to rise again.

"Nytrinion is summoning his demon army," Caethys deduced. The beast's energy was silently being absorbed by Kaiser's hungry chrysm. "I couldn't face him in my state. Kaiser, do you think you could manage him?"

"I guess we'll see."

"Good enough. The men and I will help reinforce the rebels."

"All right, but stay alive, Cae. I didn't spring you so you could go die two hours later!" Kaiser took the nearest staircase while the others continued on.

What awaited Caethys and his threadbare posse was a scene of madness. Loyalists and rebels hacked away at each other while demons materialized around them, slaughtering either side. Caethys spurred his men to join battle. The barbarians suddenly found themselves relieved by some four-dozen fellow Kasurites as grungy and starved as they were.

Caethys's rapid sword brought down two loyalist opponents before Jeth's body hurtled by to smash a gold-framed portrait off the wall. The Archaic dizzily took to his feet.

"Kaiser freed us from the prisons, Jeth! We are here to help you!" Caethys spoke quickly before Jeth's opponent was upon them.

This creature sported a conical head with one eye and four arms ending in lobster claws. A lizard tail wriggled behind its beetle-shelled body. It seemed possessed of a dark pride, as though it had long enjoyed the fear of other creatures in its realm.

"If you have holy magic, Federal, now is the time to employ it!" At Jeth's recommendation, Caethys blew coolly along the length of his sword. His breath set waves of twinkling turquoise magic up the face of the steel.

Chapter 19

Sword and shield at the ready, Kaiser breezed through the mayhem. Those balls of red magic were flying and birthing fiends everywhere. Here and there, the carcass of a loyalist would be dashed across the floor or scattered on the wall. Nytrinion had apparently not taken pains to keep his demons from murdering his own men.

Kaiser came upon the gore-stained wreckage of a lounge. Besides the light of a low burning fireplace, six winged demons with heads that curled back like snail shells feasted on the remains of handservants. Scorpion tails played at their flanks.

"Oh, you are too kind, Lord Zothre. Are these all for me?" Kaiser praised. One beast looked up from its feast, its tusks dripping red. It roared with gore bubbling in its gullet. The others rose to attention, slathered in sacrifice.

Kaiser made his intentions known when he threw his sword into the nearest demon's abdominals. It howled like something between a wolf and a goat, spraying blue blood from wound and mouth. The rest charged Kaiser quick as hounds.

The Cypolonian front-kicked the first one and flattened it.

He plucked his pick from his belt. He pivoted to avoid the raking claws and deflected the next demon's hand. He spun to slice open its leg with his shield edge. An adjacent beast attacked. Kaiser tumbled and rose to plant the pick's beak into its chest. It screamed as Kaiser abandoned the weapon and backed from the wounded enemies. Four had now been injured.

He threw his shield then, which bit into the fifth enemy's throat. The attack severed the creature's airway and sent it sprawling. The only uninjured enemy came on and closed the gap. It clawed a wealth of blood from Kaiser's armored shoulder blade as he maneuvered. The wolf-eyed fighter lunged, grabbed the demon's tusks and threw his knee into its skull. Tiny teeth and blue liquid squirted over his thigh.

Sensing an attack from his periphery, Kaiser ducked and rolled backward. It was the demon with the sword in its torso. The Cypolonian grabbed the lodged sword and wrenched it from the spraying wound that crumpled the demon.

In a flowing whirl, Kaiser sent his lengthy blade on a course through the neck of the beast that had been kneed to the face. Its head rolled from its shoulders as sapphire fluid poured down its chest.

The demon that had been floored by Kaiser's kick had recovered and charged again. The Cypolonian shifted in briskly and drove his blade into its chest so deeply that the cross guard pressed into its ribs. He drew out his mace and exploded the demon's head into flying blue gelatin.

The creature with the pick in its chest arose now. It tried to escape, but Kaiser was on it at once. It swung a claw that only managed to get broken by his mace. He seized the handle of the lodged pick and pulled it sideways, opening a crevice across its abdomen.

Its tail whipped over his shoulder and hooked into his armored back. Kaiser kneeled at the pain. Before the demon could follow up, the mace swung high to knock its jaw across the room.

Kaiser put the pick into its chest again to pull himself to his feet. He dropped both weapons and gripped the thing's head. With a twist, he cracked its neck. It dropped.

The Cypolonian found himself alone in a room of half-eaten servants and six slaughtered demons. He closed his eyes and calmly slid the hooktail from his back wound. He could feel the freshly released infernal energy of his victims. It siphoned into his chrysm, and he could enjoyed his primal magic strengthening. Some of the energy though, he saved to expend in the battles to come.

Kaiser prowled the richer-looking chambers that he assumed Nytrinion would frequent. A half dozen more demons died in his search, and Kaiser's powered chrysm made him feel ready to duel a crazed aristocrat.

He finally found himself crossing a smooth floor in a circular room. A fine map of continental Kasurai had been rendered into the marble at his feet, with mountains and lakes labeled in a strange dialect of Civilic. His footsteps echoed off the statues of late Potentates that stood around the chamber.

"I thought you might find your way back to me," Nytrinion opened, half-hidden in a doorway's shadow, as eminent as the statues surrounding him. Kaiser fought down a sudden rush of panic; in just the few hours since their dinner, some terrible, spiritual change had come over Nytrinion.

"I will laugh over your demise with the next Potentate." Kaiser reasserted his role as punishing avenger. "You've been seduced, Nytrinion. The Helix has won your soul, and I'm going to send it there."

Clusters of alien light kindled in the shadowy hall behind the Potentate. Floating in from the dark came the blade Imperium and a round shield of demon skin. Fiendish crystals were set in the center, fueling the vascular currents branching across the shield. Both items gravitated right into the Potentate's outstretched hands.

"These weapons were locked away in our vaults centuries ago. The capital sits on a wealth of demon artifacts that most are too afraid to exploit." An unholy color welled up under Nytrinion's skin as he spoke, and it did not escape Kaiser's notice. "And cowards have no place in my kingdom."

Nytrinion may be a lazy noble, Kaiser cautioned himself, *but those weapons have done something to him. I'd wager he's twice the warrior he normally is.* Even so, Kaiser became a one-man stampede rushing his enemy.

The Cypolonian's barrage of hacking and slashing confirmed his thoughts. The Potentate leaned and stepped, avoiding the cuts by a slender margin. Nytrinion was somewhat shaky however, unfamiliar with his new athleticism.

Kaiser received a sudden punch against his shield with the Potentate's own. He skidded back on his feet and had to circle his arms to regain balance.

Oh, yes, he is stronger indeed.

Nytrinion wore his excitement plainly on his face. His teeth glistened hungrily as he pressed with his own whirlwind assault.

Kaiser absorbed the blows to his shield, but all the while a vibrating pain welled up in his head. He parried a blow with his sword, and a sudden mindspite spell raged like a fire behind his eyes.

Desperate for some space from his aggressor, Kaiser fell backward into a roll and rose to his feet some distance from a chuckling Potentate. Blood started from the Cypolonian's nose as the pain in his head abated. It was Nytrinion's devil sword; once struck, it cast the sensation of a mindspite spell.

Nytrinion's laughter brewed up as he slashed again from some twenty feet away. A gash ripped through the floor as a crescent of distorted air flew from Imperium at the Cypolonian. Kaiser's shield took the hit, scarred red hot along its surface. Nytrinion was *throwing* his slashes.

Nytrinion tried again. Kaiser braced his shield against it, and in a moment felt the lower half of it drop off, sheared clean. The Potentate rushed in, but Kaiser was determined to remain aggressive.

They closed and swirled over and under each other's blows. Kaiser wanted to avoid any contact with the devil sword to keep his senses about him, but Nytrinion's speed was mounting. The air whooshed heavily with rowing steel. The Cypolonian was losing momentum to the Potentate's offensive.

In the span of a blink, Kaiser found the narrowest of openings to Nytrinion's throat. His sword would not make it, but his shield might. With a backhand, he struck out with his broken shield edge.

Kaiser was rewarded with a sudden splash of arterial crimson. A killer stroke. Nytrinion stumbled, clasping at his throat with not so much horror as . . . annoyance. While his throat spilled over his robes, he rebalanced. The jewels set into his shield flickered to life, working their profane magic through his flesh.

The skin stretched over his wound and sealed up, completely reversing the cut. Nytrinion had lost a little blood on his robes, but otherwise was left unscathed. The shield jewels went dark again.

"Thank you, Kaiser. I'll remember to keep my guard up." He grinned, some redness slipping down his lips. But Kaiser was not discouraged. He had been cheated out of a kill, but Nytrinion had lost blood, and it may have weakened him.

Confident he could match the Potentate's strength, Kaiser expended a share of his saved demon energy. The brisk, crackling sensation made him feel like a god. Nytrinion seemed to notice and set his shield squarely before him.

With speed rarely seen in humans, Kaiser was upon the Potentate again. He slashed down heavily on Nytrinion's shield. To the

Cypolonian's surprise, the impact on the shield squirted a yellowish chemical. Kaiser spun away to avoid it, but his naked arm caught a dose of a caustic acid. It sizzled in patches, discoloring his steaming skin. Nytrinion was so taken with laughter that he allowed Kaiser to fall back and shake the caustic juices from his arm.

"Oh, don't stop now! There are volumes of pain I must teach you!" Nytrinion boasted gleefully. "I stand among the world's foremost infernal warriors. You are moments from a sorry end."

"Please, I've killed larger things than you tonight," Kaiser retorted, diluting his opponent's levity.

Nytrinion was perplexed to see the Cypolonian shoving his sword into the marble and dropping his shield. He also compromised his chest plate bindings and removed it entirely.

"Well, it seems the only thing standing between you and supremacy is a half-naked, unarmed foreigner. Don't lose here, Nytrinion. They'd laugh at you for centuries."

Nytrinion saw little more than a hunk of meat ready to be carved before him. So with boundless gusto he threw himself again at the Cypolonian. Imperium swam in the afterimage of Kaiser's dodging form, nicking tiny cuts against his arms and sides.

Another trick of Nytrinion's: The little cuts by Imperium produced incredible burning pain, like a branding iron on the skin. The cuts reddened and aggravated Kaiser's veins, but he kept his composure as he shifted out of range again, keeping his fists high.

He's not very inventive with his attacks, Kaiser noticed, trying to ignore the acute scorching in his little wounds. *But he's fast, I'll have to be ready.*

The Potentate tired of the game and lunged for Kaiser's center mass. A Cypolonian foot kicked the sword off course, and Nytrinion found himself a hand's width from Kaiser's face. A backfist and a full on swing, and the Potentate was sent on a dizzied spin.

Kaiser was gratified to see that a heavy front kick to his enemy's shield was not enough to trigger the acid spray. The Cypolonian pressed, hammering the demon shield with energized kicks and shoves. Nytrinion gave ground, retreating into the shadows of the hall again.

The two passed into the darkness. Nothing could be seen on either of them save for the satanic gems in the Potentate's weapons and Kaiser's golden eyes. Before Nytrinion could think out a plan of attack, the Cypolonian closed his eyes and became totally invisible . . .

The quiet moments flew off with Nytrinion's confidence. He couldn't even hear Kaiser's breath. He swung blindly in all directions, succeeding only in illustrating his position to his stalker.

The shadows were suddenly filled with the blunt, meaty sounds of a savage beating. Nytrinion's head was knocked about by merciless fists, knees, and elbows. At last, he was thrown from the far side of the hall, his face a purpled, bleeding caricature. What was more, Nytrinion found his shield had gone missing.

Kaiser emerged now, his knuckles painted crimson. The demon shield was in his hand. He noticed that he did not enjoy the healing benefits from it that Nytrinion had.

Convinced that he was still twice the man his foe was, Nytrinion rolled to his feet and angrily launched cutting waves of force at Kaiser. The slicing force bit into Kaiser's newly won shield. Fresh acid streamed heavily from its surface, and Kaiser found his chance.

With a bodily twist, Kaiser hurled the shield like a discus. Nytrinion panicked, batting the projectile aside with a swing from Imperium. The loose acid, however, leaped and rained over his chest, face, and shoulders. It quickly corroded his face and robes, which dropped the glass orb containing Norang's heart. It broke into large pieces at his feet.

In the innermost chambers of the Meridian, the mania of Norang's laboratory drowned out a short-winded gasp. The mage was struck by death in the shadows of his chamber where the Planar Coil still hurled out infernal spawn. Norang crumpled to the cobblestone, finally freed of his bondage.

Doubled over and face dissolving Nytrinion unwittingly signaled for Kaiser to move in. He tackled Nytrinion to the ground, straddling him.

"Fool! Kasurai will not survive if we do not—"

Too livid to suffer conversation, Kaiser gave the Potentate a brain-rattling hook to the temple and did not stop. Each successive punch came harder and harder, throwing saliva and scarlet across the marble. When he was satisfied that Nytrinion had been subdued, Kaiser forced Imperium to the tyrant's throat.

The blade slid deeply across the jugular. Hot, thick blood rushed over Kaiser's fingers. A rose-colored disc widened under the tyrant's head. In his last moments, Nytrinion conveyed something like remorse through his frightened gaze. When stillness came over his victim, there was guilt in Kaiser's breath.

"I pray Tethra will still welcome you as a guardian soul, brother. But you should have placed more trust in your people." Kaiser sighed. His eyes wandered to the gothic blade in his hand. He abandoned Nytrinion's corpse.

Kaiser ignored the screams of his better judgment and admired the devil weapon. It was a satisfying weight that braced together grotesque organic features. Through the hilt, Kaiser could feel a semi-sentient evil taking notice of him from within the metal. The enriched craethune sent a seductive wave of corruption up through his veins. He would have to be careful.

Chapter 20

The walls rattled, inciting the aristocrats to whimpering. They crowded the center of the chamber, still confined with rope. A few barbarians had been left by Jeth to keep them in check.

"One's coming! It's coming!" one captive hollered. He pointed into a black hallway where a great, blood-red eye was peering in. Realizing it had been spotted, the shrouded demon thrust into the room at top speed.

It resembled nothing so much as a massive, floating head. Cancerous rot bulged and drooped from a cyclopean face, with black tentacles hanging from either side of its skeletal jaws. It's wobbling scarlet eye narrowed as it hurtled for the quivering partygoers.

The beast didn't notice an armored figure walking to intercept it. There was a wink of polished steel and a gush of white cranial juices. The flying ball of flesh and teeth was brain-dead. It struck the ground and bowled over a group of banquet guests. They were unharmed, but blubbered like children.

With his axe dripping in his powerful hands, Arcton's body stirred with the thrill of true combat at last. His old heart pumped warrior's blood. Monsters from hell were raising mayhem in the Meridian itself. Arcton praised Zothre in his mind to be thrust into such a magnificent battle!

"Drop that weapon, Federal!" A young Bloodletter commanded. Arcton halted him with a glacial stare. The rebel youth was insistent. "The Bloodletters are in control here! We will fight this battle!"

"If this is control, I'd like to see what you call a real mess!" Arcton laughed. "This is my fight too, boy. So stay out of my way.

Caethys had weakened the lobster-clawed giant with several cuts. Syrupy ichor was dripping off its arms. Dizzily, the demon lunged. Caethys sidestepped, and his blade licked in an upward arc that found the beast's neck. Caethys took a spray of slime. The monster dropped dead, and the corporal sought out Jeth, who was bashing some demon's head into the fractured marble.

"Jeth, we cannot sustain this fight! We must close off the source of these creatures!" came the corporal's desperate cry. It dawned on Jeth what he must try to do.

"My son!" he cried out. Sobol looked up from his archery. Jeth gestured for him to follow. Sobol joined and the two raced from the battle in the direction from which the red energy balls were flying.

No one seemed to notice the blue energy ball that had passed through the chamber and out a window to fly into the night sky . . .

The ensuing roar rattled the foundations of the Meridian itself, making the debris dance on the floor. Every human ear was raked by the noise. Even demons took pause, hearkening to the new predator that had crossed into the world.

The restaurant owner in the slums of Evanthea was as confused as anyone about the rush of the Potentate's mercenaries to the Meridian. He stepped to the window of his establishment on the streets, toweling a glass mug. He cast an eye toward the Meridian and froze, the moonlight playing off his eyes. There was a violent crash as the mug slipped from his hand. He stepped outside, ignoring the rain.

The storming skies above the Meridian churned like witch's brew. The electrified clouds were being pulled apart, opening a hole to eternal chaos.

Stretching down from the vortex were spidery legs long enough to arch over city blocks. A bulky abdomen squeezed from the portal suspended by silk. Blue lightning danced over the strange barnacles that armored its body.

It was a god to all blood-drinking creatures that haunt secret places, and it professed a magnificent hunger. If not by how the pedipalps twitched, then by how the gaunt hands on its front four limbs clenched and plucked at one another.

"It is we who are vermin to be crushed underfoot." The restaurant owner kneeled and paid homage to his new god with bitter tears.

The marble floor and walls suddenly ruptured. Piles of masonry tumbled to the lower levels through the disintegrating floor. Humans and demons were plunged into the pitfall of rubble. Among them was Caethys, who landed upon a dais one floor below. Then his eyes told him something he could not believe.

A mountainous, sopping exoskeleton heaved beyond the demolished brickwork. It was encrusted in hardened mildew. It had an overpowering chemical stench, as though it hailed from an ocean of poisons.

Another hulking shape smashed into the room in an avalanche of shattering stone. Through the dust clouds Caethys could see the vast, dripping appendage crushing rebels into red streaks. Caethys realized that these two shapes were both part of the same, impossibly huge demon.

The sound of thunder, galloping Whitecloaks, and screaming finally pulled Sidna from her slumber. She roused from her bed, little more than a stuffed mat with layers of old clothes for covers. Adjusting her eye patch, she squinted to look out the dripping window. She couldn't see much more than people hollering in the street.

But above the yelling was another noise. A tumbling roar like an avalanche, and it sounded from the center of the city.

Tethra, are we under some sort of attack? A banging noise from above made her jump. Something was on the roof.

Words refused to form on her quivering lips, so she jammed her hand under her bed, pulling out a short sword she had purchased for home protection. She began pulling on her campaigning boots. Aside from these, she wore only patched slacks and a sleeveless work tunic. She turned back quickly to the two children dozing in her bed.

"Get dressed, Shaden girl. Keb, wake up, sweety." Sidna patted the little boy on the rump. As Shaden rubbed her eyes, she noticed Sidna held her sword.

"Are we in danger?" the girl demanded, rising from bed.

"Don't worry, I'll keep you two safe. But we have to leave now."

"Where we goin'?" asked Keb, kicking off a quilt.

"To the barracks. Put these on or you'll freeze." Sidna buttoned large coats onto each of the children. She had promised to get them shoes when she had the money, but tonight they would have to do without. She threw a cowl over her own shoulders.

"Are we gonna die?" Keb's eyes widened as the roof creaked. Dust fell from the rafters, and the planks bowed under tremendous weight.

"Listen, now!" Sidna pulled the children into a whispering huddle. "We've got to be real fast and real quiet, got it?"

"Like mouses?" Keb hissed.

"Right. Now stay close," Sidna commanded. She led the children into the kitchen, where she peered out an old side door. There was nothing out back but a weedy yard, plus some hanging laundry soaking in the wind. She held the knob to keep it from rattling and bumped the door open with her hip.

The midnight rains spared them nothing, chilling them as they stepped into the squishy grass. Sidna turned her head in every possible direction, trying to identify threats in the black shapes. The electrified sky briefly lit a path to the alley.

"This way." She palmed the children forward with her unarmed hand. The sound of tumbling pots and pans rang out from her home behind them. Something was hunting them, and it had already broken into her kitchen.

Keb was quickly scooped into Sidna's arms, while the woman trusted Shaden's speed to match her own. They padded through the alley and descended a slippery ladder down onto a concrete trail beside a waterway.

Sidna had jogged between her home and the barracks a thousand times and knew every possible route between them. She wanted to lose her pursuer, but also to get to the barracks as quickly as possible.

Keb's weight finally made Sidna's arms ache, and in the absence of any noticeable threat, she led the children underneath a willow tree on the bank of small body of water. Shaden needed a rest anyway.

A tall concrete dam gushed across the lake, fed by the storm. Sidna had hoped the sound of crashing water and the midnight darkness would conceal their presence.

"A little cold out here, isn't it?" Sidna smiled to the children. They were obviously miserable, but the redhead's beaming warmth was always welcome, just as it was when they worked loading produce at the marketplace.

"What's happenin', Sidna?" Keb asked, scooting closer to her under the tree. The woman shrugged, squeezing the two to share her body heat.

"It's always something, isn't it?" Sidna lamented. "You two should know that life isn't always so hard. I know you miss your mama and papa, but there will be more good people in your lives. And good times too."

The children had been very strong in the days since their rescue. Sidna sometimes found them pouting during their work at the storehouses. She tried to be a friend to them, but her duties as a soldier and farmhand made it sparse.

"Some things you can't change. So the best thing to do is put your head down and barrel through. Can't cry all the time, so you might as well laugh," Sidna said. "Believe me, I know it's hard to lose family. But you do get through it."

"You don't cry," Keb asserted, transfixed with the strands of her wet cinnamon hair.

"Yeah, I got tired of it, I suppose. I bawled myself inside out after my city got captured. A time comes though, when you realize strength isn't a talent. It's a choice."

It felt good to catch their breath to the sound of rushing waters and nameless demolition booming in the distance. Sidna took turns looking down on the sopping hair of the children.

They were beginning to love her. It wouldn't be long, and she would deploy again for the frontlines. She considered getting permission to stay in Evanthea for a few more months, but the troops needed her too. At least she knew she had to be a model for these kids. It would probably mean not drinking so much . . .

"Give me a moment, I should take a look around," Sidna whispered to them. They let her out of the huddle, and she gripped the sword in her teeth. She reached up into the branches of the willow and pulled herself up into the crown with the ease of a true athlete. The children watched some bubbles gurgle along the bank.

Sprouting from the top of the tree, Sidna cast her eye toward the Meridian. She almost lost her sword when her jaw dropped and her eye expanded.

A demon arachnid blundered over the towers of the Meridian, banks of flame illustrating the features of its monstrous hide.

"What in the holy name of—"

"*Sidna!*" Shaden's shriek jerked her attention back to the ground. A long hump of slippery black flesh had hauled itself out of the lake like a slug. Nubs along its oily body functioned like little legs, paddling along the rocks for the children.

Sidna took her sword in hand and dropped through the branches. She succeeded in landing on her side between the slug beast and the children.

The creature's head lurched forth on a surprisingly elastic neck, its skin folds stretching smooth. Sidna, sore from her drop, chopped at the thing's tubular mouth. The beast flinched a bit but kept extending.

Sidna kicked at it: a mistake. The sphincter-like mouth sucked her foot inside hungrily. She pulled, but dozens of angled teeth in its esophagus hooked into her leg. All the while, the thing's lip flaps worked to draw her leg deeper inside. The monster's nostril holes whooshed with the effort of trying to swallow its prey.

"Go! Take Keb and go, Shaden!" Sidna screamed. But Shaden had rushed to claim a hunk of broken driftwood. "I said go, Shaden!"

Sidna's swipes into the creature's skin did little more than cause dents which reinflated. *I'm going to lose my leg*, she thought as she felt clammy muscular action push more teeth into her foot.

With fright burning her from within, Shaden approached the side of the creature, unsure of what she meant to do with this length of wood.

A lump on the side of the creature's body split open lazily, revealing a melon-sized eyeball. It was white with a gray-blue iris that made it look distortedly human. It settled its jiggling ocular organ on Shaden, its nostrils huffing.

Shaden's first-ever battle cry carried the notes of abandon and fear at once. She jammed the broken end of the plank under the pupil of the eye. The wrinkled eyelids closed on Shaden's lodged weapon as the beast groaned humanlike through its nostrils. The girl caught a dose of flying green ooze.

Sidna slid her sword beside her leg into the mouth, using it to pry the opening wide. She wriggled her foot, trying to dislodge from all the little spikes inside. Shaden swatted the plank again, trying to deal more injury. It was enough to widen its mouth, and Sidna jerked her leg free, minus a boot.

Did I black out? Sidna asked herself, because she could not remember up until this moment: Keb on her back and Shaden jogging beside her. The running had pumped a lot of blood out of her injured leg, and it was making her dangerously cold.

But somehow, the barracks was finally before them, a warm glow in its windows. An Apogee soldier that Sidna knew was waving for her to enter.

"Glad to see you're all right, Sidna," he said, gesturing for a healer. The redhead was seated on a brick outcropping and had her pant leg torn off to the upper thigh where the healer began cleaning the bleeding tooth marks.

"What the hell's going on out there?!" Sidna asked.

"I don't know, but they're not letting anyone inside the Meridian except Whitecloaks," came the answer.

"Did you see that thing climbing the Meridian?! Whitecloaks can't handle this. I'm heading over there." She pushed the healer away and quickly finished the bandaging of her bloody leg herself.

"You leaving us!?" Keb asked, standing in a puddle of rainwater. Sidna knelt down to their level.

"It's okay, Sidna," Shaden said, still out of breath. "We're safe in this place. Just please be careful." She mustered a deliriously tired smile.

"Thank you." Sidna kissed them both on the head and stood up. She turned to her comrade. "Can I borrow your coat? This thing's worthless." She pulled off her drenched cowl.

"Of course." He shrugged off his long coat and gave it to Sidna. She slipped it on and suddenly appeared much larger for the padded shoulders. She noticed a couple of the young soldiers she knew were eyeing her.

"Boys, we can't sit this one out," she said, putting a hand on her hip. "When the Helix comes to my capital, I call that a deal breaker. So, if you've got the stones to come along, hurry it up."

Many of the men loafing around had been inspired by her on battlefields past. The captains cursed and threatened and even tackled some, but Sidna was followed out of the barracks by nearly twenty volunteers.

Chapter 21

The arachnid leviathan raised up from the wreckage and opened the Meridian to the storms outside. Caethys watched how the demon's legs lifted its mottled body. Rainwater poured off it into the building like rivers.

This spider demon was as large to these soldiers as any man was to a cockroach. Vast hands, shaped like that of a human but layered with grime, grasped the crumbling edge of the chamber's ruins.

The spider's muddy fingers fed morsels into its mouth. The orifice was guarded by concentric layers of teeth. Caethys watched until he noticed his breath became visible in the rain. Somehow, it was getting colder, very, very quickly.

"It's some sort of attack! Run!" He raced barefoot for cover behind the remains of a fallen balcony. Dazed Bloodletters could not hear Caethys's warning above the driving rain.

From the spider's mouth came a pillar of white vapor. The funnel of icy mist splashed out, washing the chamber in waves of cold. Caethys gritted his teeth and hugged himself tightly. He thought he was going to die as his sweat froze to glass beads on his body.

Finally, it stopped, and Caethys surveyed the damage with frost in his hair. The Bloodletters had been frozen alive. Icicles spiked like crystal bouquets from piles of frosty rubble. Rainwater continued flooding in over the broken walls, splashing over the freshly frozen marble.

The corporal arose with bones achy from the eldritch cold. His sword seemed pathetic against the mountainous hellspawn. Its great humanoid arms plundered the frozen wreckage for meat. Rebels, loyalists, even demons were plucked from their encasements and tucked into the grinding maw above.

Someone grabbed Caethys's shoulder. He turned to see Kaiser, bloodied but standing tall, his eyes jagged with amber light. He was splattered with multicolored blood. Then the corporal realized that this was the Kaiser he had not seen for a long time. The Red Rapture had claimed him again.

The Cypolonian was off then to take on the impossible challenge. Caethys noticed that Kaiser had a fantastic black sword, lit up with all the colors of a sunset. Kaiser's primal sorcery blended with its infernal magic to sire an exotic enchantment.

The monster's leg plowed up the floor as it raced toward Kaiser. He threw himself on and began to climb, using Imperium to puncture handholds. If this creature was vulnerable anywhere, it would be at its organ-filled body cavity.

Up the barnacled leg Kaiser crawled in the rain, a struggling mite with a glowing weapon. The rain and the slime made the pebbled hide difficult to grasp.

The monster climbed too, spearing great holes in the towers with every leg it moved.

The Red Rapture kept him focused, but Kaiser's arms shivered for the task at hand. Still, this was precisely the challenge he had always sculpted himself for. He felt Kronin's commanding stare from beyond the grave. Surrender would be a sin.

But there seemed to be no weak point. Kaiser surveyed the beast's anatomy while rainfall spilled through his eyes. As the limb stretched, Kaiser noticed the demon's joint opened, revealing white muscle inside. With black hair sprawling over his face, he grinned at the possibilities.

He launched from his slippery hold and managed to catch himself on a ridge above the joint. He stabbed down savagely with Imperium, whose enchantments sizzled the white muscle like strong acid. Kaiser enjoyed his amplified strength with every strike, but it was not as vivid as Nytrinion's had been.

He spilled gallons of the creature's blue-purple blood that reeked like fish rot. He cut halfway through the limb before it nearly bucked Kaiser off, but he continued to attack. With madness in his muscles, he finished the cut. Cataracts of stinking blue ichor poured down the side of the Meridian's buttresses. The leg severed just beneath Kaiser's perch and fell to the heights below.

What began as its scream deepened to an apocalyptic roar. Even the thunder could not drown it out. In an unprecedented jerk, the great demon shook Kaiser too hard, and he slipped off.

He felt the pull into the battlements below. His holler was loud and stark, but he kept his mind on survival. Imperium floated at his side. The Cypolonian swam frantically in his fall for an incline of white stone.

It was like a dream. For the moment before the impact, the wind passed like a massage through Kaiser's flying hair, and the rain drops hovered next to him as his view of the slab below grew. The experience was intoxicating, but not enough to sedate the pain that awaited.

At impact, everything was radiant crimson, like the world was flushed in blood. His shoulder had taken the brunt of the landing on the incline. Kaiser could feel an unwelcome change in his shoulder bones.

Chapter 22

Had only seconds passed? Kaiser felt like termites were burrowing behind his forehead. He lay on a concrete balcony and couldn't feel the raindrops that smacked his skin. His good arm pushed up a body gone cold. Blood from his head crept through the sprinkling puddles.

He stumbled to kneel at the railing and vomited. His body was trying to black out, but the Red Rapture kept him shivering for vengeance.

Rainwater ran in glassy veins down his face as he looked up for his enemy. It was still lumbering up the Meridian like a crawling mountain.

Woom. The beast's sounds made the universe feel immense and hideous.

Kaiser spotted the seductive devil sword lying nearby like a sliver of diamond, popping in the raindrops. He felt like he wore a suit of needles as he grasped the weapon.

Urges to betray, torture, and blaspheme started to needle his drowning thoughts, but Kaiser needed the strength of this evil sword. Before he knew it, he found his way back inside and was climbing every staircase he could find. He was ready for another attempt.

Treachery and honor wrestled in the sick brew of bloodthirst that Kaiser had become. He tried to narrow his thoughts down to killing the great demon and nothing else. But his juggling feelings aligned a little when he spotted a warrior lying in the dance hall.

The old secretary lay encircled by crushed monsters. An axe resting nearby wore the strange blood of each specimen.

"Arcton?"

"Kaiser?" Arcton gurgled. He kept his eyes closed. He didn't have the strength to wipe the sweat or hair from his face. His mustache fluttered with breathing that sounded like a weak laugh. "I should thank you."

Kaiser wanted to apologize, but in his Red Rapture, he could do little more than contain his murderous impulses and kneel.

Woom.

"Can't move anymore." Arcton's voice was getting quieter. His eyes squeezed tight; the pain was getting to him. "I'm out of this one, boy. You steel yourself, and you get out there. I'm counting on you to do what I've left undone."

"I . . . will."

"I go to my ancestors. We'll watch over you, comrade." Arcton wheezed, smiling blindly. A coldness passed over him, and Kaiser touched his forehead, leaving droplets of water. With expired restraint, the Cypolonian left.

Bursting through the door to the stinking laboratory came Jeth and Sobol. It was like a mad aquarium of blood-colored light, with the hellpods swimming like tadpoles for a place to spawn their demon cargo. Jeth knew he had finally tracked down their objective. They got into position, flanking the Planar Coil that produced the pods, giving Norang's curled body only a passing glance.

"Are you ready for victory, my son?" Speaking thus, Jeth passed one of his enchanted maces to Sobol, who dropped his own instruments and accepted the gift.

"More than anything," Sobol insisted. The duo poured more primal energies into their maces. They spared nothing, giving all but their energy to keep standing. Their weapons became tiny supernovae, spitting blue-orange pyrotechnics.

"Sobol. Nothing has honored me so much as calling you my son."

"Thank you for a life of meaning, Father."

Despite their sapped strength, Jeth and Sobol each delivered a mighty blow to the summoning spire at opposing sides. The conflict of energies blasted the flesh from their bones. The Planar Coil remained, but the silvery billows of flame collapsed the connection to the demon world.

Chapter 23

It was either blood loss or bloodlust that numbed Kaiser enough to make good time up the gory staircases. A loyalist without a lower body had stretched his entrails down a hallway, but Kaiser only saw his javelins and made them his own.

Kaiser climbed out onto one of the rain-pelted minarets and withdrew the first one. He palmed the length of the missile with magical flames.

Kaiser's throw was an orange comet crossing the rainy gulf. The javelin planted between the base of two legs. The demon retaliated with a clawed hand, but swung too low. It did, however, collide with the base of Kaiser's minaret. The hand disintegrated the brickwork, breaking the tower in half.

He could feel his tower caving. He saw that the threshold of his chamber had cracked and his minaret was quickly sliding down the side of the Meridian's walls. He threw himself through the falling doorway and hardly made it through in time to prevent being cut in half by the descending tower.

The minaret that Kaiser had escaped thundered into broken slabs far below.

He eased up on sore legs. The monster lost interest in finding him. Now it mounted a spacious courtyard. Stabbing legs smashed the cobblestone like giant pestles. Concrete garden baths exploded into wet craters.

There was an overpass that the monster would have to crawl under. Kaiser was already racing to make it there. The demon became delayed between the snug columns. Kaiser positioned himself above.

A shake from the beast sent a tremor up through the bridge and into Kaiser's heart. He stepped off of the colonnade, and let gravity guide his rainy fall down onto the spider demon's back.

As the moment of landing approached, the he prepared to force the fall's impact into Imperium's point. Kaiser hoped his shoulders could endure it all. The creature's pebbled hide seemed to fly up to meet him. He concentrated all force into this one thrust.

There was a sound of crunching chitin as Kaiser's weapon bored into the monster's head. He followed through until the entire blade was buried. His injured legs buckled, and his arms hadn't fared any better. Kaiser collapsed from the pain blitz as rain water ran through his joyless grin.

Though small by the demon's standards, the sword had damaged its tiny brain. Purple blood bubbled from the injury. Demented, the demon flailed, raking apart a shining dome in its pain-fueled dance.

Kaiser rose, trying to work his failing bones. Curses escaped him as he fought to pull his blade from the wound.

Suddenly, a dozen fishhooks entered Kaiser's ankle. Or at least that's what it felt like.

A metallic maggot the size of his foot looked up at him with a face like a wailing theater mask. A strand of his own muscle still snagged to its ticking mandibles. Kaiser bisected the creature the instant the sword was free.

A sound like tumbling silverware heralded hundreds more such creatures. They jangled from their barnacled trenches and tumor hives in a musical march of hunger.

A growing list of injuries made escape a labor unto itself. Kaiser sliced several of them away, but he would have had more luck bailing out a lake. They piled over each other, scissoring their mouth parts for this rare sample of human meat. Kaiser dragged himself onto a plateau of demon hide for a final stand.

Two great, black fingers slammed down between Kaiser and his would-be devourers. The spider demon's claws raked across its back, crushing the silvery mites with their vigorous swaths.

The rush of vermin had incited the spider demon to scratch itself! Kaiser saw an opportunity to escape these little monsters for good. There was a clear path to the great hand. He shoved his sword into his belt and jumped onto a curling finger.

He held on for a sickening ride as the hand returned to hanging below the beast's head. The little journey flipped him upside down and forced what blood he had left into his pounding brain. Perhaps that was what inspired him.

Gulping away the nausea, Kaiser climbed onto a ridge of the hand. He drew out his sword and flushed his reserve primal magic into his arms.

He stabbed the palm of the hand he rode, and the great hand closed, attempting to crush Kaiser in the magnificent fingers. He used them as stepping platforms to reach the real target above . . .

With deliberate caution, Kaiser lashed out with the blade and detonated the first quarter of his reserve magic. A swath of arcane light sliced deeply into the demon's wrist. To his delight, Kaiser confirmed that like humans, this beast bled profusely at wrist injuries. Thick veins spewed gallons of cold, blue blood. Beneath the demon's groan, Kaiser could not hear himself laughing . . .

A second hand reached for Kaiser like a slimy leviathan. He leaped from the bleeding appendage to land on the oncoming hand, stabbing his sword deep into the upper forearm. As he had hoped, the third hand came on, seeking to grab him. He ran beneath it as it hovered over him. He swung overhead and ignited the next quarter of magical energy, slicing open a gash down the third arm's wrist veins. Swampy juices showered as he raced along, shearing open a terrible cleft above.

Jolted by injury, the creature pulled away the arm Kaiser was dashing across. In an instant, the Cypolonian found his footing pulled out from under him. There was only empty space between him and the rainy pavement twenty stories below. Visions of the afterlife suddenly shot in and out of his mind.

The monster's fourth hand passed beneath him, cupping the ooze that cascaded from its slashed wrists. Kaiser kicked in the air as he fell and managed splash into the slime-pooled palm. The hand could overturn or squeeze shut anytime, so he was quickly again on those weary, weary legs.

He conjured the remainder of his magic and mixed it with the devil sword's essence. His eyes were a striking, solar gold, and he gave a war cry of unbridled destruction. He swung for the wrist.

The attack was twice as strong as his first and hatched an orange light so marvelous that it shattered his sight. He crumpled at last, cradled in the palm of the hand that was now *severed*. The disembodied appendage fell heavily to the ground. The flesh, though tough, was enough to cushion the fall for Kaiser. The wounds of the beast had all the while been draining, flooding the concrete below with demon lifeblood.

The demon wailed its fatal pain. Kaiser was deaf to it, curled up on the severed hand below. Geysers of alien fire tore shrieking crevices across the beast's body. Disintegrative flames crawled up its legs.

The monster's cries quieted to the cheers of people in the streets. Some still wept with terror, others laughed as the demon spider puffed into flames, some praised the Covenant with their hands folded in worship.

With blasted vision, Kaiser looked through slit eyes up at the falling jaws of the demon. Its mouth was a fiery hellstorm of two-foot fangs. It became larger in Kaiser's vision as it fell, coming to engulf the little Cypolonian. Kaiser was too tired to be afraid.

"I wanted more." Mercifully, darkness enveloped him before the fiery jaws of the beast descended.

Chapter 24

The night had seen betrayal and blasphemy like only the Helix could provide. In the end though, the rainy moon glowed over a city restored to justice. The hollers of conflict waned, and the victorious rebels asserted their control over the Meridian.

Caethys hadn't seen any demons for some time and reasoned they must have been mostly exterminated. He had spent his remaining energy chasing Whitecloaks. Without Nytrinion, they scattered easily.

Only now did starvation finally take its toll on the corporal. His knees grew weak, and he slumped down, bare back to a cold marble wall. Sleep crept up on him even while his damaged arm pulsated.

"Cae!" Like a red-haired angel, Sidna came bounding down the hall. The beginnings of the corporal's smile faded. Her left pant leg had been torn off from the thigh down to reveal a bloodied bandage running to her foot. She wore a coat that he knew was not hers, and her sword was stained to the hilt.

"Sid, are you alright?"

"Better than you, by the looks of it. What in the Helix is going on, Cae? I woke up to demons on my roof! I ran the children to the barracks and almost lost my leg doing it! And what was that thing climbing up the Meridian?!"

"The Potentate, he conjured them all, Sid. He was mad, secretly killing and jailing people." Now it was Sidna's face that dimmed.

"Is the Potentate still here?" She seated herself at the corporal's side.

"No, he's been killed."

"Where's our Tireless Butcher?"

"I lost track of him. But I'd bet my oathkey he had something to do with the death of the spider demon."

"He's a savvy killer. It would be a shame if he bit the dust already." Sidna put it as delicately as she could.

"If poison couldn't kill him, why should a twenty-story hellspawn?" He noticed then that Sidna was taking him in.

"Cae, you're all bony. And dirty. And these don't look like battle wounds." She scrutinized a conspicuous gash on his chest so close he could feel her breath on it. The hot blood in her veins receded like regressing tree branches. Her heart distended, becoming tender and pushed moisture to her eyes. "Someone took their time with you."

He almost didn't want to tell her, for fear of shattering the precarious composure making little tics in her white forehead.

"A few fellows and I, Nytrinion had us locked up. But Kaiser sprung me just in time, you see. It wasn't a prison, it was something worse, I'm afraid."

Sidna's face was made for laughing, not for this. It was the confusion tensing all the lines around her eyes that hurt the most. For all she had endured, life was still able to dredge up pains keen enough to strike her dumb.

"Just a few days," he said to her head, which seemed to float on her neck. "I know you would have helped, Sid. You didn't know."

"I never would have found out what happened to you." She tried to put an angry slant to her eyes and accidentally spilled the tears warming behind them. "I could look my whole life, and I'd never find you."

"But it didn't happen, Sid. I'm all right."

She put her arms around him, gentle as if she feared he would break. She put her head on his chest and felt the tempo of his living body. Her hot tears trickled down his stomach.

"It'd be a pretty pointless world if you weren't here, Cae." She managed a very solid voice.

Suddenly thinking on Sidna's lost family, Caethys felt a little selfish for being so selfless.

Armor, tools, skins, and other supplies swung on the wagon ride through the woodland one late afternoon while the birds were still fussing in the treetops. Kaiser would have offered to help, but he was certain that his comrade would decline. After all, the white-maned warrior had pulled the wagon for miles as easily as any three oxen.

Kronin was his name, Kaiser learned. One of those loner Anthromes that wander the country, seeking demons to kill. Demons were rare, but Kronin and his kind had found enemies aplenty in the demon-worshiping Septunites.

They camped just outside villages. When residents learned of an Anthrome making camp nearby, they always brought out offerings of food as thanks for the protection of their presence.

Kaiser ate and watched as Kronin consumed an entire roast deer by nightfall. They gulped some water and rested a bit. Every night they camped, Kaiser dreaded this hour. It was time to train.

A morning star in his hands, Kaiser pitted his all against the Anthrome's talents with a war hammer. They slammed at each other with the same force that collapsed skulls and exploded organs.

Kaiser had to think quick; his comrade's huge weapon surged on faster and faster. It took all of his focus to repulse those tremendous hits that shook him so hard it put a lapse in his consciousness. Tendons strained and bones creaked. Kaiser had dueled Kronin like this dozens of times now, and he had never managed to return an attack.

Curious villagers lined up among the torches on the outskirts of town. They watched as the two strangers barraged each other on into the night. Anthromes always seemed to wander alone, causing some to mistake Kaiser for an Anthrome himself. If he was, they surmised, he was obviously a runt.

When at last the conflict had made pulp of Kaiser's every muscle, the morning star was bashed from his hands and he was kicked over. Kronin had again reduced him to gasping human debris.

Kaiser plunged into unconsciousness, spent beyond health. Kronin dug his fingers into the dirt above him. He traced designs in the soil until a halo of glyphs encircled Kaiser's head.

"Mend this one, Sister Tethra." Kronin addressed the heavens in a voice like suppressed thunder. "I won't be able to keep him alive by myself."

His warm-up finished, Kronin was free to begin his real training, a regimen of physical challenges that would make masochist monks vomit. The Anthrome would slave on through much of the night. In his sleep, Kaiser would not be able to sense the chill of angel magic that quietly knitted his injuries.

"He's in here. Please don't wake him up. His body needs all the rest it can get to fight off the fever."

"I see. So this is the man who killed Nytrinion?"

"We think so. And there are over forty people claiming that he was also the one that slew the spider beast."

"Marvelous. Well, I won't keep you any longer. I just needed a face to go with the name Kaiser."

"You don't need anything else?"

"No, let him rest. I will have much for him to do if he recovers . . ."

"Is anyone there?" Kaiser tried through a rusty windpipe. He couldn't open his eyes, something was folded over them. He could barely hear anything. "Is anyone there?"

"Only me," came the reply, a woman's voice. Tight bandages made moving difficult, but Kaiser managed to uncover his eyes.

His ailing vision painted the image of a seated teen girl with great green eyes and a large forehead that made her lips look small and indignant. Her fine, delicate eyebrows were the same pale blonde as her hair that she wore smoothed back.

Her white robe marked her as a light mage, as did the platinum that glittered on her choker. Light mages dotted Kasurite history like diamonds. Kaiser knew he was in good hands, for their magic was as healing to humans as it was deadly to demons.

"Pardon?" he asked, missing her words.

"You have hearing loss, it will pass. You have also three breaks in one wrist, two broken ribs, a break in your left forearm, and sprains in the other. One shoulder was dislocated *and* broken, both knees are sprained, you have two twisted ankles, a badly sprained hip, chemical burns, and an old knife wound that reopened," she recited.

"Pardon?" Kaiser repeated. She sighed and leaned in.

"I'm fixing you." Sleeplessness had put an edge to her voice. She had spent most of the last two days in the windowless little room with Kaiser's unbathed body.

"For all this, I feel rather well," Kaiser admitted.

"You can thank my spells for that."

"I can't tell you how grateful I am, miss."

"You should be combat ready in a few days." She lowered her head to the paper on her lap. She was writing something with a piece of coal.

"Caethys. I need to see my friend." Kaiser sat up a little.

"Corporal Cavawix is alive and well, I promise. You're not leaving yet."

"He and I fought too hard to—"

"You can leave when my drawing is finished," she interrupted, and reached out to touch his forehead with cold fingers. "Now sleep." Mesmerized, Kaiser's eyes closed again.

She prayed silently for him as her sketch took shape.

Kaiser arose finally to a silent city. The country had been humbled by a tyrant who ruled too long. With most fighting men and women ushered off to the battlefields, the civilian populace was left to flounder in mounting uncertainty. Some suspected Nytrinion's guilt, but just as many blamed the Bloodletters or the Septunites for the domestic misfortunes.

Ceremonies honoring the martyrs of the Ousting, as the revolution had been labeled, were bygone events. Evantheans had already entombed the remains of Bloodletters and other fallen rebels. Architects were penning plans for a statue of Jeth and Sobol. Their reputations had gone from anarchists to saviors overnight.

Kaiser spent the afternoon wandering from funeral to funeral on a cane (more for a makeshift weapon than a walking aid), but everyone was calm and treachery seemed unlikely.

Great bonfires had been lit in city squares. It was no ceremony, at least not intentionally. Citizens were incinerating Whitecloak garments, happy to see the remains of the cruel police force glut the orange fires.

Kaiser entered a two-story saloon in the slums and felt immediately at home. Every laborer and soldier herein was as sweaty and unshaven as he was. He waded through the smells to the bar as cups clinked all around.

"Black maple and something sharp from the highlands," he said to the tired-looking barmaid behind the counter. A highborn laugh rang out above the chuckles of the riffraff, beckoning him.

And there he was, Caethys, alive as the light mage had promised. Sidna was there with twice as many empty glasses in front of her, telling some humorous story that was making it difficult for the corporal to swallow any wine.

"Hey! The Cypolonian lives!" Sidna pointed with a dripping vessel. The urgency in the rising corporal's gaze provoked Kaiser to hug him hard enough to hurt Caethys's slung arm, but no complaints came.

"You are alive, you invincible bastard!" Caethys stood and laid his palm on the Cypolonian's ear. "You were a state secret for days, where were you?"

"Somewhere in the Meridian. Healers got to me before any Whitecloaks did, praise Tethra." He looked down to see Sidna glowing with rum and warmth and couldn't resist taking a loving fistful of her soft red hair. She giggled merrily. "Gods above, I'm glad you kids are all right. I was checking tombstones for your names."

"You would have been proud, Kaiser. Jeth and I put down at least ten demons between us," Caethys regaled. He turned a chair and they sat.

"Feh. Me and the boys from the barracks cleared thrice that. And a whole slew of Whitecloaks after the chumps started shooting at us," Sidna boasted, tipping a tiny glass of red liquor down her throat.

Kaiser just shook his head a moment, lost in thought. He couldn't even be distracted by the vast bosom of the server girl when she placed a black beer and a whiskey before him.

"I didn't come to Evanthea to start trouble," Kaiser said, pouring the whiskey into his foamy brew. "We sat down for dinner, and Nytrinion went off about the virtues of demon calling. I mean, what did he expect?"

"Better manners from me, apparently. That's why he bashed me over the head and hung me like a poached rabbit," Caethys stated, gesturing to his cast. "There's no sense in feeling guilty, Kaiser. It's all very sudden, but you illuminated a cancer."

"Turns out he spent loads of money gathering demon toys. We might have rebuilt our navy by now if he hadn't been so stupid," Sidna groaned.

"But I killed Nytrinion." Kaiser grinned into his beer. "Does that mean I'm Potentate now?"

"Sorry, friend. A new Potentate has already been elected," Caethys answered. "He's chosen to remain anonymous until his investigation of the cabinet is finished."

"There's a lot of cleanup to do. There are six vaults where Nytrinion experimented with Helix power." Sidna held up as many fingers. "They've only found five. Caethys and I were looking for the sixth all day until our captain told us to have a rest."

"So there's still a demon threat. You tell your captain if he needs help, this Cypolonian is at his service," Kaiser offered.

"He doesn't really trust foreigners, but I will tell him," Caethys replied. "When all this is sorted out, maybe my poor city can liven up a bit."

"For a few months, maybe. The Seps are getting closer, and our army's in sorry shape." Kaiser drained half the beer in one distressed gulp.

"Hope springs eternal. In his inaugural statement, the new Potentate promised to reopen talks with barbarians. Oh! And some of our trading partners across the seas!" Caethys put in.

"We still have allies out there. Despite Nytrinion's garbage diplomacy." Sidna caught a waitress by the arm and wagged an empty glass. "More please!"

"Still, it will be months before allies can be mobilized. And any day now, we're going to see Sinra's banners rising over those hills. Taking this city is probably their penultimate goal." Kaiser emptied his drink.

"They'll never take Evanthea. This is my city." Caethys pushed away his cup, panning for sincerity in his wine haze. "I've made a lot of mistakes. But I was made a soldier inside these walls, and others share that honor with me." He put a hand on Sidna's shoulder. "Kaiser, if ever this place is threatened, I pray you'll fly to its defense."

Kaiser rolled the empty stein in his hand. "Defense." The word chewed like hardtack. Something in his stein was fizzing softly, or rather boiling. The remains of his drink had become a curling white gas. "Aren't you tired of playing the defender, Corporal?"

His stein turned a dull red and flopped inward. The tin softened to slag, and strands of boiling metal dribbled from his squeezing fingers. He seemed nonplussed at the crucible heat that rippled the air around his fist. It was *his* heat.

"If I protect this country, it's fortuitous, but incidental. I'm getting stronger, and I'm doing it so I can kill and keep killing until Opagiel is a forgotten name." So saying, he rose and excused himself, leaving his cane and a smelted disc on the table.

"My Cypolonian's a little rusty," Sidna said, propped over her latest drink, "but I think that means 'yes'?"

Kaiser was jettisoned from a sleep too viscous for dreams to take shape. Fists were drumming over the door to his room at the Dreaming Quail. Too late for the inn staff to be bothering him. He palmed his eyes and went to the door with Seriath behind his back.

"What do you want?" he asked through the wood surface.

"Federal business, sir. Open the door," returned a voice. If it was an assassin, he had no qualms about being loud. Kaiser swung open the entrance, keeping most of his body behind the door.

It was a husky warrior with armor shimmering over his great belly. His hair was a phalanx of upstanding bronze. His eyebrows were strikingly black and bushy, while his bulldog face had exiled every whisker.

"Master Kaiser?" the man began. The Cypolonian nodded. "I'm Captain Victon Clayborn. We have little time, so will you come with us?"

"I don't even know you."

"Sources say you have an arm for fiend slaying. I won't suffer demons, but I won't suffer hesitation either. Are you coming or not?" Clayborn demanded, the keys at his green sash jingling.

Demons...

"Of course I am." Kaiser pulled a repurposed suit of barding from a hook beside his door. He'd bought it on impulse from a vendor, thinking this city was a bit too unstable to go with nothing between his skin and hidden daggers. He buckled it on like a tunic and followed Clayborn down the hall.

Chapter 25

Clayborn strode like a man half his girth. He did not speak a word to Kaiser as they saddled up the horses at the city limits. Five figures were already mounted, sporting uniform green-hide outfits and filigreed capes. Specialists of some kind. It was not until they had left the confines of the city that the captain broke his silence.

"It's time to fill you in on a few things," Clayborn said.

"Please. Where are we going?"

"We think we found Nytrinion's final demon vault. If the last ones have taught us anything, it's to be ready for trouble."

"And that's why you brought me along?"

"Actually, that's why we brought her along." Clayborn looked to a rider behind Kaiser. Behind him rode a hooded woman in a white robe with a glittering pendant at her throat.

"You," said Kaiser. It was none other than the young light mage that had treated his wounds. Her large green eyes remembered him, but would not meet his gaze.

"Velena. She'll take care of them. As for you, this is a test of character. Killing a despot and a handful of demons has gained you infamy, but not trust. Understand?"

Recalling his duel with the enormous spider creature, Kaiser was amused by Clayborn's reference to his achievements as "a handful of demons."

"Yes. I do. What else can we expect from this vault?" Kaiser asked.

"Bad dreams."

The riders' trek cast them into the grasslands outside the city. They rode into a shadowy orchard where the trees were gnarled like a dead man's fingers. Clayborn was following the secret directions in his mind. He slowed and dismounted, walking up to a tree.

"This is the territory where our Paragon Tethra was conceived from the last recorded xerecite crystal. This is sacred ground, Kaiser. You are not ever to come here without a light mage," Velena warned him as the two lowered from their horses. Kaiser could hear the captain counting his paces moonward from the tree.

". . . Eighteen, nineteen, twenty." His words came on white vapor. He stopped and investigated a nest of misty thistles.

Kaiser hissed through his teeth as he stretched his aching limbs. Velena sighed under her hood, impatient at his company.

Clayborn knelt and waved away a sheet of fog to reveal a bronze disc set in the dirt. It was crafted to resemble a demonic skull, a keyhole in its forehead. He called out for a soldier by the name of Maethro. The latter walked forth and offered Clayborn an iron key.

"I had hoped Nytrinion was pious enough to respect holy ground. You were right to put that man down, Kaiser." The captain drove the key into the demon seal's forehead. The metal face seemed to cough as the gears underneath sprang to life. It parted at the teeth and widened until a man could fit inside.

"Velena, you're behind me," the captain instructed. "Stop me if you sense anything unpleasant." The light mage obeyed, and the four Federal soldiers aligned behind them. Kaiser took up the rear and they lowered in.

The ladder was crusty orange. At the bottom, Clayborn found himself in a cylinder of moonlight. The blackness around it looked hard enough to touch. When Velena was beside him, she worked a watery incandescence into her oathkey. It became a tiny blue star that sat on her chest.

They were in an antechamber no larger than a closet. The mortar leaked mud, giving rise to all manner of pestilential rot that perfumed the air like a flooded ossuary.

Their footsteps crunched. A brittle fungus resembling knotted flesh had flourished in the damp solitude.

Velena's groan was muffled by the inflammation of her light. Its rays strangled the growth into gray crust.

"This place has been left unattended for a while," Clayborn reminded them. "Be on your guard. If there's anything down here, it's going to be hungry." Velena took the lead by the captain's command and led the party down a staircase. Demonic mold crumbled in waves under her aura.

Before them opened a putrid chamber stinking with blasphemy. Organs wriggled in jars, weird skulls glared from troughs, and round flasks of blood were chained to the ceiling like fruits. A trio of huge glass spheres containing rotting specimens bubbled with septic green light.

The main study table was a city of grinding bowls, dusty jars, slime-filled vials, and stacks of wrinkled documents.

"All right. Velena, if it's infernal, kill it. We'll take the artifacts to the church foundry," Clayborn ordered.

Nearly every surface in this dark cesspool reacted to the light mage's glow. Every spill, every embalmed specimen, disintegrated in a crescendo of crackling and hissing that died as quickly as it began.

Clayborn and the others stepped quietly, keeping their voices low. While the others plundered the trove, Kaiser simply kept out of the way, feeling he might best serve as a ready sword.

Velena visited the three globular glass tanks. She touched each one in turn, making them cauldrons of blue light that boiled apart the demons inside and cast a healthful glow around the room.

Two men were chiseling the lock from a cabinet. Their metalwork echoed softly before the lock dropped off.

Something butted its way out and pounced on Clayborn. The wiggling of its eye stalks conveyed astonishment. Clayborn let its weight bear him down so he could work his sword into position, and the creature, resembling an insectoid sow, was impaled.

Other men raced up to run it through. None of them noticed it was dead by the time it reached Clayborn. Kaiser's sword was already happily dripping.

Clayborn shoved off the deadweight, and Velena was a little disappointed she had missed the excitement. This sort of maid work bored her. She opened her hand to it, and the demon was digested in a flurry of tinkling blue flakes.

As he watched the corpse dissolve, something in the wall caught Kaiser's eye. A thin book resting in a brick slot. He carefully removed it, scaring out a centipede.

"Captain, Norang's writings," Kaiser announced.

"Read."

The thin journal whispered open.

"*The privacy here was flawless,*" Kaiser read. "*Nytrinion has forbid anyone, even light mages, from visiting Tethra's birthplace. I had months of peace to work . . . and explore. I have not told Nytrinion, but I have discovered a confounding specimen, buried secretly under this holy ground.*" He checked for a reaction from Velena. There was none.

"What specimen?" Clayborn asked.

"Doesn't give it a name. I don't think he knew exactly what it was. But it says he '*closed off the undermost chamber again permanently, where it shall vex me no longer.*'" Kaiser stopped to look to his feet. A ring was bolted to the concrete. Clayborn didn't say anything, so Kaiser reached down with one hand to pull open the cellar passage with an exertion that stung his recovering joints.

The slab locked upright, icicles hanging from its underside, leaving the portal to gape hungrily. A cold, sour breeze drifted from the hole like a dead man's breath. Kaiser tucked the journal in his belt and lowered into the passage first, none seeking to go ahead of him. The marshy stench made his skin feel oily. Before going too far, he looked to the light mage.

"Would you mind?" He offered his sword in both fists. With a touch of the light mage's pale hand, she breathed godly light into the weapon, making it twice as deadly against anything demonic.

"Maethro, Velena, come with us. The rest of you finish up here," Clayborn ordered.

With his sword doubling as an aqueous torch, the Cypolonian descended, the others following suit.

He dropped into a tall chamber possessed of the cloying chill inherent of winter swamps. The lingering echoes made it feel twice as old as the corridors above. He kept his ears sensitive and his sword arm ready as he unfolded the journal a second time.

"Never again will I attempt to speak with this creature. After our first discourse, I had forgotten certain spells, memories of my childhood, even secrets Nytrinion had entrusted to me! It drunk up my thoughts like wine, and now I have stirred it to a wakefulness that all my sorcery cannot reverse."

The shadows crackled, hiding something at their core. Velena didn't wait for a request when she arrived and removed a delicate silver censer from her cloak. With great care, she unlatched the three catches and pulled up the lid.

"What's she doing?" Kaiser asked.

"Light mages tend and harvest that invisible paradise we call the Loom," Clayborn said rather bookishly. "She's opening it."

Kaiser understood enough of the Loom to know that it was all around them and yet inaccessible to all but the most attuned holy men and women. Like a heaven locked beneath the guise of reality.

"Velena's little place in the Loom is a fruitful one," Clayborn elaborated. They watched as the light mage unleashed a golden miasma that piled around her.

When the radiance faded, Velena was being danced upon by tiny little human shapes with moth wings. They were made of light so refreshingly pure that Kaiser had to grin. Velena kissed one that glided next to her face, the most joy she'd expressed in his experience with her.

The faeries were not her only conjurations, however. An elephant-headed brute knuckle-walked into view on six gorilla arms. It was covered in clean, white fur. Its billowy ears were pierced with dozens of colorful jewels, and its tusks were tipped with gold; it was delightful to look upon. It recognized Velena and wriggled its trunk like a dog wagging its tail.

"Are you sure you need me here?" Kaiser stared up at the summoned beast.

"You're right to be impressed," Clayborn put in. "Light mages seed these creatures in the Loom with their own virtue. If this creature is any indication, Velena's a very good girl indeed."

"Pity my pay doesn't reflect it," Velena commented.

The faeries hovered in front of the explorers, banishing more darkness with their natural glamour. Clayborn had Kaiser follow the light mage and her thousand-pound creature.

The frosted path led to concrete steps looping with thorny vines. At the top was a huge face of frozen brass. It had been built into the wall where vines clambered up its cheeks, tiny icicles supplementing their thorns.

"Don't go near it," said Clayborn.

"That's a bust of St. Veristice," Velena noticed.

"I know this one . . . he was a monk, tortured and executed during the Great Eastern Genocide. He saved hundreds by refusing to reveal their hideout to the Hegemon's perfectors—" Kaiser stopped. It was an ugly bit of Apogee history that most found distasteful.

"Very good. Veristice was the Keeper of Secrets." Velena was a bit gratified to find someone else who acknowledged that period, much less understood it. She turned to a cringing Clayborn. "It makes me think what's hidden here is not for us to uncover, Captain."

Maethro was gawking at the metal face when he nicked his finger on a thorn. He thought to mouth it, but something clutched his every nerve. The conversation of his fellows sounded like distant echoes.

"The energy here, it's not demonic, but I can't recognize it."

"Then I don't like it." Clayborn found Velena's words alarming, and he wasn't one to chance things. "Let's scram, we'll come back when we get some questions answered." They began backing away, except Maethro.

"Soldier, it's time to leave," Velena said to his back. No one liked how still Maethro was standing, or the way he just stared at the blood on his finger.

"Maethro, what's wrong?" Clayborn approached. "We have to leave this place." When the young soldier looked back, a poisonous green glow shone through his eyes.

"I couldn't agree more," he said in a voice that was not his own. It sounded like a chorus of insect chittering. It sucked the sweat from Clayborn's pores to know that something straddling life and death was using his soldier as a mouthpiece.

Maethro tromped up over the thorn-piled steps, not caring how the barbs clawed at him.

"Dammit, kid, I'm not going to let a spook sink its fangs into you . . . ," declared the captain as he followed to the protest of his trembling knees. Maethro wheeled like a frightened cat and crossed Clayborn's stomach with his short sword.

"Captain!" When Velena's attempt to catch her wounded comrade failed, Kaiser zipped ahead to break his fall in ready arms.

"I'm fine, I'll be fine, this is wound-staunching armor!" Clayborn pointed with a glove stained by his cut. "Stop Maethro!"

"Go!" Velena commanded her elephant-headed creature, knowing it would subdue a human without harming one. It trundled ahead and arrested Maethro in melon-sized fists.

That's when the thorns began a serpentine locomotion. They heaved upon the beast in great knots and cinched into its furry flesh.

"I suppose I will have a drink, if you're offering," commented Maethro's possessed body just as the tightened vines gulped out the beast's blood. The beast weakened, and Maethro pulled free.

Kaiser left Clayborn to his men and darted in. He cut enough vines to buy the elephant beast's freedom and lunged for Maethro. The possessed soldier would have opened Kaiser's belly same as Clayborn's, but Seriath's superior make and velocity sheared the blade in half.

Maethro employed various strikes, but Kaiser's fighting formulae was rife with snares. The latter achieved a headlock that squeezed tears from Maethro's alien eyes.

"Velena, can you help him?!" Kaiser called, and at her will, the faeries congregated on Maethro. They pulled something from him like threads of elastic green mist. The little faeries squeaked at the effort, but their collective strength yanked the cursed presence from Maethro, who went limp in Kaiser's arms.

"Get him over here!" Clayborn hollered. The green vapor slipped from the faeries' grasp and into the nose and mouth of the brass face on the wall.

"Will he be alright?" Kaiser asked, laying Maethro next to Clayborn. Velena was transfixed on Veristice's face and the creaking sounds it made.

"I think we've made a grave mistake," she said, watching vines slither into St. Veristice's rusty lips. With a fibrous exertion, they began to pry open the mouth. Thick icicles pantomimed teeth as they parted.

Inside, something patiently basked in clouds of cold.

Velena had called her injured white creature back to her side, where the Cypolonian was considering what to do.

The suit of frost on the mummified detainee began crunching off. A hand as knotty and black as a crow's foot reached out to grasp the lip of its prison.

It was born again before any sensible moves could be made. Its feet sounded like the slap of twigs as they landed on the concrete, as fleshless and time-curdled as the rest of its cadaverous physique. It set eye sockets on the first living things it had seen in ages.

Velena's elephant-headed creature attacked without her command; something she thought was impossible. This ghoul was no product of the Helix, but something about it was profane enough to aggravate the Loom beast.

Its fists whirled about, but the ghoul was suddenly as spry as a contortionist. It dodged like it could see several seconds into the future, while its opponent's knuckles drove pockets into St. Veristice's likeness.

The corpse thing discreetly formed claws of ice on its finger bones. Having analyzed the Loom creature's attack, it returned with deep slashes. Velena's breath was snatched away as her creature's blood spiraled off in all directions.

Recognizing its sudden disadvantage, the Loom creature backed away before the pain could take hold. And when it did, a rapid putrefaction accompanied it. The ghoul let its huge victim stagger back, trumpeting at its quickly rotting wounds.

Unwilling to let the enemy catch its breath (if it even needed breath), Kaiser tumbled in, trading strikes. He employed a recently mastered tactic: unloading with a particular fight pattern, then suddenly switching to another.

Seriath landed on its waist above the hip, but the bone endured like an oak many times its thickness. Annoyed, the ghoul forced Kaiser back by tearing gouges out of his barding like a child tears gift wrapping.

As Kaiser had hoped, the elephant creature was not down yet. A head-sized fist bashed the corpse to the far wall. Neon green juices squirted in all directions.

It was no time to let up, so Kaiser charged. He'd have to be fast and careful after seeing this foe cripple Velena's beast. This thing could be several times as powerful as him, so there was no room for error.

With strength to compensate for the ghoul's dense flesh, Seriath chopped an arm from the shoulder. Again, neither the injury nor the holy magic on his sword seemed to bother it much.

The ice claws forced Kaiser to back-step. His dodges saved him from the ghoul's remarkable speed, but even a scratch might cause the same rotting wound that injured Velena's beast.

Soon, he deciphered the attack rhythm. He threw his arms around the enemy, pinning its arm. As he squeezed, he worked Seriath into its back, hoping to skewer something vital.

Ice piled up around the ghoul's mandible. It built and built until an exaggerated set of fangs formed, complete with articulating pincers. Kaiser abandoned his sword in the thing's back to grapple with both hands. Using four times the effort human bones could endure, he cracked its head to one side.

But the freed claws nicked Kaiser's neck. As he staggered back, a length of vine slipped around his ankle and pulled him off of his feet. He fought from being dragged into a greater thicket, but the rotting neck wound was suffocating him. Clawing at the ground with one hand and trying to compress his neck with the other, Kaiser began to weaken. That's when a faerie landed on his chest and began to gesture at his wounds.

"No matter what, do not let it escape," Clayborn said as he took to his feet again next to Velena. Some blood had slipped through the bottom of his armor and onto his breeks. The light mage looked to her elephant creature lying upon the staircase and agreed.

She cast a streaming light orb at the ghoul, whose head sat crooked. The magic that exploded over its chest didn't stop it from pulling Kaiser's sword from its back and hurling it at Velena.

Clayborn smashed the weapon away in time, but by now the ghoul had pounced. Clayborn was bowled over, and Velena was hoisted up by her throat.

The ghoul realized it had not heard Kaiser's deflected sword hit the ground . . .

Seriath crunched into its shoulder. It dropped Velena to face Kaiser again, but it took a second sword strike that entered its brain and blasted ice teeth from its mouth. Kaiser threw a roundhouse that knocked the skull from its broken neck. It flew across the room to explode against the wall into a mass of charnel ooze.

The body of the ghoul had resisted centuries of decay with its powers, but now the debt of time took its due. It broke into chunks, then tiny crumbs, then a fine powder that mingled with the dungeon filth.

Ice crackled, and the vine coils solemnly curled in like a dying spider's legs.

"Are we alright?" Kaiser asked. The faerie had halted his corrupted neck wound. It had grayed some of his skin, but it looked quite reversible. Clayborn didn't look worried as he checked over a rousing Maethro. "Light mage?"

Velena was at the top of the stairs, caressing the trunk of her elephant creature. Its great body was sinking into a growing pool of mist, decorated by ringlets of electricity. When it completely vaporized, the sparking mist was sucked up by a point of light a few feet above and disappeared.

"I am well enough," she whispered. Kaiser saw how her eyes gleamed and imagined it would be a grim thing to see the fruit of one's soul lost. He wondered how long she had cared for that creature.

With a heave, Captain Clayborn threw Maethro over his shoulder. His stomach wound ached horribly, but he trusted his armor to see him through.

"Everyone out now. We'll set some exorcists down here, but I think this pit is best forgotten," he declared and took to the ladder at the entrance. His beefy frame was quite enough to haul the young man up even with the wound. The other two were not far behind. They rejoined the men upstairs and, after a brief explanation, rode back into the city as the eastern sky began to bleed gold.

Chapter 26

"Sorry I'm always relying on you for everything, Caethys," Kaiser was saying, finding himself and his companion walking through a grassy terrace. The field was striped by shadows of the Meridian's towers. "But I wasn't about to do this alone."

"You must have a very jaded outlook of my Apogee by now. Who could blame you?" Caethys answered, fiddling with a clasp at his neck. He no longer wore an arm cast, which was convenient earlier when tailors had fussed over both of them.

The product was a pair of groomed gentlemen in green ceremonial vestments. They would have been the envy of most parties in their attire, but present company offered little competition. Masons of every specialty ignored their passage, attending to the construction of hostels that would house people uprooted by the Ousting.

It was a bustling work yard with sawdust in the air, but this was where Kaiser was invited to meet the Potentate elect. The city was healing everywhere, and why try to hide it? One only had to glance upward to see the wounded Meridian clutched in scaffolding, and cubes of brick suspended on wooden arms as slow as they were huge.

Armed escorts compelled Kaiser and Caethys to keep their conversation vague. But Caethys had no small admiration for these guards. They were Acolytes, the greatest holy warriors in Kasurai, whose existence had been all but stamped out by Nytrinion's legislation.

The Acolytes carried cruciphoids, wide-faced swords whose long hilts gave them the range of a spear. Their headdresses were fully a head higher than most men stood, and their armor was legendary for its reliable protection.

Kaiser felt underdressed without Seriath. Understandably, they asked the man who killed the last Potentate not to bring his weapon to see the current one.

"I was still quite young when Nytrinion took over, but I'd heard tales of former Potentates. They say that to sit on the throne of the Apogee is to become the voice of the gods." Caethys hoped Kaiser appreciated such gravity.

"The gods were hoarse indeed during Nytrinion's rule."

"We're restoring classical Apogee form," Caethys elaborated. "This is a fresh start for all of us."

"None too soon, I should say." Kaiser realized he was already taking on his finer lingual tone that surfaced in Federal company. Hopefully today it would be enough to pass him off as more than an uneducated killer.

"Thank you, anyway, for inviting me. And I'm grateful you're receptive to our ways after what you . . . what *we've* been through," Caethys came back.

"After all this, I shouldn't trust anyone who wears Federal green, Caethys," Kaiser said, plucking at his comrade's embroidered sleeve. "But there's a good man to be found in any institution. I think you might be one, so be my bodyguard until I'm out of this madhouse of a city, won't you?"

Caethys tried to unravel the mood behind Kaiser's words and wrinkled brow. It was some approximation of frailty. "All right, that's fair. But you still have to replace my brother's shirt that you lost."

Someone dressed like they were suddenly pushed up from resting in one of the half-finished dormitories. It was none other than Clayborn, looking pleased enough to be sweating so in the day's mounting heat.

"Captain!" Caethys bowed.

"Didn't think I'd see you again so soon," Clayborn remarked to Kaiser.

"Good to see you here, Captain. Your wound wasn't too serious?" Kaiser asked as he was pulled in for a handshake.

"A couple of stitches, but you can call me Victon today, son." He cast a glance at the corporal's vulnerable stature. "How'd you get Caethys to come along? You must have told him there'd be dubious women involved."

Caethys shrunk under his commanding officer's fierce grin, mumbling some response neither of the other men heard.

"I was told there's a task of high importance that falls to you and me, Kaiser. Any idea what that may be?" Clayborn asked.

"No clue, they just told me to get presentable and meet him here of all places," Kaiser replied, waving some sawdust from his face.

"Presumably, he'll thank you for his accession to the throne." Caethys was almost sorry he spoke for the look Clayborn gave him.

"So why are you here, corporal?"

"I'm Kaiser's bodyguard, sir." Caethys's comment went uncontested.

About then, the trio was visited by a tall woman in ragged clothes. She rested a sledge hammer over her considerable shoulders, but she was no laborer. She regarded them with a face whose creases were the product of a war-born grimace. The day's peace bored her, it was obvious.

"Gavel," Caethys whispered to Kaiser, noting the blue tattoo on her forearm that resembled a hammer.

Indeed, Kaiser had learned of the Sisterhood of the Gavel, a convent dedicated to protecting the Potentate. Perhaps, Kaiser thought, that should have incriminated Nytrinion earlier, that he would not suffer the Gavel to serve him.

"Kaiser and Victon? And who is this?" she asked in a thick, yet feminine timber that made the Cypolonian hesitate. Dangerous women always redirected the blood from his brain to less convenient places.

"This is my friend Corporal Cavawix. He has permission to come along," Kaiser explained, seeing how the presence of the extra man made her lips tense.

"You can go," she said over their shoulders to the Acolytes, who bowed and left. She led them up a garden staircase where children were planting orange flowers.

"When you meet the Potentate, bow to him as one, do not come closer than ten paces, do not speak until he addresses you, do not make threatening gestures nor raise your voice. Refer to him at all times as 'my lord'."

So saying, she led them up into the corner of a site where the infrastructure of a new dormitory was taking shape. Among the eunuchs tapping at their woodwork, members of the Gavel lounged leery-eyed with bludgeons and hammers on their laps. They looked more like gang members than defenders of the crown.

The tattooed woman turned to her guests.

"Now, you gentlemen won't do anything unbecoming of a Federal servant, will you?" she asked, daring them with her heat to disagree.

When they shook their heads, she turned to a man crouching in a straw hat, working a braced length of wood with a hammer and wedge. "My lord, Kaiser and company have arrived." She drew a line in front of them with her foot.

The little man tilted up the brim of his hat, regarding them with a curious expression, his mouth almost lost in a white beard. He wore a red kerchief around his neck and no gloves, allowing the work to make his bandaged fingers scabrous.

"Oh!" he hooted. He clapped the sawdust off his hands and limped right up to them. All three men's faces drained white, expecting some lethal response from the Gavel woman or her Sisters, but she simply sighed at the Potentate's willful breach of safety. He gripped each man's hand in turn.

"Fine of you boys to come so promptly. I was just about to take some lunch." At those words, one of the Gavel Sisters presented a basket and assembled him a snack from the contents. "Thank you, Toria," he said, rotating the sauced cow tongue on brown bread. He invited them to sit with him on the stone retaining wall. A Sister offered her seat to him.

"I'm Algus Equilion the Second, Kaiser. I've been named eighty-fourth Potentate, if no one's told you yet." His voice crackled pleasantly. There was authority in his words, but it was not forced, rather it unfolded in carefully hatched words, which were soon muffled by a bite of his lunch.

"It's an honor, my lord," Kaiser said.

"Is it?" The Potentate chuckled, followed by another mouthful of food. He didn't seem in much of a rush, simply chewing and swallowing a little water from his canteen before continuing. "Kaiser, Kaiser, Kaiser. You've been a riotous guest, in your short days here."

"Pardon, my lord." The Cypolonian tried to track the movement of all the Sisters in his periphery. "Nytrinion was an enemy of the state. At least that's how I saw it. My friend Caethys here was tortured at his hands." Kaiser gestured to Caethys, who seemed cowed by the invisible majesty of Algus.

"I'm glad you made it out alive, Caethys. But I'm not talking about Evanthea, Kaiser, I'm talking about Kasurai. Even when I was at the refuge out east, I heard tales of your iron empire in the south. Your tactics were inscrutable, efficient, and terribly thorough."

"My lord is too kind. How can I help now?"

"I have so much for you to do, Kaiser. But fighting is far down the list, I'm afraid," Algus said, brushing some crumbs from his beard. "The Apogee still has friends in and beyond Kasurai. And Nytrinion was a fool to forsake them as he did. You know a thing or two about Eurivone, don't you, Captain?" Algus leaned in his seat to look down at Clayborn.

"Yes, my lord. I accompanied my father on several expeditions."

"Good. Then you're the right man to accompany Kaiser when he entreaties them for aid in a few days. And the Archaics after that."

If Kaiser's body language wasn't so tightly restricted, he might have hung his head. A task of words would only keep him off the battlefield, where his enemies would vandalize to their black hearts' content.

"You've made the right decision, my lord. One I'll carry out to the letter," came Kaiser's censored response.

"But . . . ?" Algus knew when he was being humored.

"Wouldn't I serve you better on the front? I'm not called Tireless Butcher for my powers of diplomacy." Kaiser's question made the Potentate snort some food from his mouth.

"No, I don't suppose you are!" He laughed. "Kaiser, your origins are the subject of much debate. However, I'm convinced you're not Kasurite at least, so this demonstration of your competence and goodwill shall serve as your initiation rites."

"Initiation rites?"

"Absolutely." Algus finished his food and sucked the sauce from his fingers before folding them on his lap. "Nytrinion's corruption has bled into all corners of my cabinet, so I really don't know who I can trust. That's why I can't go anywhere without Celga and her Sisters to protect me." He nodded to the woman in reference; her demeanor had become no less standoffish.

"I understand."

"But upon winning Eurivonean and barbarian support, I would have no greater candidate for Executor than you, my good Cypolonian.

After all, who could be more innocent of corruption than the man who cut down a dictator?"

The sound of tools played to the blank expression on Kaiser's face. He wanted to say something, but opportunity had made a mannequin of him.

"I'm sure he'd be honored, my lord!" Caethys mercifully rang in, reactivating Kaiser with a fist to the arm.

Clayborn didn't seem to share the excitement that drew up the other men's cheeks.

"Honored is too tame a word. This is more than I deserve." The day's early heat became suddenly sweltering for Kaiser. His temples itched with opening pores.

"You are a face of hope in these troubled times. I'm asking you, as I'm asking everyone, to rise to the occasion. Can you and Captain Clayborn be ready to leave in two days' time?" the Potentate asked.

"We'll be ready, my lord," Clayborn answered, while Kaiser nodded.

"That's a relief. Now if only everyone was as cooperative as you gentlemen." The Potentate brushed off his pants and gathered the tools at his side.

"Can a corporal be of some service, my lord?" came the question from Caethys, starry-eyed from the trade in power.

"Caethys, yes, yes." The Potentate handed his hammer off to him. "Help me get this door up, will you?"

Chapter 27

The waves sparkled with the color of gemstones as the Federal vessel lumbered toward shore. Victon stood at the foredeck of the nimble *Farsider*. The navy had been virtually obliterated by the fire-lobbing dreadnoughts of Septunoth. It was a blessing, Clayborn reckoned, that they could commission this speedy little boat to make a quick and stealthy trip into the north.

The flowered islands of Eurivone unfurled before him. Groves bursting with colored fruits rolled out into a tropical vista. Mountains skirted in greenery stood as cloud-crowned kings farther inland.

"Tethra's halo . . ." Clayborn didn't have to turn to see that the breathy exclamation issued from Kaiser. He didn't get to speak with him much, since the latter was always sword training in some redoubt. Even now Kaiser wore only some cloth breeks and dripped with exhaustion. Barefoot, he carried a canteen in one hand and Seriath in the other.

"Get your gear on, man. We're almost there." His own breastplate was already cooking the captain like an oven. The wonderland only looked hot and arduous to him.

"Of course, Captain." Kaiser was about to step away, but couldn't resist first gesturing to the beaches with his canteen. "I have to ask, what's all that about?"

"The Eurivonean paradise isn't far from the Breach. It's like a hole in reality that lets nasty little things in from far away," Clayborn explained, sounding like he was paraphrasing something he'd read. "The Eurivoneans have taken it upon themselves to defend their islands. And they're getting very good at it."

It was all the explanation Kaiser needed. Staring across the sea from the white shores was a carnival of alien skulls. Wretched pantomimes of anything from a sensible world, these ghoulish effigies were planted across the shores in the thousands. They were testament to these people's cold oath to defend their civilization from the aberrant races haunting the vaults of oblivion.

When the *Farsider* anchored, Federal foot soldiers dropped into the splashing surf and dotted the shore with footprints, fanning out to secure a landing for their ambassadors.

Kaiser was buckling on his body armor: a case of compound steel symmetrically bolted with pieces of blessed metal. It had been a gift from the Potentate, specially wrought by church armorers.

Before Kaiser mimicked the captain's drop into the foaming shore, he turned and addressed the sleepy-eyed seaman leaning on the wheel.

"Vendel!" he called. The man jolted. Vendel was a wealthy retiree of the Apogee navy, though he still loaned out his prize ship for Federal affairs. Never losing his thirst for honor, he prided himself on being among the last sailors that could ferry men safely across northern waters infested with Septunites and the warships of Dragnos Cawn.

"What do you want, a kiss?" Vendel scoffed, pushing on his chin to crack his neck.

"Thanks for the safe passage. There were a lot of ways to die out there, and you avoided them all." Kaiser saluted.

"If you want to thank me, bring me back one of those pretty island girls." He winked. Vendel was a widower, and at sixty he still hadn't given up on finding another wife.

"We should be back in a fortnight or so. You're our key out of here, so stay alive." Kaiser turned to leap over the rail.

"Tethra keep you, son!" Vendel hollered over the splash. Kaiser searched his pocket as he waded ashore and pulled out the stone rendering of the paragon's eye from Ambergate, his good luck charm.

"You'll be with me, won't you, Tethra?" he asked the wet little stone.

Clayborn brought to bear a conch horn his father had received as an honor-gift decades ago from the Eurivoneans. He stepped among the seaweed draped skulls and sucked air through his salty lips. The elephantine call boomed across the canopies, setting off flights of pink birds. When silence reclaimed the skies, the captain sighed.

"They are far. That's the problem with having nomads for allies. It's so difficult to find them!" Clayborn complained.

Kaiser shrugged as he stretched his back muscles with torso rotations. He was ready for a long walk after all that seafaring.

The walk was long indeed, and offered other challenges. Kaiser and Victon's force virtually melted in the steam that enshrouded much of the forest. The bogs were long as rivers, and they had to slog through them while enduring a host of vermin that bit, stung, and sucked at their hides. The thickly knit vegetation reminded Kaiser of his trek through the Quane.

"I'm glad you've made this trip before, Victon. I'm a decent tracker, but the heat and all these smells confound my senses," Kaiser huffed as he and his comrades marched along.

"It was long, long ago, but I remember everything." Victon wiped his glistening forehead. "However, these Eurivoneans move around constantly, never settling long enough to construct more than a little campsite. What's more, they believe in symbiosis. They take only what they need, and clean away any trace of their presence behind them. All the rainfall doesn't help our search either."

"It'll be worth every drop of sweat, I'm sure."

"Still, I'd keep this war a Kasurite affair if I could. I don't like having to beg to islanders." Clayborn's boot plunged into a moist spot of soil. He cussed, though his feet had been invariably soaked for days already.

"It can't be helped. We need soldiers. And nature magic."

"It's all wrong. Before the front started crumbling, before Nytrinion and his foolishness, the Apogee was untouchable. For centuries, every generation inherited a stronger nation than the last." Clayborn slapped a yellow spider off of his ear. "We were purebloods, conquering distant lands and erecting arcane cities, we were the sage-kings of the world. Now we toil through the rotten, stinking muck to entreaty for help from islanders."

Kaiser glanced over to see a blue vein clenching in the captain's forehead. Clayborn was high-born military pedigree. Schooled to idealize country and lineage, Clayborn held all other peoples in lower regard. Greatness was slipping for the Apogee, and diehards like Clayborn could hardly stomach it.

On the third night of their march, Victon had fallen asleep by the fire, still holding a hardcover book. He awoke to the gentle sounds of breaking twigs. Kaiser was near.

"Hey, Vic. I'm just going to stretch out a bit," Kaiser stated.

"Don't you ever get tired, Kaiser? You train every night."

"Since I recovered from that Ousting brawl, I feel much stronger. I have to get used to it and stay sharp if I'm going to carve apart Synod troops in a few months."

"Fair enough. Just don't get eaten by any pitboars out there," Victon warned.

"Ha. If I do meet any pitboars, we'll have bacon for breakfast."

"Oh, and Kaiser,"—Victon held up a pair of books in his meaty hand—"if you really do take our mission seriously, you'll read these."

"What's this?" Kaiser gripped them.

"Eurivonean history. You should know these people if you're going to deal with them."

"Why didn't you tell me you had these?" Kaiser frowned, fingering through the first few pages. "History is my favorite subject."

"Really? I never see you read."

"That's because no one shares their books." Kaiser snapped the pages shut and turned away. "I'll get right on this."

The light of the moons was enough to get Kaiser through half of the first book. His training schedule did not allow him to read often, but when he did, he binged. Presently, he was reading tales of modern pilgrims to Eurivone.

> *"Perhaps the most tragic fate fell to the crew of the* Sun Spear. *These mariners sought to escape great sea serpents that had begun moving inland, consuming entire cities.*
>
> *So they endeavored south, seeking a new homeland. They survived well over thirty attacks by pirate fleets, and they quickly adopted warrior lifestyles as the years progressed, often in the face of famine and thirst.*
>
> *They hopped from coast to coast, never able to establish more than a small encampment before headhunters fell upon them. Brief warfare with*

the natives saw many of the Sun Spear*'s mariners enslaved or sacrificed.*

Continuing south, a terrific storm finally broke the ship to pieces only miles from the safety of Eurivone. The entire crew was thought to have perished."

But soon, his focus failed him. Kaiser began to think on his own past. . .

The wind threw Kronin's hair like white smoke as he breathed in the dusty air inside the castle walls. The sorcerer warlord that had consumed hundreds of lives from these mountainside towers had been smeared across the blade that Kaiser brandished nearby. He watched the surviving victims walk freely over the butchered Septunites below, as every portcullis had been pried open and every door pulverized.

"We saved more lives than we ended today," commented the Cypolonian of the revelers below. Every emotion between ecstasy and grief raced through their numbers, making them laughing, wailing lunatics.

"I know what you're going to ask. My answer is no." Kronin often began with closing statements.

"Crushing demons and Septunites with that hammer, is that your only ambition in this life?" asked Kaiser.

"Yes."

"You would be a leader without match, Kronin. Can't you see the opportunity here? It doesn't have to be just the two of us." The Cypolonian gestured his stained blade over the freed captives below. "They're homeless, dozens of them. A few more swordsmen following your instruction could accomplish so much more."

"I have shared knowledge with you because you are different, but I have never claimed to be your master. It is not my place to direct the deeds of men," Kronin breathed. Kaiser folded his arms, expecting this sort of obduracy.

"Say what you will, but the truth is you are passing up an opportunity to do more. You are capable of more," Kaiser declared. A few moments passed.

"I think you mistake your opportunity for mine," Kronin stated. "My kind aren't even supposed to be here, Kaiser. That is why we

cannot sire children and why we cannot exert our will over men. We are fated to honor the gods with our strength and pass away."

Kronin seldom spoke of his heritage, so Kaiser kept silent. He reasoned that Anthromes were more than human and less than angel, but his comrade was secretive about details.

"The very most we can do is set an example. It was humans who won these lands from the powers of nature, and it is humans who must maintain them against the aggression of demons and the men who follow them. This opportunity is yours, Kaiser," Kronin said.

"I'm half the leader you could be."

"Then think twice as hard," came the answer matter-of-factly. Kronin pinched some sand from his nose, a simple act that made his arms writhe with muscle. *"A wise man once said a king is only a peasant that has discovered his own worth."*

"Honor dictates that I do everything I can. I might not be a king, but I know that I can cast warriors from the mold of victims," came the Cypolonian's declaration. He left then to meet with the freed captives, earning praises amid their tears. He began to take their names, listen to their stories, and make known his plans.

Kronin made a decision. *"Then I will set an example for them as well."*

Seriath seemed to leap into his hands when he finally put the books down. His addiction to the martial arts deepened as time went on. He always felt on the brink of unfolding greater skill.

Shaking out his legs, Kaiser heard something jingle at his feet. He knelt to discover a tiny chain. He pulled it from obscurity to discover a metal demon face attached at the end. *Opagiel's* face.

No . . . Questions flooded his mind. Were Septunites near? Had the Eurivoneans come to harm? The trees around him suddenly seemed menacing. Just as he thought to return to camp, the chirping insects around him hushed.

The fog that began pushing in from the trees came too fast and too deliberately. Kaiser backed up as the fog began to flicker with electricity; little notes of blue light skittered within the fluff. It finally dawned on Kaiser . . .

I'm being herded backward! Just as he wheeled, a pair of rough appendages fell over his shoulders and pinched tight over his arms. He was pulled toward a set of horizontal jaws that splayed wide to receive his face.

To resist the pull, Kaiser's knee went up against the thorax of a green insect of enormous height. Magic or breeding had embellished the mantis-like creature with meaty proportions and a crested hide. Those claws clamped down with a strength that threatened to break his arms and pushing with his knee made it more painful.

But Kaiser's strength had grown, and outrage made him eager to employ it. He kicked with his other leg at the creature's shoulder. The bizarre limb lurched from the joint, dislocated in some fashion, freeing Kaiser's sword arm.

The attacks from Seriath were almost afterthoughts. Off came the creature's other arm, and the backswing claimed both of its front legs. With splashes of yellow fluid flying from its injuries, the mantis fell in an injured bow to Kaiser, who sent a fist crunching through its chest. It didn't have a heart as men have, but Kaiser was content to rip a fistful of dripping cords from its body.

Turning back to the electric mist, Kaiser noticed it was receding. He tried to listen to his surroundings, but the clicking mandibles of the dying creature made it difficult. As insect blood melted from his fist, his feelings warned of danger above.

He was more than ready when the attack fell. Kaiser parried a slash from a falling enemy with a lengthy axe. The brown-robed assailant took a knee to the jaw, but didn't fumble as Kaiser had expected. He recovered quickly, earning space with cycles from the strange poleaxe. Kaiser flew back in, but met with a burst of sparks and heat when the assailant clapped his hands.

Startled, Kaiser absorbed a series of slices that ended with an electric slash. Seriath conducted the blue energy up Kaiser's arm and into his heart. For a moment, the Cypolonian felt shaken and drained. But seeing that blade sweep in for his stomach sprung him from thoughts of surrender.

Kaiser darted back to miss it, then forward again with primal magic fueling his muscles. Waves of red energy pulsed from Seriath as he came down with a powerful stroke. The assailant's block came up in time, but it didn't matter.

The axe's shaft was severed so neatly that it made no sound. What did make sound was Seriath passing over the man's rib cage. Hot blood from the chest wound speckled Kaiser's face. He enjoyed the assailant's look of astonishment as his weapon halves fell from his hands. It was then Kaiser noticed the man's long, pale face and sunken blue eyes.

Definitely a Septunite, Kaiser thought, observing the man's features. *Though he uses a strange flavor of magic.* Plenty of time to ask questions, Kaiser reasoned, as the wound he inflicted was grievous, but would not kill him.

The assailant tipped, his eyes rolling up into his head, when something landed behind him. Another cloaked figure who caught his falling body. Kaiser caught the gaze of the second figure, seeing eyes that held untold secrets in their frosty, blue-green fusion.

He tried for a second subjugating strike, intending to slice the new enemy across the chest as well, but the foe leaped back, taking a shallow cut across a gloved hand.

With a smooth movement, the figure swept off its cloak and hurled it at Kaiser. The flying cloak was neatly swept in half by his sword stroke, but when the fabric fell, the two assailants had vanished.

"Kaiser!" Clayborn came racing over a nearby hill and had men following with bows. "Who the hell were they? What is that?" Clayborn flinched at the insect carcass that still shuddered reflexively in death.

"The Septunites are here."

"Gods, I hope you're joking."

"I found this in the soil before I was attacked." Kaiser produced the blasphemous amulet.

Clayborn's eyes narrowed on the demoniacal jewelry. "Then we have a problem. If they're here, they could sabotage our negotiations."

"Time is crucial."

"Yes. We can't rest right now. We have to rouse the men and find the Eurivoneans before the enemy does. If those were Septunites and they tell others about us, we could be overrun before we make our destination." Clayborn sighed, as he was perhaps the most tired of them all.

Kaiser followed his comrades back toward camp.

Chapter 28

Clayborn spotted smoke snaking into the sky the following evening. They had been marching straight the entire time save for one half-hour break. The sweaty captain laughed with relief and madness. He called for Kaiser, who was helping the rear guard with the gift cargo for the natives.

"Eurivoneans." Clayborn gestured to the totems of smoke.

"Are you sure?" Kaiser asked, sweating generously.

"You can tell by the aroma. They're burning sacred herbs to the Genephim," Clayborn explained.

"The Genephim, they are something like the lords of nature, right? Your books tell me that they take the shape of giant blossoms in the far corners of the universe. Pretty curious."

"They're not gods, anyway. They are the authors of natural law. But for all their power they are as ferocious and fragile as anything outside civilization," Clayborn added. "Just the type of inscrutable nonsense these people fawn over."

"Now, Victon. Is that any way to talk about allies?"

"No. No it isn't." Clayborn was quiet for a while, having some internal session before adding, "Thank you for reminding me."

Clayborn hollered the news to the men, whom grunted their satisfaction.

Once they neared the Eurivonean settlement, the Kasurites adopted a nonthreatening gait. A mile out, they could feel the calculating eyes of hidden guards and hunters. They allowed their footsteps to be heard, and by the time they were walking through the high grass near camp, their host was already gathering.

These were a cosmopolitan people, refugees and pilgrims from the disparate continents beyond this jungle paradise. Some were black as panthers, others were ruddy colored with straight black hair. Some were golden brown and still others were white.

These people brought customs of their prior homelands to Eurivone, so their attire was diverse: gowns, loincloths, vests, robes. But there was a proud efficiency in their garb that was accented by hypnotic jewelry, marking them all as a unified culture.

Standing out among them was a clay-colored man built like a tree trunk. He had a flat face that flared wide at the jaw. He had little dark eyes planted below the brow of his smooth scalp. Overlapping leather armor, gleaned from some black-and-white striped reptile, barricaded his blocky waist. Save for his fauld, his legs were exposed, looking like earthen pillars. As he made for the visitors, a braid of black hair swung behind him.

"I don't know many Kasurites, but I know this one," he said with a striking accent. "Can it be Victon? I have not seen you since you were a child. What a man you have become!"

Clayborn removed his foraging glove. He extended his wet, rank hand and was immediately embarrassed by its clamminess. His acquaintance didn't notice and swallowed it up in his mahogany paws.

"Chrasmos. It looks like time has been good to Eurivone," the captain said.

"Thankfully, yes. We receive many broken people in these troubled times. They bring good wisdom with them." Chrasmos released Clayborn's hand and looked to Kaiser, who felt cunning beneath the Eurivonean's gaze.

"This is Kaiser, my associate," Clayborn explained.

"I see. But you are different. Are you not Kasurite?" Chrasmos took Kaiser's hand next.

"Very observant, comrade. I am from Cypolon."

"Cypolon? I have never heard of this place."

"I don't think you ever will." Kaiser grinned. "But now I fight on the side of Kasurai in the war."

"War, yes . . . I can see you are tired. Our sun is not kind to strangers. I will have some volunteers show you a place to relax. Then we can talk."

The Kasurites were taken to a shaded recess where they could unload and wash up. A troop of natives carried in brimming jugs of cold water. Children carried wooden pails of the same. A woman with eyes drawn up at the ends, seemingly from the distant east, offered around a tray of green juice in porcelain cups. All the natives wore shining smiles, teeth bright and white against their various skin tones. Even the grumpiest, sweatiest Kasurites grinned back at such conspicuous cheer.

"Be welcome at our Eurivone," many of the natives said. Most were fluent in modern Civilic like the Kasurites, but some had only a meager grasp.

Later, Kaiser and Clayborn were tending their faces over the pails. They were too happy to be out of their armor for a while.

"So Chrasmos knew you when you were a child? How old can he be?" Kaiser asked as he clipped the whiskers at his short black beard.

"Oh, the better part of two centuries to be sure," Clayborn answered. At this, Kaiser turned his wet face. Clayborn went on. "You know how they revere the Genephim? Well, some worshipers achieve an elevated state of being through them. It's called *transcendence*. It promotes purity of mind and body by cinching up one's link with nature. The lifespan of a transcendent is practically indefinite."

"Fascinating. So Chrasmos is a transcendent." Kaiser scrutinized his trimming work in the reflection of Seriath.

"I think it's silly. I've always seen this life as a means to make your soul strong, so we can help Tethra fight the demons climbing through the universe. These Eurivoneans, they spend their afterlives tending to nature." Clayborn dabbed his razor in the bucket, sneering.

"You are such a purist, Vic." Kaiser chuckled.

"It was so much simpler when Kasurai was stronger. In my great-grandfather's day, the Church of Calphinas wasn't choice, it was law. We didn't have to tolerate this mystic nonsense. Now here we are begging for help from people who pray to giant flowers." The vein in his forehead was clenching again.

"Kasurai's greatness will be renewed, friend. We'll just have some Eurivonean names in our history books, hereafter."

"Greatness isn't what it used to be." Clayborn dropped his blade into his water bucket with a solid plunk. He got up, toweled off his face, and left Kaiser to his thoughts, which were not all pleasant.

Chrasmos was not a leader in the traditional sense. He was part of a caste of transcendents known as Shydrons that championed the way of the Genephim. While he was a decision maker, he was also expected to embody objectivity and discipline.

Kaiser and Clayborn felt quite honored when Chrasmos seated them in his hut and served them a broiling pan of food. Each man was given a skewer to share it: tadpoles, minnows, crayfish meat, snail meat, and even tiny lizards. The smoky blend of spices melted away Kaiser's skepticism in short order.

Chrasmos poured the tea that had been sitting on a cauldron at his side. The dusky Shydron filled three globular vessels with fragrant liquid.

"I believe I know why you've come . . . ," he began, setting the pot back to the hot stones.

"Please . . . ," Clayborn invited.

"It must have something to do with Septunoth." Chrasmos extended a pair of cups to his guests. Eurivone had no part in the war, but they shunned Septunoth for its demon worshiping. Kaiser caught the Shydron's gaze and felt obligated to speak up.

"The short answer is yes." Kaiser brought his cup into his crossed lap.

"I can't say I'm surprised. Defecting Septunites come to us, bringing dark tales of persecution." Chrasmos sat back, enjoying the scent of his tea.

"Kaiser, show him what you found," said Clayborn. Kaiser produced the amulet by its chain and offered it to the Shydron. Chrasmos frowned for the first time since the Cypolonian had met him. The former took it and absorbed the details with his eyes.

"Do you know what this is, Chrasmos?" Kaiser asked.

"I know that it is Septunite. I'm afraid to ask where you found it," Chrasmos answered.

"In the hills south of here," Kaiser replied. "That is the sigil of a hellbringer sorcerer. The white rim suggests that this was a mage of modest power, but he could have been in the service of a greater hellbringer."

"Hm." Chrasmos scrutinized Kaiser's face. "You're telling the truth. How distressing."

"I was attacked by scouts when I found it. No doubt trying to recover the amulet. Unfortunately, I didn't manage to kill any of them."

"So they are here already."

"We would have kept them from your land, Chrasmos, if we could. But our navy was crippled years ago when the Septunites virtually conquered the Northern Sea. It was by Tethra's grace that we made it here safely," Clayborn commented.

"The fault is not Kasurai's." Chrasmos seemed to regain his serenity as he closed his fingers around the amulet. He felt the dark magic chew weakly at his fingers. "The Septunites have evaded our detection. The other tribes must be made aware of this intrusion. Also, I must mobilize the Sojourners."

"Pardon. What is a Sojourner?" Kaiser asked, sipping his tea.

"Oh, you'll like them." Clayborn snickered quickly.

"There is a Breach not far off Eurivone's coast, and creatures issue from it constantly. It is the reason for our diverse wildlife," Chrasmos began to explain. "The Sojourners use their talents with ice, wind, flame, and stealth to exterminate beasts that are overly predacious. It is because of our Sojourners that our beaches are ornamented so."

Kaiser thought back to the gigantic skulls on the shores as they arrived on the Eurivonean coast. *Expert magical assassins? I'll bet I could learn a thing or two from them.*

"I'm afraid I must adjourn this meeting," Chrasmos said, standing quickly to his full six and a half foot height. Kaiser and Clayborn stood as well, respecting his sudden shift in demeanor. "Apologies, friends. We'll have words again soon enough, but a Shydron is firstly compelled to defend the people."

"That's understandable," Kaiser said, spearing one last crunchy lizard from the pot. Clayborn said nothing but did not even try to hide the displeasure on his face. Nevertheless, the two Kasurites bowed and exited.

Chrasmos took just a moment to think. He looked to the demoniacal amulet tingling in his grasp. He put a thumb to it and pressed. His burly wrist clenched. His two-hundred-year-old thumb raised then, and the amulet fell from it. The metal face of Opagiel had been replaced by an oval groove.

Chapter 29

The next morning, Eurivoneans emerged from their tents and huts. They remained silent until the key moment, and then all at once they broke into a loud prayerful song. Sleepy faces belted out in a foreign tongue.

Startled Kasurites whipped open their tent flaps, wondering what on earth was happening. The chorus, it seemed, was a morning ritual, as all the Eurivoneans sang in perfect harmony. Others even danced and clapped.

Kaiser, squinting his eyes, looked for answers in the faces of his men. When he found none, he prayed this wouldn't happen every morning.

Clayborn lay tight-lipped in his tent. He was familiar with this custom and its meaning. It was a musical oath that they would live this day with grace and courage. For him, it was a reminder of how much enthusiasm he would have to fabricate.

Clayborn's moodiness was beginning to wear on Kaiser, so the latter did what he liked best; he practiced his swordplay, this time on a secluded glade rising above the fruited trees of the Eurivonean settlement.

He had been thinking to himself how best to make his plea to Chrasmos. Assured that an audience would be granted in the next day or so, Kaiser kept his head cool and his body warm. He noticed a pair of people had broken from the shade below and mounted his hill.

One of them, the woman, was sleek and muscled like a young jungle cat, with brown skin that glittered with sweat. The riveted trappings at her chest and waist were made from some extraterrestrial hide. She was probably a beast slayer. Tresses of black hair framed her angular face like a mane of raven feathers.

She used a spear as a walking stick and had katar in her belts. Razor discs were strapped to her thighs. In either boot were the ivory hilts of hunting knives. Kaiser was even convinced that the jagged pieces in her arm bands were throwing wedges. She sported hide gloves, one of which was cut and stained from a recent injury.

Her companion walked on a cane beside her, and he was her opposite in most every way. While he too was lean and vital, he was bald and pale and wore bandages across his wounded chest, carrying as much shame as she carried pride.

"We've some words to trade before you come any closer," Kaiser warned them. They paused, the pale man panting a little. "It was you who attacked me. Wasn't it?"

The woman set her gaze evenly on the Cypolonian. Her eyes were strangely colored, like washed-out aquamarine.

"You are Master Kaiser?" she asked. He nodded. She turned down her spear and thrust it into the dirt, a gesture of humility. Her comrade shuddered in discomfort. He fell to his knees and put up his palms.

"My friend . . . ," began the pale man, "in a passion I attacked you, an ambassador from Kasurai who came in peace. With the amulet in your hand, I mistook you for a Septunite infidel. My ignorance has tarnished my honor and the honor of my Sojourners. Forgive my foolishness, I implore you, and let the troubles end here."

"Sojourners?" Kaiser put his blade over his shoulder and chewed the thought. Remembering his role as diplomat, he unfolded his grimace and cleared his throat. "Yes, I see now. Of course, I forgive you."

The man looked up, nodding gratefully. He gathered his cane and stood. The woman put a hand on his shoulder, dismissing him.

Kaiser and the woman watched the man make his way back down the hill. When she turned back to the Cypolonian, she plucked her spear from the ground.

"Nestre is his name. He is a good man," she informed Kaiser.

"Nestre is a Septunite name."

"His family defected from Septunoth long ago. He is a Eurivonean now, and no lover of Opagiel, I promise you." She watched as Kaiser's expression morphed with thought.

"You're a leader, I presume?" Kaiser asked.

"I am Azurae Iron Feathers, anointed Sojourner of the Third Tier. Nestre is one of my warriors."

"I see." Kaiser sighed, and the woman could see his heart was softening by how his eyebrows danced. "Ah, perhaps I owe you and Nestre an apology too."

"No, the fault was his. Now that he is not here, I wanted to thank you."

"I can't imagine why. I injured your fighter, killed his pet, and broke his weapon."

"He made an attempt on your life, Master Kaiser, and you let him live," she countered. "Your compatriot Victon Clayborn told us about you. I'm relieved the Tireless Butcher has some restraint."

The Cypolonian crossed his arms and shrugged. It was chance, really, that he didn't cut down Nestre out of anger. Kaiser wasn't going to say anything, so Azurae hung her arms on her spear behind her head and began walking toward him.

"May I ask you a question?" As she neared, Kaiser could see that her toned, elegant features were crisscrossed with scars. Perhaps more than he had. An old slash had left a streak of lighter skin across the bridge of her nose.

"Certainly."

"Does Kasurai bring us another war?" Her strong eyes held a glimmer of childlike innocence.

"A Tireless Butcher is no harbinger of peace, I'm afraid," Kaiser answered with a weak smile.

Azurae's mouth stretched at the comment. She savored a breeze as her gloved hands wringed her weapon. "Peace." She tried the word before turning away. "It was a foolish question." She bowed away. "Thank you for your time."

When she turned, Kaiser could see a peculiar tattoo rendered across the nape of her neck. It looked something like a pair of crossed feathers, wreathed by a circle of chains. It continued around her neck to her throat.

"Your neck, is that the crest of a Sojourner?" Kaiser asked. She paused and glanced over her shoulder with contained outrage in her expression. Had he just insulted her?

"No." Her whisper was lusterless, but Kaiser scolded himself for his sudden curiosity.

Chapter 30

Clayborn and Kaiser were quick to break from sleep when the summons came. Chrasmos had sent for them at a dark hour when the wilderness droned with insects. An escort led them into the midnight trees until they came to the rim of a vast jungle canyon.

Chrasmos sat cross-legged on the ledge, transcendent eyes scanning the wilds for villainy. The escort bowed and left Clayborn and Kaiser to the unsettling silence of their host.

"I dispatched trackers to investigate the route you have taken," Chrasmos uttered.

Suddenly, Kaiser didn't like where he was. A cliff before him and a jungle of hidden Eurivoneans behind him. He let his fingers graze the leather hilt of Seriath. His heart banged against his ribs. He thought he smelled blood . . .

"What have you found?" Kaiser lengthened his words to sound at ease. Chrasmos eased up, sounding tired and turned.

In the Shydron's hands was the head of a young man whose black hair drifted over Chrasmos's fingers. The eyes and mouth were scrunched shut in final agony. His death had not been quick, to judge by the ragged neck stump.

"This is the head of Soga Owl-Eyes, last of the Owl-Eyes family. Now his line is lost." Chrasmos's fingers tightened.

Clayborn thought of speaking, but the Shydron's quivering mouth made him rethink it.

"Menace has taken root. I am wondering what you have to say now," Chrasmos invited.

"Your people must be grieving," the Cypolonian opened. "Comrade, may I?" Kaiser held out a pair of hands.

"Kaiser . . . ," Clayborn scolded. But Chrasmos sensed no disrespect. The Shydron handed the head to the Cypolonian.

Kaiser sorted through the wound's hidden odors. He inspected the neck, scrutinizing the broken vertebrae and the color of the clotting.

"His head was removed ceremoniously, using two different weapons. Both weapons were made of hellfrost. That means this was done by a pair of Synod battlemages," Kaiser concluded.

Chrasmos put his hands on his hips.

"Then some Synod plot is underway," Clayborn put in.

"So it would seem," Chrasmos uttered.

"What will you do, Shydron?" the captain asked, sweat starting on his forehead.

"There is no choice but one. I must expel the demon lovers," Chrasmos returned. It wasn't quite the answer Clayborn was hoping for, but it was a step in the right direction.

"If you need help, we have plenty to give," Kaiser promised, offering Soga's head back to Chrasmos, who swaddled it.

"As it happens, I need it tonight." The response was airy as Chrasmos knotted the cloth together. "There's a recluse out in the wilds, and I have long called him friend. The Septunites endanger him and any rescuers I would employ. Kaiser, you know how to fight this enemy. You will retrieve my friend with my warrior Azurae."

"Tonight? Yes, I will help her." Cooperation seemed to assuage Chrasmos a bit, Kaiser noticed.

"Seeing how things have developed, perhaps you and I could have words about—" Clayborn wasn't allowed to finish.

"There will be time to speak of this on the morrow. I cannot make decisions until I hear from the rest of my scouts." Chrasmos started off to the jungle, walking between Kaiser and Clayborn, who could feel the heat of his anger. When he was gone, Clayborn took out a handkerchief and mopped the sweat from his eyebrows.

"Time is wasting, and we still haven't even been able to speak about a war package." The captain hiked up his tasset, annoyed at the chafing.

"The Shydron's temperament is difficult to navigate, but you shouldn't worry. The Septunites have forced his hand."

Kaiser made the rendezvous point early, but Azurae was already there, looking as if she'd been waiting. Back against the shaded tree, her eyes gently reflected the astral colors of the green and gray planets in the late-night sky.

"You're here, good. Please keep up. Delay could mean failure." She gathered her spear and passed into the night-stained ferns. She was set to purpose, so the Cypolonian raced to catch up.

Kaiser wore thick leather instead of his trellised chest piece, but it was not long before Kaiser regretted donning extra leather padding on his arms. Azurae was so fast, she could have eluded Kaiser with her silent footfalls. Refusing to be a hindrance, he challenged himself to match her step for step.

Their full-bore sprinting concluded when Azurae mercifully ducked inside the hollowed stump of a wide tree. She was winded as well, but the Cypolonian was nearly spent. He employed old breathing exercises to recover his stamina.

"You run fast for a continental, Kaiser," she complimented, pulling a bladder of water from her belt.

"I'm not a continental . . . by birth . . . ," he managed. Knowing he was representing Kasurai, he stood tall and shook the sweat from his bangs. He noticed Azurae reaching back for some white flowers that hung like bells from the broken wood. She tapped the petals to let a few seeds fall into her gloved palm and handed them to Kaiser.

"Keep them under your tongue. They will give you strength." She took a breath. "Careful, they're quite addictive."

"This must be an important man for Chrasmos to set a Sojourner after him," Kaiser commented, taking the seeds into his mouth.

"Rastli is his name. He's my grandfather. I insisted Chrasmos dispatch me as soon as possible."

"And Rastli chooses to remain a recluse? Away from all of you?"

Azurae's eyes glazed over, and she held out her hand for silence. She numbed all other senses but her hearing. She hearkened to a sound so faint that it wasn't a noise so much as a feeling.

"There are people moving out there . . ." She detected a tinkling noise in the distant medley. "They wear armor and are traveling quickly from the north."

"Septunites. How many?" Kaiser asked, one eye winking as sweat ran into it.

"Fifty... wait, closer to seventy... no..." Her pupils shrank.

"Oh, beautiful," came the Cypolonian's lament. "Then there is almost certainly a hellbringer. They never go anywhere unless they've nearly a hundred men with them."

"How is a hellbringer best approached?" she asked.

"Please leave him to me, if it must come to that," Kaiser insisted. "I've put down his kind before."

"Agreed. But let's avoid him entirely if we can. My grandfather is an asset to my people and mustn't come to harm." She was suddenly seized by urgency. "Step just as I step; he has many traps around his home." She threw herself out and broke into a blinding chase again. With the strange nutrients of the seeds percolating in his veins, Kaiser pursued.

The two scrambled over a pile of black rocks. Cold water bled over the rounded stones from a spring above. There was a tall wooden hut on top, disintegrating from age. The mossy walls bowed out to resemble a furry green belly. The two neared, and Azurae rapped the front door with the butt of her spear.

"Grandpa?" Her words dissolved. There was a hook that Azurae plucked out of place before palming the door open.

Azurae's grandfather was at once a hunter, mystic, craftsman, and herbalist if anything could be presumed from his home. Fur-bearing totems and religious hangings all seemed to center on a bubbling spring in the middle of his living space. The stones around the sacred water were all painted with white characters.

Surveying the trinkets and baubles cluttering every surface, Kaiser lost track of Azurae, who became a whirlwind rushing through the house. Up the stairs she went, repeating her call. The Cypolonian gazed out the lower portals to see nothing but rodents prowling in the spice gardens.

"He's not here. Probably gone to the eastern river beds, collecting material," she said upon her return. Her face took a bluer cast.

"You're certain the Septunites don't have him?" Kaiser asked.

"I shouldn't think so yet, they come from the north—" She stopped when Kaiser touched her arm. It was his turn to look pale as he looked high for some hidden danger.

"Dark spirits, I can sense them. Damn it, they do have a hellbringer."

"Spirits cannot enter. My grandfather's wards will stop them." She gestured to the doors and windows; every frame was etched with religious scribbling, while sacred herbs hung above.

"They won't be alone. Is there a quiet way out of here?" he asked.

Before an answer could be made, something rumbled quietly outside the shack. The jungle heat was suddenly flushed away. A perverse cold starved out the candle flames.

"What . . . ?" Azurae asked.

"These spirits are the unliving echoes of torment. Hellbringers control them, even strengthen them. We have to move, Azurae. Which way?"

Azurae knelt beside the spring.

"This water comes from deep in the earth, but it empties into a lagoon to the south as well," she said.

"Is it far?"

"The swim will be considerable. But if you empty your water skin, you can keep a breath or two inside." Azurae's answer did not thrill Kaiser.

"Can we catch your grandfather before the Septunites do?" He was not about to swim in armor, and so tore at his straps and pulled the leather from his chest.

"That depends on you, my friend." She clicked off the bonds that held her metal armor in place at her back. She cast the piece away, leaving her cloth harness. She looked to a high window. Taking a hop, she cast her spear through the window with a power that defied expectations.

"Why did you do that?" Kaiser asked, emptying his water skin.

"Deep breaths now. Follow me closely." She leaped into the cool waters of the spring. With no choice but to follow, the Cypolonian filled his lungs with cold air and dove after her.

The jagged underwater tunnel went straight down, and the mixed fear of drowning, tight spaces, and blackness threatened to turn Kaiser's muscles to jelly. It got colder as he followed the Sojourner's fanning legs, and dark enough to challenge even his night eyes. He trusted the sound of her swimming through what became a black trench no wider than a coffin . . .

The door to the shack creaked open. A black silhouette stood before the army's torchlight outside. He was a tall, cloaked man with unruly white hair. A third eye quivered in the center of his forehead like a globe of glowing blood. He groaned, looking around the inside of the door arch. With a finger, he ordered in a group of his reprobates.

Eagerly they scratched off the holy characters around doors and windows. Others snatched charms and hangings from the rafters. Anything religious was stamped to pieces. A fire was started and fed with the books and charms they found.

Soon, the dark spirits could enter, and they slithered in, their faces stretched through gaseous ectoplasm. The hellbringer finally stepped inside. His acuity to fear helped him find at once where the two victims had escaped. He stepped to the spring, where an underling was busily breaking the stones that had been inscribed.

"An invitation to Opagiel's Court cannot be refused." He snapped his fingers and pointed to a bowl of guppies on a crowded shelf. A reprobate brought it to him, and he grinned at the creatures inside. "And you are cordially invited."

The guppies shuddered as their water turned brackish. Weird cancers began speckling their bodies, which swelled with devilish power. The hellbringer dropped it into the spring with a splash. The bowl exploded into floating pieces. The creatures were long like eels or great tadpoles, with skinny claw arms that scissored hungrily.

Chapter 31

Kaiser was getting anxious as he swam cold and claustrophobic, but he churned his emotions in his gut, trying to mold his fear into something more useful.

After following Azurae's whooshing feet for several minutes, he was overjoyed to see moonlight beaming over the rocks ahead. He rewarded himself with a gulp of air from his deflating water bladder.

Azurae glided out of the little cave, turning to give Kaiser a pleasant gaze as she pointed to the surface. A seafaring childhood refined her swimming into a hypnotic ballet.

As he squeezed through, something wriggled up past Kaiser's ribs. He felt hooks stick into his sides. He flailed as long creatures with skinny arms mobbed him. They latched onto his skin with sucker mouths that pumped desperately to exsanguinate him.

He became lost in a cloud of his own blood, blindly seeking the parasites out to crush them in his hands. Azurae's fist shot through the drifting crimson and seized Kaiser by the throat. It felt like the water itself was biting him when white electricity brought an instant of daylight to the pond floor.

When it was over, he was awash in rising bubbles, and the creatures around him fainted; she had stunned them all with her Genephim magic. Wasting no time, Kaiser rowed madly for the surface.

The two emerged in the center of a gloomy bog, equally starved for air.

"I apologize . . ." Azurae heaved, hair like black velvet draping her eyes, "if I harmed you, Kaiser. I had to think quickly."

"Better than being eaten alive," he gasped back.

"Those fiends, did the hellbringer make them?" She waded for the shore.

"Yes, but don't fret for the water's safety. When they transform men in such a fashion, they don't live longer than a day or so. Transformed animals like those fish die even sooner." Repulsed to see a disembodied claw still stuck in his shoulder, he yanked it out and climbed through the reeds with Azurae.

Remarkably, Azurae's spear had landed nearby, jutting from a mound of mud. Her knowledge of this land was impeccable, Kaiser realized as she pulled the weapon free with a squelching sound.

"My grandfather shouldn't be far, the river beds are just across the glade," she said, wringing a splash of water from her hair. "Are your wounds serious?" Kaiser's torso was dripping red. She felt silly for asking, noticing his gallery of scars.

"Not at all. We should hurry," he insisted, gripping Seriath's hilt and looking back at the house they had left beyond the forested hill. He could hear things being smashed and broken inside.

A run brought the two to a field of high grass taller than either of them. Azurae slowed Kaiser with a hand gesture, and she began to turn her head at every sound.

"Senlu?" She called, taking a knee.

Kaiser flinched when something trotted in shaped like a leopard, but built with bony green segments like a great insect. Its eyes glimmered like beetle shells, and its strange mandibles gnawed playfully at Azurae's hand. It recognized her and its tail flared like pineapple leaves.

"Gods, that gave me a start," Kaiser commented.

"No, don't worry, Senlu's a big sweetheart." Azurae seemed suddenly very relieved. Kaiser watched as she inspected its complex jaws.

"Adorifying."

"Grandpa can't be far, if Senlu's here." Azurae stood again to look around.

"Right here, little girl," came a voice from the reeds.

There appeared a man in his sixties, darker skinned than his young relative. His hair was in a gray braid, and his face was quizzical and adventurous. He wore a sleeveless skin jacket, with tails of brush-dwelling animals hanging from the shoulders. His muscles drooped but were clearly used often. He was burdened with a basket of mushrooms.

Kaiser saw a moment of discomfort pass between the two.

"You finally get married?" he asked Azurae.

"No, Grandpa, I'm here to retrieve you. There are Septunites in Eurivone and they're tracking us!"

"The devil you say?" He dropped the basket, lumpy fungus heads bouncing in the mud. He looked across the field to see fire playing upon his old shack. His leathery esophagus rumbled. "Lead the way, child."

Azurae led the two men and Senlu southward out of the field. Kaiser was soon impressed at how well the old man's legs carried him. Life in the wilds made for strong people, he reasoned.

They vaulted down muddy slopes and through low-growing trees that had to be hopped and ducked. Senlu mocked the humans with playful bounds that made no sound. Kaiser watched Azurae's gaze dart about, looking for landmarks.

"Quickly, this way." She spoke perfectly clear and quiet. They trudged up a black trail with a ceiling of hanging moss.

Blue shapes, like handfuls of moonlight, weaved above in the branches. She took quieter steps, and her followers mimicked her. A slithering blue light rounded her feet and blossomed into a melted face before her.

The spirit screamed something, perhaps the last words of the body it once inhabited. The mindless cry roused bats into the starlight. Other spirits joined the howling, pointing with vaporous appendages at the racing adventurers.

A fiery shape passed before Azurae before she could think of using her weapon. Kaiser's empowered blade had cut the specter into twinkling vapor. He leaped from spot to spot, banishing whatever spirits were near with strokes of Seriath.

"We've been found out." Azurae, dismayed at her failure, looked to her grandfather. He straightened, but she could see that he was tiring. Septunite voices were converging.

"They won't relent. We have to fight, Azurae," Rastli said, his chest heaving. He slid a knife from his leg straps.

The lines on Kaiser's forehead deepened.

"Azurae, Rastli, please leave this to me," Kaiser insisted, considering the challenge ahead. "I will blunt their pursuit, but you'll have to deal with the ones I leave behind."

"I'm not going to let a younger man die for me, son. These are *my* woods." Rastli gripped the foreign soldier's wrist.

Kaiser threw off the hard, old fingers, trying to end the argument quickly. "These are *my* enemies." The Cypolonian set like concrete.

Azurae handed him her spear. She wished she had more to offer, but he was glad to have it.

"Make tracks, dammit!" Kaiser bolted for the torchlight parade bobbing behind them.

Rastli probably would have argued further, but Azurae knew the choice had been made. She took the old man's arm and led him into a sprint alongside their insectoid pet. She spared one look for the Cypolonian who flew to meet the outrageous opposition with a spear and a sword.

Kaiser rushed through moon rays toward the living mass of killers. Torch flames made their faces orange, pitted, and identical.

Azurae and Rastli had made impressive headway, but the spirits hounded them without pause. As the ghostly things swept by, they sucked the heat from their bodies, leaving the two strangely hot and cold at the same time.

Annoyed, Azurae tapped her chrysm, drawing electrical power into the katar she pulled from her belt. Lightning fizzled over the face of her blade as she sliced at one of her ghostly pursuers. The enemy lost only smoky bits of its essence.

"The elements do little against their kind, Azurae. Only heavenly magic truly harms them," Rastli puffed by her side.

The spirits veered high above and mashed into an orgy of vapors. All became one, and it spilled heavily like black cream to intercept the fleeing duo.

"We don't have time for this." Azurae meditatively crossed her katar. Her weapons became magical instruments, striking secret chords that the universe itself would reciprocate.

She scraped off a sparkling ember that blossomed into a fiery tornado as tall as her. It gained speed and began sucking away bits of the spirit mass that obstructed their path.

Suddenly, the tornado was blasted away as if the feeblest of tricks. Azurae's opponent had become an *agonism*, one of Septunoth's spirit weapons. Like a carcass rising from a plagued swamp, it rose up dangling sticky shadow liquids. At its center was a spot of yellow light, strangely accented with spoiled shades of purple, red, and green.

Rastli seemed more curious than anything as he gestured to the creature. His spell work washed away the enemy's outer gases in a rush of artificial starlight, but didn't seem to bother it overmuch.

The creature squashed down, rolling vapor at the two Eurivoneans. Energy of horrendous colors, like light beaming through a glass of mucus, ripped at Azurae's body.

"Grandpa, your magic!" Azurae pointed at her relative with her two katar. He clasped the weapons in his hands and let holy enchantments bring twinkling radiance into them. With her weapons smoldering like blue coals, Azurae pressed the creature.

Just as the thing appeared to weaken, it rose up and melted over Azurae's body like black mud. It filtered into the cuts of her arms and wormed into her mouth. She thrashed violently until every last bit of the cursed essence was absorbed into her body.

"Azurae!" Rastli cried, watching as his adopted granddaughter seized.

Her giant eyes shimmered as she struggled for her soul. All of her thoughts mingled with the mindless bloodthirst imposed by the spirit. A spiking coldness threatened to explode her heart.

"Grandpa . . ." She stretched for him. Rastli watched as she fell to her knees, raking the dirt with her fingers. He considered exorcising her, but stayed his hand.

Steam slipped from her wounds as her eyes watered uncontrollably. A holocaust in her mind made her teeth grind. After some terrible climax, she picked up one of her fallen katar, squeezed her eyes shut and cut the front corner of her scalp. Sick light and black blood sprayed from the wound. She held a hand to the stinging affliction and felt the wickedly cold fluids leak through her fingers.

When she opened her eyes again, she could see a puddle of bubbling pitch on the ground. The squirming fluids took on the features of a burbling face, and she knew the spirit had been vanquished.

"Why? Why didn't you help? You could have . . ." Azurae said to her grandfather, palming the black blood on her eye.

He took a breath and smirked a bit. "You didn't need my help, little girl."

Azurae's breaths came angrily that he didn't even seem ashamed. "Come now, before more foes are on us!"

Azurae joined her grandfather in trying to catch up with Senlu. It did not take long for the young Sojourner woman to forgive him.

Kaiser surrendered to outrage. The fear in his guts crystallized into malice. He had hoped they would come scattered at first, but they were too smart for that. Eight reprobates thundered in elbow to elbow.

Still, the first kills came easy. Kaiser swung the spear from the base. The necks of the first two enemies split open, and even a hand flew from one of them. He stepped through the hot, tossing blood and opened another man's torso with a downward slash from Seriath. Three losses was enough to make them hesitate and break apart their tight group.

That's better. He quickly remembered how much he enjoyed the range of spears. Turn, thrust, sidestep, back slash with Seriath, hop forward, low spear slash. His wicked dance was charted out second by second, influenced by the enemy's moves. It tore the life from the other five men in moments.

Now came the rest. A trio tried to flank Kaiser and close him in, but he wouldn't have it. He dashed in, speared the youngest one to a tree and abandoned the weapon. Kaiser guarded the tree that would keep him from being surrounded on all sides. The impaled Septunite groaned things as his chin became painted red.

A simple shift saved Kaiser from a swinging flail. The spiked ball whipped around the spear instead, and Seriath was quick to pass through the enemy's elbow, hanging the raveled weapon with the arm still attached.

More Septunites soared in, drunk on adrenaline with their swords jabbing. Kaiser had to give ground before the wall of points, waiting for an enemy to overextend. To the sound of blood-gorging steel, Kaiser found his chance, sliding past a headless reprobate into the midst of a small squadron.

Four bodily rotations passed Kaiser's edge through a forest of flesh and bone. A lucky cutlass had opened a gash across his pectoral, but the Cypolonian's foes were reshaped into blood-squirting trunks.

He could decipher death threats in the foreign screams, and his cut stung badly. Kaiser growled away his fear as more assailants moved in. He jogged backward, trying to avoid being encircled. To his left was a foe with a hefty iron hammer. Kaiser leaned back and let the weapon's head sail in front of his face, steely breeze filling his nostrils.

The Cypolonian sliced through the man's torso on the backswing, but something twirled around his feet, binding them. Kaiser let himself fall into a backroll and raised his feet, using Seriath to slice the bola from his boots. Two spears came on just as he arose. One jabbed his belly, the other his thigh, but he turned and kneeled to throw off their penetration.

The wounds were considerable, but didn't slow him. He grabbed both spear heads underneath his arm and broke them with Seriath. But before he could retaliate, the snap of bowstrings set him running.

"I hate, *hate* archers!" Kaiser declared as he had in a hundred previous skirmishes. He was chased up an island of raised earth, where a pair of arrows arched overhead. A stream of attackers clambered after, bullying Kaiser to the foot of a muddy ledge.

To the rear of the Septunite force, the white-haired hellbringer watched from his perch. He had counted nearly twenty of his own crushed by the desperate defender.

"A black-haired warrior with dark facial hair, from what I can see. A dour countenance, scarred heavily from battles past. I cannot place his age," he observed.

"He definitely does not fight like a Eurivonean," added the sorcerer's bodyguard.

"I am moved to recall a man from the Kasurite south that fought like this. Stories of a Tireless Butcher whose legacy resounded even among Archaic berserkers. But that name eludes me now."

"Perhaps Kaiser, Master. He disappeared from the south after he escaped our fortress at Coyote's Ball. But why would he be in Eurivone?" asked the bodyguard.

"To make friends," the hellbringer surmised as he watched the dripping Cypolonian eviscerate another human being.

"Shall we take him, my lord?"

"No, he won't let our poor reprobates capture him. Just call them back," the sorcerer commanded. Just as soon, the bodyguard raised the appropriate flag. It was quickly acknowledged by captains who had been eager for retreat.

Steadily, the enemies around Kaiser backed away. His body cried out for reprieve, but he wanted to keep them afraid. With a stolen craethune scimitar in one hand and Seriath in the other, he charged the ebbing tide.

The kills came easy again as fleeing enemies kept their backs to him. He brought down four more as they raced down the hill.

Just as Kaiser sipped a little pride, a shining whip flicked out from behind the tree that still had the reprobate speared to it. The painful wound against Kaiser's arm cost him his craethune sword.

A fully outfitted lictor emerged from the shadows with a blade and a craethune lash. The new enemy vaulted in, his sword crashing against Kaiser's. As the lictor twirled, his whip striped Kaiser's bare torso.

An angry boot to the gut drove the lictor back, and Kaiser yanked the spear from the tree with the flail still wrapped around the shaft. He jabbed at the lictor's whip arm, trying to monopolize range. The spear tip finally caught the lictor in the shoulder, lodging through the bone. Before he could scream, the lictor took Seriath to the torso.

Kaiser's opponent fell against a mossy log, a punctured lung wetting his growl. He looked with disbelief at the mortal injuries that he had been trained so long to avoid. But his conqueror was not finished. Kaiser gripped the flail's haft and unraveled it.

The Cypolonian pulled the helm from the lictor's head and threw it into the mud. And with a prejudice found more often in demons than men, Kaiser cycled the flail, making the spiked ball trill.

The hellbringer in the distance watched as his minion's head was blasted into gelatin.

"I thought for certain Teramax would at least take a limb," lamented the sorcerer's bodyguard, having known the lictor for his lethality.

"I will have gain for these losses," glowered the hellbringer. "Send message with all haste to our friends on the sea. Tell them to look for a Federal vessel returning from Eurivone. Scour it for one known as Kaiser and destroy him."

"They will be eager to strike at Federals, I'm certain."

"The Kasurites have revealed our presence to the Eurivoneans. We must proceed with discretion."

Chapter 32

Azurae had pleaded with Chrasmos to dispatch reinforcements for Kaiser, but it was not to be. The shydron would not move any more of his pieces tonight, stating he was confident the Cypolonian would return.

Azurae was left to focus on her grandfather, for whom a tent had been raised. The pent-up words were nearly tumbling from her mouth by the time he had been settled.

"Honestly, child. I'm safe now, I need no company." Rastli was rubbing his ankles as he sat before the coals he lit inside.

"Are you joking?! I've been aching to see you again, Grandpa!" Azurae was unfolding some of his skins across the rugs. "It must have been five months since your last visit! I need to hear about your discoveries."

"Truly, I don't want to take up your time. In fact, you should probably go address the warriors in your trust, they need to learn about the Septunites," he said, rising. Senlu, who'd been coiled at his feet replied with a chirp.

"At first light, I'll brief them on everything, of course. You must be tired, let me prepare a little tea for us!" Azurae found a kettle and dipped it in a vase of drinking water.

"Azurae, you really must not. I'm not in the humor for it." He watched with heating frustration as she set the kettle over the fire. Rastli gripped her wrist. A spoonful of herbs spilled from her hand. "Damn you, I said no, Azurae! Now leave!"

She looked hurt, but not surprised. He removed his fingers from her bloodless wrist. She set down the spoon and pushed up, turning.

"There must have been an instance long ago when I shamed you," she whispered, not expecting him to listen.

Azurae could hear him seat himself by the fire and sing softly. It was some mantra, lulling his mind far away. Her words were aimless of course, but it felt good to speak them.

"In my ignorance, I have forgotten it. Maybe instead of skill in battle I should pray for forgiveness. I would strike harder and run faster if only I knew I wasn't a failure in your eyes."

Leaving her grandfather to his privacy, Azurae went home, Senlu trotting beside her. The insectoid animal often split its time between Rastli and her, traveling between their dwellings with unearthly tracking abilities. Senlu had missed Azurae, and so was obedient as he accompanied her home.

It was the twelfth shack Azurae had built for herself since she had joined the nomadic Eurivoneans. While her neighbors would have their tents erected in moments, Azurae spent days binding stick walls to create the sound atmosphere she had come to prefer.

The entrance was a cloth flap, but a string of bells across it never failed to alert her to company. The place was just large enough to house her bed (a nest of pillows layered with skins) and a squeaky wooden cabinet crafted abroad before it had eventually been traded to her and stocked with curios.

She removed the heavier portions of her outfit and did her nightly stretch. Moving to her crude window, she pulled in a purple glass vessel that caught the condensation off her roof. Sipping on the night-chilled water, she lit a candle above her bed and a sprig of incense on her cabinet before removing an orange book.

It was her grandfather who had insisted she learn to read, and *Forever East* was a book Azurae had possessed all her waking life. It was a portal reaching back to a sort of warm innocence she enjoyed early in her childhood. They were precious years that predated her discovery of cruelty.

Opening the book, there remained pressed between the pages a delicate flower, whose blue leaves had dried black. She hadn't dared to touch it for years. Lifting the book close, she enjoyed the ancient perfume that clung to the crusty blossom like the breath of an infant.

Old visions played in her head. Wandering through sunny thickets, marveling at colorful, finned beetles that wallowed in the sea foam of a breezy beach, of laughing naked with her friends in the warm mist of a gushing geyser.

She was torn from a pleasant haze when something thumped outside her shack. She pinched out the candle hanging above her and made for the entrance. She stood to the side and swept open the curtain.

Standing in the dirt was her spear, dripping with victory and its tassels swinging in the black winds. The deliverer was gone.

***

"Ooh, the Eurivoneans come to see the glories of a continental body!" crooned one of the Federals who had begun the following day in the cool bathing falls. There were smiles and giggles aplenty as a troop of Eurivoneans paced down the stones, some wearing bathing robes while the less modest girls drank up the admiration of the adolescent Kasurites.

Some of the Eurivoneans began playing king of the mountain on the rocks, which was soon joined by the Federals who wouldn't miss a chance to impress. Staying out of it was Clayborn. He was reclined in waist-deep water, hands folded over his great bare belly, eyes closed. It was a sublime reprieve from the island heat.

"Captain Clayborn?" He opened his eyes to see Azurae there. She was nude, but had thrown a cloth around her shoulders to conceal her upper body while her stomach remained below the water line. "Did Kaiser make it back last night?"

"Of course. That kid eats Septunites for breakfast."

"I'm glad. He should be commended for his deeds."

"You're damn right he should. I hope Chrasmos realizes that."

Azurae understood his comment. "Forgive his delay, Captain. We are a peaceful people and had hoped to never war with humans again." Azurae bowed and looked around a little. "I must thank Kaiser."

"Well he's not here, love. He got up before the morning song. A night of killing makes bed a haunting place."

"I understand. Thank you, Captain."

"Glad your grandfather's safe," Clayborn said with forced courtesy before he closed his eyes again.

Down the stream some distance was a woman with powder-white skin soaking up to her shoulders in the water. Hers were the eyes of the far east, and they angled elegantly in and down as if stenciled by an artist. Azurae waded to her side, taking a moment to appreciate the perfect smoothness of her compatriot's skin.

"How is it you're older than me, Nagarei, and you still have no scars?" Azurae's eyebrows turned up as she dropped her cloth. Her own sun-browned skin was smooth and bright, but lighter-colored scars crisscrossed her arms, striped her torso, and lined her legs. Her strong body was possessed of vulpine curves, but her scars kept her pride in check. She sunk to her shoulders in the water next to Nagarei.

"I choose my fights carefully, Zuri," Nagarei said with her signature aloofness. It was a front only her close friends could see through, and Azurae was much more than that; secret pain had made them a very special kind of sisters.

"Are you saying I'm a promiscuous fighter, Nagarei?" Azurae pinched her arm under the water. Nagarei was probably holding her sword under there.

"You see a fight, you throw yourself at it. You don't ask questions or get to know the fight, you simply give yourself to it."

"I think you're jealous. Because you haven't had a good fight in a long time."

"I can get a fight whenever I want."

"Mind the seasons, Nagi. Fights are harder to come by for women of your age." Azurae knew she had won when Nagarei hissed at her. They made ripples with their laughter.

"Have you spoken with grandpa?" Azurae asked.

"Yes, he dropped by this morning."

"Of course, he visited you."

"Was he cold, Azurae?" Nagarei guessed.

"I don't understand that man anymore. I thought becoming anointed would surely rekindle his pride in me."

"Don't waiver. Your path is an honorable one, and Chrasmos will invite you to gain more honor tonight."

Azurae raised her head. "What do you mean? Have you heard something?"

Nagarei turned her big black eyes on her sister. "No, but Chrasmos wants vengeance for his friend Owl-Eyes."

"The Shydron wouldn't act on anger. He is the most peaceful man I know."

"Ah, but Shydron Chrasmos has fallen out of practice controlling his anger. The last hundred and fifty years he has known little but joy.

This affront from the Septunites comes as an outrage." Nagarei had a valid argument. While monsters from the Breach regularly threatened the land, the people had prospered in most other ways.

"Our lives are about to get very complicated, I think," Azurae mused, raising a hand to watch the water glide down her wrist.

"So it seems."

"If I am sent to Kasurai, will you come with me?"

When Azurae pleaded, Nagarei realized her voice had not changed much from back when they were children. "I suppose. It might be exciting if we were in a fight together," Nagarei said with the faintest smile on her lips.

***

Clayborn wondered if the lighthearted aspect of Chrasmos would ever return. Meeting again in the intimate dimness of his quarters, Kaiser and Clayborn held tea cups that had grown cold in their anticipation.

"In these flowered hills, killers march against my people, and I don't know how many," Chrasmos uttered.

"If we can make enough progress in the Kasurite west, we can have ships encircle Eurivone again," promised Clayborn. "We just need a little support from your people. Septunites aren't accustomed to Sojourner magic."

"How is it in all of Kasurai, you cannot muster the ships to reinforce our seas now?" came the Shydron's question. "It seems such a large continent would have the resources."

"Because Kasurai is a divided nation," Kaiser answered, wanting to scratch the bandages under his armor. "Our new Potentate is trying to improve relations with the Archaics, but it's a slow process."

"But your resources. You are a wealthy land," interjected Chrasmos.

"The barbarian Dragnos Cawn rules a dominion as large as the Apogee itself, but he refuses to join our fight against Septunoth. Instead, he's been laying claim to cities destroyed in the fighting," Clayborn explained. The captain decided to try his tea.

"Cawn? Then the cancer of Kasurai has swollen over the years. His family has aspired to rule all the land since before you were a child, Clayborn. I remember that," Chrasmos commented.

"He is too dangerous to confront at this point, but we are getting off topic," Clayborn put in. "Chrasmos, we need your warriors or we may not be able to thwart the Synod."

"You ask a lot from a nation that has just been invaded," added Chrasmos.

Kaiser's expression grew grim enough to gain attention. "They have been able to keep hidden, so their numbers cannot be large. What is the head of the hellbringer worth to you, Chrasmos?"

The Shydron appreciated the conversation's direction. "Kill the hellbringer and any mages under him, and I will see you get your share of warriors from my tribe, at least."

"Will you support us when you finally speak with the Shydrons from the outer tribes?" Clayborn was quick to ask.

"On my honor, I will argue for your support."

"Then let us be done with this bloody deed," Clayborn said.

***

Entry from Kaiser's Journal, Day 8 of the Entreaty to Eurivone

> *"I had figured since the Potentate insisted we entreaty the Eurivoneans, that these diverse jungle-faring warriors would possess a certain military value. Yet their manner for dispensing death has forever changed my conceptions of soldiery and indeed the laws of nature.*
>
> *Did you know lightning can be made to act as a liquid? That sunlight can be carved and shaped as readily as stone? Perhaps my practice of the simpler primal magic has stifled my imagination, but the Sojourners fight in a way that makes my understanding of magic seem comically incomplete.*
>
> *My appreciation came after the fact, of course. Last night, as the Sojourners combated Septunite infantry, I managed to eliminate the hellbringer after Clayborn triumphed over the elite guard. I was elated to be able to add a second hellbringer to my list of kills. They say there are*

only about a hundred of them in existence. (One less now, ha!)

But our endeavor was not without cost. While our Federals came through with only minor injuries, four of the Sojourners were killed by the hellbringer's spell work. Azurae, the leader of the force, came through unharmed, but the one she calls her sister has been badly poisoned. As luck would have it, I recognized the toxin and administered an antidote. I hope it was enough.

Among the victims of the dark arts was Azurae's good friend she called Brother Tan. This resonated bitterly among the Sojourners, who behave more like a family than a league of arcane assassins.

It was a dark reminder for me that while these people occupy a combat niche that Kasurai sorely lacks, they are untested against the spells of the Infernal Helix. When (if?) I become a leader again, I will take it upon myself to educate our Eurivonean warriors against demon sorcery.

Tethra keep me wise.
Kronin keep me strong.
Zothre keep me vengeful."

***

The Kasurite troops were cowed after Clayborn returned from another meeting. He cursed so ferociously that none responded, save Kaiser.

"Victon, you need to relax. We've all but secured a war package, Chrasmos said as much," the Cypolonian reminded him.

"I'll relax when we've made a difference. Every moment that Shydron delays, more of my people die back home," Clayborn spat, unbuckling and shoving off his breastplate.

"He is unused to such danger, which is why he hesitates. His islands haven't known peril for years except from those monsters from the Breach. But he will help us," Kaiser added.

But that night when Kaiser parted from the encampment, he couldn't help but share some of the captain's frustration. When he made for the isolated hill on which he had trained before, he noticed Azurae had beaten him there. She was rehearsing some series of movements as raindrops began to fall. He was undiscovered, so Kaiser resolved to take a knee and just watch a moment.

Her spear trilled in its course. Well-conditioned muscles kept her performance fluid and sturdy.

The skies soured, and the rain became a downpour. Azurae's battle dance quickened. She carved the rain into shredded mist. Lightning tore up the sky, filling the land with light and giving Azurae a nimbus of sparkling vapor.

Azurae was low and still then, spear frozen in a thrust. She let her shoulders burn under the lens of dripping rainwater and rose.

Kaiser walked casually to let her hear him. When she turned, she smiled through the sluice.

"Master Kaiser. I thought I'd find you here if I waited." Her chest heaved.

"It's a good hill for training, isn't it?" Kaiser answered, running a hand through his soaked hair. "How is your sister?"

"She has held strong. Your antidote will see her through, I think. She wanted me to thank you."

"My friend Sidna taught me how to mix it after she treated me for the same poison. The thanks belong to her."

"Such a nice evening to be alive," Azurae said, turning her head up and letting the water kiss her heavy eyelids.

"I am sorry about Brother Tan, Azurae. Septunoth will be punished for its sins against our countries," Kaiser offered. Azurae either ignored the comment or didn't hear him.

When she opened her bleached-teal eyes to him again though, she wore a mask of contentment. "It's time for a good fight. Will you accommodate me?"

"Certainly." Gladness stretched across Kaiser's dripping stubble.

"Thank you. It's the dogma of Sojourners to confront our fears head on. To advance our resolve."

"A good mandate for warriors. But are you saying that I'm frightening?"

She didn't answer but took up a deep stance. Kaiser accepted her silence and pulled Seriath from his belt with a loud shriek of metal.

The two collided in an explosion of dynamic slices. The clangor of their combat belted out over the forests, sounding through the trees that thrashed in the drenching gale force.

When the watery darkness was illumined by the lightning, they caught glimpses of each other's faces. Kaiser thought he saw the Sojourner grinning.

When finally their muscles could take no more, they lowered their weapons and watched each other gasp for breath. Kaiser liked how she stood tall as the downpour tinseled her body. She looked half insane the way she smiled behind the wet hair.

"Thank you," he said, feeling a shallow cut open on his cheek. "For taking me seriously."

"Same." She turned her head and let him see the little cut on her neck. "More people need to fight like you. You can tell a lot about a person by the way they fight." She ran her fingers up her arm, savoring some aerobic sensation. "Oh, Kaiser, what a story you tell . . ."

"When I asked about the mark on your neck . . . ," Kaiser began, daring to sober the moment, "I hope I didn't offend you."

Azurae looked him over. "No, Kaiser. I was only unprepared."

"I see. I wonder if you are prepared now?" Kaiser pushed without really knowing why. Her past seemed a delicate topic.

Azurae looked more or less at ease, regarding him with a lowered gaze. "You know Eurivone is a sanctuary for exiles and refugees, don't you, Kaiser?"

"Yes."

"I'm no different. A great disaster destroyed my homeland, so my people and I struck out to find a new home."

"Eurivone?"

"Well, eventually. Our odyssey was a difficult one. I was very young, but I knew that to protect my family, I must become a warrior."

"You've been fighting from a young age," Kaiser asserted.

"My elders marked me with the crossed feathers on my neck when I was eight. They honored me as a fighter and a bringer of good fortune."

"And the chains encircling the feathers?"

"I received those at . . . different hands." Azurae knew she was being vague, but she didn't feel like delving deeply. "It is still a nice night to be alive, isn't it?"

Kaiser deciphered more than Azurae had intended to disclose; her youth had been fraught with captivity. She turned her face to the spilling heavens again, and the Cypolonian regarded her with new eyes.

Azurae moved her hand up on her spear. Kaiser noticed she wore the same sliced glove that she had worn when first her warrior ambushed him.

When Azurae opened her eyes, Kaiser was standing close enough to touch. He reached up and took her hand.

He regretted carving that slit on her fist. He politely kissed her knuckles and wrapped her fingers in a two-handed grasp.

The Sojourner connected gazes with him when he looked up. Dusky as she was, she blushed beneath her eyes.

"Yes, Azurae. It is a nice night to be alive."

Chapter 33

In the cloudy afternoon, Clayborn's weight loss became obvious to Kaiser. It had been ten days since the Eurivoneans had received them, and Clayborn's hopes were teased to their limits. He burned to return and present something to the Potentate. His confidence was rooted in productivity, and barring a few Septunite kills, he had achieved virtually nothing in his sweaty foreign labors.

He and Kaiser stood out awkwardly in the company of their hosts. Ten Shydrons, Chrasmos among them, had secretly convened on this scraggly mountain top. These elite sages didn't speak much at all as they passed around the preserved head of the hellbringer that Kaiser had recently cut down.

"How do you expect to resolve your war?" asked one Shydron, a tan, slender man whose leather armor looked curiously similar to outdated Federal armor. Perhaps he had once been a Kasurite, Clayborn wondered as he thought out his response.

"As quickly as possible, by adopting a modernized plan of counterattack. In addition to barbarian commitments, which we hope to curry in the next few months, we are reviving the Apogee's ultimate fighting force, the Acolytes, who—"

The Shydron cut short the answer. "Yes, that does sound promising."

Clayborn felt like a dog being told to speak. Kaiser, on the other hand, was annoyingly quiet.

Chrasmos stepped in closer to them, drawing the attention of the other Shydrons. He had, at last, regained some of that warmth that Clayborn had been counting on.

"It will not do for us to watch as Kasurai is ravaged," Chrasmos began. "And so, we are prepared to entrust you with a thousand Sojourners."

Kaiser's folded arms fell quickly to his side, but his distress was reined in by Clayborn's stern gaze.

"A thousand master fighters. It is a gesture we can never hope to reciprocate in full." Clayborn did a gracious, traditional bow.

Kaiser spoke up. "And yet, duty compels us to test your kindness."

Clayborn tried to interrupt. "Kaiser . . ."

"Forgive me, Shydrons, but as the soldier of a beleaguered nation, I beg you to consider two thousand," Kaiser said with all his humility.

"Perhaps you do not understand the value of a Sojourner, my friend," suggested one of the Shydrons. "They are extensions of the living earth, their every waking moment committed to martial purity."

"They should not be regarded as soldiers, but as specialists," said another.

But Kaiser noticed that some of the Shydrons looked more contemplative than outraged, others flattered. "On every drop of my honor, I swear your people will be respected. We come to your island because we covet the rare power only a Sojourner can dispense. Federal command will handle them preciously."

Clayborn dropped a hand on his comrade's shoulder. With a set jaw, he conveyed to Kaiser that he must not say anything else.

"I could part with . . . another eighty, I suppose," stated one Shydron. "Granted my brothers share the burden." He set his gaze on one of his comrades that had complained.

"Then I shall see you another hundred and twenty. That totals twelve hundred," came the promise from Chrasmos.

"Thank you, old friend . . . ," Victon uttered.

"I think between the rest of us," Chrasmos went on, gesturing out with his huge, brown arms, "we can scare up enough to meet your need."

Chrasmos must have wielded more clout among his people than Clayborn understood, because while silent, they did not so much as grimace.

"Dear Kae'Asha. Your fruitful wanderings in the northwestern beaches have grown your tribe. Won't you muster a little more help?"

Chrasmos asked the golden skinned goddess at his side, whose flowered braids fell past her knees. She clearly had some admiration for the powerful warrior sage before her, because she smiled beautifully.

"I mustn't turn away from needful friends. All right, another hundred then," she said.

Chrasmos playfully tended to the rest of his fellows, and between them, a promise of two thousand Sojourners was achieved.

"If we are *well* done here, I have much to tell my tribe, and many things to do," said one of the Shydrons.

"As do I," concurred Kae'Asha, who found herself holding the hellbringer head. She handed it to Kaiser, glad to be rid of it. They began shuffling off, while Chrasmos lingered behind.

"You know, the last time you visited me, decades ago, all it took to make you happy was a sugared fruit crisp," Chrasmos reminded Victon.

"'Happy' doesn't begin to cover it. You have come through for me in a way I will never forget. I promise we will take care of your Sojourners." Clayborn took the Shydron's hand tightly.

"And they will take care of you. With my blessing, bring an end to this terrible conflict." With that, the large Shydron left the two on the mountain top.

"You push too hard, Kaiser," Clayborn stated.

"The Potentate's going to have us whipped. We failed our objective by a thousand Sojourners! We needed three thousand!" Kaiser lamented, shaking the slack-jawed head in his grasp.

"Equilion secretly disclosed to me that a thousand was all he truly needed. We don't need them to fight so much as teach. With exotic magic on their blades, our men have something to pit against Septunite sorcery."

"But isn't nature magic illegal in Kasurai?"

"It's been considered dangerous for a long time, but now we need it to survive this war. And these Sojourners will teach us how."

"So this wasn't a quest for numbers so much as knowledge? Why wouldn't you tell me that?!" Kaiser fumed.

"You said yourself you're not known for your diplomacy. We were testing your powers of negotiation, and now I can report to the Potentate that you doubled our prize." Clayborn grinned as he drew his glove across his damp forehead.

A flicker of pride rose up in Kaiser's heart, but he felt foolish as well. Clayborn punched Kaiser's chest, letting a laugh that thundered across the canyon.

"We did it, boy! We can go home!" He began marching back into the woods. Kaiser decided not to think too much, drop-kicking the head off the mountain side. "Let's have some supper. There are a lot of different animals on this island, and I want to try every one."

***

A hot day melted into a breezy, pink-sky evening. Balmy winds off the distant waters seasoned the groves with the smell of fresh salt.

Kaiser and Azurae chased into the jungle depths, making steely music with their practice combat.

The Cypolonian insisted upon learning some of Azurae's techniques. He was determined to continue until he tagged the Sojourner with one of her own moves. Their duel had been a lengthy one.

"You're a natural!" Azurae cheered.

Kaiser didn't believe her for a moment as he chased his "prey" up through the shadow of the mountain. Azurae glided through Kaiser's volleying sword thrusts like a reed bending in the wind. He tried moves that she had mastered years ago, but he was not altogether ineffective; he kept her guessing.

Finally, Kaiser bullied her against a rock wall. What he hoped would be a subjugating kick caught nothing as Azurae weaved out of the way.

"Just hold still a moment, would you?! You move like a hummingbird!" Kaiser's complaining made Azurae laugh, so she spun away and held up a pausing glove.

"Don't give up, you're using an unfamiliar style," she encouraged.

"Flexibility, balance, and stillness. It's all my weak points mixed together. But I'm lucky you're showing me. It illuminates a lot of ways for me to improve."

"That's precisely how you should see it."

"We passed some water earlier, do you think you could show me some river-fighting before we head back?" Kaiser asked.

"You really like fighting don't you?" Azurae noticed.

"Oh, hell yes."

"But it's never enough, is it? You want to be invincible."

"Every soldier wants to be invincible,"

"Some only want it with their words, others want it with their actions. You could have admitted my fighting style is simply not suited to you and given up. You actually appreciate it when your weaknesses are laid bare."

"I don't know if I like seeing how weak I am, but I like clarifying my path. If that means getting stomped a few times by a foreign woman, fair trade." Kaiser shoved his blade away.

"So what makes this Butcher so Tireless?" Azurae suddenly needed to know Kaiser's motivation. He shook his head thoughtfully.

"Past failings. A dead friend. A lot of dead friends, but one in particular showed me what real strength was. It made me feel like I could win the war if I just discovered it for myself. What he did for me, I want to do for all the Kasurites. Anyone can fight, you know? But when I do it, I want it to be a spectacle of hope, not just carnage."

"That sort of message is easily misunderstood." Azurae took a drink from her water skin.

"Which is why I have to be clear. I'll be out there again soon. And I have to glow for all those burnt-out soldiers that have forgotten they can win."

"I hope you mean that," she said. "Because hopelessness hurts all the worse if your respite is only temporary."

Kaiser smoothed over his beard, certain that he couldn't validate himself with pretty words. "Maybe it would help me to learn what hopelessness feels like," he started again. "You're no stranger to it, Azurae. In your darker days, what transpired in your young mind?"

"Mmm . . ." Azurae hesitated. "I'd really rather not muster those thoughts tonight." She received a nod.

"Of course. I don't know what you've gone through, but I know it wasn't pretty. Nevertheless, you've become a diplomat, a martial artist, and a leader. It's inspiring."

Azurae rolled her eyes and shrugged.

"I really do feel like a villain for asking you to fight in our war. For ripping your people away from this peace."

"Septunoth has to be stopped. If there are two evils, Kaiser, you are the lesser." But she could see guilt grinding between his jaws. She bit off her glove and put a palm on his arm. He didn't react, so she explored his crisscrossing scars with her fingers.

It had been a violent life for him as well. Maybe that was why she felt an unspoken kinship with him.

"Please don't feel so guilty. Of course, we cherish this life, but the best way to spend it is to safeguard the lives of others. If I die in Kasurai, it will be a good death."

Her words made Kaiser feel worse, but he nodded. "What was the name of your ship? The ship you arrived in here, when you were a child?"

Azurae thought for a moment, resting her palm on the hump of his tricep. "It was the *Sun Spear*. That was its name." She looked up when she felt Kaiser's skin go cold.

He sighed and took her hand. "Forgive me, Azurae, for what I am about to do." He gently took the side of her face and kissed her on the lips. They were cool and soft. He slid his other hand up to her neck and pulled her in a little harder. Azurae's breath was shallow and warm.

When their lips parted, Kaiser just held her and swam in those large, aquamarine eyes.

"Why did you do that?" she whispered.

"It just felt right."

This time, it was the young Sojourner who pulled the Cypolonian in. She let her spear fall and put her arms around his neck. She kissed him with an unrestrained hunger for his mystery. Their chests compressed tightly.

His gentleness had somehow survived a life as cruel as her own, and she wanted to nurture it with her kiss. She let the locked up feelings fly and burn through his aching muscles.

When the kiss ended, Azurae threw her head over his shoulder, and he dutifully squeezed her slim, breathing body. The stars glittered to life above. They embraced without words, healing each other.

***

"What's all this about?" Azurae asked Chrasmos as he moved out into the circle where a crowd of his people grinned in anticipation. Chrasmos had his great scimitar unsheathed. The bejeweled weapon was twice as long as most swords of its design.

"Kaiser asked me to test his spirit. He said it was his new policy to challenge all his fears head on to advance his resolve." He smiled back at her. The implications were not wasted on Azurae, who began scanning the crowd.

"To challenge Chrasmos right after negotiations is a slap in my face, Kaiser. This is foolish." Clayborn glared as the two made their way to the circle.

"Don't worry, Clayborn. I was respectful when I asked," Kaiser answered, unsheathing his blade.

"You understand that the Potentate will hear of all of this," Clayborn reminded him.

"Chrasmos is my friend now, Clayborn. As with all my friends, I ask to spar now and then. I am still waiting on the day you will accept my offer." Kaiser replied. Clayborn tsked.

In the throng Chrasmos came forward, sword in hand, to hug Kaiser. In Eurivone, embracing with drawn weapons was a sign of self-control, as Azurae had told him. They parted and Chrasmos turned to the crowd.

"My friend Kaiser has offered this test out of good will. There will be no blood here."

"Just a little sweat," Kaiser added.

"Just a little," Chrasmos agreed, taking up a loose battle stance and raising his heavy blade.

In her life, Azurae had never seen Chrasmos fight. But she knew transcendents were people that were no longer restrained by hesitation; their strength, focus, and precision were cultured to superhuman heights. Kaiser had the courage to challenge Chrasmos simply because he didn't realize what he was getting into.

The combatants circled, awaiting the bell. Chrasmos looked as peaceful as he might standing before a child. His saunter was easy and steady.

The bell sounded, and Kaiser felt like a protective cage around him had been lifted. Something about Chrasmos's serenity was strange.

Nothing happened. Kaiser had half expected to be rushed asunder by the transcendent. Was Chrasmos as strong as Kronin, he wondered? The Shydron certainly didn't look as aggressive. Chrasmos only bobbed along, supremely assured.

Get in there, coward! Kaiser scolded inwardly. Slowly, carefully, he approached. The onlookers held their breath. His instincts, usually so clear, demanded a dozen different actions.

Chrasmos's smile widened as he raised his sword. Finally Kaiser flared to life. Shifting back, his guard foiled a plummeting slice from the five-foot scimitar. Sizzling dashes of fire spat from the crashing blades and nipped Kaiser's face.

You are representing Kasurai! The Cypolonian recycled his backward momentum into a forward series of slices. Chrasmos's massy weapon weaved a cone of defense around him, thwarting with sparking parries.

Kaiser could sense an impending attack from his left. He ducked and rolled, evading a singing slash and feasting on the confidence.

So far, so good . . .

Trusting his own speed, Kaiser darted for Chrasmos's right, but thrust low and left. Chrasmos shifted back, but it was clear that he had not anticipated this.

Kaiser had a little time and ducked a heavy retaliation. Spinning low, he kicked out. The Shydron's blade chomped into the dirt, its face taking the kick. Chrasmos stepped around and scooped his own foot under Kaiser's ribs. Not kicking so much as lifting Kaiser flatly into the air. Kaiser found himself back on his feet. There was a breeze of laughter from the crowd. Chrasmos had given Kaiser his stance back.

He decided not to be embarrassed. Kaiser took up a low stance again. This time, Chrasmos came running, a transcendent with a sword as long as a man.

Chrasmos darted out of Kaiser's vision. The Cypolonian's head whipped about to find him. The sandy crunch of footsteps teased Kaiser from behind, but even as he chased around with his eyes, Chrasmos stayed just out of his periphery.

Could he really be so fast?!

Kaiser tried intercepting Chrasmos's unseen dash by lashing out at varying heights. He sheared a complete circle around himself, hoping to connect with anything.

Kaiser ended crouching and panting. He felt a weighty tap on his shoulder. Chrasmos's scimitar was resting on it.

"Victory! Chrasmos!" someone shouted, starting an applause. Kaiser's grip loosened. He turned and rose as the scimitar slid from his shoulder.

"Is our contest fulfilled?" Chrasmos' eyes sparkled.

"I guess it is. Chrasmos, your skills are unbelievable," Kaiser stated.

"Well, I've got two hundred years of practice on you." The Shydron patted his muscular stomach.

"I hesitated badly. I seldom hesitate."

"Probably because a transcendent radiates a sense of impassive serenity in combat. If my enemy cannot equal such peace of mind, they are plunged into panic."

"It's a potent ability. And how did you manage to evade my sight at the end? You were so fast I couldn't even lay my eyes on you." Kaiser had to know.

"It's not so much speed as it is knowing the route of the eye. I knew where you would try to look, so I simply kept myself beyond it. We call it *ghostwalking*. Very good for hunting."

Looking over Seriath, Kaiser saw that the Shydron had done something no Septunite ever had; Chrasmos had cut chips into Seriath's fine edge.

He cuts even into coroneum, Kaiser thought. *It's just as well. They will remind me of today's lessons.*

"Stay your course, Cypolonian. You're well on your way." Chrasmos shook Kaiser's hand.

"Thank you, Chrasmos."

A short distance away, Azurae let herself breathe for the first time throughout the entire fight.

***

It was nightfall, and the Kasurites were verging on departure from the settlement. When he had a spare moment, Kaiser chased a mirage down into a precipice hanging with flowered moss.

He found Azurae watching the planets hovering silently. The colorful stars were joyous in their cold brilliance.

The Cypolonian was guessing what to say when she turned. She was holding her arms out, both were sleeved to the elbow in curious fireflies. She blew on the fireflies to dismiss them and nodded for him to join her. Kaiser obliged, weaving his fingers into hers.

"I've been wondering. What exactly do the Genephim do with their followers' souls?" Kaiser asked. "Once they . . . pass away, I mean?"

"We are reborn," she replied, as if expecting the question, ". . . if we've honored the earth and striven for peace. We become a part of nature, tending to cosmic forests in a place where time has no power."

"That sounds peaceful. Sounds like I'll have a hard time finding you, though."

His sweet smile would have brought tears to her eyes, so when Azurae didn't react, Kaiser just pulled her in. His mixed scent of wood smoke and sweat lulled her. Her fingers roamed his back and his hair as if trying to claim him forever.

His kisses were pleasantly prickly on her neck, jaw, and cheek. His meaty palms caressed her like warm bath water, careful to experience her every contour. Their hearts drummed loudly to each other, pleading for oneness.

"I'm sorry. I can't stay," he said.

"It's not your fault. I enjoyed this." She nuzzled his shoulder. "I suppose this was foolish, wasn't it?"

"Who cares? It feels good. Given more time, I'd get very, very foolish with you." Kaiser chuckled.

She smiled at the implications and took his face gently in her hands. "If times were simpler, I would be honored to call you mine." Her eyes were an elixir of oceanic colors.

Kaiser's crinkled his brow, unable to find words. She put her head on his chest, and he kissed her wind-feathered hair.

***

All the *Farsider*'s crew drank that night to the sound of fiddles. Except Kaiser. It felt important to watch the island paradise shrink away. Just in case anyone might be watching him too.

His fingers moved absently on the banister as he tried to memorize the feeling of Azurae's skin and the taste of her breath.

Suddenly, death on the battlefield seemed a little less glorious. He was a warrior first and a human second, that's what he had always believed. Companionship was tantalizing, but detrimental to the warrior's way.

Seriath became heavy, urging him to practice. The chips Chrasmos had left in his blade proclaimed he was still very much a novice in the face of true warriors.

I have to become stronger, he admitted inwardly, thinking on mighty Chrasmos, then further back to memories of Thel, and how he had dismantled great Kronin.

As Kaiser quested, the world seemed to populate with grander challenges, yet his own fighting skills improved only a bit at a time.

There was no time to be human.

Chapter 34

Several days later, the *Farsider* was a wooden ghost gliding quietly through bile-colored waters. The same weather conditions that kept Eurivone tropically heated in the north had raised a fog over the seas.

The mood of the crew was as dismal as the sun trying to glow through the mist. These were dangerous waters, with Septunites patrolling, and the men knew they sailed over the graves of a million victims.

Clayborn shared the men's concern. Putting his nose to the air, he wondered if there was any truth to what sailors said about the scent here. Clayborn figured if shattered dreams indeed had a scent, they would smell something like the salted rot that thickened the air.

"One day left . . . maybe two," he whispered to himself, anticipating the jutting shores of northern Kasurai as much as any. Peering over the rear deck rails, he grimaced at the shadows morphing in the gloom.

At the forecastle deck, Kaiser was catching up with Vendel, who recounted becoming a folk legend in his small territory in northeastern Kasurai. Apparently, he was something of a career volunteer, with no family to hold him down.

"To this day, whenever I visit the docks of Shallowmoore, I eat for free," Vendel was saying, one-handing the helm.

Perhaps the only person enjoying their afternoon was Kaiser, who hungrily listened to the triumphant memories. Hearing the exploits of the Apogee's veterans gave him hope. Iron souls like Vendel did not lose wars.

"I'm not sure if I look for trouble, or if it looks for me," Vendel continued. "But the headhunters around Shallowmoore are still looking for me. So I don't visit as much as I'd like."

"You think they would recognize you after all this time?" Kaiser asked.

"Nobody missing a left ear is safe there," Vendel mentioned, wiping graying hair from the tunnel of scar tissue that used to be his ear. "I hear—with some difficulty, heh—that they're using my ear in witchcraft. Trying to curse me, I suppose. It hasn't worked yet, thank the—"

"Vendel," Kaiser interrupted, raising his nostrils to the mist, "do you smell something?"

"Broken dreams, you mean? It's an old wives' tale, pay it no mind."

"No, I smell fire, I think. And the stink of animals."

Kaiser cast his view back to see Clayborn staring over the rails. An enormous, hungry shadow was in their wake, fisting through the haze like a living mountain.

"Vendel, what is that?!" the Cypolonian blurted.

The wrinkles scrunching around Vendel's eyes turned him from a brave shipmaster into a frightened survivor. "That's impossible . . . this is impossible." Vendel's sheepish words did not suit his lusty voice.

"What is it, man?!"

"I swear, I stayed to the secret routes, Kaiser, I don't know how they found us." Vendel put a hand on Kaiser's shoulder. "It was an honor to be of service, my friend."

The fog burst like strained fabric when an enormous ship reamed through. From the bow there leered the bronze figurehead of a shapely woman. The statue's arms were fastened high, and her smile was indifferent to the panic below.

Like a floating fortress of iron-banded oak, it gained on the little *Farsider*, whose highest mast did not even peek over the pursuer's deck. Above, rows and rows of glowing portholes were wreathed in barbed wire.

Clayborn could sense depravity in the odors that settled over them. Kaiser's sudden appearance pulled him from awe.

"Victon!" he panted, having raced the length of the ship. "What in the Helix do we do?!"

"Listen carefully, Kaiser. These warriors belong to Dragnos Cawn, the Hungerer." Clayborn spoke with a sort of reverence.

"Fine and dandy! Are we killing them or what?!"

"No, do nothing, Kaiser. Nothing, I mean it."

"Clayborn, if they lay hands on our boys—"

"Listen, you damn fool! You don't know anything about Cawn law! Do you value our lives here?!" Clayborn grabbed the Cypolonian's head and impaled him with a gaze.

"Of course."

"Then you will not be a warrior today. You will bow your head and do exactly what they say!" Clayborn took back his hands.

Ropes began tumbling down from the invading vessel.

"You will see things, Kaiser. But we must endure them, are you with me?" Clayborn warned.

The Cypolonian could hear the zip of gloves on rope. Barbarian boots began thumping across the deck like hail. "I'm with you, Vic."

The Federal crewmen knew well not to anger these warriors, especially not in territory they believed to be theirs. Dozens of captors thumped on deck and began a festival of pain. Each Federal had the attention of four or more barbarians. Weapons clearly not fashioned for war were set to purpose.

The barbarians' eyes rolled in their sockets, and they salivated over the crimson puddles of their work. They fought to gash and gouge untouched skin, as if their only happiness sprang from gory wounds.

A squadron rappelled to the quarterdeck for Kaiser and Clayborn. The first barbarian met Kaiser's cheek bone with a carpenter's hammer. He went belly down, smelling blood coming from inside his face. Clayborn fell next to him, yelping as a captor clubbed his legs.

Kaiser's head was booted about so much, he almost didn't notice the spiked chains claiming little strips of his naked torso. But he knew he was being corralled, probably to the main deck. Unable to see well, he listened for Clayborn's croaks. He couldn't help, but he would try to stay close.

Kaiser emerged from a sickening lapse of consciousness. Clayborn, next to him in the line they filled, was being threatened with keelhauling if he didn't get up on his knees. Kaiser put the captain's arm around his neck and took the weight that the fractured thigh bone could not.

The rest of the crew kneeled alongside them. Teeth and blood riddled the deck. One Federal shivered, clutching an eye socket. Annoyed at his whines, a pair of captors pushed him over and stamped his head apart.

A hatch on the side of the barbarian ship groaned open, brown chains lowering the panels to lie upon the *Farsider*'s deck like a bridge. From the roaring belly of the dreadnought there emerged voluminous shapes.

Something like large wolves came first, but these creatures stood on two overdeveloped legs, like raptors, and sported sweeping, hairy tails. Their arms had degenerated to short claws, but still looked as liable to tear a man open as their nail-sized teeth. They were tall and strong, but these longhounds obeyed Dragnos's men completely.

Then came something greater. A hulk of black feathers, ambulated by four birdlike legs. It was long bodied like a lizard, complete with a feathered tail. It's crow-like head jerked about, scrutinizing the Federals with black, uncaring eyes. It easily weighed as much as ten men, and the *Farsider* groaned as the great thing tromped aboard.

The laughter of the captors lowered to the sound of iron-clad boots. Swelling Federal faces looked up to see a barbarian noble with hands on his hips. He had a short, red beard that wreathed his mouth ear to ear, and he wore silver shapes around his neck. Under his sleeveless red coat, his fat body was encased in smooth bronze.

"I am the twenty-fourth son of Dragnos the Hungerer. My name is Sotorius." He yanked a cutlass from his girdle and touched the underside of Kaiser's chin. "Upon whose seas do you sail?"

"Cawn's . . ." The cutlass skated down Kaiser's chest. The Cypolonian hunched over, giving Sotorius an irresistible target. Kaiser took a knee to the forehead, sending him and Clayborn onto their backs.

"Correct! By the gods, there is a brain among you!" Sotorius turned to punch an adjacent Federal in the ear. Kaiser and Clayborn returned to their kneel. "But trespassing is only one of two offenses. Among you, there is a special enemy of my lord and father. Who here is called Kaiser the Cypolonian?"

Clayborn's temple bulged. One Federal huffed.

"I know this is the *Farsider*, and I know it carries our man," Sotorius announced. "It's as simple to kill all of you as one of you."

Still silence.

"Think of your families. You may see them again, if you give over the Cypolonian. Now I will not ask a third time."

It had been a long, bloody road, and it had not been all bad. But as Kaiser pushed up, he could feel a thousand promises breaking over him like twine. Clayborn struggled to keep his balance, panting.

Strength, knowledge, vengeance, and victory, Kaiser wanted all of it. But in the whole mound of regret, the recent memories of Azurae seemed most incomplete.

It would have been easy enough to break Sotorius's neck as he approached, but these barbarians would begin killing his crew. Kaiser met the barbarian's gaze.

"I am Kai—"

"Brave boy, Vendel, but you're not dying for me today," spoke the old shipmaster to Kaiser. Vendel stood and beamed at the Cypolonian with whom he had switched names. "I am Kaiser."

Sotorius walked over to inspect the outspoken man. He turned his head by touching it with the tip of his blade. Vendel was putting on a genuine show; he stood as firm as his bones allowed and wore as much youthful defiance as he could muster.

"Older than I had expected," commented Sotorius. He gestured for this false Kaiser to be separated. The longhounds perked up.

"What slight have I made against your lord, son of Dragnos?" Vendel asked.

"That's between you and father. And you'll not have his ear today."

The red-haired barbarian walked behind Vendel and produced a vial of yellow liquid. He unstopped it and emptied it over Vendel.

There was a tapping sound then as the longhounds salivated heavily. Sotorius stepped back, carefully cleaning the stuff from his fingers on a kerchief.

"Tread always such that you do not offend the Hungerer, for you are never out of his reach. Cross him, and we will find you, and your families. We can enter your homes at any time and crucify you to your beds." Sotorius stepped away, raising a hand.

The longhounds lined up, large furry tails waving like serpents. Sotorius waited for his crew to fall silent.

A few of the Federals began to cry, bobbing in their kneels. For all his injuries, Kaiser monitored Vendel's conduct in stillness.

"I stand by the life I lived." Vendel hooked his thumbs into his belt. "And I stand by everything I've ever done."

Sotorius dropped his hand, and the longhounds piled on Vendel. The screams did not last long, but Kaiser listened to them like the lyrics of a song he must remember.

"You've all been atoned for harboring our enemy. But you've also trespassed on our seas. This, I will not forget," Sotorius said over the noise of carnage.

He snapped and minions came carrying troughs of smoking coals. The handles of tools were neatly arranged so that the heads lay buried within.

"And I will not let you forget," he added.

There was no shortage of volunteers to restrain the Federals. As each Apogee soldier was incapacitated, the glowing brands were lifted from the troughs.

"Tethra protect us!" cried one Federal.

"Be quiet!" Clayborn scolded him.

"The Paragon has no place on our seas," croaked the brand-wielding minion, a man whose oily face drew up like a gargoyle's as he gripped the Federal's hand.

Kaiser would have watched, but his own right hand was grabbed by a bearded minion with eyes as fierce as the brand he wielded.

"Struggle, die," the man promised. Kaiser only huffed through his nostrils. His hand trembled in his captor's thick fingers. The brand came on slow to his splayed palm, and the Cypolonian averted his eyes.

There was a slap of metal, and hell passed into his palm. His muscles quivered as if there were lightning in his blood. His skin molded in the unstoppable heat to a sound like sizzling beef. No scream could escape his bleeding teeth.

The minion ripped the brand away, taking much of Kaiser's palm with it. The Cypolonian yelped and was thrown down. He clutched his hand as boots once again hammered him from all angles.

"Go, and show the Apogee that Dragnos is lord," came the decree from Sotorius. Kaiser's mind faded in and out, but he knew on the other side of this pain life would go on. And for that gift, he had to smile.

***

When Kaiser came around, the barbarians, the beasts, and the ship were gone. Every pulse of his heart made his skull hurt. His blood had dried into a black plaster on his face.

Sliding his arm across the gore sprinkled deck, he looked pensively upon his aching palm.

It was a grilled canvas and horrendously swollen, so Kaiser couldn't decipher what the brand was supposed to depict. Certainly, he would have the rest of his life to find out. His thoughts moved to Clayborn. He found the captain, like the others, was slowly awakening from his wretched spell.

"Clayborn?" Kaiser crawled over. "Clayborn?"

"This is—" The captain suddenly had a fit of coughing. He took a moment to catch his breath. "This is what my land has become. This is what my people's home has become, Kaiser. My father, and his and his and his, they all perished on smoking battlefields because they believed in something like order." With the heel of his injured hand, he worked up to a one-armed lean.

Kaiser crawled closer.

"And for all that, my people today are whipped and murdered in their own seas. Even now . . . even now." He arrested Kaiser with a wounded eye, the other was swollen shut. "I wonder sometimes if I'm simply the latest in a long line of fools." A tear glided down his whiskers.

Kaiser put his hand on Clayborn's neck. And for a while, they and the crew just floated in those quiet, foggy waters.

Chapter 35

Seated high in the back of the auditorium, Algus Equilion digested a meal of toasted pork medallions and a glass of brandy. He strongly believed the four priestesses on stage may be the finest singers in the world. Every concert left him feeling wiser and calmer.

But the Potentate was in brooding company. The two leaders on either side observed him more than the concert. Moreover, no amount of luxury he lavished on them had seemed to stem their frustration at being pulled from their territories.

Things were progressing with more controversy than Equilion expected. He met with his diplomats to Eurivone just days ago. They brought good news of success, but they delivered it with hands branded by Dragnos's mariners.

Many called for retribution. Obviously, starting a war against Dragnos in these days would be catastrophic. But that didn't stop his critics from calling Equilion a coward for his inaction. Clayborn and Kaiser, who had more reason than anyone to be angry, actually sided with his decision. Moved by their selflessness, Equilion bade them stay in the Meridian for two weeks of healing and comfort.

"Baroness, I should think your neighboring magnates will look upon you with new eyes when they hear how much food and money you've donated," he opened to the radiant woman on his left. They had avoided talking business long enough.

"Barbarians. It would be well with me if I did not catch their eyes at all." She sighed. Her name was Corvelia; her beauty was magnified in a purple gown with golden trim, with satin gloves that came up to the shoulder of her arms. Her bangs fell in two black tresses, with the rest of her hair in a braided bun.

She did not care much for the Archaics, but then she had taken little time to understand them. Her donation had been made more out of civic obligation than generosity. Nevertheless, it had earned her the admiration of nobles. Especially since city-states in frontline territories like hers were starving.

"The barbarians are finally taking the Septunites seriously. It is a testament to Archaic ignorance that it occurs so late in the war," came the comment from Prince Norinthe. He wore his dark blonde hair back in a ponytail.

Equilion wondered how the prince's fifth ale would affect him, but drink had no power over Norinthe's cold cunning. "Ignorance" wasn't the word Equilion would have chosen.

"You've heard who I've elected to speak with them?" Equilion asked, feeling a little guilty. Norinthe had been late Nytrinion's associate and so had been stripped of much wartime authority.

"Some foreigner, is what I'm told. The word is no one truly knows where he is from, Potentate," the prince replied.

"He's from the war." Equilion laughed. Though Norinthe's tone had been grating on him most of the night, the Potentate was a man of patience. "His triumphs in the south were limited only by his resources. And now he's brought us two thousand Sojourners. He's a trustworthy man, suited to the task."

"Barbarians will listen to a blood drinker like him," Corvelia admitted, closing her eyes and letting the music fill her mind. "Ah, and with the Sojourners' magic, we'll finally have something substantial to throw at Sinra."

"I still think a Federal should draw out the agreement with the magnates," Norinthe went on. "There's too much power among all those houses. Why not send that fine lad Colygeus? He's a genius and the sort of patriot that makes me look like a turncoat."

"Colygeus would have been my very first choice, but the barbarian houses won't listen to a blue blood," replied Equilion. "To them, the Apogee is cold and greedy. Kaiser is a folk legend among the houses. *All* Archaics are the same in one regard; they respect great warriors. Kaiser masters the kind of passion that is sired in war. And if anything, barbarians are creatures of passion."

"Will Kaiser honor your commands, Potentate?" Corvelia asked.

"Better than he honored Nytrinion I hope," Norinthe put in.

Equilion arrested them with his tenderness. "My friends, this Tireless Butcher that is Kaiser is not one of our Kasurites, but in this late chapter of the war, a tired and frightened soldier can look to him and feel pride."

"But truly, do you think he will be compliant to your orders?" Norinthe asked.

"Out on the field, my good prince, my only order is that he wins."

***

"Eleven years old, I was. People thought he was a beggar. He didn't wander like a beggar, though, his stride had purpose. Loads of it."

It was Tavaryn, Clayborn's increasingly present acquaintance, that carried on. The former had a shakiness to him that he tried to disguise as swiftness as he polished the dome of his green helmet, whose steel was in no need of polish.

"He slept under the same bridge every night. Only I don't think he slept. It was the only bridge leading out of town, see. And he didn't have the look of a man that slept much. But the town guard never questioned him, because he never bothered anyone."

Clayborn, fighting his early morning haze with a mug of java in his fist, sat at the window of the stone hall. He was trying to enjoy the sound of the birds outside, but Tavaryn was a talker. Clayborn learned that only after he accepted the lad's service for the task at hand.

"Until my brother got back from his journey, that is. My mother and I met him at the bridge. Had a right good time catching up. And then we notice the barbarian from under the bridge is starin' at us."

Clayborn peeked under his palm bandages. Time to change them again. Riding and training had made the wound slow to heal. But subtle signs of disinterest didn't stop Tavaryn from yakking.

"My brother was fourteen, a kid, you know? Didn't know any better. The barbarian wrestles him down, all the same. He knew it was big brother that helped take their stupid idol. The barbarian was finding all of them responsible, see. He took his hand off then. With a bronze knife. Right in front of Mum."

"They'll be here soon, Tav," Clayborn urged, rising, finishing his hot beverage and setting his cup on the sill. "Get up top, now."

Tavaryn plopped on his helmet and shouldered a bow.

"Listen, you don't trust these Archaic types, right?" He met the captain on the wicker rug at the door. "That Kaiser, he fancies himself a barbarian, you know? What place has he got breakin' bread on our behalf?"

"If anyone can get Archaics on our side, it's him. With Nytrinion dead, some barbarians have a mind to work with us again. And Kaiser's our best olive branch, anyone will tell you that." Clayborn reached for the door knob, but Tavaryn grabbed his wrist.

"We'll have arrows aplenty up high, Captain," he said with a meaningful twinkle in his strangely long, light brown eyes. "If the barbarians, or anyone, get a little too big for their britches, all you have to do is gesture, all right? That's what Prince Norinthe is paying me for."

"Just get up top before Kaiser sees you, Tav."

Swordsong Coliseum would seat the Archaic dignitaries in a few hours. Every fighting man with a handful of brains spoke of Swordsong with the same extreme formality it imposed on all of its participants. The heights of its circular walls bristled with swords and spears recovered from its gravel yard.

Kaiser was surprised at the Evanthea councilors for their open-mindedness. They allowed him to choose the locale for negotiations and even permitted him to forego wearing any Federal regalia. "Anything to gain their help" was a phrase that leapt from a score different tongues. Somehow, he doubted the same councilors would always be so passive.

There were dots toddling on the horizon, Kaiser saw, and he suddenly felt very fake in the suit of red imported Archaic plate mail that he had never worn in battle.

Tiring of the view, he stepped from the arcade and looked down on the Federals standing around with nothing to do.

"Soldier, bring the wine casks out near the entrance. Have them ready when they arrive," Kaiser called. Clayborn appeared, sensitive to any deviation from the plan.

"Not before negotiations, Kaiser. It's a bad idea," he called up.

"They'll be thirsty when they arrive. They're not generous when they're thirsty," Kaiser insisted. The men waited until Clayborn nodded. They always checked Kaiser's orders with Clayborn first.

When night set in, the coliseum was a furnace of torchlight and pride. The seated barbarians were segregated, with their colorful banners held high.

Tavaryn's arm was getting tired. He kept tensing his bowstring out of habit. There were a hundred different barbarians down there that he felt needed an arrow in the face, but like his soldiers here, he wouldn't act without Clayborn's say-so.

So he waited, with the others, haunting the high places with enough archers to silence the whole coliseum.

One unnerving thing about Archaics, Tavaryn realized, was how their shouts of fury and shouts of joy were indistinguishable. So he wasn't sure if they were celebrating Kaiser's sudden appearance on the sands or calling for his head.

The Cypolonian raised his gaze to the crowd, dominating the coliseum like a sandstorm. He patted the air for silence, unafraid to expose the brand on his palm. Many barbarians boasted the same injury from Cawn's abuse.

"Kaiser! You saved my godson from a dungeon in Sudel!"

"And me, at the Battle of Elwin's Cairn! I'll never forget what you did for us!"

"My brothers fought with you at Castle Valengard!"

"Tethra keep you for killing Nytrinion!"

"I won't mince words with you," Kaiser echoed. His voice was carried loudly on primal magic. "I need your help."

Clayborn stood a little behind him, deflecting glares under his compatriot's words.

Kaiser continued, "I've been fighting a very old war. And for all the good men I've been privileged to fight among, I can't win it. For that I need Grasnian strength. Branic strength. Colovian, Rhinic, Sudelic strength."

The barbarians shifted to hear their territories mentioned.

"I can see Kasurai's greatest fighters mingled under one banner. I want to present Septunoth with all that is worthy of the title Kasurite. Because that is precisely what is being erased, day by day, life by life. Captain?" Kaiser gestured to Clayborn behind him.

"Last year's Federal census shows fully one-third of the Apogee's people have been eradicated since Septunoth's invasion some eighty years ago." He was careful to near the audience tall and straight.

"Whole territories have been flensed to fuel the power of the demonarch Opagiel. You've honored your summons here. Surely you've seen the waves of refugees plodding in, hungry and mutilated, from the wreckage the West has become."

"You all have the duty to defend your provinces. How much nobler than to join the Apogee and defend the entire country?" Kaiser asked.

"The Apogee doesn't want us, they want to take our land once we've died!" someone shouted from the audience.

"They would send us in to endure the worst of it and march to victory over our broken backs," came another.

"Do you really think I'd let that happen?" Kaiser returned. "Our new leader, Algus Equilion, is a man of fine character. In every way Nytrinion's opposite. Neither he nor I would dare abuse your commitment."

"Ah, but all the contracts they write and laws they pass! We'll fight for them, only to have fees and conditions drain our homes behind us! We've seen how it works!" argued another Archaic.

"That was a different Apogee!" Clayborn's tone made him twice as large. "I know, all right? Our deeds have not always been so noble. But that is a bygone time."

"This is about survival now," Kaiser interjected before Clayborn's patriotism got too heated. "An alliance could achieve what disparate territories cannot. Septunoth is united under a demonarch. Could it be they cherish Opagiel more than we cherish our countrymen?"

The bad blood ran deeper than Kaiser had realized, and an hour later not a single barbarian had voiced any interest in fighting for the Apogee. The audience had become a wall. There were always ten or more people ready to dismantle Kaiser's argument.

"The Apogee is organizing a movement to drive back the invasion. Is that really not good enough to merit some forgiveness?" Clayborn's face was a shimmering red oval.

"Forgiveness you have, but trust comes later. And you haven't my trust yet, Federal," returned one Archaic.

"Gentlemen, Federal shields can deflect a lot more hellfire than House pride. It's time to think about what the Apogee can do for you. Because the Septunites will come, and if allowed to write the history books, they will count us all as fools for not fighting together." Kaiser rose a sweating forehead. Debate taxed him the way combat never could.

The barbarians could smell weakness like hounds could blood. And in Kaiser's posture was a secret desperation that tickled their disdain.

"You have my respect, Cypolonian," voiced one elderly official, who stood with the help of his attendant. "But your words are guarded and stem from an Apogee that means to repeat old transgressions. Praise you, but I cannot trust my men to the Federals." And he began shuffling from the aisles on a curved cane.

The audience cropped up, hoisting their banners. Many were reverent enough to keep their seat but looked none the more keen to listen further.

"How do we play this, Clayborn?" Kaiser asked to his right.

The captain was shaking his head, sickened at the indifference that was shuffling the Archaics off.

"Then be mine, and not the Apogee's!" The words issued from Kaiser's throat, white-hot guilt pushing up after. He didn't dare look right, where Clayborn became a silent furnace.

But the Archaics stopped leaving.

"If a contract with the Federals won't do, make a contract with me. We'll march at their side, but you will be my soldiers alone, not theirs." Kaiser felt himself veering far from the graces of Federal royalty, but repentance at this point seemed counterproductive. Especially seeing how the brows raised among the barbarians.

"He's gone wrong." Tavaryn confirmed to himself. In the gloom of the highest arcade, he crouched and nocked an arrow on the same bow he'd familiarized himself with for five years. The gleaming point lined up with Kaiser's chest. But Tavaryn was possessed of a golden confidence and switched to Kaiser's head.

Kaiser was already a man of questionable means, but now he threatened to become a barbarian warlord unchecked by Federal law. And that was a dog Tavaryn thirsted to euthanize.

"Just give me the signal, Captain. I'll nip this thing in the bud."

But down on the sands behind Kaiser, Clayborn was puzzling together just how powerless he was. The Potentate hadn't the legal right to keep

Federal assassins from targeting Kaiser should he threaten Apogee interests, but Clayborn still figured Tavaryn's role in this was one implemented out of formality.

If I hold up two fingers, Kaiser gets an arrow in the forehead. The Cypolonian had molested Clayborn's deepest values to be sure. But ending his life was a decision Clayborn hadn't anticipated having to make.

"With a handful of injured men on the brink of suicide, I was able to protect Sudel. We grew and killed so many Septunites that the bounty on my head could raise a small kingdom," Kaiser went on. "Imagine what we could accomplish when I have fifty thousand of your most decorated killers at my side!"

"Captain, give me the bloody sign." Tavaryn pleaded silently.

Clayborn was a glistening statue. He gripped his left hand behind him, which had two fingers rigidly extended.

"Hark, some promise at last." The old barbarian with the cane had turned from the stairs to give his comment. "My men would fight for Kaiser, absent Federal meddling."

"I'd be proud to contribute to an army so destined for triumph. Given the pay is good," concurred another.

"If Kaiser leads, hell, I'll commit."

"Aye, I want to be a part of this."

Like a mist settling over a fire, the words of the barbarians lessened Clayborn's incentive to spring Tavaryn's aching bow.

"Yer not going to pull one over on me, are ye, lad? Ye swear to not let the Federals make any decisions for ye, regarding us?" One magnate pointed a quill pen as he hovered over the document sprawled across the navel-high lectern before Kaiser.

"On Kronin's grave, I will never break my promise to any of you as long as—"

"All right, all right, I believe ye." And with that, the first commitment was signed.

A line formed, and the officials began signing over warriors. Earlier than he should have, Kaiser threw his arm proudly around a Clayborn as cold and damp as a waterlogged boot.

"If you mean to kill me, do it tomorrow. We're making too much progress today," Kaiser told him. Clayborn wasn't sure how seriously he was supposed to receive that.

"Hold now! Should we throw our scepters at the feet of a foreigner?" shouted one barbarian. His gloom earned him everyone's attention. "Pray remember, he comes at the behest of the Apogee!"

"Who the hell are you?" Kaiser asked as delicately as he could.

"The emissary of House Keltheo, and skeptic of your word. How shall I receive the promises of a man who wears a Federal leash under that pretty armor?" The man's jaw jutted to endure retaliation.

"I abide by certain laws, yes. But perhaps my murder of Nytrinion will show that I am not one to suffer despotism. Least of all to good warriors who would bleed for me." Kaiser had found his stride quickly. If he had fur, it would have bristled.

"And what promises have you been made hence? We should not be so quick to trust a man sleeping among vipers. Vipers whose coils are the self-same laws that will make us slaves in a year, mark me!" the emissary went on.

The claim drummed up some antagonism. The Apogee's sins against the barbarians glowed in everyone's mind now.

"By the Covenant I won't have that," another barbarian swore.

Clayborn could do nothing, unable to choose between reinforcing a potential tyrant or losing barbarian support.

"I will die before I call a Federal my sword-brother!" The emissary was putting filigree on an argument that was being built up by adherents around him.

"Then die you will," Kaiser said, and stepped closer. "But remember this when you're happily burning in Septunite fires: Every barbarian territory west of Tarsuna that has refused Federal aid was conquered in the first third of the war. Now tell me, emissary, how does pride measure against Kasurite brotherhood?"

The emissary delivered his retort on puffing laughter. "You're not even a Kasurite. You come regurgitating the sentiment of blue bloods who think only of profit. Hang the Federals and their hollow extensions of fellowship."

"I've heard enough from House Keltheo."

The words came from a giant in a black cape in the higher seats. He was suddenly an object of intense veneration when he stood to his six and a half feet of tattooed lion muscle. Long twists of black and silver hair tinkled with paraphernalia. His black mustache grew down to his jaw.

"I am Tibernas Krale, Lord of Valathon. It bears mentioning that my kingdom shares a border with Dragnos Cawn's Ulcanea. But I see Septunoth for the danger that it is, in the eyes of refugees whom I now call citizens. Dragnos threatens my people more than anyone's. But honor dictates that I do my bit against Septunoth as well."

"Few of us can afford to be so valiant," the emissary came back.

"Imminent doom has a way of loosening your coin purse. Now the Apogee says they can triumph with our help. I for one believe them." And he went down the landing to sign.

"You repeat past mistakes, comrades! They cannot be trusted—"

The emissary was cut off by Kaiser, who knew in debate as well as in combat when to make the killing blow. "Be silent, emissary. This is a union of warriors and kings, and you are neither. Go home, and tell your lord how you have honored his House." The Cypolonian pointed him to the exit.

It cost Kaiser an ally, but it made the other guests feel like a part of something greater. The emissary grumbled his way to the exit, shoving off his attendants while others put pen to paper, swelling Kaiser's future army.

***

The negotiations eventually concluded, and the Archaics filed out of the coliseum to establish camp with the Federal detachment, an encouraging, if small, display of cultural cohesion.

But Clayborn was beside himself. He stalked Kaiser for nearly an hour, trying to isolate the wolf-eyed warrior. The magnate Tibernas would not release Kaiser's hand, for the two seemed to commiserate on a very deep level.

"It's not going to be easy on my House, but I know it has to be done," Tibernas was saying. A gold tooth glinted under his mustache. "I didn't want any part of this Septunite war unless others were going to commit as well. It would have ruined me. It's about time someone like you got this going, Kaiser."

"Well, it was a Federal decision to coordinate with the Archaics. I'm just glad so many decided to join. Tonight, we changed the course of this conflict."

"I'm proud to be a part of it. I suppose when next I see you, it'll be at the city of Insomnia."

"Yes, Insomnia will be our base of operations. City leaders are preparing for our arrival, and the arrival of Eurivoneans as well."

"I'd better get my boys ready then." Tibernas finally released Kaiser's sweating hand. "Good luck to you, comrade."

"You too, Tibernas." They bowed with palmed fists.

When the magnate retreated out of earshot, Clayborn strode in dark as a storm cloud. The look on his face unnerved even the Cypolonian.

"By all the gods of the Covenant, Kaiser! Do you have any idea what you have done?!" His round face resembled a tomato. "Fight for you?! We were supposed to conscript allies for the Apogee, and you've established a personal army out of these barbarians!"

"We have our Archaics now," Kaiser answered, folding his arms.

"The nobles will name you a radical! What if the Potentate sends for you? Should I hang next to you in the gallows?!"

"If he remembers what I did to the last Potentate, he'll tread softly," Kaiser half jested.

"Look, you have stepped far beyond your bounds! The only reason I am not ordering my men to arrest you now is because . . ." Victon hesitated. ". . . you're my friend."

At that, the wolf-eyed warrior's brow raised a little.

Victon resumed his growling. "So it is in your defense that I protest this!"

"The Apogee wanted barbarians to fight their war, and now they have them," Kaiser reminded him.

"Under your command! Kaiser, how can I be sure you aren't going to use these armies to become another tyrant like Dragnos Cawn?!"

"You know I would never do such a thing, Victon."

"Others will not be so easily convinced! These barbarians are now coming to the front by the multitudes with no legal boundaries!"

"They are Kasurites, Victon. The Apogee forgets that. They will fight the enemy, and they will respect the Federals. I will make certain they do." Kaiser's words hushed a heaving Victon. He glared at Kaiser with wild eyes.

"What if they come after you, Kaiser? Shall I stand with you and die? Or do I aid in your arrest and see a friend executed?"

"Killing me would infuriate the barbarian houses, and the Apogee won't risk losing their support."

"But the Federal soldiers you were promised in the coming months . . . they can still repeal your command of them."

"The Potentate himself admitted no other candidate could be trusted, given the corruption of the last administration, but let them do as they will. I will triumph whether or not they facilitate me."

"But the Apogee is the Federal governing power of Kasurai . . . ," Victon began.

"The Apogee governs only itself. Kasurai is a land of Archaics, Federals, and others. We are *all* charged with the Fatherland's defense. You and I are just doing our parts, Victon," Kaiser said with a note of finality. Victon sighed in resignation and turned slowly, bidding Kaiser to follow him.

With that, the two sauntered off to mingle with the others. Archaics and Federals drank and laughed together outside Swordsong Coliseum. For a night, they were all Kasurites and nothing more.

Chapter 36

Kaiser and Clayborn both hoped they weren't marching to the gallows in returning to Evanthea. Things proceeded gradually, and as the first day of their return drew to a close, both men remained with their necks happily unbroken, though news of the Archaic negotiations permeated like air.

***

Walking along with a sullen Potentate the next day however, it was obvious to Kaiser that the nobility had soured toward him. He couldn't blame them, even as the Potentate's bodyguard from the Gavel Sisterhood gave him looks that could kill a bull. She loomed like an executioner with her war hammer.

  Kaiser and Equilion proceeded along the trimmed concrete high in the arches of the Meridian. The Potentate spoke less and less, and Kaiser wondered if he was being ignored.

  Equilion seemed transfixed by the warriors drilling below. There were forty rows of them, all in armor as white as innocence. Each sported a headdress and a personalized cape that flowed with every sweep of their spear-like cruciphoid weapons.

  These were the Acolytes, the arcane knighthood that Nytrinion had dissolved for their contention. Equilion had liquidated Nytrinion's private horde to finance their revival.

  "Would it be wise to make you Executor, I wonder?" Equilion asked Kaiser. His voice was neutral as warm milk. His gaze never left the carnival of soldiers below.

"It would win you the war." Kaiser's answer was quick. By Equilion's expression, he had hoped for an answer with more humility.

"You have few friends among the aristocracy now. And by association, I have few friends. Some fear you have the makings of a tyrant, Kaiser."

"I have no desire to rule, my lord. Septunoth is the only reason I'm here. When they are gone, my purpose here is done," Kaiser confessed.

Equilion sighed. More truth-lies in the melting pot that every councilor in Evanthea was stewing for him. A pious life out east could never have prepared Equilion for the tangled politics of the day. No one could be trusted.

But honesty had a way of ferreting out lies. Liars thrived in deception, while honesty removed their armor, put them out of their element. It was Equilion's unfailing blade.

"Like many, I fear you will misuse your power, if I give it." He extended only thoughts, no hate. "So I must hear the plain truth. What is the doctrine of Kaiser the Cypolonian?"

The rising sun exaggerated the shadows on their faces.

"My doctrine? I don't have one," Kaiser answered. "Doctrines start wars. I just try to do what's right at the time."

"Your motivation, then. Why do you want to be my Executor?" Equilion pressed.

Kaiser was less reflexive now. "Because once before, it was my charge to thwart an enemy much like Septunoth. My enemy was another human empire in thrall to Opagiel. They came to my land, to Cypolon, and kindled the fire that ended a world. My honor died with my people. I must atone for that failure, Potentate."

Equilion considered his alternatives again. But other candidates had worked too closely with Nytrinion to be trusted. His thoughts always circled back to the slayer before him, a wolf pretending to be a man.

Kaiser noticed that the Potentate's gaze always returned to the heaving throngs below. It did not look like Equilion was going to reply.

"Who is that?" Kaiser gestured to the figure at the head of the Acolytes, a vibrant warrior in fantastic green armor.

"That, my friend, is Colygeus." The Potentate was delighted to speak of him. "At twenty-six, he is the youngest Sage of Arms to ever lead the Acolytes. He is the wisest and most skilled Acolyte warrior in four hundred years. That young man is keeping hope alive."

"I'm surprised you haven't asked him to be Executor," Kaiser said.

"Colygeus has too much to do here right now. The Acolytes must be reassembled, and Colygeus will mastermind it."

Kaiser was humbled. The man below inspired the confidence of Kasurites like the Cypolonian aspired to. Colygeus was a younger man than Kaiser as well. Always, it seemed, there was much for Kaiser to improve upon.

"On my homeland's ashes, I swear I will bring you victory. And when I turn the west into a Septunite graveyard, I will leave Kasurai." Kaiser drew on scarce words, and the Potentate could taste his conviction.

"So, to safeguard my flock, I give wings to the wolf," the Potentate mused. His mind looked made up.

On the verge of power, Kaiser said nothing, for fear that his hunger would show in his teeth.

***

Kaiser walked down a blue carpet in a sea of celebration; seated on either side were princes, dukes, and generals whose expressions he didn't care to analyze. An orchestra spanning the perfumed balconies trumpeted its homage.

Sidna and Caethys smiled from their seats, his guests of honor. They kept him grounded enough to smile in all this Federal mania.

"I should kill him now, before he is appointed," Prince Norinthe whispered to himself in his aisle seat, rather hoping someone would hear.

A white gloved hand slid over his shoulder from behind. Baroness Corvelia leaned up to his ear from her place. She enjoyed teasing the prince.

"I heard that," scolded the baroness flirtatiously. "Careful, that sort of talk could put you in danger."

"I'll truly be in danger when I have to answer to that hellion. He makes himself a barbarian emperor, and we heap more power on him. This is how it starts, my lady."

"You sound like my father. He fretted when power was redistributed among neighboring nobles. Claimed such times were fraught with conspiracy."

"Your father was a wise leader."

"He nearly fell ill when he heard you became prince," she concluded, her hand sliding from his shoulder.

Kaiser knelt before the Potentate, who brandished a sword so reflective that the evening's whole scene was mirrored in it. It was the Sword of the People, which bestowed power on Federal men and women for centuries.

But before it would do so again, peons assembled armor over Kaiser's shoulders and chest. The Defender's Mantle, which had belonged to forty men before him, was Kaiser's now. Its new ownership was sealed by two touches of the Potentate's blade.

The Cypolonian rose and turned to face an ovation of clapping, music, and cheers.

"He's coming to help us, Prince Norinthe. You'll be reasonable with him, won't you?" asked the baroness who stood clapping softly.

"I will watch him, and I will act accordingly. That is all," the prince answered, still seated.

***

The lodges of Evanthea brimmed with conscripts. Kaiser was pleased to see over seven thousand fresh soldiers summoned for service, but they looked terribly young. Many were sixteen or less. The war had chewed up so many older soldiers that the Apogee was moved to harvest its unripened citizens.

Teenagers with smooth faces and large eyes wandered the streets carrying uniforms and papers. Armories took these recruits in at one end and released armored soldiers out the other.

New forges had recently sprung up to meet the sudden demand for combat swords, helmets, and chest plates. The music of industry rang out night and day.

The Gavel Sisterhood had volunteered themselves as unpaid laborers. They became fletchers, stable hands, or guards, whatever the city needed. And somehow, in all the madness, Evanthea conceived a new army.

"You achieved gold status at the academy?" Kaiser asked, reviewing a document. The husky young soldier before him was kneeling unnecessarily. "Why weren't you assigned to be squad leader?"

"An offense made me ineligible, Executor," the man said in a voice too small for his size. "I . . . struck a superior officer."

"Oh. Will you ever do it again?"

"No, of course not, sir."

"All right, fine. You're pardoned." Kaiser produced his stamp and pressed it over the refusal inked on the lad's document. "Take this to your captain. You're squad leader now, son. Make me proud."

"Yes, sir, I will." The young man took the document and jetted off, not recognizing a man, none other than the Potentate, who approached down the street. His Gavel bodyguard followed.

"Everything in order, Executor?" Equilion said.

Kaiser was a little hesitant, not expecting to see the Potentate again before the march. "Yes, we're actually ahead of schedule." Kaiser smiled. "Isn't it a bit dangerous for you to be out here, my lord?"

"Celga, am I in danger?" Equilion asked his bodyguard.

"None, my lord," she insisted with a thump of her war hammer. Equilion grinned pleasantly back at Kaiser.

"Well, now you have a fine army of Federals to take to the front, with barbarians soon to follow. Are you daunted by the Septunites' millions?" Equilion asked him.

"My strategy of aggressive defense is calibrated against those odds. I will make them suffer for every step they take, forward or back, because we will make meat grinders out of our cities and forests."

"I'm glad that nothing is more important to you," Equilion said. He already knew that to Kaiser, this war was a personal test of will. Every casualty was an insult to be avenged. Equilion turned about and walked away before turning once and adding, "Upon your return, I should like to hear more about your Cypolon, whence such ambitious men come."

***

"You've got nothing to worry about, kiddos. Granny Crandle's cooking made me the woman I am today," Sidna said as she lowered herself to the level of Shaden and Keb. They looked back at the crackling smile and black eyes of the old woman that had housed Sidna when she was a cadet.

"You'll be careful, right?" Shaden asked. "Keep close to your friend Caethys. He's good at protecting you."

"Sidna's stronger," Keb voiced. He had not quite grasped that Sidna was leaving for a long time, but he had been rather quiet, sensing that Shaden was upset.

"You're gonna help out Crandle with the chores, aren't you?" Sidna asked. Keb nodded, but Shaden had a rim of water beneath her eyes.

"We'll be really, really good." When Shaden felt the tear glide down her cheek she started to sob. "We'll be so good, until you come back . . ."

Sidna tucked in her lips and scooped the two up in a hug, trying to keep herself from bawling. Their hands gripped the metal trappings of her armor.

"We'll be so good, Sidna! You'll be amazed about it!" Shaden wailed, voice breaking. Keb began pouting into the redhead's arm.

"I can't wait to see you again, kids. It's going to be wonderful. You just wait." Sidna looked up; she had left little droplets on Shaden's shoulder. "Keep 'em busy, okay, Granny?" Holding a kerchief to her face, Crandle nodded her promise.

***

When the day came to march, the gates of Evanthea opened and out rolled a tongue of steel. Like ants swarming from their hill, Federal soldiers followed a western warpath. The city was hushed with the evacuation of the soldiers. At the vanguard of the glorious host was Kaiser on a horse named Justice.

Part II

Chapter 37

It was some late-night hour, and one of the season's last downpours was washing through the rocky plains. Lightning danced on the black mountains in the distance, but there was no wind. The rain felt heavy and lazy.

    Azurae wondered if she had erred somewhere along the way. She knew Kasurai was enormous, but the muddy flats she had been treading for over four hours were beginning to seem endless.

    She sported a hooded cloak like the rest of the troops behind her. They walked in pools of yellow light from their swinging lanterns, and they all carried weapons on their packs. Azurae had told them they would march until they found the next Federal settlement. She had expected it hours ago, but they did not complain as the soaking hours flowed by.

    Senlu, ever the energetic pet, was making huge circles around them. Azurae figured the new smells were overwhelming him, so she let him explore. His playful gallop in the darkness gave them an excuse to laugh now and then.

    Azurae took a moment to look back into Meng's eyes. She did not know him well, but he was easy to speak to.

    "I thought it rained a lot back home," he said.

    Azurae nodded. Looking forward again, she caught a whiff of something in the air.

    "I smell fire. We may be in luck." She called Senlu to heel. He had a rabbit in his jaws. She let him gnaw the dead thing while she secured a leash.

Azurae led her band through the storm toward the scent. It became more distinct, carrying notes of manure and grain, as a wooden high wall appeared. Azurae told her followers to stand back while she approached the barricade with Senlu. The guards looked down on her from above.

"Oi. What's your business at this hour?"

"We are Sojourners from Eurivone!" she yelled through the pitter-patter of water. She let them see the spear fixed on her back. She did not want to hide anything. "We were told we would be provided quarter in Federal territory."

The guards looked at each other and called a third by name. The third came up and looked down on the dripping Eurivonean.

He pointed to her. "Sojourner?"

"All of us are." Azurae gestured to her people waiting in the darkness. The third guard nodded lazily and walked back. The other two guards waved for men below, and the gate began creaking.

The third guard had come down to meet Azurae and her people as they passed inside. He took off his helm to feel the rain on his scalp. He didn't look especially cheerful, but it was not a cheerful hour.

"Thank you." Azurae's gratitude was met with a nod. She fought to kept Senlu from straying, but he clearly alarmed the guard all the same.

"What the hell is this thing? Does it bite?" he asked of her insectoid panther.

"Yes, but not Kasurites. I'll keep him in check," she assured him. The guard didn't look pleased, but he had his orders.

"Every village in the region's got orders to house you, if you showed up," he informed her. "I never thought you'd end up in crummy little Dunfirth."

"That's probably my fault. Maybe I could purchase a better map from someone?"

"Yeah, but in the morning, love." Just now, Azurae was realizing how tired the man sounded. "I'm afraid I can't offer you much for shelter. Best I could probably do is the storehouse. Not much food left in it, so I suppose you could bed down there."

"That's perfectly fine." She swallowed. "Would there possibly be a place for us to get something to eat?"

"Oh. Olli feeds the guards through the night. He could probably be convinced to put something extra on."

"Excellent. We'll be no trouble, and we'll be gone early tomorrow," she promised.

He nodded again and walked off with another yawn.

The Eurivoneans faced each other, sitting on benches on either side of a hall in the eatery. They left the better-lit area to the guards, whom they outnumbered. Many of the tired warriors were still spooning from their bowls when Azurae dabbed her face and stood up among them. Senlu snuffled at her feet.

"I don't want to impose on these people, so we're leaving at daybreak," she said. "We're going to have to veer a little east to avoid one of King Dragnos's roaming armies. That's going to make our journey to the front a little longer."

In the brick chamber nearby, the half dozen guards were staring. Few had ever seen skin any darker than buttermilk, and a hundred other ethnic features captivated them as they nursed their meals by lamplight.

"We are blazing the trail for the Sojourners yet to come, so I want to get a decent map and get some messages sent early. Let's get some rest." She was speaking Civilic, feeling that in a Kasurite town that they would appreciate it.

"If it doesn't counter your aims, teacher . . . ," one of her larger, stronger warriors piped up from his third bowl, "Kasurai is known for its fantastic beer. Such a cold night, we may sleep better with a little tingle in our bellies." He made a motion like knocking back a drink.

"You're shameless, Neb'Rul," Meng voiced. "But now that you mention it, I feel rather restless too." A few others glanced up at Azurae with expectant grins. She snickered; they were like children sometimes.

"You've all been very faithful. All right, sit tight." She turned from their glow to attend the counter top in the chamber where the guards were eating. Near her at the bar was a drunken hump of a man whose head hovered over the counter.

Azurae was mesmerized by the colorful liquor bottles such that she hardly noticed the barkeep's bewildered look. Like the guards, he'd never seen any sort of Eurivonean, and her exotic armor dashed his notions of proper dress.

"You must be Olli," she said. "It's a pleasure. Could you recommend something for thirsty outlanders?"

"Eh, Bison Heart seems to do well with warrior types." He removed a white porcelain jug from a corner shelf, along with a tall, skinny clear bottle with golden alcohol. "Or you might try some Colovian Winterbrew. Not cheap, but it tastes like Tethra's love."

Azurae's eyes glittered at the variety of foreign beverages and purchased all she could carry in one arm. When she turned back, someone had grabbed her hair to stay her.

"Whassa crew o' outsider devils . . . gotta do in *my* grandfather's favorite pub?!" slurred the drunk seated at the bar. He was round and tough looking with a gleaming bald spot. His eyes struggled to fix on one of Azurae's images.

"Food and drink, like you. But a sight less drink, I suspect," Azurae said, calmly pulling her black ponytail out of the man's chubby fingers.

"Where was *you*, when grandfather . . . he captured a whole platoon o' Septunites!"

"I'm not sure I understand your point."

"Garren, I already told you not to bother patrons," Olli warned him.

"Patrons?! I'm a patron, 'n' I know who'sa mangy . . ." Garren gripped a bottle from behind the counter and swung it at Azurae's head. He followed through, but was befuddled to find his hand suddenly empty.

"For me, Garren?" Azurae asked, holding the purloined bottle. She inspected the markings. "Fourteen years old? You're sweet." She planted a kiss on his bald spot as he fought to regain balance. She returned to her Sojourners, who laughed every bit as hard as the guards at the table.

***

The prospect of midnight festivals and beautiful young men and women inspired so much gabbing among the troops that Kaiser had to swat a few to keep pace. But spirits were high even after a hard day's march, so he counted himself lucky that these soldiers were hardier than their smooth faces suggested.

Federals truly polarized as fighters, Kaiser remembered. Most were deadly warrior-philosophers, as their culture insisted, but there was a frailty among many that one would never find among the Archaics. And the weakness of the frail ones resonated disastrously in battles past. He had seen it himself too many times.

His men's admiration came easily and quickly. No doubt the tales of Kaiser's exploits in Sudel had gilded his image. So he started to admire them back, even love them, in the few short weeks of their travels. It was a tendency he had tried unsuccessfully to excise in the past. It made decisions more difficult.

But balancing his relationship with the soldiers became a trivial matter that day when Insomnia came into view.

Across the sparse grasslands, autumn had painted an orchard of witchnose trees all sorts of delicious reds and yellows, but heaps of rags sat at their bases. Bodies, many of them, lay among overturned baskets of the curved fruits.

Farther in, a lust for complexity made the city a triumph of art. Builders had stacked classical features high enough to make strange silhouettes in the sky. It was a city proud of its own mystifying excess.

Black and yellow banners proclaimed the city was Kasurite no longer. Septunites had seized the navel of Kasurai with hellfire and catapults. The evidence was in the perforated buildings and the ash-streaked walls. And there was that stink in the air, the kind that issued from burned flesh.

The map in Kaiser's mind began to darken as he noted more fallen territory. Outrage piped up among the men.

"So much for easing the men into the campaign," Kaiser growled heavily. "Our troops get their first taste of blood tonight."

"Their own, you mean?" Clayborn voiced. "These young ones don't have the experience for a siege, Kaiser, they'll be butchered."

"There must be a master hellbringer leading them." Kaiser's eyes darted from rampart to rampart, absorbing stories from the damage. The late afternoon sun glazed the stone monuments orange and made him feel like he was losing time. "They would have just leveled the city if there wasn't a hellbringer to profit from the sacrifices. Walled cities are like dinner plates to those three-eyed sadists."

"All the more reason *not* to move in. These young ones didn't march from the east to be burned alive in their first engagement," Clayborn argued.

"No, they came to kill Septunites, and they can't do it from here. I've heard this sort of argument a thousand times, Clayborn. Now, Caethys . . ."

The familiar corporal appeared from the vanguard. Caethys had shown a quiet form of loyalty since Kaiser's return, wondering how the incident on the high seas had affected the Cypolonian.

"Remind me how many light mages we have."

"Only twelve light mages, Executor," Caethys recited. "But many of the troops, including myself, can use simple holy spells in our martial arts."

"That's not even close to enough for a task like this," Kaiser scoffed. Caethys shrank a bit at the comment. The legion had been assembled in a terrible hurry, and divine magic users were in short supply.

The Cypolonian let the course pan out in his head; the untested recruits mobbing thickly at the gates. Arrows, stones, and hot oil would punish them as they battered at the walls with rams that they would make from the orchard trees.

But the hellbringer would be the real problem, as his magic would feed on the terror in their weak hearts. As troops fell, panic would rise and the magic would burn all the fiercer. Even fighters like Caethys wouldn't be able to endure it. An image of Caethys's face came to mind, bloodless, still and dead, with those soft eyes frozen over.

"You're right, Clayborn. We don't have the magic for this," Kaiser muttered, rising from his daydream. The captain looked notably relieved, but Caethys seemed to adopt the anxiety.

"Executor, you won't leave Insomnia to be devoured." Caethys's words were between a statement and a question.

"Every victory is made up of a thousand *little* victories, Corporal." Kaiser swung off his horse and kicked out his stiff legs.

"So how do we earn little victories from a fortified city?" questioned Clayborn.

Kaiser wished he knew. Insomnia sat on the lip of a canyon, so it was only approachable on three sides. Or was it? The Executor's eyes wandered to a cavernous opening that had been gouged out of the cliff face beneath the city.

"Is Insomnia a mining city?" Kaiser asked.

"That's how it got its name," Clayborn informed him. "Diggers would harvest the earth's riches late into the night. Their clamor kept the city awake until the wee hours, and so they learned to live on little sleep at all."

"It's layout is well known to me, Executor," Caethys put in. "I've spent many a holiday in those streets."

"Then we have the makings of a ploy after all. Tonight, we'll be Insomniacs ourselves."

***

A series of fireside wrestling matches proved to be enormous fun for the recruits. A young female veteran named Sidna was making off with everyone's pride in dusty bouts of grappling.

"Not today, chicken legs!" came her decree as she rolled on top of her opponent, a milky-faced lad who was hoping to earn a little easy respect. He mistakenly gave her his back, and she seized his arm, quickly seating her full weight upon his shoulder blades. He flattened and his arm was cranked taut.

He struggled a moment and managed to turn onto his back and face her again. He threw a hook that landed across Sidna's mouth. She fell back, and he took a side mount position, trying to wrangle her limbs.

"Oh, so we *are* punching, eh?" she said, a little redness thickening between her teeth. She pulled one of his hands away and cuffed him on the temple as many times as she could. When he turned his head away, she pushed him off and bashed away at his frantically waving face.

"S . . . stop!" the bruised boy uttered. The blows to the face were panicking him. Sidna slid off and took to her feet. He pushed back some distance and rose again himself. His adolescent cheek bones were taking on bluish colors as he glared at the redhead.

"Don't give up so easily!" she scolded him. "You escaped every hold I used, and I was getting tired. If you kept up the grapple, I couldn't have lasted. Don't let a little pain scare you from your potential."

"I feel like a fool." He put his hands on his hips, trying to make his voice sound as deep as possible as he turned away.

"Give it time, handsome," Sidna swatted him on the rear. He wheeled but kept backing, the blue of his cheeks drowning in pink. He was swallowed in a laughing crowd of his onlookers.

Sidna was about to call out another opponent when she glanced out over the moonlit fields. Black figures were prowling the bluish flats. She suspected an attack at first, but the figures appeared to be moving away from the camp.

Jogging through a host of soldiers reclining, visiting, eating, and sparring, she made for the outskirts of camp where guards halted her with their palms.

"This is as far as you go, comrade. Camp bounds," one informed her.

"Do you see those people sneaking off out there? Who are they?" she asked, pointing.

"We know, just back away and don't go spreading this around, understand?"

At these words, Sidna's obedience kicked in and she stepped back, a quizzical expression painted across her pale, one-eyed face.

***

It was like the nightmare Kaiser often had. But tonight, with his belly against the stone, the nothingness beneath his feet was real.

Ten others followed him on a sideways climb across the canyon wall to the opening beneath the city. They inched along, wearing their swords on their backs, feeling for handholds in the darkness.

When the black clouds thinned out, the moon's icy light caressed the cliffs. Kaiser clicked twice at his men. Each of them held still as possible as they clung to the rocks.

The walls of Insomnia above padded softly with enemy reprobates that were hardly interested in the canyon walls below. Kaiser's troops, all dressed in black, resembled the hanging shadows that melted beneath the moon's advances.

At last, clouds jacketed the moon and darkness returned. Kaiser clicked for his men to resume. It was a strenuous effort, so it was best to keep moving.

A faint crackle and a waving of black shapes earned Kaiser's attention. One man's hold had given out. He fell, eyes wide and white. A scream would have gotten them all killed, but Kaiser watched with morbid pride as the man cupped his mouth with both hands. Sailing down into the valleys below, the man kept his demise a secret.

Caethys, second in line, touched his forehead to the stone and looked again for Kaiser's lead. He did not let the loss slow them, and they followed a meandering climb until finally they reached the ledge of the mine tunnel.

Their strength was pushed to its limits, but finding that ledge spilled adrenaline into their blood. One by one, Kaiser and Caethys pulled the men onto the sweet, horizontal surface.

Even Kaiser, with his developed night vision, decided to scout more with his hearing and feet than with his eyes. He was trailed by his nine surviving men into the belly of a lightless stone corridor. They stalked deeper into the earth, sealing away all talk during a trek that felt ominously infinite. It was beginning to seem like they weren't moving at all, swallowed in blindness the entire way.

"Sir . . . ," one man tried, but Kaiser shushed him. It felt like a test of sorts, dangling from the cliffs, then being thrust into this claustrophobic blackness. If the Executor shared the anxiety, the shadows hid it well.

At last, Kaiser stopped. It smelled like moldy masonry and stagnant water when they found lamplight streaming down through a boarded tunnel above. They all took a knee under the skinny sheets of light that barred their sweaty faces.

"All right, we're somewhere under the south side of the city. Caethys, what can you tell us about the layout?" Kaiser prodded.

"The southern side is a dozen or so rows of poor homes and shops. There's a prison and a few pleasure palaces closer to the center of the city. The streets are poorly lit, with lots of alleys and bridges and dark places."

"That's perfect. It will be hard for them to search all those little homes for us."

***

A new day, and Clayborn was seated with his horse's foot in his lap. He was picking its shod hooves clean, and the animal whined and pulled.

Clayborn's grip was tight. "If you wouldn't step in your own business, I wouldn't have to be so thorough about this."

Sidna padded up to him, breakfast tea sloshing in her hand. "Smoke from inside the city, Captain!"

Clayborn gave his horse back her foot and stood tall, craning his neck to get a better glimpse.

"Yes, I've been expecting that. Don't concern yourself with it," Clayborn concluded, relief coming over his face. Seating himself back onto the stool and slapping his horse's other leg. It reluctantly surrendered its foot.

"That's one big fire, though. Don't they usually sacrifice Kasurites in smaller rituals? It looks and smells as if they're burning hundreds at once," Sidna pressed, her face paling a bit at the thought.

"Those aren't Kasurites burning . . ."

"Gods on high, Kaiser entered the city, didn't he?"

Clayborn sighed. "I'm not surprised you figured it out." He went on, pointing the soiled pick at the redhead. "Don't think I had a hand in this, I fought the idea tooth and nail. And don't go blabbing this to the men. They don't need to know their commanding officer and ten others are in the lion's den."

"What's Kaiser thinking?! He's going to get chained to a death altar for sure!" Sidna pointed out. Suddenly, Clayborn's placid demeanor struck her. "How can you be so calm about this? We're going to lose our Executor!"

"There's a lot you don't know about Kaiser, Sidna. When he fought the Septunites in the south, people assume he rushed in with swords swinging, a thousand comrades at his side. But that was the exception to the rule."

"When Caethys and I went south to retrieve him, Kaiser had dozens of warriors with him. And before that, thousands."

"Yes, but he didn't start out that way, Sidna. It began with he and Kronin entering the occupied city of Mirage at midnight. By morning, the entire Septunite garrison had been murdered. They could never find him or Kronin. It was there he became the Tireless Butcher. It was the first event of many."

"But Insomnia's got to be twenty times the size of Mirage."

"Those were my exact words to him last night." Clayborn let down his horse's foot and wiped the pick in the dirt next to him. "But he insisted that the Septunites must be made afraid before our troops attack."

"He's hoping to demoralize them."

"Seems that way. Ideally, they'll withdraw, and our soldiers can get their first taste of battle on fleeing Septunites." Then Clayborn's brow furrowed. "Now I've told you enough. Keep your mates lively and your mouth shut, got it?"

Sidna realized she had not seen Caethys all morning.

"So Kaiser grabbed Caethys and a handful of men to take on thousands of enemies. Why wasn't . . . ," she stammered, "why wasn't I chosen to go, sir?"

"This is a delicate quest they're on, Sidna. They *must* succeed. Only the most discreet, elusive, and resilient of them were chosen to go along. Your profile marks you as a fine soldier, but a poor assassin."

She broke off her gaze.

"I meant what I said about keeping quiet. If you let this slip, you'll be locked up," Clayborn said, and left her.

Caethys is out there, she thought. While Kaiser and his troops were likely the best protection any ten men could offer, it didn't change the fact that the corporal was in a sea of enemies. *If I was stronger, I could have come along. I could have helped protect him . . .*

Chapter 38

A thicket of human ash paved the converted barracks. Skulls hissed and spat under a gray haze.

Before it had burned, and before the Septunites had annexed it, it had been a music hall. Its cylindrical stories made it suited for housing soldiers. But arson had made it a tomb in one night.

Death had always been beautiful to Sanakal. To any hellbringer, humanity was a curse, and death, even their own, was the solution.

But today, the smell of seared humans did not ferry him to the usual heights of pleasure. Indeed, his hatred was so intense that his men could not stand within five paces of him. Boils and bruises mottled their skin otherwise.

Perhaps it was some trick of the heat, but the air around him seemed to wrinkle, as if reality cramped up. Spirits mewled like deformed kittens, wriggling almost invisibly from the folds of his aura.

"The count?" he asked.

"Including the sentries, and the ones who jumped from the windows, two hundred and sixty-two," replied a peon, bald and featureless as others of his low caste.

"My, my, my . . . ," Sanakal started, his cowl fluttering. "I cannot wait to meet this rascal." His men avoided his eye, for he displayed only one; a green-veined orb with a yellow iris in the center of his forehead. When this oculus had sprouted in his forehead, the second sight it offered engrossed him so that he destroyed his human eyes and sealed them behind leather straps.

His scalp was checkered with craethune studs, bolted into his skull to fertilize the dark emotions that defined the magic of the Helix. It made his white dome sore and red, but if his smiling countenance was any indication, he didn't mind.

Whether he was pleasantly amused or crucifying someone, Sanakal always wore the same thin, black-lipped smile. Rumor had it that he slept that way too, that the infection from his scalp froze his face muscles into that clownish grin. Even so, his displeasure was unquestionable at present.

But murder always left echoes in the form of spirits. For Sanakal, seeing such things was second nature. With his oculus, he looked far off the spectrum of human sight. He watched as the pain, fear, hate, and sorrow of the previous night took shape before him.

Two figures of yellowish ether appeared in his vision. These were effigies of his guards. They hesitated, molting wisps of yellow fear. A third figure, shot through with all the green shades of hatred, appeared and dropped a fatal wound onto the back of one yellow figure's head. The murderous phantom faded out and reappeared to swing its weapon into a second victim's ribcage before disappearing again.

The green specter appeared so close the third time that it gave Sanakal a start. It sheared both arms from its next victim, which fell neatly onto one of the real flesh and blood corpses at his feet.

"Our enemy is a disciplined killer. He pockets away his hatred until it is time to strike, so I cannot sense from which direction he came," Sanakal noted. He watched as other green attackers, notably duller in color than their leader, emerged to help.

"How were so many of our men in the barracks caught unaware?" asked one of Sanakal's captains. The hellbringer looked to where the upper stories of the structure had loomed before the collapse. Something he saw made him click the jewelry at his fingers.

"They barricaded the doors, blocked all entry and exit"—Sanakal watched the colorful past play out—"and pitched burning oil through the windows." The deviousness of the enemy made him giddy.

"What shall we do, my lord?" the captain urged as Sanakal's scanned the invisible sights.

"There are not many. A small nest of rats in our new home." His lips writhed strangely.

"If they are skilled saboteurs, it would be best to hunt them with skilled assassins," the captain put in, trying to be helpful.

Sanakal turned his head as his mind was made up. His two-pronged pointy beard shivering. "An appropriate task for the Disciple, then. Rouse him from his meditations and mingle him with the patrol."

"At once." The captain bowed, turned away, and crunched through the ashes. The rest of the underlings eyed their peer, curious to their part.

"The soldiers we lost here, I'm just not ready to retire them." Sanakal steepled his jeweled fingers. The men looked over the plot of soot. "Gather their remains, bring them to my gallery. The poor things, they still want to serve. And serve they shall."

***

Days later, ash and soot that still resembled the Kasurites it used to be hissed with sparking smoke. A shirtless battlemage stood there, naked feet imperviously buried in the crackling embers. His work had swirled the air with a brackish haze that stung the throat.

The two moons were a guilty shade of yellow that night, and the gravestones sweated as dew glittered down their faces. When the battlemage looked up from his prayers, his searing red eyes matched the moons in midnight splendor. His arms were black to the elbows. With one of those soiled hands, he pointed into the crowd.

"Him."

More frightened than the appointed victim was his son, who squeezed him. The man hugged his son back, knowing that the reprobates lording over the captives would fall upon them.

"No! Damn you to hell, damn you to hell, you can't take my father! I won't let you!" The boy was fourteen, but his time as a blacksmith's apprentice had put tenacity in those skinny arms that proved challenging enough for two reprobates.

The father clutched him tight, tucking the boy's head under his whiskered chin. When a sword pommel slammed into his lower ribs, he knelt, but did not let go.

The boy growled as they pulled at his legs. He took a stomp to his shoulder and yelped. He didn't care, he decided to never let go.

But his father was stronger. Unwilling to see his son take any more injury, he ripped loose and turned away, to the circle of ash where a dozen others had died.

"Come." The battlemage beckoned.

"Father, wait! Stay with me! It doesn't hurt! Stay with me! Please, gods, help me! Help me!" The boy's voice broke calling for any power in the universe to intervene. The reprobates held him while six other captives shuddered. They had suffered far too many beatings to offer any courage.

The father was a simple man in most every way: modest height, strong, yet not heroically so. His face was the type one wouldn't look at twice, and his hair was sparse. But he decided to carry himself like a giant.

The father stepped up to the ash mound. The battlemage gripped his throat and giggled through his teeth as deadly magic crackled between them. When it was enough, he threw the man aside.

The father coughed, and sparks flew from his mouth. Pain was building in his fingers, his toes, behind his eyes, and almost everywhere. With crumbling faculties, he shoved aside a reprobate that tried to subdue him. He ran back to the crowd, smoke slipping from his arms. His son wriggled free in time to collide with him, and both were on their knees again.

"Father! Why did you go!?" His father touched his cheek. The hand was hot as lamp glass.

"Briston, look me in the eyes, son," he said, speaking through the pain. Briston managed to stare into his father's gray-green eyes and took a moment to appreciate that face like no one ever did.

The bridge of his nose had a bulge on one side where he had been kicked by a calf long ago. His cheeks, always oily, sported hundreds of wide pores between his sandy whiskers. His ears were always the first thing to sunburn and resembled flaps of leather. Soot and dust and sand had collected in the folds around his eyes, and though he washed his face twice a day, it was always there.

No, his father was not the majestic, handsome sort that people waxed on about, but he was his father, and every little sin and kindness and flaw made him so important in this hysterical moment.

"Look me in the eyes," he said again. "Are there tears?"

Briston scrutinized that forty-year-old face again and found a solidness. His father let an exhale, and the heat from his body became as fierce as the heat from a forge.

"I've been a smith twenty years," his father stated. "I made more beautiful pieces than I could ever count. But you, Briston, you were my greatest."

Briston closed his eyes to the heat. He could hear the crackle of flames making their claim. The heat swelled, but he would not let his father's hand fall from his cheek. Moaning like an ailing dog, he let the flames from the hand play up the side of his head. He bathed in the smell of char.

At last, the fingers he held dissolved in a gray spill. He sifted through the popping embers with his fingers. He didn't feel anything.

Briston didn't care to be awake, or alive. So he hardly noticed his head was suddenly over the battlemage's knee.

"My Queen, your feast continues." The battlemage's words slurred as saliva gathered. He ran his black fingers across the hand shape Briston's father had burned on his cheek. It was odd for Septunites to speak Civilic, but they would if it served to torment their victims.

Just as the energy congealed the battlemage's hand, the gravestone shadows ripped loose and pounced. The captives covered their heads. Figures dressed in black raged against the Septunite guards. Steel could be heard, but not seen, and spurting wounds opened across the reprobates' bodies as if by magic.

When the last reprobate fell, the figures stood tall over their kills. The battlemage pulled a curved dagger from his boot and pointed it into Briston's throat, hard enough to free a drop of blood.

Training his eyes, the battlemage found enemies in stealth leathers with gloves and boots tailored for quiet deeds. Warpainted faces focused on the two in the ashen circle.

The battlemage said nothing, he only kept his knife ready to end another life. One of the figures entered the moonlight: a lean, powerful specimen, a head ringed with a bandanna black as his stubble. He pointed to the hostage with a sword colored by violence.

"Give him to us," Kaiser demanded.

"I cannot. He belongs to Opagiel," came the sterile reply. The battlemage knew he was at a disadvantage. This could be his last sacrifice, and he must deliver it.

"I'm not one for bargaining, Septunite. But this one time, if you let that boy go, I will let you go." Kaiser's eyes brightened to gold.

What the battlemage didn't see was that Caethys was among them, and behind his back was his dimly glowing oathkey. His gentle magic was being transmitted to Briston . . .

"You think I believe that?" The Septunite gave a daring smile. "You have nothing to gain by leaving me unharmed."

"I never said I'd leave you unharmed," Kaiser reminded him.

"Tempting." The battlemage's sarcasm denoted he was not afraid to die. "But this boy and I are both finished."

A sudden elbow to the nose interrupted his gloating.

Briston didn't know how he had suddenly recovered his defiance and managed to throw himself from the battlemage's lap.

As if his leash had broken, Kaiser threw himself in. An upward strike sent the battlemage's hand into the air. The Septunite's scream was cut short when Kaiser's gloved hand clamped over his throat. Kaiser pushed him over, strangling the prone victim in a cloud of white ash.

Briston watched with no little satisfaction as the killer of his father bled and strangled in the remains of his own victims.

Kaiser loved how his fingers sunk into that clammy neck. The battlemage's tongue banged around in his mouth. Defiance, panic, then nothingness all passed through the fading red eyes.

"That was good work, Caethys. You're getting very good at throwing your holy magic." Kaiser released the corpse. Briston's seared face was fixed on his. The Cypolonian brushed some ash from the boy's arm.

"The boy's courage is what saved him. I just stoked it a bit," Caethys admitted, replacing the oathkey around his neck.

There were stone steps behind them that would be their exit. Several of the men sensed the finality of things and headed that way. They would secure the path for everyone, including the handful of freed captives who silently accepted the rescue.

"I'm sorry, friend. We could have saved more if the patrols hadn't changed," Kaiser groaned to Briston, who was more accustomed to being called "boy" than "friend." Caethys was tying a scarf over his nose and mouth to reduce his breath vapor.

"Are you Federals?" Briston asked, his weariness returning.

"That's right. And there's more of us to come," Caethys whispered, tending hope wherever he found it.

A round of yelps sounded from the top of the staircase. The shadows concealed whatever had happened. All anyone could see was blood snaking down the steps. Keeping pace with the slow scarlet trickle was a pair of fine black boots.

It was some master assassin, sinister and majestic as a black eagle. A halo of facial hair circled his full lips, which were purple like the bags under his eyes. He had dreadlocks that fanned over a long dark coat, and his eyes were sharp red as the blood melting from his weapon; a butcher's cleaver.

In his other hand, he wore a set of treacherous claws engineered from a thousand tiny interlocking pieces.

This killer just toppled expert soldiers like children. Now, only Caethys and three other soldiers remained to defend the captives.

Kaiser pored over the killer's features, letting them fish at his memory. His innards clenched, imploring him to flee from the presence that was both familiar and surreal.

Caethys didn't like how Kaiser was becoming a sweaty mannequin.

"Just give me the word, Kaiser. I will help you fight." Caethys glowed with courage whereas his fellow soldiers offered little more bravery than the mewling captives. "You need my life, Kaiser? It's yours, just tell me what to do!"

"Caethys, you know the plan, don't you? The hours, the rally points, all of it?" Kaiser asked, backing from the steps as he palmed for the rest of them to do the same.

"I know it perfectly," the corporal answered. "But we need you for it, Kaiser."

"No, you can do this, Caethys. I will hold him back. I'm sorry, but this task is yours now. I'm counting on you." Kaiser looked to Briston. "Go with the corporal. Live a long life."

Briston hoped that the Cypolonian's last comment was just a formality. He felt awful leaving his rescuer to a cleaver-wielding menace. Caethys began rushing them all through the foggy tombstones and squishy grass.

Kaiser was satisfied to hear the footsteps fade out. He sent some thoughts to Zothre and Tethra for his people's safety and tried to kindle some courage in his frozen liver.

This man, this *Disciple*, had been there when all the Cypolonian's triumphs in the south came undone.

That dark day, hell itself walked among the southern city-states, feasting like a cat over a robin's nest. Thel and his gang of champions had been summoned by Cenobite Sinra. They reaped thousands of lives in a ballet of ruin that reversed years of freedom fighting.

Kaiser remembered Kronin's decision. The old Anthrome pitted his entire being against them. The Cypolonian thought so much about that moment that his memories were probably distorted. But he remembered that he himself had been useless.

He at last realized he was in a game being waged between a greater class of warriors than himself. Warriors like Kronin, Chrasmos, and Thel, these were the sort of men that made a difference in the world. For all of his own accomplishments, Kaiser was only the strongest of the weak.

"They turn and turn, those wheels behind your eyes," began the Disciple. His voice was scratchy from the smoke of burning villages. He put his claws on his stomach and tilted his head, studying Kaiser's expression. "I am Thel's Guillotine. Akanis, by name, but I think you may already know that. Are we old friends?"

The notion made Kaiser want to bite open someone's skull. His teeth scraped inside his head. Under the inferno of his mounting anger, however, he was glad. Rage gave him strength, and now he had buckets of it.

I never missed a day of training since that moment, Kaiser thought to himself. *I killed you all in my mind a thousand times every day, while my body went through the actions.*

He remembered bringing the torch to bear over Kronin's funeral pyre. That still, old, bearded head that had never issued a thought of arrogance or selfishness. Kronin was a vessel of noble deeds, so much so that Kaiser wanted to be like him.

Kronin had been an example for all men aspiring to be decent. His quiet soldiering made him seem untouchable. He was a better man than was ever asked of him, and he was glad to be one.

"You'll never understand what you wasted that day," muttered the Cypolonian through trembling lips.

"Did you say something? Friend?" Akanis prodded. That was enough.

Seriath's haft squeaked in Kaiser's grasp. He suddenly found himself a man's height above the ground, catapulted by malice. Akanis welcomed the assault with a wide-eyed glare.

But it wasn't prudent to be so direct. Kaiser ignored the chance for a falling strike and hit the ground in a crouch, swinging in a low half circle for the Disciple's knees.

It was nothing Akanis hadn't seen before. He soared over Kaiser, clawing biting blood from his nape. Kaiser didn't even feel it until he swiveled to return a barrage. Seriath banged against that lengthy butcher knife that shielded Akanis with its craethune steel.

Kaiser ducked a swipe for his face, but the cleaver followed and caught his shoulder. His retaliatory slash was parried while the claws closed on his wrist, pulling him off balance. This time, those metal fingers raked over Kaiser's face. Four gleaming red stripes appeared from his cheek to his forehead, barely missing his eye.

Seriath shot for Akanis's ribs. The Disciple knocked it away, but Kaiser circled his arm the other way and dropped a heavy strike from above. The claws caught the falling slash with a ringing thump, but Kaiser crunched Akanis's gut with a front kick that should have burst his kidneys.

But Akanis did not release his grip on Seriath's blade, and pulled at Kaiser's balance again. Seeing the butcher knife fly in low, the Cypolonian gave up his footing and fell to the side, yanking his sword from his enemy's grasp. Kaiser rolled back up to his feet.

The Disciple was already waiting and delivered a sidelong cut for Kaiser's chest. As he backstepped, Kaiser made the mistake of shooting his arms forward. Akanis caught his wrist again and lunged in to complete a skull-cracking punch to the face with his weapon hand.

Dazed, Kaiser discovered himself cartwheeling from some wrestling throw. He smashed his back on the corner of a cubic marble slab but he was back to his feet instantly. This time, Akanis was just glaring at him.

Wiping his black sleeve over his bleeding face, Kaiser was surprised to see how wet it made his arm. He could feel even more blood dribbling down his back from the scratches at his nape.

His hands were shaking too much; he was too excited. Kaiser knew he was outmatched. He let his breath carry out the heat, let his heart settle and his shoulders loosen. In a moment, he was ready to try again.

"Don't try to be calm. Your anger is your only strength," Akanis declared in his rustic voice. The Disciple suddenly looked to the moons and something shifted in his expression. "It's getting late now. I'm supposed to have you by morning."

Kaiser threw off the comments, as they were probably meant to aggravate him. *Run your mouth while you can, demon kisser. It'll be hard to boast with your ribs stuck into your windpipe.*

"Time to go," Akanis insisted. As he walked to meet Kaiser again, the butcher weapon issued a sort of red-hot vapor. It reminded Kaiser of molten rock, but it was wispier and drifted like glowing cobwebs in the night air. *Hellfire.*

"It really is," Kaiser answered, deciding not to imbue his own weapon with primal energy. He needed speed, not power, and also to conserve his stamina. As the Disciple drew closer, the diseased heat reminded Kaiser of dark days past and all the nightmares hence. It was time to redeem himself.

The Cypolonian suddenly served up a slew of strikes with half again more speed. There was more than one instance that Kaiser felt his blade must have just barely missed his enemy's neck, and so he redoubled his efforts. But even as Akanis gave ground, it became clear that he was not tiring.

A sweeping counterattack blasted Kaiser back. All of his injuries felt like they had been salted as Akanis's burning weapon flew by again and again. Hellfire magnified pain, he remembered. He had to be careful not to sustain any more injuries from that grisly blade that molted strange neon flames.

He had to remain calm. He tried not to imagine that hot edge cleaving down through his skull and into his brain, sizzling away all his thoughts and memories.

Backpedaling between the headstones, Kaiser swept his free hand down the back of his neck and lunged back in. With a flick of his off hand, he cast a splash of his own blood across Akanis's eyes, blinding him.

The moment happened too quickly to even form a memory of it. Kaiser dove in. Their weapons cycled madly, hellfire and moonlight frolicking over the steel before they each launched a front kick into each other's chests.

Each man backed away and found his footing. Kaiser panted, noticing Akanis's gray-blue skin was dry as a bone with not a drop of sweat. Was there nothing that even jarred this opponent?

Winded, Kaiser tried to point his weapon at Akanis, but his arm wouldn't obey. Because it wasn't there.

That's when he noticed a long, black object draped over a tombstone not far away. His sleeved arm hung there, Seriath still clutched in that leather-gloved hand.

His free hand floated to his shoulder where a stump still exhaled a grilled odor. The pain set in shortly after.

Akanis patted his belly, taking a moment to watch his prey crumble, hit the ground, and fume through clenched teeth. The suffering unfolded beautifully and with so much energy. This victim was screaming less for the agony and more for the loss of a dream that he now felt foolish for having.

"Hellfire. Either you consume it, or it consumes you." Akanis pulled up the hem of his coat and kneeled next to Kaiser. "It hurts, I know."

The Cypolonian was foaming and writhing, inebriated by the intensity. It was the sort of pain reserved for the torture cauldrons of the underworld. Akanis placed his clawed hand gently on Kaiser's head.

"Believe me, I know."

Chapter 39

The Federal encampment outside Insomnia was every dull shade of brown and gray from the dust carried in by adjacent scrublands. The wind was powerless however to alleviate the sun's hot rays. There was much to do, and so the men sweated the morning away, making mud of the powder on their skin.

Clayborn knew the hour of action was near and sweated more than his share. Kaiser had signaled with a great pillar of smoke inside the city. It meant things were supposedly going as planned, and the siege was imminent. There was no reason for things not to work. So why the gross anxiety, Clayborn wondered?

Not far away, a horseman on the edge of a gnarled forest entered the daylight. He found the Kasurite encampment rippling with heat waves just beyond firing range of the city walls.

Insomnia itself looked tarnished and subdued. The tallest government monuments had been thrashed by supernatural forces. Handsome white stone had been gouged with fire-scarred openings. Chains were arranged over the minarets and swayed under the weight of crow-eaten bodies.

It was Prince Norinthe who took pause atop his horse, soaking up the scene while the forest behind him began to rumble with a heavy march. His domestic guard broke from the trees, some two thousand in number. Norinthe's scouts were already padding far ahead at the prince's insistence.

"Insomnia has fallen?" The prince's words were to himself, but never fell short of the ears of his subordinate, keeping close on his own animal.

"And recently, at that. Surely the good Cypolonian has some retaliation in the making," the subordinate returned.

"He has a mind for repayment, or so I've heard." Norinthe looked back over his company; his legion would be in dire peril far sooner than he expected. He regretted bringing so many of his best, but he was determined on showing the strength of his state.

Then he remembered the Eurivoneans. He had crossed paths with them on their southward trek and was relieved he had the generosity to escort them. They looked hardy enough. They had the headiness to come all this way to fight a foreign war, after all. They would make a fine buffer for his own troops.

"We'll be thrust into some ugly business sooner than I had foreseen." Norinthe sighed, turning back to the scene. He had hoped to leap out of his armor and soak in some cool, treated waters to mend the saddle soreness of his thighs. Now he'd have to trade news with panicky yokels until nightfall.

He produced the decorative, round canteen from a compartment behind his hip and pulled the ringed bung out with a pop. He enjoyed a smooth draught of the mint tonic and immediately felt better. Restoring the canteen, he licked his lips and thought of what he might gain from this sudden enterprise.

"It would seem a siege is inevitable. Pity we didn't bring our stone-throwers. Marching on high walls that spit arrows . . . what a mess that will be," the subordinate commented.

"Honor grows well in such messes, and I'll have my share of it. Come, we'll learn nothing from up here."

When Norinthe's forces merged with the encampment, they were met with excessive courtesy, but the prince didn't notice. He started looking for someone in charge, sifting through mobs of low-ranking soldiers, most no older than eighteen.

Clayborn, who'd become doubly observant in Kaiser's absence, was already on his way to greet the prince.

"Prince Norinthe, you've arrived at a delicate hour. I'm Captain Victon Clayborn, I'm in charge here presently," he opened with a bow.

Norinthe looked disgusted. "You're in charge? This is Executor Kaiser's army, isn't it? Where is he?"

Clayborn groaned in his mind. "That's what makes the hour delicate. Our wayward Executor is inside the city, undergoing a plot of sabotage against the occupying Hellbringer."

"On Tethra's halo, I swear I have never heard such a thing," said the subordinate, whom Norinthe had forgotten was there.

"I hope you're joking," the prince added.

"I'm not, sir. Kaiser's powers have passed to me at the moment. I will be conducting the siege with the rest of his officers."

"And I suppose you have plans for my men and the Eurivoneans I bring?" Norinthe asked.

"You bring Eurivoneans?" Clayborn's grim eyebrows floated up like feathers. "We have a place for everyone, to answer your question. I'm sorry to burden you with this when you are weary from your travels. The longer we wait though, the more people are sacrificed, and Kaiser is put in further danger."

"So. I'm to obey a captain, am I?" The thought made Norinthe curl his upper lip a bit.

"Nothing so preposterous, my prince. You're obeying the delegations from the Executor." Clayborn's words made Norinthe scoff disdainfully.

"He's dead, most likely, the madman. What business does he have playing saboteur when his legions dawdle out here waiting for mine?"

"Our men are greenhorns, prince. Too soft to handle a siege all their own. The Executor aims to weaken defenses from within and make some room on the wall for our toys." Clayborn nodded to the wooden scaffolding protruding over the tents. Wheeled staircases, ladders, and siege towers were being swarmed over by shirtless grunts hammering and sawing.

"So, there's a hellbringer commanding the Septunites inside?" Norinthe asked.

"Almost certainly. The damage to the city appears to have been done with sorcery, not siege craft. Only a hellbringer with some carefully planned spell work could take a walled city in such short time."

"Hasn't that barbarian lord Tibernas shown up yet?"

"No, sir. We don't expect him for another month, at least." Clayborn gestured to the rear of camp. "Please, have a rest. The coming task will make us busy men indeed, and we'll all need to be sound and sharp."

"I'll obey well enough, Captain. But don't think I'll march my soldiers into a slaughterhouse just so your adolescents can take the easier path."

"Have you ever fought a hellbringer before, Prince?"

"I have not."

"I have, and I can guarantee there is no easy path to take."

Nearby, it was still a bit unsettling being surrounded on all sides by Kasurites in the heart of their own country, but Azurae and her Sojourners had been treated kindly enough. They had crossed paths with Prince Norinthe a week ago and joined his march, expecting a few days of rest. But rest was the last thing to be found here.

The air was alive with the lopping, scraping noises of woodwork. Shirtless Federals sweated to assemble what looked like crude war machines. They roped and nailed together rough beams and covered their skin in shavings.

"The hell you're finished, this still needs crossbeams!" came the reprimand from a red-haired woman with an eye patch. She was pulling workers to their feet who were taking an obviously undeserved break. "I wouldn't climb that thing if the Potentate told me to. Get it done!"

Azurae pushed on her chin to crack her neck and decided to address the woman.

"Hello, Federal, we have just arrived with Prince Norinthe. How can we be of service?" She wanted to appear helpful.

Sidna looked up from her work in the yard to take in Azurae and her people. They looked almost angelic compared to the dust-caked Kasurites. The Sojourners wore an exotic array of armor made from the hides of multiform creatures. Shells, scales, and horns were arranged whimsically over metal and leather to color them as the lords of nature that they were.

Sidna looked to a man standing nearby and shrugged.

"They're the martial artists we've been expecting. From Eurivone," he reminded her. Sidna turned to them again, her eye bright.

"Oh, martial artists." She tossed a hammer into her associate's hands and curled her finger at the Eurivoneans. "As it happens, we do have something you can help with."

Sidna led them to the center of camp where Federals were drilling in swordplay. The monitors nearby marshaled them to duel without pause before switching onto some other exercise.

"I notice many of them fight two on one," Azurae voiced.

"Yes, see, they're all academy graduates. Book smart, but they need to be toughened up. Executor Kaiser's real serious about making the most of these kids, so he puts 'em through some vicious training."

"Executor . . . Kaiser?" Azurae repeated. She slowed her pace. Her nerves fired up at the warm memories. *No, don't be foolish*, she thought. *Meeting him was a wonderful diversion, but it's time to move on.* It couldn't possibly be him anyway. And yet, Kaiser was not a Federal name.

"Yep. Anyway . . ." Sidna pointed to a lodge where one soldier sat holding a bloodied bandage to his forehead. "There's some water in there. When you've rested a spell, come back out to the yard and teach our boys everything you can about fighting. Word is we're taking the city back in a day or so."

Azurae paused at the statement. "Then our part in the war begins." She bowed earnestly in the Kasurite way. Sidna was a little embarrassed to receive it. "I promise we will awaken new strength in these men."

"It's going to be a madhouse, but Kaiser's going to hollow out the defenses from within. If we can just keep our heads down and our eyes up, we should manage," Sidna added.

"Executor Kaiser's inside the city?" Azurae asked reflexively. Anxiety made her shoulders feel heavy.

"Yes, everyone knows that now, so I suppose you may as well too. He and a few of our best"—Caethys crossed Sidna's mind—"they're trying to keep people off blood altars." Sidna left then, ending the conversation.

***

The air was rank with human filth. But to the growing army of refugees, these mining tunnels were a sanctuary. Gatherers had been dispatched to the ravaged houses above to retrieve food. Many were starving, and provisions were wiped out as quickly as they arrived. Nor could they cook their meals. The Septunites would be quick to investigate smoke wafting up from grates.

But the people were being strong. Their lives were ruined, but every time Kaiser came back with a load of food under one arm and a bloody weapon in the other, most decided to carry on.

The Cypolonian had not returned however, and none fretted more than Caethys. Many days of dried sweat made his stealth leathers stiff and scratchy, but he attempted a little sleep anyway. It was the middle of the day, but they only quested at night.

A woman was tiptoeing over the forms of the sleeping people. She was holding a young child in her arms, and Caethys could see the grayness around her eyes. He raised up a gloved hand and waved her over.

"Take a rest here, ma'am." He rose from his tight little spot among others on the moist sediment. She smiled and thanked him in some Archaic accent.

He wasn't tired anyway. When he wasn't sharply alert, he was downright paranoid. He scratched at the stubble on his face that was the longest it had been in years. Resting his shoulder against a wet beam, he watched the sleepers' bodies inflate and deflate.

Caethys found himself wishing again that he was half the healer Sidna was. His holy magic could restore injury and disease from demon magic, but these people suffered infected lash wounds, dysentery, and malnutrition, against which his magic could do little.

He was lonely. There were only a few other Federal spy-soldiers among these hundred or so refugees. Caethys wanted to speak with them, find strength in their brotherly words, but they had time for little more than a passing nod.

And where was Kaiser? He had not seen him since the run-in with the enemy assassin. The siege would probably begin tomorrow. If the Cypolonian did not return, Caethys would have to assume command in the morning.

"Corporal?" A familiar voice addressed Caethys. It was a man with a gray, receding hair that curled over his ears. He carried a manic smile under heavy eyes that had been rubbed bloodshot. "Corporal, Kaiser is dead, I think, yes?"

"We don't know that, Suraq. Look, I know what you're going to ask . . ."

"No no no no, Corporal, you have others!" The man's smile melted into the grimace he'd tried many times. "We have enough men, don't we?! You don't need me out there, please! The Septunites have already taken them all, my boys!" Suraq cupped his hands, kneeling to Caethys.

"Don't do this, you know I can't disobey him. That would be treason. I'm sorry."

"And if I go too, my family's wiped out! The whole line, Corporal! Let me live out my last few years in peace! For them! Have mercy!"

"You were archery champion two years in a row, friend. We need you desperately. Please, find your strength. Do it for the ones you lost."

"The ones I lost? I didn't lose them, they were stolen! My boys, and their strong little legs." He buried his face in his hands, then became disgusted by his own fingers. "They were torn from me. That bastard put his hands on my boys. Twelve years, ten years, and four, gone to ash in moments. Corporal . . . corporal, my sons are *under my fingernails*!" He showed his begrimed nails to Caethys.

"Your pain must be unbearable." Caethys kept his head turned. "I could never imagine how you feel. I will pray for your sons and for you, but in order to save others from this kind of misery—"

"No no no . . ." Suraq grasped the corporal's tunic, trying to wring mercy from it.

"We need you in the raid tomorrow. I am so sorry, friend, but Kaiser's decree must be upheld. I expect you to be ready by dawn, so get some rest." Caethys pulled his tunic hem away and turned from the man, who sobbed in the dirt.

Chapter 40

It was the night before the siege, and by now even the Septunites knew it. The arrival of Prince Norinthe's forces spurred Sanakal to mobilize his own.

Akanis had the night to do as he pleased. He loved this hour, when the sky was heavy and planets slept in the twinkling deep. Opagiel weaved inscrutable works above and below this little world of his. It gave him a sense of belonging to know he played a part in her sprawling ambition to devour humanity.

It was also the changing of the guards, and it would mean Akanis wouldn't be detained a moment as he dragged his captive by the legs through a sumptuous mansion. He was seldom bothered either way, for the men knew he loathed company. He spoke freely only to high-ranking officers.

And victims. He cherished the words of those near death. Mostly because they were honest. Kaiser however, had been mute with pain since the night of his injury. Still, Akanis enjoyed the desperation in his growls.

They passed into the deeper halls. Torchlight from outside speared across the hallway from the boarded windows. Night had fallen again without Kaiser's notice, as the pain magic of the hellfire still caused him blackouts.

He raised his head from its muddy drag to inspect his arm stump. He tried to wriggle fingers that were no longer there. His mind simply could not understand their absence.

With Akanis dragging him to some morose fate, Kaiser pondered how he might somehow survive. He didn't have much time. He sensed the spirits of recent victims roaming the halls, and the feelings they elicited painted a vile tale.

Akanis reached a white door with red hand prints at the base. He worked one of his metal claws into the lock, and it clicked open.

The Cypolonian was tossed face down inside. Akanis's heavy black boot rested on the side of Kaiser's head.

"Greetings, master," saluted a third figure.

Kaiser blinked away some sweat. It looked and smelled like a smoking den, cluttered with shining paraphernalia.

There was a podium where a mountain of red candles lighted an open book inked with strange, geometric symbols. The robed Septunite priest occupying the room was enjoying a pipe through his white mask that resembled a grieving face.

"More inspiration, splendid." The priest turned to scan Kaiser's prone form. He pulled up the hem of his robe to kneel down. "Your words will be immortalized, Chosen One. My colleagues will study them for ages to come! You see, I record lamentations into the Tomes of Anguish."

The priest caressed Kaiser's cheek with a red-gloved hand. A mistake. Kaiser snatched it with his remaining hand and crunched it like dry twigs. A scream filled the room.

"Put that in your damn book."

The priest was released to clutch the flipper his hand had become. The Cypolonian welcomed any punishment.

But Akanis seemed only mildly disappointed, perhaps a little annoyed by his priest's shrieking.

"Is she hungry?" Akanis asked.

"Yes, master! Very! *Iga hamash, pentili'uni!*" the priest exclaimed through his mask. Kaiser spoke a goodly amount of Septunite and recognized the last phrase as something like "*How severe, my fingers!*"

Keeping Kaiser under his boot, Akanis leaned to an iron grate in the floorboards. His claws resolved the lock and he pulled it open. A curious smell drifted from the opening. It smelled like autumn . . .

Akanis plunged Kaiser headfirst into the pit. The chamber air was surprisingly cool as it rushed up Kaiser's falling body.

The wind was crushed out of him as he hit the soil, but no new injuries occurred. He swept out with his arm. Dry leaves whooshed over his wrist.

He was in some underground garden. Short trees and ferns made it a tiny forest, lit by hanging glass lamps that once nourished the plants with their chemical glow. Now the dangling flames were strangely white, and every single leaf and bloom was dead.

"Opagiel is quick to reward faithful servants like Lord Sanakal. And so, someone from Opagiel's own bloodline has honored us with a visit. A great-great-granddaughter possessed of a particular appetite. As it happens, you meet her preferences." Akanis rolled his tongue in his mouth, meeting Kaiser's upward glare. "Did you really think I forgot you? You're the same dreg we defeated in the south."

Kaiser's stare could have frozen over a volcano. The Disciple above was lighting fires he couldn't possibly understand. The Cypolonian's remaining hand balled into a fist as hard as concrete.

"I'll bet you thought Kronin was invincible, didn't you?" Akanis went on, kneeling in closer to better see Kaiser's expression.

"You better pray to your whore demon to kill me good," Kaiser started in a baritone that sounded less than human, or perhaps more. "Because next time, I'll do things to you that would make Opagiel soil herself."

"Farewell, my friend." With a creak, the grate slammed above, sealing the Cypolonian in the crusty warren.

With the silence came contemplation. The injured priest above would be the final witness to Kaiser's crippled struggle. His remains would probably never be found.

But if a relative of Opagiel really was down here, he'd be lucky if there were any remains at all. Septunites summoned demons now and then, but now demon nobles? Tethra must be overwhelmed to let such things into the world, he figured.

Kaiser sensed something heavily evil close by. The lamps mixed ghostly light into the shadows. The she-demon couldn't be terribly large to hide here.

A shape in the leaf litter arrested his gaze. He rubbed both eyes to confirm a tiny, delicate, human shape only four inches long lying there. And there were others, Kaiser noticed, bending to see more closely. Frail of body they were, and possessed of withered wings.

Fairies, or pixies, Kaiser always got the two confused. Some people were known to keep them, benefiting from their auras of wisdom and wellness. It was an illegal but rampant habit of the wealthy.

He wheeled reflexively. What at first looked like a giant plant bulb on thick roots revealed itself to be his enemy: a creature standing on four stilt-like legs. The fleshy petals of the "bulb" receded like curtains, forming a sort of cowl for the figure inside.

She approximated a human woman from the waist up, though her flesh was like arranged fisherman scraps. Four yellow eyes narrowed on Kaiser from the kaleidoscopic bone and skin that was her face.

"So quiet. Not like the rest." There was no mouth to make words; they issued like sound waves from her mind. And indeed she was armless, but she had hands, six in all. They were resting on her body like sets of crab legs. They floated from her person with the grace of a ballet pose.

Kaiser had to marvel at her ugliness. An urge tugged at him to beg her for mercy. It was an odd feeling to mix with his sharpened prejudice against demons. Until he was able to organize his impulses, he watched her stab forward on those four legs.

"Are you Kaiser of Cypolon?" Her voice was crystal edged in psychic darkness.

She bought a look of disbelief with that question, but Kaiser quickly corrected himself.

"I will not play your mind games." His resolute words were hot with primal strength.

Her double pupils shrank in excitement. "I am familiar with the humans in this world. I have seen your failures. You were crushed by Thel once and now by his servant." One of her floating hands pointed at his severed shoulder as she took another step.

"Be very, very careful now. The more you move, the more I learn about you," Kaiser warned her.

He noticed her legs were made for scuttling, not jumping. But her floating hands seemed capable of extending far from her body, and the claw tips had a liquid sheen to them: poison, and probably the kind that could surpass his resistance.

And Kaiser resolved to avoid those eyes of hers. They were likely hypnotic, judging by their glow. The facts fell into place, and the Cypolonian began to develop a strategy.

The she-demon paused. She would not feed until he had been seasoned with the proper emotions.

"Kronin . . ." She tensed her sinewy face. "We have his soul, you know."

Upon hearing this, Kaiser forgot his missing arm. He wasn't tired or hungry anymore, he just wanted to kill. So he approached.

The she-demon was confused that this sprig of pale meat intended to fight.

She took a step back, and Kaiser's confidence mushroomed to see a six-hundred-pound creature give ground.

Her front leg swatted out, its bone ridges resembling teeth.

Kaiser had seen this move in many large creatures. If confused, they lashed out with a powerful attack rather than a fast one. A diagonal roll safely moved him closer.

But now the hands flew in like spiny crows. They clawed and grasped and forced Kaiser down onto his back. She rested a leg point on his sternum. Her full weight would crush his ribcage. The poison began to double his vision.

"Is it not a curse to be human?" Her claws stroked his skin. "A few decades of pointless misery until you die confused and regretful. I've often wondered, how does it feel to be so fragile?"

"Like this." Kaiser gripped her leg and pushed it off, kicking under her knee hard enough to cave an oak door. Her joint made a popping noise that she found as horrifying as Kaiser found it hilarious.

She prostrated, a mental scream shivering the dead leaves around them. The moment of panic allowed Kaiser to clamber onto her armless body.

Her many hands came in, their poisons undermining his stamina. They gouged and clawed, raking huge swaths of flesh from his back, arms, and scalp. Death was on the way, and Kaiser had no method of retaliation.

Except his teeth.

Her flesh would surely be the bitterest cut of meat he'd ever tasted, and her blood was probably nutritious as mercury, but he sunk his teeth into the softest part of her neck all the same.

A spurt of black liquid and yellow foam painted half of his face. It tasted like nothing he could ever describe. He turned his nausea into biting strength.

A bite wasn't enough, he had to *tear*. When his teeth had secured a hold, he ripped for all his worth. Clamping down again, he elicited another wash of oily fluids.

The smell was bad enough, but he was dimly aware of the gross dissection of his back and shoulders. Somehow, Kaiser did not vomit.

He simply worked, biting, tearing, and spitting, while claws pulled the skin from his body.

He was fading. No! Through the poison and blood loss, he found one last rush of strength. His primal magic went into his teeth, turning them into pegs of searing steel. The claws gave up, but with the neck bone between his jaws, he had one final goal.

Crunch.

The demon's head rolled off her shoulders, and Kaiser followed. His head filled with black noise.

This was death for certain. It felt very simple. His senses faded to remote observation. His fortitude prolonged his dying, he noticed. Levels of consciousness were disintegrating. It was not entirely unpleasant.

Enough of his mind functioned to remember one thing: He had killed a demon.

Echoes of himself called for him to drink the dead demon's energy. It sounded difficult; he only wanted to rest. The darkness hugged him and promised peace.

One facet of his consciousness disagreed. It rallied his faculties to draw in the nutritious power from the demon corpse.

Pain returned, and it realigned his floating thoughts. The pain was detached but intense, threatening to burst his heart.

Something was different. This was no feral demon, after all. This was a descendant of Opagiel whose power he was absorbing.

He was drinking the quintessence of the Helix itself, and it made every pore boil with agony and ecstasy.

He became a greater being, from his marrow to the surface of his skin. But the most exquisite pain played on his wounds. He could feel his sudden excess of vitality shoot into his arm stump, where bone began to extend. It was chased by layers of red muscle and fresh skin.

The pain was hellish, but it was too fascinating to faint now.

He watched through watering eyes as flesh jacketed newly sprouted fingers. And the pain crackled away, leaving a clammy but powerful new arm on Kaiser's shoulder.

For a moment, the world was completely quiet. But Kaiser realized death had ignored him once more. It was again his privilege to stand and live, and he went mad with joy.

He looked up, and his new strength made the hatch above look reachable. He swung back with his arms and leaped, nearly hitting his head on the grate. He caught hold of the bars, and curled up his lower body to plant his feet on the ceiling.

He gritted his teeth, which still had chunks of demon flesh in them, and pulled. He exerted beyond his old limits. His fingers ached, his thighs and shoulders burned. The grate warped and the lock popped apart.

Kaiser and the grate fell to the ground, but he leapt up to catch the ledge again, eager to be out of this place.

At that moment, the priest with the broken hand reentered the room, having properly dressed his injury. He was met with the sight of the missing grate and dirty fingers toiling to pull up the Cypolonian.

"Oh no." These would be his last words.

Chapter 41

It was by choice that Sanakal took a knife to both of his natural eyes ninety years ago. His growing addiction to the night and blackness broadened into a mania that ostracized him from his family. But his fascinations earned him the embrace of a new family in the growing cult of Opagiel.

He became unborn in his studies of death and pain, closely guided by the clergy whom always hinted at greater and darker mysteries. The hideous truths of humanity hollowed him out completely, and drop by drop, Opagiel's influence soaked in. Every time the ugliness of his path broke his mind, his comrades called it enlightenment.

And now he was Insomnia's God of Pain, lounging in the pitch black he had built a legacy from. The city had become his pleasure dungeon, with thousands of mewling victims waiting to perish under his invocations. With sensations his old eyes could never have provided, he could witness all at once the deadly rites his minions performed on the Kasurites across the ash-caked city.

There was a quiet tap at the door of the spacious chamber. Bashful white fingertips gripped the great panels and eased them open. The torchlight silhouetted the guest, but his small stature, round head and thin neck marked him as his pupil, Feo.

The light from the door drifted in, and hundreds of glistening creatures slithered to escape it. Feo had never asked Sanakal what these things were, but he was certain they were in his master's power. A pile of the creatures wriggled off to expose Sanakal's reclining form upon the couch.

"Master, the enemy has mobilized, just as you expected. They have brought siege weapons to bear and have foreigners among them."

The message elicited no response. It dawned on Feo that his master was not among the living. At the moment, anyway.

Sanakal had taken leave of his body, as meditating hellbringers do. His soul had fallen through a galactic inferno, streaking down into the Helix itself, where a million different atrocities surrounded him.

There in the cellar of the universe, the most smooth, delicious darkness was bejeweled with fiendish wonders. A hundred lifetimes wouldn't be sufficient to learn all the gothic history of a single shadow. Time marched on to drown every layer in demonic chaos, creating and forgetting eons of horror.

Sanakal was always humbled in his visits. He lingered over the ugliness of hell as a child might admire flowers in a field.

But years of communing had made Sanakal a part of the Helix, and his curious little soul went very nearly unnoticed by the ancient demons that haunted his every pace. He soaked into the environment to gather its power. Such journeys were as much about harvest as they were enlightenment.

The pain of it jolted him from his meditations, and his soul jetted back up to his body. In a moment, his lounging form awoke into the human world. His third eye peeled open with a rejuvenated glow.

Sanakal sighed, bored already at the cheap gloom this young world offered. He wanted to escape this realm of thoughtless colors and nestle into blackness forever. He regarded his student.

"Pardon my intrusion, master. The enemy comes," Feo began, going to gather Sanakal's outer robes. There was no response, so the pupil chose to hold silence. Meditation often put his master in a foul mood.

Quietly, Sanakal arose to allow Feo to fasten on his garments. Drawing tight the belts, Feo saw a morbidity in Sanakal's black lips.

"I will make my first journey to the Helix this year, master. Is it really so grand?" He looked up at the leather straps that concealed the sorcerer's empty eye sockets and would not have found any more emotion if there had been eyes. When there was no answer, Feo continued to tidy him.

Chilly fingers took his chin. His master's old smile had returned, and Sanakal was examining the purple sore on his pupil's forehead, the beginnings of an oculus, a third eye.

"Feo. Do you remember the visions you had as a child?"

"Yes."

"They were enough to make you flee your Kasurite home. What was it about those visions that could possibly move you like that?"

"They were unclear, they were more sensations than visions." Feo looked up, careful not to speak too long, but Sanakal seemed ready to listen. "They were frightening, even painful. But somewhere under my thoughts, I felt like something was calling me back, like a memory from before I was born."

"A memory of what?"

"That is what is unclear, master. But it was always accompanied by an ache in my skull that sunlight made worse. The shadows protected me like a lover, and cradled therein, I answered another urge . . ."

Sanakal pulled back the young man's sleeve. Feo's arm was interlaced with script carved by glass, needles, rocks, whatever had been at hand. Sanakal read the scars with his metal nails. They captured fantastic moments of inhumanity.

"The Felsong calls for us to undergo our own rites," said Sanakal. "You confronted yours bravely. Perhaps I angered Opagiel when I resisted mine, for they lasted years. In the end, I offered up my father, my mother, and others. When I gave her my eyes, she gave me the blackness of night that I had wanted for so long."

At these words, Feo sobbed. He was vastly jealous of Sanakal, but at the same time adored the inspiration he provided. "I'm too pitiful a thing to be a part of her Felsong, aren't I?"

"Feo . . ." The sorcerer pressed his pupil's head to his chest. They were both students of pain, but a sort of fatherly affection shined through now and then. Neither ascribed humanity to it, and neither ever spoke of it. "Your struggle is evidence of a greater destiny. You were called, child, and you answered. Trust in Her."

"With every rustle of pages, with every footstep, I hear the gods whispering. They want me back." Feo pressed his forehead into his master, trying to absorb his resolve.

"Of course they do."

"Every day, I am harassed by this world's beautiful lies. I fear if I am further tempted, She will abandon me."

Sanakal carefully slid a knife from his belt. It was an unremarkable thing, like an item from a poor bakery. He had surprisingly little menace in his stature.

"Resist it long enough, and you'll see that temptation is of your own making, and the gods were powerless all along," he promised. His student focused on the knife and understood. This was the same instrument that had rid Sanakal of his eyes.

Feo religiously adopted the small weapon.

"Perhaps it is time for the rites to continue."

***

Daybreak lit Insomnia's buildings like rows of golden boxes. Mist drifted off from the wet bridges as light fanned in between the cold spaces.

Patrols were thinning out, Caethys noticed. Reprobates came down this wide market road every ten minutes most days, peeking into windows with crossbows. Caethys had been observing for an hour, hidden behind skins in front of a tannery. He had seen only two patrols, and they never even looked in his direction.

Caethys raised an orange to his lips but stopped, listening to the voices of the enemy as their black boots carried them away.

"I keep hearing them say '*serem.*' They're talking about the siege," Caethys explained to his companion. After getting the burn wounds on his face bandaged, Briston could not sleep. He was thankful Caethys allowed him to join the morning rounds. He didn't want to be alone with his thoughts.

"There's much more noise at the gates today. The Federals are going to attack for sure," Briston remarked. Nodding, Caethys pointed to a veranda high in a trading den.

"We'll shoot from there. That place is built above a huge tent city. If they chase us out, we'll be able to lose them pretty easily, I should think." Caethys failed to contain a yawn.

"Insomnia will be free soon." Briston looked to Caethys, who waved to join him inside the tannery. Caethys took a small bite of the orange and handed it off to Briston. They sat in the stillness of the tools and hanging skins.

Briston chewed and Caethys stared. The latter was letting himself daydream about the bath houses where he could rinse away days of sweat. After that, he'd find an abandoned house and collapse under some heavy covers.

"Before we head back, let's see if we can scavenge some more arrows. We'll need to shoot a good twenty volleys to make it worth our time." Caethys never broke his stare.

Squatting next to the corporal, Briston palmed juice from his lips. "That's a lot."

"Kaiser planned to gain so many more archers. But then, he had also planned to help us do it."

"Too bad Kaiser died."

Caethys chuckled before he realized how inappropriate it was. "I won't believe he's gone until I see a body. Kaiser dies all the time. Hell just spits him back out." Caethys saw the confusion in the lad's face, but he just couldn't bring himself to believe a man could kill the Cypolonian.

"I can shoot pretty well. And I can run!" Briston said, a little too loudly. Caethys hushed him urgently, his tired eyes glittered a warning. Briston cupped his mouth.

Caethys peered out the door to see if any attention had been drawn. He returned to his seat.

"Septunites can run and shoot too, you know. If you join the attack, be ready to die. Because I can't protect all of you." Caethys was too tired to include his usual pleasantness. "I just can't."

"I know." Briston was careful to be quiet.

"Maybe we can get some fruit with less rat droppings when this is over."

"I won't get in the way. I won't slow you down. I lost a lot, but I can handle it." Briston was confident, as if nothing had happened to him.

"When we attack, you stay glued to me until it's over. Victory or defeat, you're my shadow, understand?" Caethys crawled to the door to peek out again.

"If you still want to get some arrows, we should try the hunter's den up the road," Briston suggested. "The Septunites have picked the armories clean."

"Have they? Then our course is clear. Let's hurry."

***

The elder Septunite priest had not seen his comrade at the morning's rituals. He had a mind to flog him for the offense.

"Brother! Did you not think Lord Sanakal needed our blessings for the siege today?!" He pushed at the door to the chamber. The lock fell into jangling pieces.

The elder priest was greeted with a murder scene. His peon lay underneath a crimson splash on the wall, mask broken.

"Brother . . ." The elder noticed the floor grate to the feeding chamber was missing, as if the matron had broken loose. But would she have really killed one of her own servants?

Something was very wrong. He glanced into the feeding chamber. The matron demon was dead, headless, decorated in her own blood.

"Opagiel protect us!"

With more fear than he had ever known, the elder priest chased out of the room, robes flying. He turned down a hallway to a closer exit, but a dozen dead guards bleeding on the hardwood gave him pause.

And to think, he had turned his bodyguards away this morning for privacy.

Kneeling for a short sword from one of the dead, the priest cursed the loud popping of his knees. He stalked down the hall, trying not to slip in the gore. Protective mantras coursed through his mind, but he could feel danger fuming from every surface.

Through the archway ahead, a guard lounge was in similar condition. A plate of potatoes was broken next to a dead warden whose head had rolled a shimmering trail some distance under the table, where a scimitar had pinned yet another reprobate to its surface.

"Hello."

The priest turned to the corner he hadn't checked. Wearing Septunite blood was a muscled brigand sporting black spy apparel. He was missing a sleeve on one arm. It was Kaiser, seated on a cabinet. He toyed with a wavy knife, a pipe hanging from his lips.

"Put it down." He eyed the priest's trembling weapon. Knowing nothing of fighting, the priest clunked the sword onto the table and held up his hands.

"Are you going to kill me?" asked the priest.

"Every hellbringer has a pylon that connects them to every other hellbringer. They need it close, so Sanakal's pylon must be in the city. Where is it?"

The priest went a few shades paler. Licking his lips, he answered, "The barracks on the eastern plaza. The fourth floor."

Kaiser stood. He took one last pull of tobacco smoke before dropping the pipe, crushing it under his boot. He reached out his hand.

Perplexed and afraid, the priest cautiously took the Cypolonian's hand. Kaiser studied the rhythm in the man's veins.

"Liar." Kaiser clamped onto the priest's throat and hoisted the man's two hundred pounds from the hardwood. He let the man strangle for a moment before kicking over the table. The sword driven through it now pointed upward.

Throwing the priest to his knees, Kaiser forced his mouth over the tip of the sword, wet with salty blood.

"Your mouth can lie. Your pulse cannot." Kaiser snatched off his headdress. "Where is the pylon, priest?" He forced the bald head deeper onto the sword point until he choked.

"La roal lahary!" Kaiser let up on the pressure for a clearer answer. Coughing blood, the priest repeated, "The royal library! Top floor!" This time, his pulse indicated honesty.

"Excellent."

"Will you let me go?" The priest fought hopelessly to get his face away from that leering steel point.

"Promise me you'll stop killing people. Promise me you'll help heal the damage you have caused," Kaiser offered, holding tight.

"I will redeem myself! I will be a balm to those I have hurt!" The priest gasped, sweat trickling between his eye and his nose.

Kaiser's fingers wrapped over his throat again, counting the heartbeats. "No, you won't."

The priest's head was shoved down the length of the blade, his lies squirting to the beat of his dishonest heart.

Chapter 42

The heat outside the curtains made Sanakal curl his lips. It was time to confront the sun's dreadful rays. Of course the Kasurites would strike in the early morning, when he would be most uncomfortable.

"Are you ready, master?" Receiving a nod, Feo peeled open the balcony. The sunlight was hot, and it made Sanakal sweat between the studs in his scalp.

The veranda jutted from the top of the city embassy, supported by brass-ringed columns. The vast marble face of the first Potentate was set high on the wall above Sanakal, gazing toward Evanthea in the east.

Feo was more confident. The sweat stung the new script rendered underneath his eyes like tear trails. Tiny symbols had been cut as neatly as any book page. Feo felt empowered, as if pressure had escaped from the bleeding words.

Feo kneeled and presented a bone goblet to his master. Metal-dressed fingers clinking on the vessel, Sanakal observed his wavering reflection in the drink, a brew of twisting yellows. With a savory draught, he imbibed fully the cup of congealed fear and nightmare extract.

Sanakal's third eye watched the Federals arrange into phalanxes. He enjoyed the pomp of their formations. Thousands of skinny teenagers stuffed into green army padding. They stood behind shields painted with goblets and crowns.

They were like little gifts, ripe in their fearfulness. Sanakal could already imagine these fleshy tidbits erupting into blood and ashes. But he would only be able to collect three, maybe four souls. Their paragon Tethra spirited most souls safely away upon dying.

His third eye became darkly radiant. Hellfire winked above his head. The wind itself rotted to resemble black saliva. It congealed into a set of black wings around him. Ornaments of condensed fury budded like devil fruit.

The self-styled God of Insomnia offered his sacrament with open arms.

***

Clayborn dismounted his horse, trying not to think about the bizarre transformation the sorcerer had just undergone. He had just finished inspecting the formation. He didn't care if the stable boy saw or heard him mumble things to his horse. Goldie had put up with his restless adventures for four years, and he came to love the animal. He was glad she would have no place in this mess of a siege.

Clayborn finally addressed the boy. "The balm for her rib sores is hanging from the water trough. You'll give her some of that, right? She's been squealing a little."

"We'll take good care of her," came the promise.

Goldie's big brown eyes wandered over the captain. She jabbed his arm with her nose. He scratched the white patch on her forehead and handed the reins to the boy.

"But I might forget, Captain," the boy said in a hopeful voice. "I think you'll have to do it yourself, when you get back."

Clayborn bobbed his head a little. The armor-bearer had his turn now, handing over the headgear. It was smoothly domed, with no feathers, horns, or any other nonsense weighing it down. Clayborn shoved it on and creaked up the visor which came to a point over his nose, making him look angry.

He took the shield next: a kite-shaped piece of steel framed in brass, the red bull on its surface nearly erased by sword scratches.

With his bastard sword on his back, he shared the uncertainty of his men filed before him. Open-field battle was something Clayborn felt good at, but sieges felt like waiting in line to die. For the third time this morning he counted how many light mages were dispersed throughout his troops.

Twelve light mages had been placed evenly in the ranks to share their spells among the men. The mages would walk behind full body shields on wheels. They needed to stay alive because they kept troops alive.

Even Velena was there, that aloof introvert that kept finding herself in the captain's company in Evanthea. Like many others, it would be her first battle. And while she stood a foot shorter than most of the shivering soldiers, she was still as a lighthouse in a hurricane.

Velena was a talented one, but Clayborn still didn't want her here. She was like a daughter to him, but he had no power to keep her from battle when she was conscripted for service.

But for all her talents, an average light mage could only muster a quarter the power that a hellbringer could. Tethra, the lone Paragon, could only manage to dole out so much power to humans by herself.

The soldiers busied the Paragon with pleas, Clayborn noticed. Everyone with an oath-key clutched it, whispering prayers into the backs of their shields.

But one person seemed confident enough. He rode behind his charioteer to meet Clayborn. There was something about his excited face that the captain didn't appreciate. It was a sort of self-assurance that most men couldn't afford. Prince Norinthe was certain he'd survive the day. More than that, he was certain he'd win.

In appearance, Prince Norinthe was Clayborn's opposite. He donned a helm with a red feather that bounced merrily on his ride. His tight-fitting metal armor was lusty green and in mint condition.

It was difficult to look from Norinthe's glowing expression to the soldiers who'd never seen battle. Many of them looked on the verge of throwing up. They breathed through their teeth, and their shields wavered.

"I hope the Septunites can't see your soldiers' faces," Norinthe began.

"Fright will make them vulnerable to Hellbringer magic," admitted Clayborn. "Prince Norinthe, your men are more experienced. If your men made up the frontlines and set an example, it might help—"

"No, no, no. I don't think so." Norinthe chuckled, plucking at the wicker that laced up his bow. "The contract dictates that I support your troops, not do their bleeding for them. They'll be all right, Captain. It's baptism by fire. My men will take the reins when yours get tired."

"To reap the glory our dead have earned?" Clayborn wished he hadn't said that. Wearing full plate made him bold of tongue.

"My contributions are insufficient, are they?" Norinthe's smile betrayed his wounded pride. The prince savored the tension. "Just get your little lambs on the siege ladders. Your dead can keep their glory. My men and I will take our own."

"Forgive me, prince. I'm only concerned for these greenhorns." Clayborn glanced at his army again. Would half of them die? More? Norinthe's ire seemed smaller compared to such worries. "They have a lot of promise, they shouldn't be used carelessly."

"But they did come to fight a damn war, Captain. In the bid for victory, one mustn't become overly attached to one's coins."

Clayborn was silent. He settled into the same killing mode that had carried him through danger in the past. It had been a while since his last engagement, but Victon Clayborn was a professional soldier. He smoothed over each of his bristly eyebrows and sniffed through his big nostrils as if to suck back weighty thoughts.

"True enough. We shall commit until the task is done," Clayborn said in a baritone that carried to the front men, whom he approached.

"If only I'd arrived sooner. Kaiser might have left this task in more capable hands," the prince whispered to his charioteer as they turned away.

"You're all thinking too much," Clayborn began, knocking on his own helm with a fist. "Thinking of what's going to happen. I'll tell you. We're going to close on that wall and weather some dark sorcery. A lot of us are going to meet the Paragon today, but keep your magic strong and it won't be you. Listen to what the light mages say, because they're going to keep hell out of your soul, and your soul out of hell."

He gestured to Velena, who was watching from behind a shield that was quite taller than she was. He went on.

"They're counting on us to be afraid. Hellbringers can use fear, so don't give them any. They're the ones hiding behind walls, with nowhere to run. They're hoping their demon-bitch's magic is enough to see them through, because if it isn't, they are all going to die.

"We are the Hand of the Gods today. March strong over that wall and leave behind all pretense of mercy. As they resist, kill them. If they flee, pursue and kill them. If they surrender,"—Clayborn watched his words solidify a few faces— "...kill them. At day's end, Insomnia will call us saviors. Stay alive for that moment."

He threw down his visor and backed into the front row, a few of the soldiers made room. He didn't know why, but he always took a moment before battle to take in the magnitude of the enemy, to get a little scared.

Insomnia's walls were originally made to thwart Dragnos's family raids. Cubes of concrete were puzzled together to a height of forty feet, where the ramparts flew the black banners of Opagiel's faith. The wall's length was staggered by turrets, each one occupied by white-scalped, black-uniformed archers. Behind them, soldiery bristled in the severe shapes of Septunite armor.

It was said that when part of a human world is desecrated, a duplicate of that part appeared in the Helix, and that was how Opagiel's dominion grew. If true, Opagiel had made a tremendous gain. Corpses were worked into chain nets skirted along the high wall, where pikes and nooses boasted other victims, or parts of them.

Clayborn nodded to his flag crew. The green eagle flag was hoisted, and the drummers made their musical welcome.

Like sunrays off tropical water, energy crackled from the light mages in the ranks. They used rings, orbs, and scepters as implements.

The Federal soldiers felt heavenly courage and corrosive terror dueling for place. At the whistle, they took four steps in place to find their rhythm and began their march. The legions' movement gave a heartbeat to the grassy flats.

Clayborn hoped the men felt as strong as he did. In this rumbling formation, the men were all a part of something huge and daunting. It was good to know that if his strength failed, the wit and will of others carried on.

Sanakal's gruesome wings dripped a syrupy, yellow-hot ooze. He swept them forward. Out flew hundreds of glowing spindles leaving threads of smoke.

The shields of the Federals rattled to the hail of cinders. The screaming began. Men dropped, grasping at the burning darts in the wounds.

Snapping noises sounded above. Federals tried to shrink behind their shields as the arrows fell, slamming like fists against the wood and metal. The missiles found toes, padded elbows, knees, and eyes.

Sidna was a few rows back. She hated shields normally, finding them cumbersome. Today in the siege, she felt quite the opposite. It had caught one arrow already and deflected another. She wondered if the archers were aiming for her. The red hair issuing from the back of her helm sometimes earned unwelcome attention.

Beside her, a young man was huffing. She could hear his armor rattling. He was about to fall apart.

"Hey! You're not dead yet, little brother!" Sidna hollered to him over the metal plinking. He looked over, tears had already streamed down into his teeth.

"I don't—" An arrow slid past him and jabbed the man behind. "I don't want to die, please!"

"Easy, you have to be calm, you know," Sidna warned, and she reached out with her sword hand to tap his weakly glowing oath-key. "If you're fearful, their magic burns hotter!"

"I don't know what to do! I can't do this!" he sobbed. Sidna peeked over her shield for a brief moment and ducked back under.

"Here, hang tight." She sheathed her blade and pulled her necklace over her head. Reaching over, she touched the oath-key at his chest in the same hand her own was in.

The items glowed a joyous sapphire that painted the inside of his shield bright blue. Sidna groaned a little. Casting divine magic had always been a weakness of hers. Sidna released the young man's blazing oath-key.

"Don't waste it! It should last until we're over the wall."

Chapter 43

Above the Federal army, a ball of flame was forming. A disk of smoke orbited the fireball like a tiny galaxy, arcing with currents of demon plasma.

Red lightning forked into the Federal ranks. One soldier took a blast. He knelt, but his oath-key thwarted the spell in a gout of blue light. He arose again to his cheering comrades, inspired by the holy courage that saved his life.

"That's right, boys! You're giants, all of you! Don't buckle to anything!" Clayborn reinforced.

Others were not as fortunate. The bolts shot down to blast Federals into clouds of bone and ash. But the bones did not settle, they tumbled upward to feed the brimstone vortex above. With gleaming eyes, survivors looked up to see skulls of comrades rolling in a carousel of skeletal debris.

Clayborn looked back, past the flame and bone puffing up from his army, to see the wide ladders bobbing above. The siege towers were squeaking along, but many of the laborers had perished and it was slowing, blocking the advance of those behind.

"Get that siege tower moving! Everyone near the tower, get pushing!" At Clayborn's command, men gravitated to the hulking platform that had been spiked by arrows.

Another wave of screams, but Clayborn noticed this time it came from inside the wall; Septunites were being killed.

«What is this?! Who fires on us?!» demanded a reprobate captain. He stood at the gate in a jungle of black armor and white skin. Before an underling could answer, an arrow caught him in the forehead.

The captain realized he didn't need an answer, and he carved a group of men from the flank with shoving and waving. He squinted deeper into the city heights to discover the source of the attack.

«The hostel with the yellow shutters, across the market! Storm the building, don't let them escape!» His task force charged away.

Kneeling on top of a bookcase, Caethys fired his arrows from the window. He arched them high over the streets to where the Septunites clustered. In the same room, volunteers rescued in previous nights stood or kneeled to snap off their own volleys.

Among them was Suraq, whose torment had morphed into anger. He cursed as his expert arrows dropped Septunites so quickly, he exhausted both of his quivers before Caethys could begin his second.

Spying enemy swordsmen racing to the foot of the building, Caethys shouldered his bow. He dropped from the bookcase and began knocking his compatriots' backs.

"It's time, up and out, everyone!" When his hand landed on Suraq's shoulder, Caethys was shoved to the floor. Suraq looked ready to fight him, but Caethys ignored this and continued to pull everyone out.

They breezed down a stairway where there hanged paintings of pale, soft-eyed women. Some of their portraits had been slashed during the occupation.

Caethys looked to see his hungry comrades padding over the spiraling steps above, then down over the railing to where the lobby entrance burst open. Several dark figures entered, kicking in chamber doors while others cast their eyes up to spot Caethys.

Their sudden appearance tightened up Caethys's chest. He wheeled back up the stairs, waving for men to follow him into one of halls. They trotted behind him to a window at the end of the corridor.

He slammed open the cheap shutters. As he remembered, smaller inns and tents were present below. Perhaps a bit too far below. He imagined leaping from the sill to the tile roof of the home across the alley.

"We have to jump. Onto the roof, then the street. Now!"

"Should we really jump so far?" a volunteer asked.

"Unless a Septunite sword is less painful! Don't think, just go! Everyone!" came the command. The man tried to blow out his apprehension and stepped upon the creaking wood. Caethys watched as he jumped.

He dropped to pound the slanted housetop. Several of the clay tiles slid with him onto the cart path below. He stood and looked up to his fellows expectantly.

Finally goading the next man upon the sill, Caethys saw them hop one at a time onto the opposing building like sacks of feed. Even Suraq mustered the angry gumption to cast himself down to rejoin the men.

Caethys finally jumped forward into empty air. His legs flailed, desperate to find ground. He struck, and the old woodwork beneath him popped apart, releasing Caethys into the chamber below. The corporal and a hundred pounds of scrap wood fell over a row of kegs in a kitchen.

He lay across the humps of two barrels, praising Tethra he didn't break his back. He swung onto the floor, crunching tiles, and looked up. His bow had been caught on the hole in the ceiling and was too high up to worry about now. He heard his men calling for him outside. He jogged for the cement stairway. He kicked the door open to find his men.

"Everything's gotta be so flashy with you, doesn't it?" someone commented.

"To the rally point, we'll stick to the underwalk." Caethys budged ahead and pointed across a slum of shacks and tents. Suraq was off before Caethys could finish.

They could hear the gallop of pursuers on the far side of buildings. Caethys zigzagged his party through the dirty tent yard.

"Over here, let's see if we can lose them," he whispered. They followed him onto their bellies behind a wagon dangling with foreign wares.

They waited, breath fluttering the dust as Septunites ripped open tents and demolished shacks. They shouted things, and Caethys recognized the word for "skin" and didn't care to learn the context.

"They're over here! Come here!" Suraq hopped up and screamed at the pursuers. He threw down his bow and held out his arms in welcome.

Caethys thought about killing Suraq, but opted to get his men out instead. Suraq waved and pointed as the reprobates chased by him on their route. One stopped to confront him with unreadable body language.

"No more love Apogee?" began the reprobate in his broken Civilic.

"No. I want peace. I want purpose," Suraq said as tears leaked down his cheek.

"Purpose. I know this word," the reprobate acknowledged. "Come, new brother. You have purpose." He put his sword away and gently put his arm over Suraq's back, guiding him to a different life. Suraq turned one last time.

"Caethys! You and that tyrant Kaiser can rot in hell!" Suraq's curse carried to the corporal as the latter urged his men through the ghetto.

"Just keep running!" Caethys veered everyone down an alley. Suddenly, a throwing wedge spun into his back. He stumbled and crashed into a dead fireplace, spilling the pot of old stew and blackening himself in soot. One of the younger, quicker archers loaned his shoulder to Caethys. They would have to remove the wedge later.

They rounded a great potted fern, following the cement decline and turning into a tunnel stained from runoff.

As they emerged from the passage, discus blades kept whisking past them. A four-point blade stung Caethys's upper back now, but only barely pierced his leather armor. The corporal kept his head down and tromped along on his comrade's shoulder until they reached the bathhouse entrance.

The bathhouse was cool and shaded but for the morning light from the windows. Sunrays rippled in the baths and played on the statues.

Insomnia nobles favored such diversions, and their business made it a huge place with a high ceiling hanging with censers. The footsteps of volunteers echoed. Caethys turned for the enemies nearing the entrance, wincing at the pain of his back wounds.

When the last Septunite crossed in, ambush defenders exploded from the pools. Javelins streaked in, and spearmen appeared. The Septunites thrashed at the sudden wall of points, but Caethys and his group joined in as well. In seconds, the Septunites were down and the blades of the ambushers were dripping.

"We lost one," Caethys explained over the dead quarry. "Now we rotate, just as Kaiser said. Defenders, take up bows. Archers, stay here to ambush the next group. We won't get tired from escaping by doing this."

That's when the archer who had aided Caethys put a hand on his back. "Deep breaths," he instructed. The higher wedge came out easily. But careful as the archer was, the lower wedge clung.

"Damn!" Caethys took a knee. He put his glove between his teeth. An ugly sound, and the wedge was out. Caethys's groan sounded like an old man's.

"You're in luck, they forgot to poison these." The archer held the bloody thing in the corporal's vision.

"Huzzah, praise my fortune," Caethys huffed, wiping his forehead.

***

Perched on an exposed beam of a half-destroyed building, Akanis was trying to read a rare book as the battle raged visibly in the distance.

Oh, how Akanis wanted to be out there. All those tender little soldiers would glut his blood-red desires completely. Sanakal was an effective leader, but too frugal in using his assets like a Disciple. The hellbringer tended to stretch the value of little pawns like his reprobate legions. Perhaps, thought Akanis, Sanakal would achieve greater things if he were a touch more reckless.

But Akanis was a servant first, and he refused to challenge authority. Service to Thel had put him on a path of macabre glory, and it was all he ever wanted. Still, being put to heel while others fulfilled their gory potential set his iron-clawed fingers to tapping.

Something wasn't right. Akanis turned to see exactly what he shouldn't have. In the littered study hall below stood the whelp he had already condemned to a demonic execution.

Kaiser looked like a battlefield scarecrow; he had stolen spiked armor from a reprobate and wore razor-finned greaves and bracers. His arms were coiled in barbed wire. The Cypolonian had taken pains to make himself as untouchable as possible.

Akanis was less concerned with Kaiser's attire than his presence at all, let alone the arm that had only recently been cut off. Regardless, it appeared the Cypolonian had a mind to fight, judging by the way he aimed one of his two long daggers.

"Get . . . your ass . . . down here," he demanded.

Akanis's brow furrowed in confusion, but he sucked in a breath and dismounted. Even in his flowing military coat, he was remarkably nimble, bounding down the broken obstacles.

He landed a few yards away in the room where papers scattered like carpet. Lying among their beloved books were dead librarians, who would leave their decaying odors in this place for years to come.

"I left you to my Lady's appetites. How is it you come here with the arm I have taken from you?" Akanis asked. He fluttered open his coat to unhook that same cleaver that had done the deed.

"A gift. From your Lady," Kaiser answered.

It was then Akanis noticed a greater presence in this man than before. The magic of Kaiser's chrysm, indeed his very appearance, seemed more vigorous. Lady Sarshel, as her inner circle referred to her, would never release an offering. Impossible as it was, the only explanation was the Cypolonian had escaped. And this newfound strength?

It could only have come from her.

"She's gone then." Akanis confirmed to himself. He glanced at his reflection in the blade and saw a failure.

"You lost someone important?" Kaiser jeered with slit eyes. "That must be just *devastating*."

If Akanis *had* been in any mood for humor, it was gone now. It was as much his duty as Sanakal's to honor and comfort their demonic envoy.

It was Akanis who had thrown Kaiser to Sarshel as a sacrifice. It was his fault; he had utterly failed his charge.

What would Master Thel think?

"You have destroyed my name." Akanis's whisper was candy sweet to the Cypolonian, whose emotions all aligned for a death match. A lush new power coursed through Kaiser's veins. He had assumed it would be enough to match this enemy, but now the Disciple's claws scissored with anger.

Breath streamed from the Disciple's purple lips, and he became still.

"I will suffer for this failure. But I promise, you will suffer more." Akanis stepped closer, and Kaiser did the same. Papers rustled across the floor. Ruby eyes met golden ones in the tense seconds before mortal combat.

Their contest began with forearms and elbows thumping back and forth. They tested each other with blocks that made their bones ache.

They were eager to risk injury for an early triumph. They circled and began trading steel with such vigor that dust fell from the rafters. Blood dotted the papers at their feet as light injuries were forgotten as quickly as they appeared.

Knowing Akanis's penchant for grappling and throwing, Kaiser opened his left side to invite a grab. In a calmer state of mind, Akanis might have recognized the ruse, but his metal claws swooped in to spring the trap.

The spikes on Kaiser's elbow jabbed into Akanis's bicep. The Disciple recoiled, but lunged back in. Kaiser nearly lost his hand as that butcher knife arced under. The Cypolonian flailed to avoid the death strokes that came thick and fast. Akanis succeeded in putting Kaiser on the defensive.

But it was another ruse. Just as Akanis's claws clasped Kaiser's neck, an uppercut raked barbed wire over the Disciple's face. Akanis spiraled away to avoid being blinded, leaving his enemy's throat unharmed.

Kaiser followed up with dual knife jabs, keeping Akanis moving past a table. Kaiser plugged both of his daggers into the surface of it. In his battle rage, the table seemed weightless as he swung it around and smashed it to pieces over Akanis. The Disciple was thrown down, but fought to regain his feet. Kaiser had already hooked a chair with his foot and crashed it against Akanis's guard in a burst of curved wooden shapes. As Akanis's injuries mounted, Kaiser began to have fun.

Akanis, always so calm, suddenly erupted. His eyes became blindingly red like a burst of sulfur, and that deadly hellfire began to curl over his blade and his claws. Fury consumed him, and the Cypolonian had to give up the offensive as weird devil fires crawled up the Disciple's arms.

The glowing strands doubled the sting of Kaiser's injuries, but it was not the time to be weak. He had to ignore that pain. When they collided again, Kaiser utilized his kicks to keep the effigy of pain at bay, but those fiery claws tore through the armor at his stomach.

It was surprising how much it hurt. The slash on his abdomen made Kaiser want to curl up and surrender, but he kept focused. He looked for *any* faults in his enemy's form. The Disciple was unaccustomed to fighting so angrily, and his barrage betrayed a hidden pattern.

Kaiser's dagger found its chance: a slash across Akanis's hand. The butcher knife connected with the same arm Kaiser had lost before, but this time it penetrated only lightly.

After all, Akanis could not wield the weapon properly with so many fingers suddenly missing.

Akanis couldn't cry out before his foe's daggers disappeared into his stomach. A gust of foul wind blasted the hellfire from the Disciple's body in a storm of shredded heat that rushed loose papers in waves around the library.

The cool reprieve from the extinguished flames almost lulled Kaiser from the duty at hand, but he left the daggers in Akanis's gut to pull the butcher knife from his own shoulder padding.

A second later the butcher knife was buried deeply in Akanis's forehead. His claws tinkled eerily as his brain emptied. Kaiser watched in triumph as a great enemy spilled volumes of blood before falling to the papers curling at the floor.

This tender slice of vengeance would have to be savored another time. But before Kaiser continued to prowl the library for the Pylon, he knelt and unhooked the bindings of Akanis's metallic claws. The Guillotine Gauntlet was Kaiser's now, and it clicked with splendid lethality on his fingers.

Moments later, the Cypolonian located the gruesome Pylon that was supporting Sanakal's power. It was like a black spine tall as a man, curved 'round to form a partial loop. In the center of the loop was suspended a glass ovoid gripped in obsidian filigree, while a smaller glass orb hung from the loop's tip. It was from the larger glass ovoid that Kaiser could sense disgustingly rich demon energy.

His new claws clinked over the item, and with a yank, he broke the chain that suspended it. He held it far from his body, sickened at the hellish radiation. He stepped to the window and kicked open the pane. With something like a "yech," he cast the heavy thing out from the library's seventh story.

The ovoid plummeted sharply for several moments before it crunched against the pavement. The glass broke into ten thousand sparkling chunks. A green slime bubble inflated among the shards. It grew fat and popped to release a hundred red-hot spirits shrieking in excitement.

Having enjoyed the spectacle, Kaiser turned and plucked the smaller orb from the Pylon. As he walked from the room, he chucked it against the wall, where it popped far less impressively.

***

In the screams rising from battle, Sanakal's own went nearly unnoticed, except by his apprentice. The nourishing flow of demon magic stopped, and his spell casting quickly robbed his body of power.

Sanakal threw his arms over the banister while his shadow wings evaporated, dripping yellow toxins.

"Is it the light mages, master?!" Feo asked, helping him find a feeble stance.

"I am cut off . . . from the Pool." Sanakal salivated from his black lips.

"Something has happened to the Pylon, then? It has been attacked! But what of Akanis?"

"It doesn't matter." Sanakal's third eye trickled black liquid. "I can no longer sustain the maelstrom spell." He gestured to the firestorm cloud above the Federals, who enjoyed less red lightning.

"We can't resist the Federals without it, master. The saboteurs in the city have reduced our numbers too much," came Feo's grave reply. Sanakal sleeved away the black tears of his third eye.

"Feo." In a strange arrest, Sanakal's third eye gazed into the apprentice. "Feo, I'm sorry. My power was rooted in the Pool. Until it is restored, I am useless here. Your power, however, is still entirely your own."

"Yes."

"The responsibility falls to you, my student," Sanakal admitted, inky lips bobbing an attempt at apology. Feo stood to overlook the enemy army that labored against the wall like a flood of stabbing metal.

"Then please leave. You are in danger here without your powers," Feo remarked. Withdrawing the dagger that was gifted him, he stitched his own magical powers into the firestorm cloud.

Though faint from the episode, Sanakal refused to slouch any longer in the face of his brave pupil.

"Restore your power, master! If I can be a stepping stone for a *true* hellbringer, then nothing else matters!" Every gout of lightning sucked away a fraction of Feo's power, but he was prepared to expend all of it. Already, the wounds under his eyes smoldered with effort.

Feo wasn't prepared for this task, but Sanakal hadn't the time to entertain affections. His turned for the door and forced himself to not look back, ignoring the ache in his chest.

Chapter 44

Septunites were bundling their arrows in oiled linen and igniting them. They sent glowing shots at the wooden hulks that the Federals were rolling forward. Arrows prickled them thickly, but the lumber had been treated during construction, and flames struggled to catch. As the machines rolled closer, the caricatures and curses carved by the Kasurite troops became readable to the archers, who seethed at the blasphemy.

Clayborn huffed as he helped push along the rolling staircase. The damn wheels wanted to jam on every rotation. As he pressed at the rear, he could feel all the little arrows biting into the higher parts. Inwardly, he thanked the Covenant that the machines were drawing so much of the fire. Turning to survey his ranks again, however, it seemed the dark magic was still doing its work. The spell was ripping fiery bones from the ranks at a pace that was sure to diminish morale, and that would only make them more vulnerable.

Above the sound of surging energy and clanging armor, Clayborn could swear he heard another round of screams come from inside the wall.

It had to be Kaiser's saboteurs. Perhaps he was still alive, then? Taking leave of his labor for a moment, Clayborn climbed the stairs of his siege machine and raised his visor to the troops.

"Hearken to the screams behind the wall! Executor Kaiser lives!" he said, holding his palms beside his mouth. "Septunites are already dying in the city! Hurry, lads, while there are still Septunites to kill!"

Clayborn slapped down his visor and got back to shoving the staircase. With a creak, the bumper fell from its suspension and tripped him. Pushing himself up, Clayborn found the eyes of a nearby soldier he had seen on the construction yard.

"Is this thing even going to hold us?" he yelled. The man made awkward gestures until he decided to turn away from the captain.

An arc of blood-red lightning raveled around one of the soldiers. The weird pains from deep inside him made it difficult just to stand. Someone's hand landed on his shoulder.

It was Sidna's, taking it upon herself to take some of the demon energy into herself to lessen the man's burden.

"It's . . . no problem, brother! We've got this! Just—" But Sidna was interrupted as the man crumbled like dry leaves under her hand. His armor wasted down to charred shavings and his sparking skeleton clattered into the hellstorm above.

Sidna had never known the man's name, but she had known him. He was a gambler, indulging every time they made camp. It had probably bankrupted him, which was why he signed on for additional paid duties like cook, smith hand, and guard. He often referred to a woman back home.

He had his own story, and it ended in a bouquet of cinders.

She had to live for him. And for the others. A wooden clatter drew her attention to the heights. Sidna knew the ladders would make it to the wall first, but they were always tremendously unsafe. The rickety things offered no protection against arrows and could be shoved off or broken apart.

"To the top, men! Don't stop a moment! Press to the top! Hurry now, hurry! Claim the turrets! Don't hold up the line, go, go!" Squad leaders in plumed helmets and outrageously tall flags were throwing men onto the ladders.

Sidna watched as the front ranks were bullied onto those flimsy wooden tracks. The enemy archers were merciless, pelting the climbing men with darts. Some of the men rolled off of the ladders on purpose, favoring a thirty-foot fall over the barrage of bowshots. One man fell through the rungs as crimson lightning crumbled him into glowing flakes. The other lads crawled right over the sparking stains to meet similar fates.

"Stop holding up the line! Get moving!" yelled a squad leader. Daydreaming about all the ways she could die, Sidna was herded to the ladder. She had to tuck away her sword, but kept her shield out.

Her legs felt full of glacier water, and her back was wet. She wanted to roll off, dig a hole in the ground, and disappear. If she climbed this ladder, she would die. The squad leader slammed her helm with his fist, cursing her to get moving. She managed one step, then the next, and a man mounted the ladder beneath her. There was no going back now. She looked up, following the boots of the trooper ahead.

Already Sidna didn't want to look down. She was perhaps ten feet up when her gloves smeared some blood along the rungs. At the top, a trooper was wrestling helplessly against a battlemage, who had already put a blade through the trooper's stomach while reprobates eagerly helped throw the bodies over the wall.

This is so stupid! Gods, this is ridiculous! We can't make any progress like this! Casting her gaze down, Sidna could see a litter of casualties crumpled at the base of the wall. But they weren't all dead. While many were prickling with arrows and sprinkled in ash, a few anguished over bent limbs or tried to staunch gashes in their heads or torsos.

A woman was looking up at her with an arrow in her neck. Her helmet had fallen away and her auburn hair was fanned out over the bloody armor. She held a gloved fist up to Sidna in some gesture and unfolded her fingers as if to give her something.

Maybe it was the gods sending a message, or perhaps the dying woman was delirious. But Sidna somehow realized that she wouldn't have a chance unless she made one.

I am not fodder. Not for the Septunites, and not for the Apogee. Sidna looked at the troops ahead of her. One after the other, they staged a feeble affront against the enemy only to have a variety of weapons chop and hack them off the walls.

The battlemage ahead was too quick to be taken by another Federal's attempt. Slick as can be, the Septunite blade struck the head from the neck. The man's body fell over the ladder. Catching the head in his arms, the battlemage cradled it like a baby, never minding how it bled over his hips.

«Sing of your end to us, little one,» the battlemage cooed to its working face. The Federal head, kept magically alive, was held toward the ladder climbers. In the tortured mind of that victim somewhere between life and death, a song formed, and it took shape at the end of a purple tongue.

The sound crushed away all other noise of arrows and steel. Without words, the "song" conjured a feeling in listeners that made them wonder if they were already in hell.

Sidna pushed back at the artificial terror that the song evoked. Sleeping fears cropped up in every Federal brain, and the red lightning above feasted more easily. Branches of ruby energy dismantled them into sizzling debris.

The soldiers on the ladder bled from their ears and noses, but Sidna pulled her loaded crossbow from her back. She trained her smeared senses to send a bolt into the Federal's screaming head. The battlemage was astonished and dropped it. The shriek trailed off, alleviating the ladder climbers from their torment.

Fed up with playing prey, Sidna loaded another bolt, fully intending on sending it between the battlemage's teeth above. She climbed furiously with her shield hand in her mad bid to become the aggressor.

Keeping her shield strapped on her left, she managed to turn aside what arrows flew for her. She aligned all the lessons her uncle had recited in the years they spent darting small game in his backwoods property.

The quarrel popped from her weapon. It would have caught the battlemage in the right breast, but a nearby reprobate threw himself in the way, taking the missile.

The battlemage laughed at his fortune and laughed harder when he slipped a small axe from his belt and hurled it down at Sidna. It bit into her shield, and immediately she could sense some magic in it. With a flick of his fingers, the battlemage willed the axe to pull to the side. Sidna's balance was lost, and she fell.

She cartwheeled her arms and caught herself on a wall chain. Thanking all the gods above, she threw her leg over the chain links and hooked her crossbow back onto her belt clip. She was not alone. Her burden made the cadavers on the chain sway like butcher shop product.

She couldn't drop from this distance without dislocating something, nor was the chain connected high enough to make it over the turrets. So she straddled the chain to one of its wall fixtures and pried the stakes out with her shield. Finally the chain fell loose, and holding fast, Sidna fell with it for a few more feet.

With what little remorse she could afford, Sidna removed her sword and cut the hands from the corpses sharing her chain. One by one, the cadavers dropped. Hanging now by a dozen feet of chain, Sidna ran along the wall, building up a swing of movement that she hoped would gain her the top of the wall.

Meanwhile, figures in foreign costume were slowly clambering up the walls. With minds as disciplined as their bodies, the Eurivoneans found footholds in even the barest surfaces. They hugged tightly to the sheer face, grasping at javelins they had thrown themselves or employing metal palm claws.

Clayborn watched in delight as the Septunites appeared oblivious to the imminent threat rising. Before he could praise Calphinas, tangles of red lightning hit the box of the siege tower he pushed. Fear made bombs of the men inside. Arcane explosions ripped the siege tower apart, throwing charred planks spinning over the ranks.

There were probably twenty men in that tower. Suddenly, Clayborn couldn't stop his own legs from tramping angrily for the front lines.

He found the ram squad. They had stopped, and one man was bawling over a bed of ashes where a compatriot used to be. With a kick, Clayborn smashed the man over.

"Sniffle one more time, you bleating jackass!" Clayborn waved over all the men that had noticed his rebuking. "I want to see less piss and more sweat! Get this damn ram moving! More men, get over here!"

Clayborn started the ram by himself, and it moved more easily when a trio of lads joined. The path was bare before them, except for the bodies thrown from above. They could not hesitate and crushed their own dead under the wooden wheels.

"We get this gate open, we win! Don't be just another pawn, make a difference!" Clayborn demanded.

The ram was a woodshed on six stubborn wheels. A roof of sloping boards sheltered the pushers below from arrows, but Clayborn knew the real threat would come when they closed in on the vast doors.

The ram trundled at growing speed. At last, the blunt head of the log touched the tall doors. Grabbing the dowels, Clayborn and his crew heaved back and threw their weight into it.

A tapping on the roof of the ram alarmed Clayborn. Soon oil sloshed over the ram's canopy, drizzling off the sides in long, sticky strands. A moment later, flaming arrows zipped in to hatch a cloud of flames.

"We don't have much time! Push and pull, lads, make it count!" came Clayborn's command over the crackling fire. Other troops moved in. While their comrades held shields up to protect them, they brought lumbering axes to bear against the gate doors. By the way they crunched at the barrier, they appeared to know as well as Clayborn that when the protective ram canopy collapsed, the next oil spill would spell their doom.

A Septunite archer was having an easy day, sending shafts into the green soldiers below. But his surprise was second to none when he was suddenly headlocked by a Federal soldier popping up from the outer wall.

Sidna threw her leg over the wall. Bringing herself in, she kicked the archer's feet up and over, sending him face first down the outer wall.

Ripping out her sword, she realized she may very well have been safer suspended from the chain. Mobs of enemy infantry were fighting for a view at the turrets. She was a mouse among cats.

But that's not how she felt. Knowing how her boys struggled to get up that ladder, Sidna raced down the walkway. Surprisingly, few of the Septunites noticed her, and under the commotion, few responded to the calls to attack her.

The reprobates that did notice were bull-rushed or bypassed. Sidna couldn't afford to be waylaid, she needed to help the lads on the ladder. It was a sight, a woman in green racing for all her worth behind rows and rows of black-clad foes.

At last she reached the ladder. She began a spree of backstabbing. Her blade saw the insides of seven different ribcages by the time she pulled the first Federal onto the walk alongside her.

"Come on! We've made a stand! Get up here!" At last, some progress had been made. Sidna exploded with pride as the first squadron made it over the turrets. She bashed desperately with her shield to make space. Soon, the same battlemage that had menaced her before shoved through the ranks.

His weighty scimitar whacked her shield from side to side. By the time she realized it would be better to team up against this enemy, he pressed her against the turrets. Once again, Sidna felt the awful space beneath her head.

"Our city now! Soon, our country!" He was interrupted as hands armed with palm spikes gripped his face. Sidna thought she recognized the clay-colored muscles of her rescuer.

Azurae clambered right over the battlemage, using her hooked spikes to turn him about on the catwalk. She dislodged from his face and swung her iron spikes through his throat, tossing arterial spray over the reprobates that came too late to aid him.

The first reprobate would have tried his hatchet on the Eurivonean, but her palm spikes found his cheeks. Azurae slipped her hands free, leaving the spikes in his face. She whisked out her twin katar in a course that separated the man's arms from his shoulders.

Azurae simply walked into that wall of spear points and sword edges. With all her parrying and tripping, she made the reprobates look foolish. As they struggled just to keep their footing, she left one after the other on the walk behind her, shivering under their bleeding lacerations.

They would win with this momentum, Sidna realized, shaking her numbed arm. Rejoining her fellows in the other direction, she was overjoyed to see other Sojourners flipping over the walls and plunging into the black rows of Septunites.

Feo labored to transmit magic into the burning storm cloud his master had created. Clutching each of his temples, the oculus tumor on his forehead throbbed.

His vision relayed only smeared colors now, and all he could hear was the creak of his joints. His magic malfunctioned as his arms grew cold and rigid.

But Sanakal was on the far side of the city by now, perhaps he had even escaped. It would have to be enough.

"Forgive me!" Feo dropped his hands and toppled. His oculus tumor burned, heavily fertilized with dark power. He watched as the vortex quickly puffed away its outer layers. He crawled to watch his master's beautiful weapon starve away.

A fat glowing shape from the storm cloud fell among the Federals. It smashed to pieces among their ranks like an egg of red-hot glass. An inky shape tossed ash about in sudden wakefulness.

Feo bit his knuckles, proud at his master. Sanakal had seeded the creature in the firestorm and nursed it with the terror and sorrow of the Federals. He never let anything go to waste.

The creature's mournful face lazily drooled a sluice of glowing lava, as though sick at its own existence. It was something like a giant's torso made entirely from cancer. A lumpy head grievously surveyed this world that angered and frightened it. It floated up, burning entrails hanging from its open waist. One arm was a rope of malignant flesh, ending in muscled jaws. This it extended in sudden hunger.

"You are not welcome here, fiend!" Velena was backpedaling to avoid the lava it vomited. She produced her censer and tore open a portal to her own little piece of the Loom, thrusting the area in mist.

From her cloud came charging something like a giant golden scarab with a rack of diamond horns. It gored the hellbeast only to be thrown aside by its tentacle jaw.

But other light mages followed suit, and soon holy wrath took the shape of a variety of animals that flew, leaped, or stampeded in to combat the Worm of Suffering. Sanakal's creature boasted far greater size, but it was harassed at all angles.

The heat from the ram's burning roof drank away Clayborn's breath. He labored enough to get concerned looks from compatriots in equal danger.

He glanced up to see another crucible of iron overturned. A black sluice stretched down for them in shimmering ribbons. Clayborn screamed his warnings as best he could.

The scalding liquid splashed through the ram's weakened roof and blanketed the whole squad. Soon, the Federals at the door all wore cloaks of flame. The screams spiked just above the roar of the conflagration.

Pain and panic set the captain off. His armor heated up like a potbelly stove while fire clung to his arms and back. He shoved through men like a minotaur. By chance, he found a patch of mud crisscrossed by old cart tracks and threw himself into it.

"Captain!" Velena parked her wheeled shield. The Worm of Suffering was quite occupied with Loom monsters, so she risked rescuing him. She pulled off her cowl and fell upon Clayborn, trying desperately to cover him. "I've got you, I've got you!"

Soon, Clayborn was a steaming rollup of muddied fabric that sucked breath in hoarse gasps. Only his helm was exposed, but it had nearly fallen off. Somewhere between concern and relief, the light mage let a huff that may have been a laugh. Clayborn sat up in his steaming blanket, letting the helm slide off of his face as he looked to the wall.

His ram troops were beyond help. He wanted to shoot to his feet, drag them to the mud that might spare their lives, but the way their blackened hands reached up from the thicket of shivering fire, he knew death would be a kinder fate.

"My lads . . ." he said, spittle in his lips. His head fell back. Even with the arrows pelting the ranks around him, he couldn't muster the will to stand. Though his armor still held a painful heat, it faded, as did his consciousness.

Chapter 45

"What . . . what happened here?" His magic spent, Feo had retired from the balcony to join a squad leader at the gate. He arrived to find his force drastically reduced. Piles of reprobates had been prickled with arrows and dragged off to corners.

"Enemy archers continue to fire on this position from somewhere in the city, my lord. Every time I dispatch a force to hunt them down, they do not return and the arrows keep coming. It is not safe for you to be here!"

"True enough, but the enemy is tired. You are all fresh, more than ready to extinguish their battered forces when this gate breaks. They have no more miracles to help them," Feo assured him.

That's when a four-horse wagon rumbled a few blocks away. A wagon there was, but it was a Cypolonian hauling it, the yoke in his fists. Several clay urns spilling petroleum were his cargo, fixed with burning torches. Still muscled by Sarshel's energy, he prepared to employ his ballistic weapon.

Running ahead, Kaiser swung the yoke aside. The wagon rotated, nearly spilling as Kaiser wedged himself underneath its tilting side. The forward momentum kept it hurtling forth, but now he pressed it from below. The wagon was launched high into the air.

Teams of reprobates watched in horror as the wagon careened above, the greasy liquids flying loose. A crash of wood and clay doused scores of men in petroleum. A second later, the torches fired up the spill. Waves of flame surged in the ranks, thirsty to ignite every drop of the slippery sludge.

Many Septunites were hopelessly immolated. Some twirled madly, but others chose to drive their swords into their own hearts. They became living pillars of fire, throwing cinders in their tragic thrashing.

Feo, who had been tackled to safety by his captain, raised his head to see Kaiser painted in the light of his burning victims, a dagger in one hand and familiar claws on the other. Razor disks that were thrown at him were foiled by slaps from his metal fingers. Reprobates flew to meet him, and Kaiser initiated his brand of tireless butchery.

The gate had held, though flames gnawed anxiously through the planks. However, that did not stop the Federals from teeming over the heights. Green clad Federals began dropping from the heights and charging down the ramps, while those on the walls dropped stones and arrows against the reprobate defenders.

Caethys's hidden archers sent another hail of arrows to kill off another slew of reprobates. The wall above was shuffling with green Federal armor now, and the Sojourners supported them. Kaiser had drawn away a squadron of enemies to dispatch at his leisure, but vowed to return to the greater fight in good time.

By noon, a nimbus of smoke hung above the ravaged city. Colorful magic clawed through the doldrums as Eurivoneans dominated the urban combat.

Federals scoured the city room by room. Ambushes were stomped out, and lone reprobates that surrendered were pulled from hiding and slaughtered. The green army's march was haunted by red footprints.

A pair of muddy battlemages were leading six reprobates. They had been twice their number, but their retreat had been disastrous. They stayed to the quieter parts of the city, avoiding combat. Spying a graveyard, they cut open the gate chains and filed in.

"Praise Opagiel, a graveyard. Our magic will be stronger here," exhaled the battlemage known as Galister. "Nydross, absorb what power you can and divide it among the men. I will prepare to combat them up close."

"You don't mean to make a stand, Galister?! We've got to catch up with Sanakal!" exclaimed the other. The reprobates stood around blinking, as they were not allowed the sort of free thought superiors were. Individuality came with promotion, and not before.

"We aren't joining him, Nydross, we are delaying his pursuers. The hellbringer's survival is what's important," replied Galister.

"We'll be slaughtered, brother! The city is lost, the Kasurites will kill us!"

"Then rejoice that this miserable chapter ends, Nydross! You are happy that we will no longer have to live as humans, aren't you?" Turning wide-eyed to Nydross, Galister put his hand gently around his neck. "We are eaters of fear, do not let your fear eat you. Give your power to the men."

Nydross had heard the same metaphors, mantras, and declarations as Galister had, but at his core, Nydross still appreciated being a living human. It was a sin he could never have disclosed to his comrades.

Nevertheless, he stuck a hellfrost dagger into the soil and invoked the spirits in the air. In a moment, he retrieved the blade. A purple, jellylike substance was squirming over it as though alive. He bid his men to kneel.

"I decorate you in the tears of infidels, that you may decorate yourselves in their blood," Nydross explained. He swung out his arm, speckling them with the sorrow slime.

At the same time, Galister's muscles glowed like electric eels under his skin. It was a strength spell he had only practiced four times in his life, as he was often too exhausted to stay conscious afterward. Today, that wouldn't matter.

There was a solemn creak, and all gazes shot for the smoggy gate. It was Azurae, but to the Septunites she was a battered warrior woman who wore a confident expression like she wasn't outnumbered eight to one.

Tall and imperious with her grand spear, Azurae's muddy hair hung like black vines over her shoulders. Jabbing her spear into the ground, she gathered her hair and tied a ponytail, pulling it tight with strong arm muscles.

"Two, four, six, eight . . ." she counted, a thousand thoughts plying behind those aquamarine eyes. There was little chance of her winning this particular fight. Perhaps none at all, she realized.

A handful of reprobates, even ones that resonated with dark power like these, wouldn't be a problem. But two battlemages would manage to land some critical strikes. No strategy she could think of resulted in anything less than her taking a blade. She plucked her spear and looked over her shoulder.

"The rest will be here soon." She returned her gaze to Nydross. He seemed miserable and frightened. She pointed to him. "You know, you might just survive, if only you run right now. Fast as you can."

"Nydross, remember your oath." Galister's reprimand made it even less appealing, and the next moment the cowardly battlemage was flying off through the headstones. Galister took on a frown as toothy as Azurae's grin.

"Heed the Felsong!" Galister marched to face her. His reprobates doubled his pace, vaulting forth with axes and swords.

Azurae almost looked bored the way she lowered her eyelids to filter distractions from her vision. Taking her spear in both hands, she welcomed their falling strikes with angled blocks that banged their weapons in odd directions. It wasn't long before two reprobates were thrown back by a pair of kicks that shattered their teeth.

The battlemage came on, but Azurae didn't feel ready for him. So she somersaulted over his guard, landing between the two that had been flattened by her kicks. She flicked out one katar with her free hand and, spiraling both weapons, jammed them into either Septunite lying beside her.

Galister put his increased arm strength to use and hurled a small axe at Azurae. Though she blocked it with her spear, it was enough to make her take a step back. She flicked the blood from her katar and returned it to her belt.

With heightened strength, the reprobates lashed out with a sort of recklessness that Azurae was happy to exploit. Her spear rowed thoughtfully, thwarting their strikes with ringing collisions.

A punch she delivered immediately encrusted one reprobate's face in ice. He panicked, unable to breathe, but after Azurae slashed his chest, he no longer needed to.

An axe swung for her head, but she snatched it and redirected it to Galister's shoulder. The squirting abrasion put him on his knees.

From then on, Azurae danced with the three remaining reprobates as their leader clutched his wound. Their attacks carved dangerous slices around her, but her masterful mobility carried her through while calculated strikes injured their legs.

One stumbled, grabbing her leg. The others gripped her arms. Azurae knotted them together with pushing and pulling until all of them were in choke holds. She snapped the first's neck from behind, the second over her shoulder, and the third she had squeezed behind her knee. She gripped her ankle and crunched his vertebrae like a nutcracker. She lay him gently down before her eyes settled on the wounded battlemage.

"I'm sorry," she said, eyes sparkling under her black bangs. "I'll make this quick." Azurae came on with her spear over her shoulder, but Galister slid a hidden dagger across his throat. In moments, his neck and chest were painted red, and he smiled at Azurae with blood in his teeth.

Shaking her head, Azurae stepped past to let him die as he pleased. She scanned the graveyard framed in smoky light. She ran a finger along a headstone, leaving a bare stripe across its filth.

This graveyard would grow in the coming days, she realized. She realized too that she was several blocks ahead of her companions. It was time to rejoin them, in case they were ambushed.

A tombstone with something on top of it drew her attention. A dirty severed arm, still clutching a sword. The weapon was a handsome piece indeed, made of some bronze-colored metal. Coroneum?

Azurae had only ever known one coroneum blade. She took a knee and produced a kerchief, wiping it. She distinctly recalled these saw-toothed lower edges and glyphs carved at the base. Kaiser was certainly too strong to be killed here. But she had to be sure.

She tore open the arm's sleeves to reveal the chalky blue flesh underneath. She knew these scars. She had touched them. She didn't realize she had remembered them so perfectly.

"Of course they got you," she mused.

Azurae recalled then that Kasurites treasured the weapons of the dead. She pulled the sword out of those wriggly fingers and turned back. Looking over the blade, she could see the chips that Shydron Chrasmos had cut into it.

"Fool."

Chapter 46

The fighting turned into hunting by late afternoon. Riding the spirit of victory, young Federals crushed demonic icons, burned flags, and demolished Septunite altars. At the same time, survivors locked down the city. Areas were designated safe or unsafe (several Septunites chose to stay behind laying ambushes). The daylight was easily used up as repairs had to be made and dwellings secured.

It became strangely quiet. Despite the hollers of triumph and misery, Insomnia was quieter than it had ever been. Mounds of rubble were busy with half-naked citizens, searching for family. While many soldiers had the good sense to help them, most paraded by with sloshing wine bottles hooting victoriously.

"I swear to sweet Tethra, I will *gut* you if you take off without me one more time!" Sidna knew full well the tenderness of Caethys's wounds, but she headlocked him anyway. His glittering eyes pleaded for help from the onlookers, but the troops could only laugh in the firelight. None had the energy to face Sidna, the Torch of the Battlefield.

"Kaiser ordered me, I hadn't any choice! I won't . . . I won't do it again!" Caethys was finally released, and Sidna let out an exhilarated sigh. She gathered a few pieces of a chair they had broken for fuel and tossed them onto the fire.

"Nice job, though. The gate defenders were prickly with arrows by the time we got to them," Sidna admitted. "We needed it. These new kids are still delicate."

"I think they're a lot stronger after today, don't you?" Caethys defended, seeing as how some of the newer recruits were listening.

Sidna glanced out at them with her one good eye. "It's not enough for us to be strong. We have to fight smart, you know? Don't think I'm picking on you, because I'm not. I have to learn it too." Stretching her arms, Sidna turned to leave.

"Hold. Won't you have a nip with us, Sid?"

Caethys's invitation halted her. She gazed over her shoulder at the crystal decanter that sloshed with glorious amber liquor. She hoped they didn't hear her whimper.

"Not now. Maybe save some for me?" she asked and left the light of the fire.

Caethys could not recall Sidna turning down alcohol once in their whole friendship. "Mercy. She's injured her brain."

Sidna found Clayborn on a bed in a furnished guestroom. He was lying on his belly so that his healer, a light mage, could apply salve to the blisters on his back and shoulders.

"Who is it?" he asked into the pillows after Sidna had rapped at the door.

"I don't know," replied Velena, who barely glanced away from the work she was doing on Clayborn's sores.

"It's Sidna, Captain. Gods, what happened to you?"

She was met with a groan. "Oil at the gates. I was the lucky one, if you can believe it." He sucked breath as Velena medicated an especially gruesome crater near his backbone. "We never did get those damn gates open. Not even close. What did you do, take the ladders?"

"Yes."

"Damn fool thing to do."

"Weren't many smart choices to make."

"Fair enough. What do you want?" Clayborn was tiring of the conversation already.

Sidna wondered if the light mage would be kind enough to give them some privacy, but she didn't look the patient type. Clayborn needed the medicine anyway. "I'd like to start elite training."

"What? During the campaign? You'll die of exhaustion."

"I know. But I'll be more useful when I'm through."

"That's for sure."

"When are the tryouts? I can be ready any time."

"Don't bother. You're thick, but your record shines like the sun. I'll sign you over in the morning."

Clayborn's comment made Sidna want to hug him, or maybe slap him hard on the back. Either way, she got what she wanted. "Thank you, sir."

She spiraled from the room after a speedy salute. Having considered it for several nights, Sidna was convinced it was the right thing to do. It would likely tear her apart, especially since a year's training would have to be condensed to three or four months. So be it. It would be worth becoming a better soldier. No, a better *protector*.

***

Somewhere among the rescuees was Azurae. Widows, widowers, and orphans were cramming just to touch her shoulder as she gently returned their affections, trying not to smear blood on them, for her arms were decked with it.

It was overwhelming, so many broken people lavishing her with tearful praise. She had penetrated the nightmare that their lives had become, striking off their chains and ripping open cages like a goddess.

It had been many years since she had seen traditional warfare. Once she was adopted by Chrasmos's clan, most of the violence she experienced was at the claws of monsters from the Breach, whom she hunted for honor and balance. Hers was a dead smile today.

She was able to break from the crowd in time. Scanning the teams of Federals, Azurae managed to find several of her compatriots, fixing on one. Meng, that sly, cunning man of eastern complexion who had faithfully followed her to Kasurai. She had not seen him since this morning.

"I don't know why I worried about you, you're too lucky to die." Azurae threw an arm around the man's head, pressing her cheek to his forehead.

"Strategy and luck are bedfellows. I plan to serve you a long time, so I plan to stay alive," Meng declared, smiling chin digging into his patterned scarf.

"All right. Final count?" Azurae looked apprehensive.

"Final count . . . all alive," he reported, unlocking Azurae's tensed shoulders. "The Gray-Dog twins are both bedridden with arrow wounds, but they'll live. Most everyone else came out with less than a few bumps and scrapes."

"My warriors are most genuinely talented." Azurae closed her eyes, reining in excited emotions. "I'm not terribly surprised."

"Yes, I did not foresee things going so well."

"Don't say that too loudly," Azurae advised, hooking her thumbs in her belts as she looked around at gloomy civilians.

"Oh, Executor Kaiser is debriefing his captains, by the way. He wanted the highest ranking Sojourner to attend as well. I suppose you had best get over there."

"Executor Kaiser? Kaiser's alive?"

"Very." Meng noted a tremble that played on Azurae's chin.

"Ah, but he must be horribly wounded." She remembered the arm.

"No, he looked spry enough to me. What did you hear?"

Azurae pulled Seriath a little way from her belt and examined the details again, trying to disprove what she had figured. "I must be losing my mind. Make sure the warriors all get something to eat, Meng. Have them bed in the large property four blocks east. I made sure to claim it." Azurae excused herself.

Meng spied the furnished mansion in the distance. "Ah, continental beds. Yes, teacher."

***

It was obvious that Kaiser's time with the Archaics had influenced him in the way he proudly wore his enemy's blood. His officers were not accustomed to being debriefed by a man in such shambles (or raveled in barbed wire). Kaiser didn't even bother to stand as they encircled him. He palmed his forehead, reclining on the steps of the governor's headquarters.

"We lost too many men to strengthen the front. We must consolidate until barbarian reinforcements arrive. I'm calling for the frontline troops to fall back. As the barbarians trickle in, they'll cover the retreat," Kaiser said.

"How soon can we expect the barbarians?" asked one.

"About a month or so."

"Bah, they can hardly track the seasons. We can't plan according to their estimates," another put in. "Sanakal could make another attempt on the city in that time."

"A notion I myself have pressed," Prince Norinthe added, toying with a leash. At the end of it was Feo, blindfolded on his knees with tied hands. The young apprentice did not make a sound.

Kaiser sneered at the strange bondage. "Impossible. Sanakal's magic has been crippled, and three-quarters of his army lay dead in our streets. Now from this city, we will intercept enemy incursions with Archaics until our Federal veterans are healed, rested, and fed."

Norinthe scowled. "It's a pity. Once again we must fight defensively."

"Not for long. Before spring, we'll have enough barbarians to retaliate. We are going to root out hellbringers with force, then assassinate them with Sojourners. This will tear the heart out of their demon magic and make them vulnerable by the time Colygeus can march through with the Acolytes in a year or so."

"A good plan in theory. But you depend heavily on barbarian loyalty," returned the prince.

"I depend on their zeal, and Archaics are nothing if not zealous. If I feed them glory, they'll die for me."

Azurae materialized, absorbing stares as she entered the circle.

Kaiser's glance was deliberately brief. "In short, Insomnia is our forward barracks, the stake of our efforts that must never be uprooted."

"Is that all?" Norinthe asked.

"You were all brilliant today. And you, Prince Norinthe, capturing a hellbringer's apprentice, excellent indeed." Kaiser nodded, running dusty fingers through his hair.

They retired, the prince and his bodyguards brutalizing Feo. Azurae remained while the rest walked off. Kaiser felt more prepared to fight Akanis again than to speak with her.

"Pardon. It felt prudent to speak with you," she said.

"I'm sappy to hee you—" Kaiser took a slow, deep breath and tried again. "I'm happy to see you, Azurae."

"Executor Kaiser. I reasoned you might figure prominently in all of this, but an Executor? I'm not sure how much formality I should exercise," Azurae admitted, trying not to stare at his arm.

"Neither do I. You crossed a lot of land and sea to help fight this battle. My thanks must come as little reward." Kaiser shuffled through a million things to say.

"We're here to safeguard liberty. No reward is needed. But we are very excited about the clean beds." Azurae joked, but she began to realize herself just how much she had to censor her words.

"Have at them, by all means. It was a day from hell, and I really could not be more pleased that you're here and that you're safe." Kaiser stopped himself.

"I can empathize. Just moments ago, I still thought you were dead." Her large eyes took on a grateful sheen.

"Heh, not yet. Not quite yet." Kaiser watched as she pulled his sword from her belt. He brightened to see it had been recovered, but then remembered the circumstances in which he had left it. "Ah."

"I knew this sword to be yours, more by the dead hand that gripped it than by the make itself." She offered it in both hands to Kaiser. "It was . . . it was your arm I saw there." Now she failed to resist glancing at his arm. Kaiser just gently took Seriath from her hands and slid it through his own belt.

"I expect you would be puzzled. I'm puzzled myself."

"How did you recover from something like that?"

"I want to understand it, but I don't. You mustn't tell anyone about what you saw, Azurae."

"As you wish. I won't say a word." It felt like the end of the conversation, so she palm-fist bowed and began stepping away.

"I'm . . ." He started, trying to keep her from leaving, but he hadn't the slightest idea what to say. Her stare turned his thoughts to mud. "Nothing. Never mind."

"Please get some rest, Executor. You must be tired as well." She left.

Chapter 47

"We had never been so close to breaking the Apogee's back. And you, you lose Insomnia! The very crux of our plan!" Festel's echoes flew high in the Cathedral of Joy, or as its current occupants had christened it, the Cathedral of Pain.

It was here the greatest hellbringers squirmed under the direction of Sinra. She surveyed the accusations from a high window's ledge.

She had quit ritual meditation years ago. People said it was because projecting her soul into the underworld, as hellbringers do, was redundant; hell was inside her now. Nor did she sleep. She was slavishly present, positioning every pawn with an attentiveness that no four generals could hope to rival.

And for all her pawns, she had yet to meet one as tall as her. She was a proud seven feet and more, every inch of her bandaged in strips of linen like a mummy, which was changed by blind, tongueless eunuchs every seven days. Aside from her eyes and her oculus, the only aspect of her free of the linen was her gray hair, worn as long as men are tall.

The subject of scrutiny tonight was Sanakal, who knelt before a row of his elders on the altar. He had brought wailing offerings here in the past, to Sinra's quiet delight. Now, he could feel his victim's spirits jeering him in this hour of disgrace.

"And now they have time to assemble their barbarian allies! You have cost us *months*, Sanakal! And thousands of soldiers!" Festel's oculus beamed orange with joy disguised as outrage. He was in position to inherit Sanakal's authority.

"I have conquered Insomnia once already. I can take it again. Please let me redeem myself, brothers," Sanakal tried, his harlequin lips downturned.

Sinra said nothing.

"You are broken! It will take too long for you to calibrate a new Pylon. Until you are reconnected to the Pool, you are useless!" Festel countered.

"Useless?!" Sanakal stood, all black teeth and pink gums. "Is Opagiel's cup not filled with tears I have stolen? Have I earned no lenience for the rainbow of suffering I have painted in Her name?"

There was a great cracking noise from the altar. The hellbringers scurried off as heat flared. A black hulk pushed upright from the broken stone, strands of hissing lava dripping off its sides. It was the same sarcophagus that had taken Kasurite nobles and holy men to the eternal appetites below.

Sanakal paled, looking up to see Sinra's triad of red eyes pinned on him.

"Before Velucephes was chancellor of Septunoth, he and I raised up the weak, eventually grooming the world's finest sorcerers." Her mesmeric voice threaded into his brain. "And now, we are all strong. Except you." Latches on the coffin unlocked, and the lid split open like the arms of a poisonous lover. "Get in."

Sanakal's unique brand of sight settled on the gaping sarcophagus. It promised suffering that would intensify forever and ever. But wasn't that bliss? To become one with Opagiel through holy pain?

It was over. It was time to have ultimate faith. He stepped upon the altar.

"Wait."

Whoever it was that spoke, they curdled Sanakal's blood. He did not look. His brethren were clasping their amulets and mouth breathing like fools. Sanakal could burn a village with his own hatred, but what he felt in the presence behind him made him yearn for the safety of the hellbound coffin.

"Heretic! You dare show yourself in Sinra's presence?!" Festel had found his courage at length, doubtless using spells to keep his composure.

Sinra seemed unmoved by the intrusion.

"I would know the fate of my Disciple," the stranger voiced. But something in his inflection suggested he already knew everything.

Sanakal licked his lips.

"Akanis was defending my Pylon when it was destroyed. It can be assumed that he was martyred."

A hand slid onto Sanakal's shoulder. It was gentle.

"Sinra. This one is weak, but wise. Give him to me, that I may strengthen my remaining Disciples." The stranger's breath was winter wind on Sanakal's neck.

"You would have the servitude of a hellbringer? Even a broken one holds secrets you have no right to learn," Festel reminded the stranger.

"Those are the only secrets worth learning," the visitor returned.

Sinra finally seemed invested. She flexed her bandaged fingers, which crunched cadaverously as the stranger gazed up at her.

"Take him, then. And I should think we are mended, Thel," she replied.

Sanakal was whirled around. His tall, new master was a man of obscene beauty, almost mythical with his upswept eyes and high cheek bones. He wore his dark hair in braids that hung like serpent tails off either side of his head, separated by the fingers of black metal on his headpiece that resembled horns.

Seemingly eager to violate his handsomeness was a central, vertical seam running from crown to chin. Rivets of flesh marched up his countenance as if his beauty was the product of a seamstress.

Festel's oculus was dilating. This cult prophet, this *Thel*, represented a brand of faith that flew in the face of Septunoth's church. Why Sinra suffered his blasphemy, Festel fretted to know. But Festel had no more scolding to give. He would avoid Sanakal's sorry fate at any cost. And like his brothers, he took leave of the chamber.

For his part, Sanakal was uncertain how to act, subscribing to gracious servility. "Gratitude, new master. You have saved me from death this day."

Thel put his cold hand on Sanakal's heart. "Have I?"

***

Days later and still stiff from battle, Kaiser exited the governor's mansion at sunrise. As always, the Sojourners were in the city square in front of a lion fountain that had failed to issue water since the occupation.

They were put to work tutoring Federals in nature magic, and Kaiser could already see some progress. The young soldiers looked invariably surprised to see that this power had always been theirs when energy played at their fingertips. It would be a long time before it was battle applicable, however.

Azurae was speaking with a compatriot. Her native language was so lyrical Kaiser couldn't be sure if she was lecturing or reciting poetry.

Kaiser would have watched, but it was to be another busy day. He strode to a ramshackle forge situated behind a small barracks. It was a hilariously messy place, its walls little more than metal sheets bolted to posts while tools and materials were scattered to some weapon master's whim.

"Briston? Briston." Kaiser knocked gently on one of the panels.

"Good morning," muttered an old man who approached from the alley. He sported white madman's hair while liver-spotted arms swayed from his dirty tunic. He set a lunch pail on the railing. Pulling an apron from a nail on the post, he continued in an Archaic accent, "Briston sleep too much. I wake him." The old man disappeared into the forge.

Kaiser heard him holler at the boy for his laziness. Metal rattled, but soon the curtains were thrown open. Briston emerged, fastening his own apron.

"Kaiser! So sorry, Executor, I didn't hear you arrive!" The boy's eyes were almost as red as the handprint scar on his cheek. They widened a bit, as they always did, when they laid upon the Defender's Mantle that sat gracefully over Kaiser's uniform.

"No worries. I was just concerned about my dear Seriath. Have you finished her?" Kaiser wiped a little bath water from behind his ear.

"Oh, yes, indeed." Briston whirled back behind the curtain. There was another tirade from the old man. This time Briston retaliated with defensive hollers. Briston returned proudly bearing Seriath in both hands, only this time, the hilt was blue rather than red.

"Well, she looks nice. Was the tang bent like I feared?"

"No, actually the hilt was just falling apart. So I reconstructed one from materials I had laying around to feel just like your old one." Briston was hoping that his choice was alright.

"Oh, fine. I was afraid the metal was breaking."

"Heh, you can't really break coroneum."

"Not on Septunite skulls, anyway." Kaiser took a moment to give it a few slow swings. It felt wonderfully solid. "That'll do fine. How's old man Norving treating you?" Kaiser glanced into the shop where the old man was deafly stoking coals.

"He's a little intense. But a good teacher. I really appreciate you getting me an apprenticeship."

"He's in high demand, so don't waste his time. Get up earlier, and you'll get more practice. You're a good smith, but I need a great smith." Kaiser tried to mix discipline with encouragement. Strangely, Briston never seemed to grieve, so the Cypolonian wasn't quite sure how to treat him.

"I promise I will. I really do work hard."

"I know, I know." Kaiser reached into a small satchel, not seeming to care how many coins he grabbed and slammed it into Briston's skinny hand. "That'll cover it, right?"

Briston sorted the currency with his fingers. Federal king-silvers, the largest amount he'd ever seen, let alone possessed. "Yes, about ten times, actually."

"Well, buy Norving a haircut then." Kaiser's reply put Briston at ease.

"A thousand thanks, Executor. Where are you off to now?"

That's when Kaiser noticed green light in a distant cellar window. "Hunting for Septunite stragglers. I think I just found some." He nodded and left Briston to his work.

Kaiser stalked to the leaf-littered stairwell. Rust had stained the concrete. The door at the bottom was peeling.

The glass was rippled, so he couldn't tell what was inside. He thought about using the knob but decided to simply kick the door open. It swung in with a crash, exposing Kaiser to a wet cellar dimmed by neglect. He scanned the racks and shelves.

Grain sacks hunkered in the spidery corners. Kaiser could hear mice shuffling inside them. He walked into the rows of wine racks. Most bottles had been stolen away, but a few spirits remained bottled fast.

As he considered touching one, something pricked his senses. Seriath was primed like a scorpion tail as he investigated.

With eyes accustomed to parting the darkness, he spied a great store of lumber set against the far wall, but no enemy. There was no way for anyone else to enter except the door he used. Even so, a voice.

"Kaiser." It addressed him from the air itself. His eyes went gold and his blade flushed with the heat of primal magic.

The darkness *wrinkled*. Strange matter bled in from another world, like light filtered through swamp water. It was not infernal magic, but certainly something unearthly. Kaiser could feel his soul thwarting a presence. Something was trying to examine him.

"You've been busy, haven't you, Kaiser?" They were the words of a young man, but strangely frayed. Kaiser silently watched as strands of essence weaved together a human likeness. Ectoplasm slithered over the form, hinting at youthful features.

A Septunite spirit perhaps. Divine magic would be most appropriate. Kaiser began powering up the Defender's Mantle. As he took on the awesome light of the Covenant, the phantom raised a hand.

"No need for that."

"You know my name." Kaiser was eager for answers.

"Your reputation is fast spreading west, Kaiser, by Kasurites and even by Septunites, albeit with less reverence."

"So which are you?" Kaiser murmured, poised for a hasty exorcism.

"Neither. I am a product of Ixolil's short-sighted ingenuity. I was hoping we could strike a bargain?"

Kaiser had to dig through his mind for facts about an Ixolil. Each one he found put more lines in his frown. A goddess, but not one from the Covenant.

"Ixolil's an exodeity, and crazy, even for their kind. I don't think I care to talk to you."

"Given our confrontation a while back, I shouldn't expect you to."

"What are you talking about?" Kaiser asked.

"Not that I hold it against you, but you did skewer me, cut off my arm, and decapitate me."

"I'm afraid you'll have to be more specific." Admittedly, Kaiser had to think back hard on his lengthy list of victims. He adroitly remembered most men he killed, but one memory did stand out.

"Now you remember," the phantom cooed as the realization swelled Kaiser's veins. The phantom's eyes even glimmered with the same aberrant green light . . .

"You're that *thing* Clayborn and I fought in that hidden laboratory outside Evanthea!? *You're* what we unleashed from that iron face!?"

"I cannot thank you enough for that, by the way. I've been sealed away since you were a twinkle in your great-great-grandmother's eye. My name is Izlou." The specter took a shallow bow.

"Well, Izlou. Which hell am I sending you to this morning?" Kaiser took a menacing step forward. Izlou's effigy seemed unmoved.

"Any hell's preferable to the one you're putting me through," the phantom remarked. Kaiser was perturbed, but Izlou's easy demeanor made him curious.

"What do you want?"

"To cooperate, you excitable thing. Do I look vengeful to you? Come now, let's observe some of the etiquette these Federals are so taken with." Izlou expressed nothing in the way of aggression.

Kaiser lowered his sword. "You're no demon at least. Go on."

"The cursed ice in which I was encased has left me terribly weak, and thanks to you, I don't even have a body any more. If you provide me with another host body, I would be happy to divulge what I know about Septunite movement."

"A host body?" Kaiser's nostrils upturned. "That's a bold request."

"Well, it doesn't have to be Kasurite. I know for a fact that you're a leading producer of Septunite corpses. The more you help me, the more I'll disclose about Septunite strategy."

The concept made Kaiser think. "Why doesn't Ixolil help you?"

"We are . . . estranged."

Izlou's admittance elevated the Cypolonian's suspicions. "What? Was the goddess Ixolil your bride or something?"

"Shocking, I know. I'm barely in my third millennium, too young for that sort of commitment."

"Are you hiding from Ixolil?" The phantom seemed reluctant. "She's trying to find you, isn't she?"

"You have no need to be concerned, Kaiser. Remember, she's *not* a Covenant deity. Helping me wouldn't violate any of your precious principles."

Kaiser had to think for a moment, scratching at his short beard. "Why did you choose to approach me? Why not ask a hellbringer? They're fantastically powerful."

"There's no help to be had from those soul-brokers. They would feed me to Opagiel first chance they get." Izlou touched his cheek in exaggerated concern.

"Yes, they probably would."

"Besides, infernal magic is all about suffering. Too one dimensional. You however, have unlimited resources and everything to gain by my knowledge."

"I'll have to think about it, Izlou. I'd hate to turn an exodeity's wrath on Kasurai if she discovers our work together."

"I understand. But think on it. I'll contact you again."

"Very well," Kaiser agreed, turning.

"Oh, and Kaiser . . . keep our dealings private. Or my offer is voided, and I keep the Septunite secrets to myself."

"How can I be sure you even know anything?"

"In the northeastern part of this city, in the sewers beneath the mansion with the cherry trees, eight Septunite swordsmen and two battlemages are planning to surface tonight and abduct citizens for sacrifice."

Could that really be? Kaiser wondered.

"That one's on the house. Farewell." With that, the phantom soaked back into the gloom like green ink into a midnight swamp.

The Executor was left to his thoughts, scratching the back of his head. "Decisions, decisions . . . ," he muttered.

***

Hope was cropping up again the weeks following Insomnia's siege. In addition to helping with reconstruction, Federal troops formed choirs to help sing the citizens back to peace of mind. But that was something this generation of Insomniacs would never really know again.

Naturally, panic exploded when an exodus of warriors was spotted snaking in from the north. But the oncoming army was identified as friendly, and the calm returned.

Clayborn had not used his breastplate while his back burns healed, but a barbarian magnate heading the army demanded to speak with someone in charge. Clayborn was armored and at the gate in moments.

A pair of bodyguards emerged from the side portcullis, flanking Clayborn. He came face to face with the grisliest lot he had seen since the Archaic negotiations.

"Greetings. Lord Tibernas, isn't it? I remember you, we're elated to have you join us." Clayborn heaped on the cordiality. The tall, mustached, dreadlocked warrior-lord he was addressing seemed none too cheery.

"Why do they send out this fat man? Where is Tireless Butcher?" the man growled in a voice salty as sea brine. War mementos jingled as his tattooed arms crossed.

Clayborn chuckled, knowing full well barbarians liked to antagonize Federals to gauge their character.

"Executor Kaiser will return in a few days. He is raiding Septunite outposts to the west. But he is eager to meet with you when he returns. Please, let's bring your men inside. You must all be very tired." Clayborn's reply did not uncross the magnate's arms.

"Insomnia. I see arrow marks in the stone. I smell old blood. What has happened here?" Tibernas suspected a trap. Clayborn was careful to remain calm.

"A lot has happened. We discovered the city occupied by Septunites. Through sabotage and siege, we reclaimed it. The cost was grievous, so we're all relieved th—"

"A siege? You assaulted this city, took it back? In so many days?" Tibernas interrupted, unconvinced.

"That's correct." Clayborn stood firm. "We even sent a hellbringer running, tail tucked." He folded his arms this time.

"Defeated a hellbringer . . ." Tibernas wondered thoughtfully. He produced a canister and opened it, dipping his fingers into the green powder and poking a bit into either nostril. He rubbed a little more onto his gums where some gold teeth glittered. He nodded finally. "Well done, fat man. But we will top that, by Zothre, in the days to come. Right, lads?"

His men answered with a thunderous bark. Clayborn waved to the gate master. The portcullis unplugged from the stone slots and raised. The warriors lumbered inside.

But Tibernas himself climbed back onto his horse alongside a party of his greater warriors. He rumbled off something in a barbarian dialect and the riders turned about, poised to ride again.

"Wait, Lord Tibernas, you're leaving? Why?" Clayborn trotted after them.

"I agreed to meet Kaiser in person. If he is out west, then that is where I must go." Tibernas took a deep breath as the refreshing buzz of his drug powder took effect.

"But he'll be back in just a few days! Please, stay."

"Be assured, your city is safe so long as my ten-handers are here. They are sworn to never lose a battle. Never, Federal!" Tibernas kicked his spurs. He and his posse fired off then to whatever destiny they damn well pleased.

Chapter 48

With her knees up to her chin, Sidna waited inside the barrel, breathing quiet so she could hear the signal noise. She had been curled up like this for an hour, and her legs tingled unbearably.

A clanking sound perked her ears. A cage opening. Peering through the tap hole, she made a final evaluation, and carefully lifted the lid from the barrel.

She pulled her sleeping legs out and quietly replaced the lid. She set to work jimmying a loose brick from the wall, hot breath puffing in the night air. It unplugged in moments, and she checked around the corner.

A spearman with layers of padding tied around his helmet glanced in her direction. Panic put speed in her arm, and she crashed the brick against his temple. With an irritated grunt, the guard imitated coma and tipped. Sidna claimed his long weapon. His wooden sword and keys also found their way into her belt.

She whisked down the alley, barefoot in nightclothes. She came upon a set of bars and discretely worked the key in the padlock. She opened it just enough to slip through, resetting the lock to delay possible pursuers.

A door lay between her and the wooden stairway ahead. Before she could make her dash, a guard swung through the door (a surprise). She jabbed her spear tip for his throat. The padded blade thumped his trachea. He croaked, and she successfully caught him.

But she failed to notice the bottle. It slipped from his fingers and crashed on the wooden floorboards.

"Damn you!" she whispered, tiptoeing barefoot through the broken glass for the staircase. Another guard at the top received a javelin toss of Sidna's spear. He caught it and fell to imitate death. Sidna raced up the stairs to catch him before he made noise. She whisked out her wooden sword and slid it across his throat to finalize the kill.

She turned onto a catwalk where two guards were tying a noose next to a kneeling prisoner. Her footfalls drew their attention. One drew a practice sword, but received her flying knee too quickly. She collided her blade with the second soldier's padded helmet. He dropped, and she jabbed the floored one to finish him.

Throwing the noose's slack off the catwalk, she took the rope in her hands and gripped the prisoner under the arms with her legs. Her cramping muscles complained to bear all the extra weight down the rope.

But she made it to the ground and, hefting the skinny prisoner over her shoulder, made for the horse tied against a nearby post. The prisoner feigned extreme weakness, so she had to help him onto the saddle. She untied the horse and threw herself on behind him and flicked the reins.

She steered it for the arch across a plaza, where a guard was racing to drop the portcullis. If he reached the lever, the gate would drop and halt their escape. Sidna cracked her palm against the horse's rump. She had to use her other arm to keep the limp prisoner from tipping out of the saddle.

And as she shot through the arch, her legs relaxed and her mind lightened.

"*Yes!*" She shrieked, turning the horse about. In moments, she reentered the arch to meet up with all the mock guards and the tablet-wielding elite trainer.

"Gods, Sidna, you nearly killed me with that blow to the throat," complained the man that had portrayed the bottle-dropping guard.

"You're supposed to go for the throat so they can't scream, Jeven. Read the book for once." She swung off the horse. She turned to the trainer. "All right, don't sugarcoat it."

"Seven out of ten. You need eight out of ten to pass, Sidna."

"Son of a . . . !" She stopped herself, knowing the trainer took outbursts as a slip of discipline. "It was the bottle, wasn't it?"

"And you're too loud on the catwalk. Your stomping almost gave the hangmen enough time to kill the prisoner," he recited, lifting a page of his notes. "Same problem you had last time. When you get close to your objective you panic. You need to stay focused."

Sidna would have loved to punch each of them in the face, even the prisoner. But she was slowly learning how to save up her anger for constructive purposes.

"Then let's do it again."

***

"Why can't the Septunites horde real loot? This sorcery garbage doesn't fetch a tin coin in mountain country." Tibernas spit on the array of fiendish weapons that had been recovered from the raid.

"The Church is experimenting with redeeming demonic weapons, hoping to step up our presence in the arms race. We'll collect a chunky bounty on today's winnings." Kaiser looked relaxed; the day's skirmishes had left scores of Septunites dead and added half again their number in freed prisoners.

But Tibernas still grumbled. Kaiser didn't stop him as the magnate gripped one of the battlemage swords. His teeth suddenly glowed like coals. Kaiser wasn't sure if it was the metal curdling or Tibernas's growl he heard as the magnate's teeth sunk into the metal.

The blade burst under the pressure, sending sparks skittering into Tibernas's dreadlocks. The fire here would not hurt him however, because it was *his* fire, *his* primal magic.

"Tastes like cowardice." Tibernas spit a steaming metal shard.

Kaiser turned to the Federal troops that hefted the body of a battlemage. They were adding to the vast grave pit haunted by a halo of crows.

"Not that one."

Tibernas watched the Cypolonian hoist the body over his own shoulder.

"You going somewhere?"

"Don't follow me," Kaiser ordered.

"What are you going to do with that?"

"Practice a sword technique. Need a body," Kaiser answered dismissively.

Moments later, Kaiser was alone with the body in the dirt, its hands crossed at the chest and bound in manacles. He had removed the chest plate and produced a dagger. He sliced open the shirt where a spear wound had penetrated the ribcage. Kaiser dabbed a cloth to his sweating brow and used it to wipe the dried gore from the wound.

"Are you here or what?" Kaiser sighed, looking around.

"Present," came the airy voice of Izlou. A faint imprint in the air took on features that implied Kaiser's acquaintance.

"We did good again today, thanks to your information. Remember the second part of the deal. I do this, and you tell me where the Septunite 115th Shock Army is." Kaiser pointed his dagger at the specter.

"If this one works," Izlou corrected.

"Why can't you use just any body?"

"Only battlemages and similar spell casters have a chrysm fertile enough for me to commandeer. Now please, I must make a connection with his departing soul so that I can be pulled into the body."

Kaiser pricked his finger tip with the dagger. He dabbed little red dots at six points around the wound.

"Perfect." Izlou said as his own essence funneled into the earth.

A tiny black plant curled out of the dirt. Its bud snapped open, and a seed like a green pearl hummed with the majority of Izlou's soul.

"Please, there's no time." Izlou's bodiless voice sounded agonized.

Kaiser prayed to Tethra in his mind one last time that he was not making a huge mistake and plucked out the seed. He placed it in the spear wound. "Izlou, take residence in this mortal clay, by my invitation."

His designation made the eddies of magic shudder and enfold the spirit of Izlou. The Cypolonian watched as the smell of charged ectoplasm played strangely in his nostrils.

The dots of blood skittered into the wound. Emerald light pulsed from the corpse's skin like a gentle storm as Izlou made millions of connections between nerve and muscle and bone. The only thing that really confused Kaiser was the way the corpse's hair slowly turned a clean silver gray.

The fingers twitched, and the whole body shivered as the dead tissues were resuscitated. If the skin was pale before, it went ghost white now. The only color it harbored was under the eyes, where strange workings flushed it black.

Izlou's new eyes opened green. He eventually recognized Kaiser observing his revival with an unreadable grimace. Izlou managed to coordinate a smile and lifted up his arms to try a stretch.

"Looks like it went well enough," noted Kaiser.

"Oh!" Izlou jolted a little and touched the wound at his ribs. "Kill the next one more gently."

"All right, give me the truth." Kaiser gripped the man's cuffed wrist, preparing to gauge his honesty by his pulse. In a moment, the Cypolonian went cold. "Gods, you don't have a heartbeat, Izlou."

"Because I'm not alive." Izlou chuckled. "I can repair, sustain, and even strengthen this body, but I can't do it naturally." He sat up with little difficulty. Kaiser looked increasingly uncomfortable.

"What unnerves me is that there's nothing stopping you now from breaking our deal." Kaiser's hand drifted to the hilt of Seriath.

"The 115th is camped just south of the ruins of Castle Teravina. Feel better?"

"You're a free man now. But do yourself a favor, and never, never consort with Septunites," Kaiser warned, standing. "They will ply you with promises. Do as I do, and take the words of dead men with caution."

"You're so certain I'll betray you. But there's so much more I need you to do for me. I don't mind telling you who's where when, because I think we'll both have what we want in the end." Izlou held out his cold hand, and Kaiser dropped into it the key to the manacles.

Chapter 49

The sky was a turbid gray stew that breezy day, contrasting the autumn-dappled trees. They fanned in the same breeze that carried fresh forest scent into the busied heights of Insomnia.

Clayborn was enjoying his rounds on the wall entirely too much. The colors abroad, the cool air, and the rapid healing of his back burns lit a twinkle in his eyes usually only present when hounding troops into compliance.

He imagined that when Kaiser's van approached, it would be with an air of victory. But the refugees and soldiers scurried like muddy rats when they first appeared in the distant rocky woodland. Almost as if something was chasing them.

"Get those gates open," he called to the guards below. He rang the bell for more sentries to man the wall.

Families herded through the gate carrying hastily packaged belongings. Tibernas's men were among them, perhaps one for every four refugees. Clayborn could only imagine the strain on housing that would ensue.

Tibernas was among the crowd, governing the flow with menacing authority. The magnate wore a dour demeanor fueled by the ruckus.

"Magnate! Who are these people?!" Clayborn thundered.

"They are all that's left of Turningham!" came the reply. What had just seemed a great many people suddenly seemed far too scant. Turningham was a city equal to Insomnia in size.

"Where's the Executor?!"

"Bringing up the rear! The wounded are straggling!" At Tibernas's answer, Clayborn peered over the turrets to find the end of the staggered parade. Roving through the forests behind them were enemies aplenty.

"Damn it all," Clayborn voiced, recognizing Kaiser's mantle even at this far distance. He was on foot, escorting a wagon being pulled by slow horses.

It was unclear what sort of enemy was chasing them exactly, or how many. But if two brutes like Kaiser and Tibernas had chosen fleeing over fighting, Clayborn had to assume the worst.

There was a huge gap between the main body of the Turningham survivors and the wounded still a distance out. Gulping down the protesting lump in his throat, Clayborn addressed his underlings again below.

"Seal the gates, do it now!"

Tibernas was already off his horse when he heard Clayborn's order. Hemmed in by escapees, he was powerless to stop the vast doors from closing. But he plowed his way to the stairs, climbed them, and gave Clayborn a strong slam to the jaw.

"Fat fool! Open the gate, our Executor is still outside!"

Clayborn steadied and thumbed some blood from his nostril. "You're the fool, Magnate! We cannot risk enemies reentering the city!" Tibernas threw another punch, but Clayborn swatted it away and clocked the barbarian off of his feet.

"Kaiser is out there! Are we to let him die?!" Tibernas argued, regaining his legs.

"Kaiser is the one who ordered these gates sealed if enemies break the tree line! I'm not going to endanger Insomnia again for anyone, barbarian!" Clayborn turned from him then and watched the crisis unfold.

"Tethra, they've already locked the gate," Caethys huffed, having handed off his horse to an old couple long ago.

"These bastards would have caught us before we reached it. We're going to have to fight them." Kaiser roared to halt atop a stony mound with scraggly trees. He commanded all noncombatants inside the wagons. While fleeing in armor was enough to make anyone tired, it was his spirit that was crushed; this was not a fight he could win. By his expression, Caethys knew it as well.

"They're barbarians, hired out by the Septunites. They won't have much in the ways of black magic," Caethys figured.

"They won't need it, with their numbers. Treacherous rats must breed well in the west."

"That is a lot of hired swordsmen. And pikemen. And cavalry."

"I'm sorry, Caethys. I can't tell you how sorry I am."

"Time enough for apologies at Tethra's table. Be the man that they say you are, and help me protect these people," Caethys asked with a gentle glow to his fine features.

Kaiser arranged Caethys and the soldiers into a line of twenty along the incline of the mound. Behind them were the wagons, stocked so full of wounded and elders that many lay underneath or behind.

"In case you are unclear as to our task . . ." Kaiser began, his men trying to listen as a hurricane of killers neared, "we are here to punish these barbarian traitors. Treachery, after all, is something all of our gods detest. That we can protect these elders and children at our backs is happy coincidence."

With that, they kneeled to him as he took Seriath up in both hands for the blessing. Something like blue sunlight crackled through his Defender's Mantle, and the rays shot over his soldiers. Kaiser had graced them in the same way many times in the past weeks. It absolutely cemented their souls with courage. Doubt and anything like it became a forgotten dream. They felt ready to fight for days.

"Once again, the valor of the Apogee's late heroes is in us. Once again, we honor their legacy, and shape our own," Caethys put in, and he was the first to draw his saber. The rest did the same. Kaiser walked down their line and ignited each weapon with holy magic by striking it with his own.

"Stay alive, until *they* are not," Kaiser finished, taking up the spare shield Caethys had been holding for him.

The enemies were like heaps of metal, decorated with the rusty scrap of wasteland battlefields. Their hair and body modifications were Septunite inspired, severe and gothic. In their staggered march, their group was long as the city walls.

Trudging along with them was a giant cat-beast with an extensive neck, outfitted as a living weapon.

"Tethra, watch over my foolish friend." Clayborn pulled his oathkey from his belt and kissed it, watching a flood of killers surge meet the defenders.

The mob steered pikes into the defenders on the incline. Kaiser's shield fell like a portcullis, snapping the heads from the weapons. His defenders jutted in, avalanching like angels with glowing swords.

Caethys unlocked enemy defenses with meditative finesse and tapped wellsprings of hot blood from chinks in their armor. He was almost gentle in the way he ruined them and tilted them away.

Throwing hatchets bit into Federal armor. The defenders reflexively pulled them out, forgetting the injuries at once. Their clockwork martial arts dismantled lines of attackers, making the rock shelves droop with dripping bodies.

Even in his heaven-powered valor, Kaiser's grim perspective refused to be silenced. His men were gaining injuries, whether they acknowledged them or not. Above the skirmish he could see the river of wicked barbarians flowing in.

Having earned a wide berth, Kaiser addressed the screams up the hill. Raising its halo of antlers on a long neck was the barbarians' *megalynx*. Once they were worshiped as cat-headed demigods of the western deserts by nomads. This specimen however, had been tortured into a tall, ferocious man-eater.

The megalynx had locked its arm-length teeth onto the wagon and pulled the load toward the edge while war trophies dangled from its antlers. Children inside screamed their lungs empty.

Kaiser shoved through his defenders to the wagon, stabbing Seriath into the earth to catch the yoke poles. The great cat growled at its halted progress. Kaiser climbed atop the wagon to be met with a yowl that exposed the creature's spiny tongue.

It swiveled its antler tines into the wagon, no doubt killing someone inside. Kaiser threw himself onto the head. He punched his shield in like a shovel, breaking the creature's nose. He was thrown off instantly, but laughed for his success. The wranglers on the megalynx's back could not persuade the offended creature to attack the wagon again. Uprooting his sword, Kaiser resolved to rejoin his defenders.

But an enemy lineup had somehow made it atop the plateau. It fell to Kaiser, he realized, to hold off those who scaled the rock face with hooks and ropes. Orange primal magic slithered from Seriath like saliva, and Kaiser's protective massacre began.

Clayborn cupped his mouth in prayer, wincing at every ringing crash. He could hardly pry his eyes from the scene when he sensed things dropping from the city walls. Eurivoneans, perhaps ten of them. They had rappelled down with ropes and flew across the field to join combat.

"Tethra, protect these fools too."

"Neb'Rul, the pond." Azurae gestured to the reedy body of water they passed. "We will take the rock wall and climb it to join the defenders' line." Saluting, her subordinate broke off and dove in, seating himself at the bottom of the water and working his energies.

They rounded the barbarian army and loosed a volley of moonsaws, fireballs, and ice streams, expending much of their energy for an aggressive start. But as Azurae had hoped, the watery likeness of Neb'Rul had sloshed from the pond.

It had a gleaming firmness to its eight-foot height whose mechanical sprint plowed over a section of the warband. Neb'Rul's water surrogate broke apart, only to raise out of the puddle again to deliver huge bodily slams against the raiders. He spent his water with each reincarnation, however, becoming a little smaller each time.

Alternating between impaling attackers and kicking out grappling hooks, Kaiser left a bloody graveyard encircling the wagon. Caethys, he could see, was one of four men remaining on the incline. The rest had fought to the death.

"To me, all of you!" Kaiser called, knowing that in so doing he had pulled the stop that had stemmed the raiders. Now, it was about stretching the lives of his remaining warriors.

"I'm proud to die with you, Kaiser!" Caethys roared, sliding his soaking blade from another torso.

"Die later, we've got people to protect!"

Together, Kaiser and Caethys navigated the bloody moments alongside their surviving men, pouncing between dynamic fatalities.

A missile breezed through the melee to lodge into one barbarian's chest. With sudden clarity, Kaiser saw it to be Azurae's spear, and indeed she had clambered up the wall with her fighters to fortify his last stand.

"Too early for martyrdom, Executor," she stated, bringing her twin katar to bear against a brute in full plate. The defenders found themselves suddenly visited with a squadron of fresh Sojourners.

On the battlefield, Kaiser always sought sources of strength. The visitation of the Sojourners provided it. Throwing off his shield, Kaiser scoured an axe from the dead and continued the impossible fight.

But coming up the incline now was the megalynx, lashed into compliance again by its riders. Its weighty steps carried it up the incline where it lowered its antlers to finish off the shrunken defenders.

Azurae leaped, taking a step off a raider's face and caught the reins of the beast. She disconnected it from the beast-riders before the megalynx flicked its head. Azurae held tight as the leather cord swung her high around. She managed to swing under, and over once again to tie shut the creature's catlike snout. She put her boots to its jaw and pulled with all her strength to twist the creature's head sideways.

Its antlers scooped aside barbarians like the claw of an even greater monster. Azurae wrangled her giant quarry to stumble back off the incline. Its great angry eyes threatened a hundred deaths in their clenching hazel, but as long as it struggled against her burden, it ignored its barbarian riders.

Caethys saw the opportunity to push back at the incline, with the raiders there toppled like figurines. His fellow warriors followed suit, with Kaiser's masterful dismemberments seeding fear at last in the enemies that still tried to move in.

The sight of their dead had made many of the barbarians turn back, but it was Azurae's beast-taming feat that did capital damage. Animal pride had focused the megalynx on ridding itself of the swinging pest on its snout. It had lost all interest in the battle, throwing off its riders while trampling gaps in the war band.

Spirits frayed, and the barbarians broke off, fleeing from those cursed rock shelves that should have been a simple triumph. Caethys and Kaiser lacerated stragglers to keep the enemy falling back.

The megalynx's growl was like the groan of an old skiff's mast bending in the wind. Azurae had hoped to drop off on her own terms, but a flick of the creature's head at the wrong time broke her grip, and she was sent careening across a patch of mossy stones.

Her arm bleeding from the fall, she rose quickly to meet the approach of the megalynx. It was intelligent enough to unwind its muzzle and shake the bit from its mouth. Great gobs of saliva stretched from its chin while its long-tipped ears bent back.

"I know, I know, I'm sorry," Azurae admitted, taking up a low horse stance with both of her katar back in her hands. She spoke then in slower, soothing words. "Let me go, just this once?"

Kaiser trotted up with her spear, still full of fighting spirit that the megalynx could sense. Azurae gestured for him to stay back with her hand, but the beast had already switched all its frustration on him.

"Hey! Don't ignore me! You just leave. Get something to eat, I know you're hungry." Azurae fought for its attention. It regarded her again with disdainful hunger. Azurae scraped her katar together, letting off a blast of sparks. "Go!"

Tired of the whole ordeal, the creature turned away in a run that was far more enthusiastic than it had ever done in service to the barbarians. Azurae watched its tufted tail waver gracefully behind it with a sigh.

"Whatever we're paying you," Kaiser started, handing her spear back to her, "it's not enough." They turned to retrieve the wagon, where Caethys and the others were hooting and hopping for their inexplicable success.

"She was mad at you. Are you the one that broke her nose?" Azurae asked Kaiser, who was mopping the blood from his face and neck with a kerchief. He only stared at her as they walked, disbelief sewed his lips. "Rude," she added.

"It was trying to eat us." Somehow, Kaiser felt his argument was insufficient.

Neb'Rul emerged from the pond to find his comrades pulling the wagon along to the city, where the gates were swinging open.

Clayborn was at the front of the crowd. He looked like he was waiting to be beaten, and Kaiser noticed he already wore a purple bruise on his cheekbone.

"Executor."

"I know you would have helped if you could, Clayborn. You did what I asked you to do," came the Cypolonian's medicinal reply. "I hope for the city's sake, you'd do it again."

"Glad you're safe, friend." The captain was not mended, obviously, but he would not bother his gore-bathed Executor any longer.

"Well done, little brother." Tibernas budged in, gripping Kaiser's shoulder plate. "Surely, Tethra was expecting you at her table tonight."

"After that march, I never would have lasted. Those Eurivoneans saved our lives." Looking back, Azurae was helping the elders from the battered wagon, to be reunited with hysterical families.

Chapter 50

Even after Insomnia's occupation, the citizens had always believed the gods cherished them deeply. It was why the city celebrated the Festooning four times a year as opposed to the traditional three.

Azurae watched the tortured city turn into a suite of fireworks, alcohol, and dance. The people became colorful devils in glittering masks that trampled their grief in midnight carnivals. And while the barbarians plunged merrily into the spirit, the Sojourners shied like cats through the smoke and ribbons.

But it was so terribly interesting to Azurae, nursing a decorative water pipe under the shade of a statue. She made off with a few pillows and blankets to make a perch away from lustful barbarians.

She gathered her glittering braid and smelled it; it was gingerly perfumed. Maids had bathed and dressed her like royalty. She felt her tanned, scarred skin wasn't suited to this sleek, dark green dress, nor these elegant sandals that made it difficult to walk.

They had decorated her arms and neck with bangles and henna, probably to conceal her scars. She was a little envious of those near-nude, ignorant girls down in the pits of celebration. To them, fighting was someone else's business. To look and feel charming, that was their concern.

For some time, Kaiser had just watched her smoke and relax. Behind the statue, he clutched a pair of full glasses and a vessel of imported fruit spirits. He knew she loved fruit. He let the glasses clink in his hands to alert her. She looked over her shoulder.

"Executor." Her voice was ferried on smoke.

"You strike me as a dancer, Azurae. But I find you up here?"

"What transpires in that melee below is hardly dancing." The fireworks above suddenly painted her pink and violet.

"I wanted to share this. But maybe you'd like to be alone?"

"Shh." She curled her finger at him. "Bring those drinks over here."

He obeyed and sat, setting a tumbler of the deep blue liquor next to her basin. "I wouldn't have survived that fight if you hadn't appeared. I've been trying to thank you for days."

She reached up with her smoking tube, offering it to him. "Just paying you back for grandpa. Try this, it's my blend," she told him as he accepted. She lifted the glass to her mouth and hesitated. "Oof, this is going to kill me."

Kaiser drew on the tube and watched her sip, watched the fireworks twinkle in her eyes. He had to remind himself to breathe out the smoke.

"Mmm, smoother than I thought," Azurae commented on the beverage.

"Good. I thought it might taste a little like home to you."

"Home is wherever I am together with my people. That is the Nomad's Fortune." The explosions in the sky painted her green and yellow. "Kasurai makes a fine home, presently."

"Listen, Azurae." Kaiser kept his eyes in his glass. "You're smart, you know what's on my mind. I've got a hundred thousand things to say to you, but they're all jammed up in my throat somewhere."

It was like pulling barb wire from his gullet, but he said what he came to say. He would have liked to throw himself from the heights if Azurae hadn't rested her head on his leg. Her braid fell into his lap.

"Please relax a little, Executor. I can hear your heart above the music."

***

A server presented Caethys and Sidna a pair of drinks on the restaurant patio; Sidna received a tall, sudsy stein of beer that made Caethys feel rather silly for his stemmed glass of purple wine.

"I've barely seen you the past few weeks, Sid. You must be well into your elite training by now." Caethys reclined in his wicker seat. He picked something from his gleaming brown leather boots.

Sidna realized at once he was attempting to be polite, but was quite distracted. "It's killing me, cramming it all into a month."

"You do look thinner. You have courses every night?"

"And drills early in the morning. They work you until you feel like there are termites in your muscles. They play mind games too, Cae, insisting you won't make it, daring you to quit. And when you absolutely cannot take another horrid second, you're about half done."

"That sounds about right. I'm glad I went through it when I did. But you'll make it, just . . . persevere," he said over his glass.

"Get out of here, Cae, I know you're itching to celebrate. I'm too tired to be much fun right now. Maybe I'll find you later, alright?" Sidna waved him away. His guilty smile was charming as always. He rose with his glass and hugged her head.

"I really do wish you health, Sid." He kissed her hair and set off.

Prying her eyes from his handsome hindquarters as he walked away, Sidna decided to unfold some parchment from her pocket on the table. She took out a coal stylus and began penning a letter. They worried, she knew, so Sidna wrote the children every week.

Hello again, Sweeties!

I hope fortune has found you lately. I'm safe, as always, and I still mean to visit you at first rotation. How is Granny Crandle? Be nice to that old bird, she took care of me when I first transferred from Narthalm. I wasn't much older than Shaden then.

Is work going well? I'm sure the market is working your little bodies to pieces, but keep at it! Every bit you save pays for more schooling. I rather wish I had gone to school. I know teachers hit hard, but captains hit harder!

You've become so strong. Shaden, I think you really will be a genius stable master someday. You're so good with animals and calming down the cattle. It's a little early to think of a career for Keb, but I think it will involve muscle. I heard he dug up Granny's turnip patch without even being asked . . .

Sidna gave her hand a rest and remembered her dripping beer mug. Sipping, she spotted Caethys across the swirl of dancers below. Blooms dangled over him and a girl, a very young brunette, her skin inked in crawling patterns. She cupped her mouth excitedly at his every jest. As was Caethys's nature, his arm was around her soon, to take her some place more private.

The beer suddenly tasted extremely weak, so Sidna set it down.

> *I promise I will try to stay safe. Barbarians keep lumbering in to help us, and they're big as oak trees. We're going to hit these Septunites hard. So hard, I hope, that you'll never have to fight them.*
>
> *I'm eager to see how you two have changed by the time I get back! So stay busy, keep the faith, and I'll see you soon enough. I think we'll all have stories to tell!*
>
> *Gods' favor,*
>
> *Sidna*

***

"I think you've danced your injuries away, my dear," the governor's wife commented to him as they retired from the floor. She clutched his arm proudly.

"This is precisely what we needed, isn't it? A display of fiery resilience reminds us that we are not defined by our losses."

A peculiar sight greeted them as they neared the governor's seat. An Archaic was sprawled across it, and the lady's seat was kicked over. The intruder pretended not to see them as they approached.

"Oh, dear," said the governor's wife.

"Worthy soldier, your cups have betrayed you. You are in the wrong seat!" the governor said.

"I think my cups are the only ones telling the truth anymore." The Archaic put the cup suddenly to his ear. "Ah, my cup says I'm more suited to this seat than you. That tonight, I should sleep in a pillowy mansion and you should be the one to sleep in a stable!"

"If you have a grievance with your lodging, there are more expedient ways to address them." The governor noticed the man wore a sword.

"So whom do I address about my pitiful pay? The ratty food? What are you drinking, governor? Some priceless vintage? I bought mine from a street vendor and it tastes like spit."

"If you're still of a mind to talk on this, I will speak to you directly the day after tomorrow, when your head is mended. But I don't trade words with drunks. So get out of my seat, and get out of my sight," the governor demanded, throwing off his wife's arm and smashing his own cup to the ground.

The barbarian regarded him calmly. His free hand moved to his blade and slowly pulled the weapon from its sheath, resting it over his belly. Heavy footfalls turned the governor's head. It was Tibernas, who had been watching, deep in his own drink, but far cooler headed than both men. He put a hand on the governor's shoulder.

"Carabas is not wrong, Governor. He lost a cousin not two days ago in an engagement outside the city. Every night, he must retire to a stall that reeks of manure." Tibernas illustrated.

"Some of us can't even bed in the stalls," said one of Carabas's backers, who tottered drunkenly onto the scene.

"Some things to contemplate, Governor. But not tonight. Come, Carabas." Tibernas beckoned.

"No. The governor had this seat all month while I bled outside these walls. He can find a different seat."

Tibernas groaned and approached, leaning into Carabas close enough to smell his breath.

"You're a fool if you think I don't understand. My men eat and sleep no better than you, but they know to show allies respect. If you start trouble tonight, Carabas, I won't be able to help you."

"Then you're no longer an Archaic."

***

Azurae must've fallen asleep, because Kaiser's squeeze on her arm shook her from a different world.

"Pardon, Azurae. I have to tend to something." Kaiser said, pushing up. He sensed a tremendous fury mounting that could only be Tibernas's, and he dropped into the crowd to shove closer. Azurae let Kaiser gain some distance, then followed discreetly.

More men had arrived to back up Carabas. Liquor had made them all brave, and they crossed their thick arms watching Tibernas scold the seated barbarian.

"If you want to fight so badly, Carabas, I'm your man. But let's have it where you won't be embarrassed in front of the city's finest." Tibernas tilted his head, and his buffalo neck cracked like corn stalks.

"A fight? I've had enough pointless fights. No, tonight I will have change."

Carabas kicked Tibernas in the chest, throwing the magnate down the stair. Carabas and his barbarians joyfully burst into violence, attacking all Federals and barbarians that were not as drunk as they.

The governor intervened when Carabas attempted to bludgeon his wife and was struck by his own seat. The dancers in the crowd below needed punishment, Carabas decided, and his gang made to injure as many as possible.

Masked merrymakers were beaten and sliced in Carabas's warpath. He was no stranger to the Red Rapture, and it had gripped him tonight. Sweet power made him a destroyer of weak Federals as he moved to the fountain ahead.

Tibernas arose with a roar, throwing off his black cape. He put his great fists to work, laying out any barbarian that had sided with Carabas.

"Hear me, my Archaic brothers!" Carabas began, taking a bottle of alcohol from a comrade that had a flaming cloth in it. "We are worth more than the crusts thrown to us!" He leaned to cast his fiery weapon when his arm was caught.

Kaiser whirled him around and swatted the bottle from his hand. It fell and broke, starting a waist-high fire at their feet.

Surprisingly, Carabas had the audacity to retaliate. While Kaiser retreated from the blaze, Carabas swiped his sword at his throat, striving for a decapitation.

A full trial played out in Kaiser's mind in the short time he was ducking blows, and the verdict was clear.

A final drunken swing, and Carabas's arm was caught in Kaiser's hands. A practiced movement broke the elbow. The sword fell into Kaiser's grasp, and proceeded into the barbarian's heart.

Carabas fell backwards onto the puddle of flaming alcohol.

"*No!*" Tibernas howled, throwing off an attacker.

Kaiser turned to absorb everyone's gaze, waiting as his victim burned at his back.

"I didn't bring a sword tonight, because I didn't think I needed one," he said. "But Carabas was eager to die in battle. Pity there were *no enemies here.*"

"You've killed our captain, you madman!" someone howled at him from the crowd.

"And I'd be delighted to kill more of you, but there's something I want more. An army that doesn't destroy itself!"

"Carabas didn't deserve to die! He wanted a better life for his men!" one barbarian argued.

"Ah, I didn't see how noble he was being, because you see, he was killing fellow soldiers like a traitor. Let me make something very clear." Kaiser put his hand horizontally. "Septunites." He lowered his hand a bit. "Demons." Lowered it again. "Traitors."

Tibernas chewed his remorse as archers shoved into position above, securing balconies.

"Nothing is more important than winning this war. I need a seamless army to accomplish that. If you want to attack your own countrymen, try your daggers on me first." Kaiser soaked in stares as he stepped down from his perch.

***

As expected, Tibernas soon appeared in Kaiser's chambers.

"You'll find no apologies here, Tibernas." Kaiser plucked rings from his fingers and dropped them in a brass basin on his desk.

"I thought Federal law included warning, arrest, and trial. I thought Federals were bureaucrats like that."

"But Archaics aren't bureaucrats, are they? I know I stink like a Federal to barbarians. They have great respect for me, but a moment of weakness and it will be snatched away."

"It was wrong of him to hurt those people, but Carabas deserved better. He was a good soldier."

"I don't doubt that. But he was a better rebel."

"Just wait, the guilt *will* catch you. You're no tyrant, and if you try to be one you'll go mad. Myself and others can back you if trouble brews again. You should stay your sword where a broken jaw will suffice." Tibernas spat words like stakes, and when he felt he had pinned Kaiser down, he wheeled to leave.

"Was Carabas your friend?" Kaiser asked to his back. The magnate's heavy head rotated back.

"Fourteen years, Kaiser." And he was gone.

Suddenly alone, the Cypolonian numbly removed his coat. He angrily thrust his bloodied hands into a water basin and slapped water across his face.

"Disgraceful." He wasn't quite sure who he was talking about as the water dripped from his beard.

He assembled the same drink he had every two days for a long time. Into the tin measuring cup went a dose from a bottle of Septunite poison, then a teaspoon of slowing agent, and plenty of water. In his advanced treatment, he expected little more than a mild migraine in the morning.

He was getting rather used to his puffy noble bed, and it called for him to retire from thinking. But Tibernas's prophecy was already coming true, and Kaiser began to hurt for what he did tonight.

"You would have done the same thing, wouldn't you, Kronin?" he asked his comrade in the afterlife. Severe as Kronin could be, Kaiser wasn't sure about the answer. The Cypolonian could have stocked ten cemeteries with his Septunite kills, but none among them resonated like tonight's victim. Kaiser raised the toxic beverage to his lips, wishing instead it was some highland liquor.

"Please don't."

A knife on the table flew into Kaiser's hand as he spun to the window. Carved out of the moon was Azurae's silhouette, fixed like a mountain climber to one of the eaves outside. She was so quiet and shaded that Kaiser thought he was imagining her.

Gladness won the race to his mind, so he stuck the knife into the table with a smirk. "This room is six stories up. With armed guards on patrol."

"Very drunk guards." Her syllables were frozen, almost brittle, and it made Kaiser wonder what must be on her mind.

"Has justice compelled you to kill me?" His question went unanswered, and it made him wonder again if she were really there. Judging by the shape of her black outline, she had changed into her battle leathers.

Quiet as a spider, she entered.

"Listen, my course is set, Azurae. I can't stop for anything. This march into the west is my reason for living." Her silence seemed defiant. "Do you hear me?! I am prepared to pay any price for Kasurai's survival."

She looked disarmed then, and not just in posture, Kaiser noticed. If she had come to assassinate him, she was ill equipped.

"Does that price include taking your own life?" Her question was met with perplexity, but then she gestured to the cup.

"You saw that, did you? It's not what you think. I'm training myself against poison. I've done this for years."

"Training. Of course. And here I suspected your guilt moved you to suicide."

"My business is killing. If you came to observe my grief, you must feel unsatisfied." Kaiser put a hand on his hip as Azurae turned back to the window. "But if one thing does poison me, it's knowing that I disappointed you."

Azurae sighed, turned back to him, seating herself on the window ledge. Her hair looked heavy the way she hung her head. "I'm not disappointed. In your position, I might have killed Carabas as well." Azurae put her fingers on her chest. "It's that twice already I had to try and accept that you were gone. And then you spring back every time like you can't die. Teasing me. Making me think you'll always be there."

Azurae's body could not accommodate her feelings, and she rounded her back while her fingers pawed at the sill. She was breaking like a statue in an earthquake.

"Get up." Kaiser refused to let her fall from dignity play out any longer and offered a hand. She rose, and he studied that scar on her hand that he had made in Eurivone. He gave it a slow kiss.

"I know you're a killer, but that's not all you are," she said.

"I don't deserve your thoughts, Azurae. My life will always be a mess of atrocities committed for what I think is justice."

He earned a thoughtful gaze from her, and he went pale, dropping her hand.

"Why are you even here?! Hellfire, when I look in your eyes, I feel so ugly and monstrous I *crave* poison." Disgusted with himself, he pointed to one of the old wounds on his pectoral. "Every one of these was made by a person whose hatred I earned."

Azurae tore open the leather harness on her chest. The color in Kaiser's face returned at the sight of her undercloth, taut with womanly bloom.

"Maybe you thought I received all these from the beasts I hunt?" she asked of her own battle scars. "If fighting against evil men is murder, then I was a murderer at seven years old. Don't try to convince me you're so irredeemable, because we are all killers, and you are my favorite."

Azurae's heart was thumping so loud, she was embarrassed he might hear it, but her pride was back. Kaiser moved his arms around her, and she squeezed his waist. Their bodies compressed tightly, from their chests to their stomachs.

"Every little thing I learn about you doubles my obsession. It's taken every drop of my will to keep my distance," Kaiser admitted. She rested her chin on his shoulder, hair falling over his arms. "Aren't you afraid I'll ruin your life?"

"You know my policy about things that frighten me, Kaiser."

"I don't know what to do with you." He took her head in one hand and put his brow to hers. "So you'll forgive me if I improvise."

Kaiser was a cage of masculine heat, but from him came a kiss as gentle and savory as a meadow breeze. The dangerous thrum of blood in his arms and chest felt like some mammoth hunger would be unchained on her. She was a hare in serpent's coils, but pinpoints of delight cropped up like flowers and compelled her to let him resume.

Azurae released a pleasurable hum, lost in the smooth confusion. She felt blocks and constrictions in her mind get washed away in a tide of passion. Her legs were powerless when the kiss ended, and she slid drunkenly to the floor.

"I don't . . . it's new. Always ignored it . . ." Her words went undeciphered by Kaiser, kneeling to her level. The architecture of his neck looked irresistible, and she claimed it with her mouth. It was Kaiser's turn to melt.

He cast her to the bed and tore away their garments in a frenzy to explore. Azurae, flushed with passion, found herself squirming and panting underneath Kaiser's overwhelming presence. Innocence brimmed in her watery eyes while the Cypolonian loomed above, poised to devour her like a wolf, and began.

Every minute was a voyage of senses, sweet physical energy given and taken. Years of confined emotion burst forth like a shattered dam. It was frightening in its intensity, yet every time Azurae was moved to tears of confused happiness, Kaiser was there to console her with his tender strength.

Their escapades seemed endless, with so much fuel to burn. Kaiser was constantly refreshed by Azurae's mystic beauty. She was the sum of his desires, and she was here, vulnerable to his designs.

When finally muscles and imaginations were exhausted, they were tangled together in the wreckage of the bed. When they had regained their breath, they used it to laugh uncontrollably about how savagely they had passed the hours.

Chapter 51

Wearing a dress inherited by her cousins that was far too big, little Lylia struggled to duplicate the same crown of dandelions her mother had used to ring her brown hair. About to give up, she was caught unawares by the thunder of hooves and a bejeweled carriage rolling up the dirt path to her hillside cottage.

Moments later, she had found her father in his field hauling a large basket of orange, cone-like vegetables whose name she still could not pronounce. Lylia blundered into his view, whipping up puffs of black dirt with her footfalls. She sometimes had difficulty speaking, but he was doubly observant to detect her when she was in need.

"I suppose you want a piggyback ride, now that I've been doing this all day, don't you?" he groaned, pulling a soaked kerchief from his rolled-up pantaloons. As soaked and dirty as he got, Lylia never hesitated to latch onto her big, safe papa. *I'm thirsty anyway*, he thought, and he decided to hike the girl onto his shoulder before going to inspect what might have excited her.

Coming in the back door to his wood-bare home, he hadn't even noticed the carriage resting in front of his porch. He was met quickly by his wife, whose eyes were wide and white enough to shame her apron.

"Dear, we've noble guests," she said, with so much fright in her voice, her husband thought to reach for the axe propped against the rocker as he set down his daughter.

In the next room, at his very simple dinner table, was seated the white-robed and neatly groomed Potentate of the Apogee himself. He absolutely gleamed among the drab surroundings, as did the large Gavel woman guarding him. And here was this husband and father, without even a shirt.

"Hello," said Equilion.

"He will be joining us for dinner, my love," the farmer's wife informed him.

After sporting his least-stained shirt and washing his face, the husband sat with the Potentate, whom he could offer no wine or beer, for the stores were empty. Soon enough, the wife emerged again. She had been crying, though she tried to hide it. She carried in her hands a great pot of steaming stew that she had diced carrots into. Following her was Lylia, who carried the plates and silverware.

The bodyguard chose not to eat, but the Potentate, who had been amicable enough the whole evening, ate in silence, as if thinking. He finished and set his spoon in the wooden bowl.

"I come from the highest point of Evanthea, your Potentate, asking for you to prepare for me the finest meal you can muster," he began. "You have managed only to bring out this stew, with no seasoning, not even any meat. This is the best you have to offer."

The family, seated at the table with him, was stark white. The wife put her hands to her face and sobbed. The husband lowered his head in shame, palming his wife's shoulder to comfort her.

"It won't do for citizens to be so threadbare. I'd wager your little one has never even tasted beef, has she?" Equilion looked to the child.

"I did at festival this year!" Lylia gasped from faulty lungs.

"Mercy, Potentate. It's been a trying season, with the war tax and all. Please don't take our modest amenities as a reflection of our respect," said the husband.

"Stop now, young man. I'm not Nytrinion, you know," Equilion said abruptly. "Forgive me. This dinner has been an investigation of the state of the people. And I see that times are grim indeed, though my well-paid officials would have me believe otherwise."

The wife looked up, feeling a little more at ease with the Potentate's crisp, friendly tone. He certainly seemed a decent man. Lylia scraped at her bowl with her spoon while Equilion held a hand out to his bodyguard, who dropped into it a sack of coins. Squeaking out his chair, he walked to the family, who stood to meet him.

"That is a lot of money, please make it last and share with those in greater need, for the winter will be a grievous one. I'm counting on you to be charitable." He took the husband's calloused hands and sealed the sack into them. "I will not forget your family's kindness. Please take this visit as my promise to alleviate the hardships that have kept you and your neighbors poor and wanting. I will not rest until I have improved the lives of the people." He took the wife's hand and kissed it, thanking her for the meal and left.

The family stood there and talked a while, an empty bowl hardly serving as evidence that the Potentate had visited. Then again, the hefty load of coins the size of Lylia's head was proof enough.

***

Fierce as the day's battles had been, they almost paled to the bartering that ensued as the barbarians argued over the spoils. Strange drink, fine armor that could be refashioned, foodstuffs, jewelry, and literature traded hands frantically as everyone sought gain from the trampled Septunite camp.

But at least they weren't killing each other. Arms folded, Clayborn watched as the Archaics exercised the same impassioned mania that reinforced his prejudice. But they had won the day, here at the east fork of the Golden Straits.

"Clayborn." Kaiser patted his compatriot on the shoulder, the latter shuddering. "Oh, sorry, you still sore?"

"*Yes*," Clayborn voiced, referring to his burn wounds. He saw Kaiser was in the company of some of his strongest, cruelest-looking Federal warriors. They patrolled bartering sessions to remind barbarians that bloodletting among Kasurites would be swiftly punished. "Are you finished being menacing?"

"I guess. They've already heard about the tax reduction that Equilion's making. This isn't going to get any more civilized. With reduced pay, they're going to fight hard for their keep, and not just against the Septunites." Kaiser sighed.

"The Federals we can call to heel, but these barbarians are going to turn the front inside out, Kaiser. What if they rob from the citizens?" Clayborn saw his question work over in Kaiser's mind, prompting the latter's hand to rest close to the pommel of Seriath.

"Then they'll only do it once," came the promise.

"I really hope you can curb them as well as you think. The contracts we signed with them are like using fences for birds." Clayborn remembered a little courtesy. "Ah, but why did you look so chipper before I sullied your mood, Executor?" Kaiser was still rather like a student to him, but outranked him now by a vast margin, and both were adjusting to it.

"Just some fascinating news, really. I'll be cleaving off a few of our boys to swing by the woods to the south this afternoon. Something requires our attention." Kaiser's teeth gleamed at Clayborn expectantly.

Clayborn humored him. "Pray tell?"

"A demon, Clayborn."

"Gods, no. It's happening. I fear for the world if we can't put a lid on this Septunite sorcery." That's when Kaiser's self-assuredness annoyed him. "And just why the hell does that please you so much?"

"Well, it doesn't, really. I just like killing them."

"Caethys was right about you. You get strange when fiends are afoot. You keep your wits, Executor. Make wise decisions."

"Has Caethys been spreading rumors about me? I'm going to flog that brat."

"If you take the craziest ones with you, I promise I'll keep the peace among these barbarians until you return."

"It's a deal, friend." Kaiser offered a hand to Clayborn. Their identically scarred palms squeezed tight, and they went their respective ways.

Chapter 52

Kaiser's team made good time through the swampy woodlands. The Executor valued speed, so handpicked warriors like today's were always fast. As ever, they had been selected from every house to staunch suspicions of favoritism.

Tibernas was honored to be the only close acquaintance brought along. Kaiser seemed to entrust most everything else to that fat man Clayborn, so the magnate was pleased to be of especial service today. He spied a hump in the muck ahead.

"Another one." He pointed, but Kaiser was already jogging up to it. Tibernas joined, grunting at the smell of the corpse's scattered entrails. He thumbed some of his drug dust up his nose, letting his Executor evaluate.

Kaiser slipped one of his journals from his satchel and fluttered it open to where his own scribblings frustrated him.

"Something doesn't add up, does it?" Tibernas guessed, brushing a mosquito from his tattooed arm.

"Now this thing is acting more like a weeping skinhound," Kaiser said, examining one of his own sketches a little closer, and hating how it didn't resemble at all the wounds on the corpse.

"What was it last time, a blue-assed baby-eater?" Tibernas was joined in his chuckles by a few of the men. "Come on, Executor, I thought you had this thing pegged."

"I'd like to identify it before we fight, but I think I just haven't seen this type of demon before." Kaiser whapped his booklet shut. Pocketing it, he tapped the tattoo of Calphinas on the corpse's bloody neck. "Clergyman, this fellow."

"I think I saw a bell tower peeking over the ridge ahead," Tibernas returned.

"Best we take a look." Then something hooked Kaiser's attention.

"Something wrong, Executor?"

"No. Head for the tower, but don't enter until I return. I won't be a moment." The Cypolonian rose from the body and entered a cage of scraggly branches decked with spider webs.

"Where're you going? You might need our help," Tibernas argued.

"Not to take a sprinkle, I won't. Just keep moving."

When finally Kaiser lowered into a trench of high plants and drifting spores, he crouched and widened his eyes. He slid out his hunting knife, preferring it in tight confines. Spying some radiance in the tall grass ahead, he crawled to inspect it.

"Izlou?" he whispered, knowing the strange outlander heard on wavelengths that didn't necessarily align with sound.

"Kaiser, I'm glad you saw my signal," came the fluid voice from the pond nearby. The Cypolonian watched as the adjacent mire buzzed with alien green light and a phantasm pushed up from the waters. But somehow Izlou's light was paler than normal, as if his ghost had aged as easily as a flesh and blood creature.

"What on earth are you doing here?" Kaiser recollected the ritual he had performed for Izlou just weeks before. "You're a ghost again, where's that body I got for you?"

"Probably still lying where it was sliced apart. There's a very powerful creature down here, Kaiser. It turned me into dog food before I could offer any sort of resistance."

"A hellspawn, right?"

"It indeed gave off demon energy. But I don't think it was a true hellspawn. More likely a man severely corrupted by Helix magic."

"Oh? What makes you think it was a man, not an animal?"

"Because I observed him in spirit briefly after he destroyed my body. He reformed into a human shape and even spoke like a man, reciting some sort of prayer."

"A prayer? In Septunite or Civilic?"

"Septunite, but strangely he did not dedicate my death to Opagiel. Rather, to some being he called Thel."

Goosebumps raised along Kaiser's spine like a centipede with cold feet. Had they found him at last? No, that was impossible. Thel and his Disciples weren't shape-changers, they were human.

Weren't they?

Once again, it dawned on him that he knew dangerously little of his old enemies.

"Are there others with him?" Kaiser pressed.

"From what I've seen, he has been traveling alone." Izlou could see the thoughts swarming like termites in Kaiser's brain. "You have a history with this man, do you?"

"I have to get back to the team. We'll speak again." Kaiser raced off.

"Kill him slowly, Kaiser, for my sake." Izlou dismissed the conversation and sunk back into the waters.

The mud fought to swallow Kaiser's boots, but he quickly regained the others on a rocky mound. The men were mumbling over another discovered corpse.

"Tibernas, praise Tethra. Grave news," Kaiser said.

"What's the matter?"

"This enemy is greater than I thought."

"I told you, we should have brought my ten-handers. But I think there's less to be worried about than you think. We caught this murderous bastard alone."

Tibernas gestured to the body that the barbarians were gathered around, and Kaiser realized it wasn't dead after all. The beaten stranger was pulled up to his knees.

His head was wrapped in a sewn hood that concealed his face. At first, Kaiser thought the barbarians had placed it on him, but it was obvious that the hood was stitched out of bloody Kasurite flags. It contrasted with the rest of his black ballroom finery. He raised his masked face to Kaiser, as if to say:

I found you.

The Cypolonian whisked out Seriath and arced it down onto the captive's head. It clanked on something metal under the hood. The chance was lost.

The enemy unzipped the torsos of his captors with two short spears that came out of nowhere. Kaiser tried to dodge, but a blade crossed his throat.

Tibernas's long mace swung in. It was ducked, but Kaiser was ignoring his wound and launched his own attack. Now the other barbarians came on. The enemy saw an unflinching resolve in Kaiser, even as blood streamed down his throat.

The window for a quick kill had been lost, the enemy realized. He scuttled back, winding through the swinging warriors before bounding into the woods toward the bell tower.

"Kaiser!" Tibernas moved up. Kaiser would not speak; crimson was spilling over the fingers at his throat. Tibernas produced a cloth but was pushed away. Then he noticed the Cypolonian had powered his sword with steaming hot energy.

His own primal magic should never have harmed him, but Kaiser willed it so at the wound on his throat. It burned, boiled, cauterized in a sort of pain that made him recall the torment he and Clayborn had suffered under Dragnos's men.

The Cypolonian punched the dirt, trying anything to alleviate the choking burn. His fingers raked through the earth before he pushed up with Tibernas.

It was a deeper throat wound than Kaiser had ever received, and it somehow gave him strength to know that he had survived it.

Cloth dangled from Tibernas's hand as he stared transfixed at Kaiser. The Cypolonian snatched it and secured the bandage around his neck.

"So who's this prick?" Tibernas asked, satisfied that his friend would survive.

"You . . ." Kaiser tested out his voice, wincing at the way charred flesh chafed under the bandage. "Will you help me fight him, Tibernas?"

"You know I will, little brother."

"The rest of you stay behind. You cannot match this enemy." Even with his charred voice, Kaiser sounded invincibly headstrong. "If we do not return in a quarter hour, get back to the division and return them to the city on my orders."

"You know this man," Tibernas suggested as he followed his wayward companion through the trees.

"He is an old enemy. It was his master and his companions that defeated me in the south. Today, however, he is alone."

"You were the quickest sword arm I've ever known until just now, Executor. Yet he was still skilled enough to cut your throat."

"That is because he is one of the best. And somehow, I sense his demon energy has tripled since last we met."

"How do a couple of dogs like us match one of the world's greatest assassins?"

"With this." Kaiser tapped the blue diamond in his Defender's Mantle. It unfolded golden-blue ether that encapsulated both muscle and sword. The Cypolonian was suddenly quickened in the way of angels.

"Well, isn't that fancy. You're going to share, aren't you?"

"This will work much better than our primal magic. I may not be able to produce holy magic myself for some reason, but the Defender's Mantle can. Enough to unravel this bastard like a cheap garment," Kaiser promised, tapping Seriath against Tibernas's mace. Soon enough, the magic took root in the magnate's weapon, and it bubbled with neon sorcery like the Paragon had kissed it.

Tibernas followed his companion over a river to the bell tower on an island of broken stone. Quaint and sturdy, the tower housed the iron bell in a stone minaret that only barely reached above the canopy.

A circular window had been built above the red door. But the stained glass had been broken, as if their quarry had leaped up through it. Colorful glass crunched under their feet as they neared the entrance.

"Careful. He'll try to take you out first," Kaiser whispered. Tibernas was becoming too battle-minded to respond.

The smell of old woodwork rushed out to meet them as Kaiser eased the door open with his scabbard. He surveyed the sparse interior and took the first pensive step inside. The pair's blessed weapons washed closer items in clean light.

There was a square brick fireplace for cooking and heating in the corner. Burning coals still sent a little smoke up the chimney. And beside the only table, one old barbarian monk stood still as a statue.

Armored boots clinking over the wooden floors, Kaiser cautiously approached the man, a white-haired chap with a black mustache. He regarded Kaiser with one eye while the other rolled up into the corner.

"He's up in the rafters," the monk informed him, supposing these two were here to eliminate the unseen menace. Kaiser glanced at the ceiling. It was dark, with wooden beams crossing the deepening shadow.

"Best you step outside, we'll take care of it." Kaiser reached out for him.

"No! Don't!" The monk turned white, flushing suddenly with the gravest fear. Kaiser retracted his hand, concerned. "Don't worry about me, Tethra's already tucked me in."

"I see. I'm sorry."

"Save it. Tethra watches you, my son. Bring that monster down." With that, the monk let his body pitch. The cut encircling his neck yawned wetly and his head separated from his shoulders, painting an end at Kaiser's boots.

Tibernas was sinking into his deep battle mania that made him feel five times his size. With typical Archaic aggression, he swung with his mace and exploded a chunk of the cubic fireplace across the planks. He leered up at the ceiling shadows, where he expected the enemy was hiding.

"Play the spider while you can! Soon I'll scrape you off my treads like one!" Tibernas sent his stormy challenge up. A bit of dust drifted down.

Kaiser gently thumbed the monk's dead eyes closed. "Seremet will not break words with the unbaptized." He rose from the growing puddle of glistening scarlet and took a seat at the table, resting his hand on his sword.

"Fair enough. I didn't come here for talk." Tibernas was a little grated that Kaiser seemed so serene. The Cypolonian even took a moment to break some cheese off of the monk's dinner plate. Chewing blankly, Kaiser looked almost drowsy, yet his sword hand was clutched in angry blue veins.

"I haven't spoken to many about that day. When I lost Sudel," Kaiser mused.

"Can it wait, Executor? Perhaps when there's fewer assassins?"

"Don't fret. Seremet waits. That is his skill." Kaiser broke off another piece of cheese and rolled it in his fingers. "He waited for a chance to strike Kronin, and he found one. After Thel had already wounded him, that is."

The sound of rushing fabric whispered above.

"But waiting was the right choice, I suppose. Kronin would have taken his head off, if Seremet had acted sooner. It was safer to let Thel do the hard work. It's always best to wait." Kaiser sighed, recalling how useless he himself had been during the baleful holocaust that withered his years of work. "I wonder how long he'll wait for Akanis to return."

The silence settled on Tibernas's nerves. He felt as though the presence above was expanding like an eclipse, shrieking without voice.

"Your brother was in many ways my better, Seremet. He was faster, bolder, an excellent grappler." Kaiser brought his off hand to his satchel.

When the Cypolonian's hand returned to the table, he rapped the wood with fingers now encased in the late Akanis's deadly claws.

"But I have suffered this memory long enough. I will not stop at Akanis. And I will not stop at you. I will send each of you to hell and heap upon you a million Septunite souls."

The sound of swishing razors preceded the fall of a large wooden beam. Rising from his chair, Kaiser halved it with Seriath in an effortless movement. The two heavy logs thundered against the stone floor.

Tibernas leaped aside as a lanky creature plummeted to where he stood. Its body was so heavily outfitted with racks of bone blades, it was unclear how many arms and legs it had. Vestigial mantis claws twitched from joints, providing it with ever more weaponry.

Its head was equipped with a gigantic set of scissoring pincers that nearly equaled its legs in size. Despite the weight of these hefty appendages, its head jerked with manic deliberation, evaluating the enemy with two rows of eyes.

Tibernas rose next to Kaiser, whose teeth were screeching. His irises were loops of gold floating in blood red. The Red Rapture had possessed both warriors, and they stared down their sizable enemy like a pair of wolves.

The thing that Seremet had become raked its claws across the floor, plowing through the planks. Suddenly, it proceeded to shake furiously, like a dog.

Webs of slime secreted from pores splattered around it. It shook and shook until it had nothing left, and the slime gave rise to gelatinous growths like little anemones. They sparked with red light that carried the unmistakable sensation of hell magic.

A wayward charge pitted Kaiser against the creature. Seriath battled to penetrate the striking bone blades that were effortless for Seremet to maintain. Kaiser shifted back to avoid those enormous pincers that tried for his wounded neck.

Tibernas spun in and bashed the pincers aside with his mace. The holy magic succeeded in breaking off chips of the creature's chitin. Tibernas swung desperately to follow up, but defensive blades beat him aside. Kaiser was quick to replace his comrade's blunt force with his own high-speed slashing.

Holy magic from the Defender's Mantle allowed Seriath to make stripes in the organic armor, but not truly penetrate. Kaiser needed time to commit a powerful blow, but the creature thwarted all but the very quickest attacks.

Tibernas ducked a swing from one of the creature's blades, which was quickly ensnared by Kaiser's metal claws. First blood went to Tibernas when his mace broke open the casing on the creature's leg. The divine energy in his weapon flared up in the wound, scalding the creature deeply.

Kaiser sent Seriath quickly across the creature's hip, opening a wound that beamed with holy light. But as quickly as the injuries were meted out, a strange second type of energy sprang from the wounds. Dashes of scarlet, like the gleam of a ruby, fluttered out. They ripped at Kaiser and Tibernas, shearing into their skin through their breastplates. Sorcery had turned Seremet's blood into a cutting energy attack.

Both warriors were beset with a sudden weakness, even in their Red Rapture, as if the cutting energy knew precisely what sort of injuries would strangle their fortitude. Backing up, Kaiser used his scabbard to occupy more of the creature's whiffling razors. He was trying to open an opportunity for Tibernas, but the magnate's mace was too large and heavy to get past those darting demon limbs.

Kaiser rolled under a pincer snap to flank. The creature turned to regard Kaiser's new position and took a blow to the back of the head from Tibernas. While rattled, the monster's armor protected its brain from even that tremendous smash, and a back kick put a divot in Tibernas's gut and sent him across the room.

The creature was confident it would find Kaiser's vitals soon, but a rumbling cast its attention back on Tibernas. The magnate was pushing the heavy oaken table like a ram and succeeded in colliding it against the monster's abdomen. It backstepped and ripped the table to pieces with its claws.

Kaiser saw the opportunity. Seriath entered the monster's back. Pulling away quickly, Kaiser still could not fully avoid the slicing crescents of crimson magic that issued from the wound. It bit into his wrist and made his fingers sticky with blood.

Tibernas had even less concern for taking injury. As the creature convulsed, Tibernas connected with a stroke that made off with part of its bony face. The cutting magic from the wound fluttered upward, missing Tibernas completely.

Snapping out with a pair of thin, whiplike tails, the creature managed to get its assailants to step back. They regarded their torsos where the tails had struck yet more painful slashes that penetrated their armor as if it weren't even there.

Two on one, the combatants heaved in their pain. Kaiser's claws were quick to shoot to the respective clasps around his body armor. It had been tailored specifically for easy donning and removal, and in a moment, he was able to pull it off and throw it to the ground, along with the supplemental pieces at his arms and hips. With only his slacks and Defender's Mantle to encumber him, he felt much lighter.

"Armor's pointless. Lose it, we'll be faster," Kaiser advised, laboring to form words in his Red Rapture. Tibernas grunted, and pulled off his cuirass, which was simple by barbarian nature to remove.

Oddly, the creature took no initiative in the short window while its opponents cast off their bloody regalia. Instead, it clomped back to where it had slimed the floor. The jelly pods had cultured bright demonic power from the spirits in the air. At the monster's command, the pods burst all at once, and their violet essence twisted together and flowed into its wounds, sealing them up. Kaiser and Tibernas watched in dismay as their hard-earned progress reversed itself.

"Now he knows how we fight," Kaiser grumbled.

"Your wrath is slipping. Don't let the fear in," warned Tibernas.

The creature's claw blades flexed inward then, and began sawing against one another. They generated a keening sound just above the scope of human hearing. The weapons of the two warrior's began to dampen in brightness. The holy magic was being extinguished by the strange wavelengths.

"Damn. If we continue, we'll die. Tibernas, go. I've left instructions—"

"*Hey!*" Tibernas interrupted Kaiser, thrusting the butt of his mace across the Cypolonian's nose. Kaiser's fear evaporated under an icy tide of rage. His eyes took on a volcanic glow that matched his growl in ferocity.

"Thank you." Kaiser's tone promised recompense to everyone present. It was a pure, unfettered aggression that he had not enjoyed for some time, and he used it to fuel his sudden rush at the creature.

Tibernas caught up soon, dropping his mace and pulling out his sword for quicker attacks. Unburdened by armor and freshened by anger, they delivered blows to match the creature's slicing defenses.

Kaiser baited one of those insectile limbs by overstretching with his leg. He managed to pull it back in time and seize the demonic blade arm in his claws. He tore it from the creature's body in a sudden burst of stinging energy that Kaiser laughed off.

Inspired by his companion's brutality, Tibernas took a slash to the shoulder to swat at one of the extra limbs. He struck off the appendage, but a blunt hit twisted his neck. The magnate's upper vertebrae wrenched.

Tibernas crumpled. The creature turned back to Kaiser, only to find him gone.

Desperate to use Tibernas's sacrifice, Kaiser threw himself onto the creature's back. Few of its attacks could reach him now, so while the monster's lobster-like armor punctured Kaiser's torso, he avoided heavy damage.

As the beast whirled and whirled, Kaiser tore off another claw arm, and shunted Seriath in between a pair of bony plates at the base of the creature's neck.

Fighting to steer the beast from Tibernas's helpless form, the Cypolonian invoked another charge from the Defender's Mantle. He could not summon as much holy might this time, but he put all that he could muster into his claws. Finding a ridge on the creature's back, Kaiser set his iron fingers to work prying the lengthy piece back. He kept it angled away so the cutting energies of the bare muscle beneath could not reach him.

The creature struggled like mad to get Kaiser off, but its limbs were built for forward combat, not grasping at odd angles. Farther and farther the plate of chitin was pried, tearing open a gaping wound that exposed ugly purple muscle.

Suddenly the world flipped strangely, and Kaiser was crushed under the monster that had thrown itself onto its back.

Kaiser's insides squished uncomfortably inside him such that he didn't know whether he was about to herniate or vomit. As he could not decide, he kept tormenting the creature. Keeping his grip on the plate, he put his legs to its back and kicked creature to its feet. Meanwhile, the chitin plate was torn from its back in a light show of zipping red magic and purple blood.

Agonized by the affliction, the creature hobbled some distance from Kaiser, who got up feeling like his guts and his lungs had switched places. Despite this, he forced himself to charge the creature, which still had Seriath jutting from its clavicle.

The creature received all of Kaiser's speeding weight. It whirled to try and steady itself, but tripped over the ledge of the large open fireplace. It flattened onto the blazing coals, which sizzled painfully at its enormous back wound.

Kaiser leaped right into the fireplace on top of the creature, pinning it to the coals. It thrashed and thrashed, but the Cypolonian refused to be moved, pushing the sword deeper into the neck to weaken it.

Then began the real punishment. Kaiser's glowing metal fist rocketed into the beast's face, sending blue sparks in all directions. Little of the cutting energy escaped to harm Kaiser, for he aimed not to break the skull, but rattle the brain inside. He bashed its head back and forth until a sudden gust blew coals from the fireplace.

Kaiser saw that red energy spinning outward from the monster's breaking armor, and knew it was time to get away. He had seen enough fiendish creatures die to know that they made a spectacle of it.

Grabbing Seriath he rolled off, sparing a look to the trembling creature. It shook apart into bits of shell armor, flaring up the coal fires while a vast glob of purple ooze emerged from the carcass. It stepped away from the flames, molting buckets of slime to eventually reveal itself as Seremet's human form.

It appeared that some of the damage to his demonic shape carried over, for as the slime dripped off, a massive wound at the base of his neck soaked through his gothic vestments. Kaiser hoped that the grievous back wound had also been sustained.

"Don't look so slighted. There's a lot more hell to beat out of you." Kaiser's lingual skills had returned now that his Red Rapture was burning out, but he and Seremet were more or less evenly injured.

With two slick movements, Seremet flicked out both of his weapons. Those strange glaives spiraled in his hands as if he had practiced two lifetimes with them. He glanced at Tibernas's prone form hungrily, then back to Kaiser. The Disciple waited, poised in a springy battle stance.

Knowing that Seremet had a thousand traps planned, Kaiser calculated how best to approach him. Even injured, this enemy could probably outmatch his speed. But he would wait for his moment, until the Cypolonian made an opportune mistake. Seremet was immovable, like a barbed shield that could not be provoked.

There seemed to be no wise decision to make. Approaching Seremet was extremely dangerous, and Tibernas needed help desperately, for Kaiser was sure the magnate's neck was broken.

But perhaps Tibernas could still help. Kaiser rolled the magnate's mace with his foot, slapping the haft into his claw hand. It was a marvelously heavy piece of weaponry, but nothing Kaiser couldn't throw to great effect.

He flung the weapon at Seremet, who twisted to avoid it. There was a thick crunching sound, followed by the tumble of bricks and red-hot coals. The glowing embers rolled around Seremet's feet. With that, Kaiser closed in, just out of reach, and waited.

Their animosity heightened like the flames surrounding Seremet. It wouldn't take more than a moment or so, Kaiser reasoned, watching his enemy's neck perspire. The flames took root and cast their waves of heat over Seremet's legs. Fire budded around his feet, but his eyes never moved from the waiting Cypolonian. Kaiser had taken the role Seremet had jealously guarded his whole career. In moments, one of their lives would end.

A piece of the floorboards snapped some sparks into the air, and it severed Seremet's mental leash. His forward dash was the fastest he had ever accomplished, and his glaives flew so cleanly that they rippled the air. One glaive would be foiled by Kaiser's sword, but it wouldn't be able to stop both.

And yet both glaives were stopped. Seremet realized that Kaiser had whisked his scabbard from his belt again to stop the second glaive like Seriath had stopped the first. Kaiser swept his arms around Seremet's.

With a pull, Kaiser broke both of Seremet's arms. The deep crunch was cut short by Seremet's cry of unimaginable pain. Both the glaives and the scabbard dropped.

Taking Seremet's throat in his claws, he gave his old enemy an ultimatum.

"Speak my name. Just once. And I will let you live."

While haggard breaths came harder and harder, Seremet would not speak to an infidel. It was well with Kaiser, who crossed his enemy's torso with Seriath. Seremet's hips fell away while a deluge of blood and guts splattered over the Cypolonian's boots.

There wasn't a drop of guilt to spoil Kaiser's enjoyment. Still holding the upper half of his old enemy's body by the throat, he felt a fragment of his honor regrow in watching the hooded Septunite's eyes roll back. Throwing the half body aside, Kaiser attended Tibernas, who was squinting and mouthing something.

"You alive yet, Tibernas?"

"Did you get the bastard?"

"I did, thanks to you. Can you move your feet, old boy?" Kaiser watched as Tibernas struggled to work his leg muscles. The ankle twitched. "Good, you're not paralyzed, but your neck was twisted something fierce. I'm going to have to make a sleigh for you quick."

"Quick would be good," Tibernas mentioned, feeling the roaring flames grow in intensity.

The men were nearly ready to leave when they saw Kaiser pulling Tibernas along. He had tied the magnate to the bell-tower door and piled their damaged armor on top of him. Tibernas was none too pleased to return in such a disgraceful state. His warriors rushed to his side, eager to know the state of things.

"Quit your yammering, I'm fine," Tibernas assured them. "Our enemy's in a worse way, I promise you." The magnate tried to wink at Kaiser, but could barely adjust his gaze.

"Tibernas sat in the corner crying most of the time," Kaiser grunted, inciting a round of laughter from the warriors.

"Ho ho, oh yes. Like a newborn." Tibernas almost felt the strength to sit up and clobber Kaiser for his joke.

"Take him, I'm too tired to pull his carcass around." Kaiser gave the sleigh ropes off to the men. His slacks were soaked through with his own blood, Kaiser realized, and he began to feel the dizziness of it. A warrior offered him a quaff from a canteen.

"Thel must be a real piece of work if he's Seremet's master," Tibernas thought aloud.

"He's a real piece of something." Kaiser splashed some of the water over his face.

"And Seremet was stronger this time. You still beat him."

"He would have turned me into pork chops if you hadn't been there. Thank you, old boy. You did me a fine service today."

"I think you'll find a happy little jar of powdered coal-ivy if you search my satchel, Executor," Tibernas said, gold teeth glinting hopefully. "If you want to thank me, would you grab me a pinch of it?"

"I'm not going to stick my fingers up your nose, Tibernas," Kaiser scolded, ignoring his comrade's groan. "You do too much of that stuff anyway."

"You sound like my first wife."

Their march back to the army was filled with such banter. It was an hour of celebration, despite the injuries. Kaiser had to rest now and again, but for all his damage he radiated more joy than any of them.

Chapter 53

"It's going to be an eventful winter," Norinthe was saying, gazing up at the night sky through the cell window.

The prince turned to the man chained to the inclined interrogation table. It was Feo, who had suffered the prince's enthusiastic sessions every night since the siege. The apprentice of Sanakal was leaner for his incarceration, and it was made evident in his writhing ribcage that was, like his face, decorated with self-scarification. But for all his masochism, he still dreaded the prince's attentions.

"You've been on that table for two days now. Still don't feel like speaking?" Norinthe asked, arms folded. Feo would not reply.

The prince was not as patient as his tone pretended. He put an arm up to lean close to his captive's face.

"This is the end of your life, Septunite. All of your years have been a blunder through deeper atrocities. And for what? So Opagiel can drink your soul and forget you?" Norinthe's minty breath swam over Feo's face and made his eyes water.

They looked almost like different species: Feo was the picture of a suicidal zealot, runic cuts streaming under graying, sleepless eyes. Norinthe was comparatively divine, his features smooth, clean, and tended, with colorful eyes awake and demanding.

"Even demons pity traitors, and you have betrayed humanity, a universal offense. In your final days, make amends by telling me what city will be attacked next."

Nearby, Velena was seated uncomfortably on a stool. She knew she would be addressed again soon. She felt the prince's attention seize her, and she pretended not to notice.

"Bless him again. And don't hold back, I'll know if you do."

Meekly rising from her seat and entering the moonlight, Velena raised a hand to the captive. The magic did not occur, and she lowered her hand. "This is an abuse of godly magic. Calphinas would never condone this, not even on an enemy."

"It only hurts him because he has rejected the gods. This is purifying him, mage. There's no sense in wasting his pain."

She did not move.

"Would you rather be excommunicated? Because I can flourish a pen and make that happen. Any of your colleagues can do this just as well as you."

Velena couldn't stand to be exiled from the church; her comrades needed her healing and guidance. She weighed her options again, just as she had four times already. Remorsefully, she placed her palm over Feo's chest and averted her eyes.

Divine magic flowed into the man. His veins glowed as if flushed through with neon ice. Demon energy had infected him deeply, it rooted in his marrow and pervaded his organs. Velena's blessing agitated all of it. A conflict of energies blazed through every level of his physicality, quaking the integrity of his body.

Feo's cuts became a thousand little geysers across his skin, crushing out black vapor in the painful exorcism.

Velena stopped, not caring if she was chastised, but Norinthe seemed amused enough, his breath pulsing with barely contained mirth as saliva flitted from the captive's teeth.

"You feel that? That is your own hubris, Septunite." When the prince saw his captive had fallen numb, he gripped Feo's head and knocked it against the table hard. "I'm not going to let you die, you know. I know that's what you want. I'm not concerned that you're not speaking. There's so much more your young body can endure."

Norinthe's predations had consumed the better part of two hours, he suddenly realized. Time went so quickly. A third day on the table wouldn't kill Feo, he figured, and so hiking up his belt, he stepped to the door, which a guard promptly opened for him.

Velena wanted to sink back into her white hood and disappear. She was becoming a monster on the prince's leash. It gnawed at her heart to do such things. She watched a set of Feo's scars begin sealing up and fading away. Divine magic was the essence of humanity's health and goodness after all. She had never dared consider it could be used for so perverted a purpose as torture.

The prince beckoned. "Light mage, come." Since he had begun using her talents, he felt the need to keep her in sight. She obeyed, praying in her mind for forgiveness.

***

The darkest rites of the Septunite church did not happen on Kasurite soil, but underneath it. Opagiel's clergy governed a sacred labyrinth deep underground, where the distinction between man and demon was blurred.

Every blood-red sin had its turn on those black altars. And with every innocent destroyed, magic was added to the Pool that connected the hellbringers. An unseen economy of death and suffering was the cornerstone of their power.

But Sanakal was outside the privileges of hellbringers now. He had become a slave, despite his abilities. The Disciples tasked him for works and knowledge like a wine press.

He was shaping the large creature in the hanging glass cylinder with his spells. The ritual caused both him and the creature great pain. He was forced to wield the *Ctheraton*, a book he did not think really existed until recently. When it was open, it sucked the warmth from the air and turned his breath white.

When he was finally finished, he made a dismissive gesture. He crumpled at his podium, and the creature was ejected from the bottom of the cylinder in a slimy pantomime of birth.

It was Purnon that emerged from the cylinder, naked and wet. He had fallen into a circle of powder that quickly dried away the slime.

"Rest quickly, sorcerer. It would please me to have another session before sunrise," he said with his iron courtesy. An attendant offered him his clothes and hat. "I simply cannot rest until my power matches my sister's."

The woman in reference was sipping a glass of green liquid, lounging in the gallery above. She sat with spike-armored legs crossed. She seldom removed all her armor.

"Then I should expect you'll grow old in that chamber, brother," she quipped.

Purnon dressed and extended a pale hand. A transformation played out on his fingers; they blackened and extended, and teeth cropped up on their undersides. A yellow webbing stretched between them. In an instant, they returned to normal.

The power he wielded now pleased him so much he giggled.

"What say you, Volter?" Purnon called out to his brother seated adjacent to his sister. "Shall we have a scrap when I'm finished?"

"Don't be so impressed with yourself," returned Volter, accepting a sip of his sister's beverage. "This advancement from Sanakal is a single step in a great road. A road Tysis and I have traveled far longer than you."

"Yes, I must remember that," Purnon said with genuine modesty. "Strength begs to be used, that's all. And I would use mine to avenge Akanis."

"On that we can agree."

"How much stronger did Sanakal make you, Volter? And you Tysis? You wouldn't let me spectate on your sessions."

Volter and Tysis shared a smile.

The door to the chamber rattled. The three Disciples turned their heads while Sanakal rested silently. Four peons entered, each hefting a corner of a traveling gurney.

It could hardly be called Seremet, what laid there, but there he was. Missing his waist and legs and his skin burned away. Still, *death would not have him.*

"Brothers . . ." he sobbed from lips like sun-dried worms. He tried and failed to sit up with his broken arms. "*Sister!*"

Tysis dropped her drink and lunged down from her seat. The gurney was set down on its fold-out legs.

"Seremet?!" She lay her hands where his knees should have been. Her zealous little brother had always come to her for protection and guidance. Not like the stronger Purnon who came on, a half smile betraying his amusement.

"Who was it?" said Volter, who came on as well, while Seremet was being smothered by Tysis's tearful kisses.

"That maggot, from the south. Kronin's companion, Kaiser," Seremet reported, unwilling to make the Furnace repeat himself.

Tysis palmed his chest. "Poor thing, gather your wits. Kaiser? We delivered him to the torture palace at Coyote's Ball, don't you remember?"

"Those were my thoughts precisely, when in my ambush, I looked up to meet those same golden eyes that quaked at our deeds. It was him. And he's become stronger." Seremet began heaving, the cross section at his waist pulsing with pain. "Mother Opagiel, he's so much stronger now!"

Purnon folded his arms. "How could he have overcome you? You were stronger than ever after Sanakal cast his magic upon you. Kaiser should have been like a plaything."

"And even though Akanis never received Sanakal's spell work, he should have made good sport of Kaiser too! And yet, dear Akanis was cut down by that mongrel as well!" Seremet's words made Tysis cup her mouth. Even Purnon lost all levity.

Volter held more composure than any of them. "So our missing brother Akanis was indeed murdered. And by the same miscreant who has done this to you."

"We swore we would witness the Felsong's Final Verse together," Purnon whispered to himself. "We swore a hundred years ago that we would see Opagiel enthroned as queen of Madon, and we would bask in the rays of her glory."

"Dead he is," Seremet announced, "but Akanis would give voice one last time." This time, he resolved to fight through the pain and forced his broken arms to sit himself up. He opened his blackened lips.

With a strong exhale, Seremet loosed a red vapor that quickly congealed into the form of a man at the bedside. Tendrils of the mist weaved into the form of Akanis's ghost, looking as majestic as he had in life.

"Elder . . ." Volter bowed, followed by Tysis and Purnon.

"I come by the grace of our bond." Akanis spoke in a phantom drone that made the air around them colder.

"A miracle of Thel!" said Tysis.

"Akanis, tell them what you told me. Tell them everything!" Seremet beckoned as he drifted off, weakened from the excitement.

"How has such a weak enemy come to vanquish two of Thel's Disciples?" Purnon demanded.

"Kaiser has become Executor of the Apogee forces. The source of his strength is unique, to say the least. He consumes the energies released by hellspawn that he destroys. He has consumed many in this fashion since our encounter in the south. Somehow, he managed to murder Opagiel's granddaughter Sarshel, despite my crippling him. It was then he was healed and took on power enough to surpass my own."

The ghost scanned the room with his senses. "Where is Master Thel?"

"In his chambers, as he has been for days," replied Volter. "Our blood harvest has earned him another chance to do battle with *her*, so his meditations must be uninterrupted."

"Indeed. *She* may be our Master's greatest adversary. But he will triumph. If not this time, then the next," Purnon put in.

"I see you have all developed new power. Good. Because it is your harvest that must usher in the Final Verse. Farewell, my family. Know that I will continue our fight whither my soul flies," said the ghost of Akanis. His essence melted away, drawn down to the realm of the godqueen he had served so long.

Perhaps they were linked, because as Akanis faded, Seremet convulsed. His pseudo-demonic fortitude was finally spent. The three remaining Disciples listened carefully to the throaty death rattle of their youngest member.

Tysis grasped dead Seremet's hand. Her teeth grated as black liquid streamed down from her eyes. One of the inky tears dripped upon the gurney and proceeded to boil a hole into it like strong acid.

"Kaiser wishes to destroy our family." She lifted her abyssal eyes to the ceiling and smiled, corralling her rage perfectly. "Oh, that simple man."

Chapter 54

It was some deep, black hour when heavy silence fell over Insomnia. Mingled efforts between the Federals and Archaics were lessening resentment and made for restful nights in the city that knew little of such things.

It was so quiet that Azurae feared she might be heard climbing the side of the mansion. She was getting very good at it, for she rarely missed an opportunity to see Kaiser when the day's duties were fulfilled. And they had both been away for some time now.

No sooner had she peeked over his window sill did a pair of great arms pull her into the room. She was thrown into the bed with a loving velocity that could only be the Cypolonian's.

"Intruder! I'll have your hide for this!" he scolded in his best impression of an old, bloated noble.

They undressed, surprised to find they both wore bandages on fresh wounds. But questions could wait, bodily kisses could not.

It was an effortless exercise, their forms powered by anticipation. A lengthy session of meaningful touching stripped their defenses completely.

Every beat of their excited hearts coaxed them deeper into meditative euphoria. Azurae's breath became rhythmic cries as intensity mounted. Kaiser savored every nubile contour, putting her through a paradise of lips and finger tips.

Two simultaneous sighs of completion made their bandaged muscles relax.

"Welcome back to Evanthea, Executor." She spoke so closely he could feel her lips moving on his.

"Welcome back, Sojourner." He touched a bandage on her back. The thought of a Septunite axe swinging down on her made him shiver. "You got this one defending the Green River cities, didn't you?"

"I did." She was proud, but Kaiser was plainly shaken.

"If only you weren't so skilled, I wouldn't have to entrust the most dangerous tasks to you. But then, endangering worthy people is all I do anymore."

Suddenly she said, "I need you to be faithful, Kaiser."

"Faithful? I'm not interested in anyone but you."

She laughed a little and kissed him. "I know that. I'm talking about the war." With mounting seriousness she said, "It's beginning to show in your face. In your voice."

"What's showing?"

"We all know what you think. We've all weighed the Apogee and its allies against Septunoth. I don't want you to suffer by yourself anymore, Kaiser."

Kaiser had never told anyone his true thoughts on the campaign.

"We can't win. It is hopeless." It felt like profanity. But to say it finally to another gave Kaiser some comfort.

She slid away then, pacing unclothed to his desk. She filled a pair of crystal tumblers with golden liquor. "Everyone thinks they're alone. But we are a fellowship, all of us, united in secret suffering." She formed a cluster of ice in her palm with her magic. "Triumph has many faces, and it never keeps one for long."

Kaiser watched her crush the ice in her fist and share it between the glasses. Her words were deliberately cryptic. It was a Eurivonean custom, to speak such that the listener is moved to think deeply.

"Do you think we can win?" he asked, as she returned to the bed, handing him a drink.

"I think we will never give up." She sipped the drink. "You once told me how you wanted to be a beacon for these people. That you wanted to glow for them."

She set down her drink. Then Kaiser received the most exhilarating kiss of his waking life. Her soft lips, tasting of bold alcohol, sent lightning through thoughts he had been too afraid to confront.

With the hypnotic authority of a sorceress, her eyes demanded his attention.

"I want you to glow, Kaiser. Through wind and rain, I want you to glow."

Kaiser felt shallow. The great woman on his arm trusted him, and he felt unequal to her. But worrying solved nothing.

He downed his drink and set aside his glass. They got to their knees and he kissed her hand. They held each other's wounded bodies. He clutched her with a strength that said *I will not fail*.

"I love you." He confessed into her soft hair. "I love you so much."

She kissed his cheek. "I love you too."

***

In the north, it was the third and hardest snowfall of the season. For House Dragnos, it was a time of harvest. Surrounding cities were getting hungry, and their defenses were becoming brittle. Their vulnerable wealth would find its way into the Hungerer's coffers by spring. Annual raids were the foundation of House Dragnos's prosperity after all.

But Corphian would have no part in those raids this year. While he had been among the first ten sons born to Dragnos, his disobedience had demoted him to something of a noble messenger.

So here he waited, with a company of bodyguards he did not trust, in a blustery thicket of dead trees on the remote western border of his father's realm. He was a man of cold ambition, every bit as unyielding as his father, but Corphian found even this task to be exceptionally repulsive.

He spared a look back into the eyes of a shivering, auburn-bearded man, the first of many in the long chain gang. There were twenty such prisoners, all clergymen, abducted from churches unfortunate enough to dwell within striking range of House Dragnos. Corphian absorbed silent grief from the prisoners and smugness from the bodyguards that sat high on their horses above them.

At last something trundled along the pass before them. A slaver band of Septunites, but without slaves. They were headed by a lictor whose horse nearly floated along on his cloud of self-importance. His polished gear gleamed like a beetle's shell as he brushed aside a snowy branch in approach.

"I presume this is an ambush then?" said the lictor from a safe distance.

"This is your tribute, fool," returned Corphian.

"Then why clutch your sword with such passion, son of Dragnos?"

"Because I want to kill you."

"Still? It seems your father desires a partnership with us." The lictor ventured forward, brave amid Corphian's outrage. Pulling aside one of the prisoner's ears, the lictor inspected the neck to find a Covenant tattoo. "Ah, godly men satisfy our Mother's hunger like no other offering can."

"This score and the bullion carts will satisfy your demands for the month. Until then, stay out of our lands." Corphian turned, happy to end the transaction so soon.

"Our business isn't finished yet, young Corphian." The lictor held up a hand that the son of Dragnos wanted desperately to sever. "Remember our second condition. We reserve the right to send your father against city-states near his realm."

Corphian had no leverage to debate. Dragnos was paranoid at the strange magic the Septunites wielded and bent to most any of their requests.

"Speak its name, and it will burn," promised Corphian, for whom battlefield glory was like a sweet, sweet orange. While he loathed to take commands from Septunites, the thought of conquest set his mouth to watering.

"The House of Tibernas Krale." The lictor was pleased to detect some give in the young warrior's demeanor. "I shouldn't think your father will need much convincing."

"The men of House Tibernas are said to have descended from giants. Were I in your position, I would ask the same." Corphian's misty breath heated with intent. "They are our old rivals. You will have our cooperation in this, Septunite."

"Sinra will be most pleased. Ah, but you have always served us well, Corphian."

An insult, or so one was perceived, though Corphian did not react. The first of his bodyguards, however, jostled with quiet laughter, amused at the noble son's short leash. The lictor watched intently, eager to see some retribution meted out, though none came as Corphian palm-fist bowed in his saddle.

"No, I am only serving my father." He turned away then with such obedience that the lictor nearly forgot he was son of the nation's most hellacious tyrant.

"Well, then. Off to the pyres for all of you." The lictor teased the chained slaves with a kick from his horse.

"The pyres, yes," added Corphian, retrieving the lictor's attention. "Please, allow me to make one more small contribution."

The lictor looked up to see Corphian crack his bodyguard across the face with a fist. A pair of teeth shot off into the snow, and the man crumpled face first into his horse's mane, which soon ran thick with dark blood from the man's broken skull. Corphian gave the bodyguard's horse a hard slap on the rump, and the animal carried the unconscious man into the ranks of the Septunites.

"An unworthy offering, but please accept it," Corphian said, seeing how the lictor's own men eagerly raveled rope around the comatose man's neck and the horse's neck while others manacled his hands behind him. "Presently, I'm feeling very generous toward your Opagiel." Corphian eyed his other bodyguards, who fought to make sure their cold shivering didn't resemble laughter of any kind.

Chapter 55

Sidna was hoping Caethys could have been here for this. She was standing in a row with eight other Federals on a ribboned platform. The commotion of the banquet was magnified by the shape of the hall, a high oaken dome whose pinnacle suspended a great chandelier of glass cylinders.

Caethys would almost certainly be fine, she told herself, maintaining posture in her green, buttoned uniform. Her hair was braided and terminated in a black bow, a look she could not wait to discard. Suddenly, she heard her name through the oration that Clayborn was delivering from center stage.

She approached him with soldier's finesse. They shook white-gloved hands before Clayborn turned to the case bearer and retrieved a handsome brass armlet. Upon it was etched a large-eyed owl. It symbolized the vigilance of the Apogee's elite forces, of which Sidna was now formally a member.

Clayborn clasped it comfortably across her left arm. Below, hundreds of infantrymen in military dress were deep in their cups, and upon seeing beloved Sidna decorated, they shook the chandelier with their applause.

Sidna could not stop a toothy grin from stretching across her face. She looked into the crowd with her good eye and saw faces that had called her a savior. Though Sidna rarely spared herself the credit, to them she was a torch.

Laughing over pipes with some enormously mustached aristocrat, Clayborn was spotted by Azurae, who had just now arrived. Having no celebratory clothes, she arrived in her armor, but had taken pains to clean it and herself thoroughly. She was met with a mild sneer from Clayborn and even less-veiled disgust from his short, fat friend.

Azurae refused to let the air of prejudice shrink her. "Hello, Captain."

"Give me good news, Sojourner." Clayborn had dispatched her days ago to intercept a shipment of spell-crafting supplies on its way to a neighboring province. It meant racing hard to make the window and destroying a vast supply of dangerous materials guarded by battlemages. He puffed his pipe expectedly.

"Our information was off. The convoy carried only a third of the materials we expected, yet had twice as many guards with them. The documents we found stated that the rest of the shipment would be dispatched at an undisclosed date." Azurae had rehearsed the words. "We eliminated them and their cargo, but the rest of the materials could not be accounted for."

"That's disappointing. We won't know where they are until some hellbringer uses it to wreck a village along the front," Clayborn put in at once.

"You'd have done well to bring some Federal riders with you," added Clayborn's mustached friend. "They'd have been able to track the other shipments, in case they were dispatched at the same time."

"We could have too, if we had been supplied horses," Azurae reminded them.

"Oh, but I thought all Sojourners could run like the wind?" The mustached man leaned in as he spoke, pipe smoke escaping his purple lips.

"Yes, but not for four full days, comrade."

"Hush, both of you. You did well enough, Azurae. The six of your party should get some rest."

"Four."

"Hm?"

"We were outnumbered, Captain, by no small margin. We lost two good warriors."

Clayborn would not show any remorse on his face, but also could not dispense any more edge at such news. He scratched his cheek with his pipe stem.

But Clayborn didn't have to respond. Sidna speared in with wine-scented breath. "Hey, the Sojourner Queen is back!"

Sidna shoved a cup into Azurae's bandaged hand. Azurae allowed Sidna's warmth to evaporate her frustration. She decided she didn't need the captain's praises anyway.

Clayborn was pleased to see the redhead again and greeted her with a hug. "You've done us all very proud, kid." He gave her a little kiss on the cheek. It made her giggle clumsily as she patted his back.

"Come on, your majesty. You're not drunk enough yet to flirt with old men." Sidna swung her arm around Azurae after breaking from Clayborn and led her into the crowd to a curved sofa.

Sidna pulled a man from the couch by the oiled hair, proclaiming it had been her seat, and he obeyed her command with a grunt.

"I suppose Clayborn was yelling at you for doing as you were told, wasn't he?" Sidna asked, accepting a drink from a waiter's tray before reclining against one of the pillows.

Azurae sat down, crossing her legs next to her. "It's no trouble really."

"So mild, Queen. Wouldn't you like a little gratitude from us continentals?"

"Why do you call me 'Queen'?"

"I don't know, you just have the presence of a noble. You walk straight, talk clean, and you smell nice. You must be a big deal back in Eurivone, eh?"

"It's true that I have more responsibilities back home." Azurae tried her beverage. It was a heady wine, bitter, but with a delayed savory flourish.

"Well, we have enough contention between all the barbarian houses and the Federals. One thing you'll learn about the Apogee is that we don't know how to say 'please' or 'thank you' very well. We're used to being the boss." Sidna drained half her cup in one swig. "I just wanted to say that we appreciate your help. Really. Even if our officers don't show it."

Azurae was still bitter enough that the gesture seemed ridiculous. But the Federal woman was being sincere, so she tilted her head a little as if flattered.

"Well, we believe in the cause as much as you do. You're welcome. And you can call me Azurae. Anyway, I've seen the burn that Dragnos left on Clayborn's hand, and on Executor Kaiser's. I heard about Potentate Nytrinion and the Ousting. I don't blame your people for being . . . defensive."

"We'll set it right. Maybe I'll even live to see this country restored." Sidna hummed thoughtfully.

"How long has this war been in motion?"

"Some eighty years."

"I see, that long. Let's make a difference, then, shall we? I don't want to be another lost soul in all these poor, shattered generations. I want to see my island again."

"You do believe we can do it, don't you?"

"I will formulate a more complete opinion when Executor Kaiser returns from his attack."

"Don't remind me. Two months they've been gone, and he's taken our best men with him." Caethys crossed Sidna's mind. "At least Tibernas and his goons are still here to keep us safe. Hey, aren't we supposed to be getting more of your type this month? More Sojourners, I mean?"

"Last month, actually. I'm a little concerned they haven't arrived yet. My sword-sister is among them, and I've been missing her greatly." Not one to lament openly, Azurae took a breath and tapped a finger on the owl on Sidna's armlet. "Congratulations, by the way. I know you've been training very hard."

"Her majesty is too kind," Sidna murmured happily into her cup.

***

Winter had settled heavily over the midnight province, caking Insomnia in windswept frost. The season's icy breath jetted freshly through the streets, to say nothing of the new watchtowers and barracks shivering outside the city walls. Dangerous-looking icicles stabbed down from every stone lip and overhang among the dwellings. Orange lanterns among the patrols were the only spark of vibrancy in the frozen metropolis.

Crawling across the snows outside the city came a long, black mass, pocking the white expanses with thousands of footprints. Gate captains hollered something over the wind, and the city gates scraped open.

In moments, one cheering guard was joined by a hundred others. Soon, awakened civilians and warriors crowded to their windows to find Kaiser had returned at the head of a happy procession. Another battle had been won.

The Executor held a pike high in his right hand, upon which had been planted two bald heads frozen and ugly. Their foreheads sported dead third eyes, one pale purple and the other orange: hellbringer heads.

Barbarians and Federals were throwing snow into the air like confetti, laughing at the defeated faces of the Septunite skulls.

"We have two less hellbringers to worry about, my friends!" Kaiser jiggled the heads grotesquely. "And a good four thousand less Septunites!"

Kaiser enjoyed his welcome only briefly, eager to return to his annexed mansion for any news. His horse and pike were taken as he arrived, and guards pulled the doors open. The warmth inside hugged him, thawing the cold of his lengthy march.

But he was not met with the same mirth the gates had supplied. Instead, his entire first floor had been turned into a healing ward. So many wounded had been laid out that some even lay on the stair landings. Kaiser shoved the cold doors shut.

"What the hell?" He had to take a moment to just realize how full the place was. There was a shortage of blankets, so old shirts and animal skins were piled upon as many as quantity allowed.

No one noticed him, for the healers were a sleepless lot skittering from bedside to bedside, trying to waylay death in all its encroaching forms.

He spotted Azurae praying softly, clutching the hand of a patient nearby. The tropical glow of her eyes was dimmed with exhaustion as she scanned the figure respiring quietly beneath her. She suddenly discovered Kaiser at the foot of the bed, the cold of the outdoors melting off of him in streams of mist.

"Kaiser, you're back." She set the hand down carefully and met his embrace. "Praise Tethra." Her hands explored the cold contours of his armor, happy that locked within was her trusted lover. She kissed his cheek, not caring who might see.

"What happened, Azurae? Who are these people?"

"They're my people, Kaiser. My Sojourners. They arrived just two days ago, torn to pieces." She sighed.

"Did the Septunites intercept them?"

"No, no they—"

"Kaiser? Executor . . ." The inquiry came from the patient Azurae had been tending. It was a slender woman of far eastern features and hair dark enough to match Azurae's. That's when Kaiser realized this was Nagarei, the sword-sister to whom Azurae often referred. She was in a bad way, it seemed. She had a bowl next to her head into which she had been spitting blood, which still stained the sides of her white, white face.

"Yes, Nagarei, is it? Don't speak if it hurts," the Cypolonian offered, but speak she did.

"It was not Septunites. They were Archaics. Carried red banners with a symbol like . . ." Nagarei gulped, thinking back.

Kaiser whisked off his riding glove and opened his scarred palm to her. "Like this?" he asked, in a timbre like a dungeon echo. The wounded girl's black eyes fixed wearily on his scar, and she nodded. He glanced at Azurae. "Dragnos's family has never in their history attacked Eurivone or any foreign power that I can remember. Why would he attack your people now?"

"But we weren't his main target, Executor," Nagarei told him. "Dragnos himself is leading a great army to conquer all of Valathon." Her words turned Kaiser into a glacier.

***

Archaic culture was a mystery to Azurae. So as Tibernas fumed through the stable, the Sojourner kept decidedly silent.

"Don't think I didn't expect this. I knew the Hungerer was eyeing my territory. He was waiting for my ten-hander army to leave, the scheming coward!" The magnate smashed his clay cup against a beam and made the penned horses jittery.

Kaiser didn't know what to say. He would have offered the magnate another beer, but the previous two had met the same fate.

"The Hungerer has always coveted my mountains. His father, Dragnos the Cold, tried to take it from my father. And before him, Dragnos the Hoarder attempted it. And I sure as hell will not be the lord that lets Valathon collapse!" Tibernas turned from Kaiser.

"Where do you think you're going?" Kaiser feared he already knew the magnate's mind.

"I'm sorry, Executor. But my own people come first. I'm taking my men north, to meet the Hungerer's forces. I only waited this long because you deserved to be told in person."

"Absolutely out of the question. I need you here, now more than ever."

"Tell me you wouldn't do the same, Kaiser!" Tibernas jabbed a finger into Kaiser's chest. "If it were your kinsmen burning in their homes, wouldn't you go to protect them?"

"You swore on your honor to follow my instruction, Tibernas. I cannot let my forces be divided. You may not leave."

"Family trumps contracts, Executor. I go." No sooner had Tibernas finished his words than the crisp sound of raking metal alerted him to his compatriot's darkened spirit. Deadly Seriath was in the Cypolonian's right hand.

"Little brother," Tibernas voiced to Kaiser in a hurt tone. "Is it really so easy to discard our bond?"

There was no response, not even eye contact. Kaiser just radiated the same absolute ardency he wore in the presence of any challenge. Grimly, Tibernas took a step back and reached for the haft of his great mace leaning against a stable post.

Azurae folded her arms, brow wrinkled. Kaiser's sudden cold militancy took her by surprise, but so did Tibernas's willingness to break a promise. It was her duty to defend Kaiser from danger, but this was a matter between friends. She waited.

"You're not going to stop me," Tibernas promised, hefting his weapon into vein-clutched arms.

"I've carved those words on many a tombstone." Kaiser swept forward with swaths that left primal energy sizzling in the afterimage of his blade. Seriath burst against Tibernas's guarding mace, throwing shockwaves of straw and dust from the padding feet of the combatants.

"I'm just another barbarian fool, right, Kaiser?!" Anger hardened Tibernas's defenses. It jetted from weapon clashes in the form of strobing sparks that started tiny flames in the hay around them. "Devotion to my family makes me dangerous, doesn't it?!"

Kaiser fought Tibernas back through the length of the stable. The magnate patiently increased his own force to try and wear down the Cypolonian, but there would be no tiring him.

Tibernas managed his own heavy strike against Kaiser at a key moment. The latter ducked and caught the mace in his hand on the backswing. Kaiser wondered if that was enough to make his point.

A fist crashed against Kaiser's jaw in response. Tibernas broke away and tried the mace again. The massy iron head came on fast enough to turn a man's skull to shrapnel.

But in that moment, Azurae saw no concern on Kaiser's face. Rather, it was as if he were just going through the motions until triumph occurred.

Kaiser's slash cancelled out the mace's momentum in a thunderous collision. Tibernas barely kept his grip on the mace as its backward force almost tipped him over. His midriff was ripe for slicing.

Tethra, stay his hand, Azurae prayed in her mind, gripping her arms in helpless observation.

Kaiser elected to seize the magnate by the dreadlocks. With strength disproportionate to his size, he flung Tibernas into a post.

A kick met Tibernas's face and spiraled him onto the hay-covered ground. His mace was not in his hand. He reached to retrieve it.

But Seriath shot down between his fingers, causing him no harm. Kaiser pulled the sword out, leaning in and training it on the huffing magnate's forehead.

"You've been my most faithful ally among any of the Archaics, Tibernas," Kaiser growled under a shady brow. "But you must obey the same rules as the others. I'm sorry."

Tibernas swallowed, the sword point just above his nose. "You know I won't, little brother. You'll have to make an example out of me."

Slowly, Tibernas reached up and slid the side of his palm over Seriath's treacherous edge. He squeezed his bleeding fist at Kaiser. "While there's blood in these veins, I am the protector of Valathon."

Azurae watched silent discourse pass between their gazes. There were layers of brotherhood between them on the verge of fraying forever, and both seemed to know it.

Kaiser removed the tip of his sword from Tibernas's forehead, barely leaving an indent above his nose. The magnate sucked the blood from his hand before retrieving his mace and pushing himself to his feet with it.

"Your men look to you as a father. If I kill you, they won't fight for me. Neither choice will stop my barbarian forces from being halved. I may as well let you live." Kaiser returned his sword to his scabbard.

"You're a real saint, you know that?" Tibernas remarked, patting some straw from his flank.

"But lord Tibernas," started Azurae. She was overturning one of the watering buckets onto the flames the two had carelessly started. "The Hungerer has ushered his siege monsters and enough soldiers against your realm to conquer Valathon twice. You may help your family escape, but your kingdom will never recover from what is coming."

Tibernas seemed insulted. "My ten-handers have never been defeated, Sojourner."

"But this is the largest invasion Dragnos's house has staged in two generations." Kaiser drew upon his historical knowledge. "And he'll be expecting you to return."

"What do you want me to say?!" Tibernas's brow wrinkled ghoulishly. He was biting back a horrible feeling of helpless shame, and like any Archaic, he flushed it in aggression. "I have to do this. I have to do this."

"He'll be expecting your ten-handers, that's obvious." Kaiser ran a thumb across his jaw where Tibernas had struck him, searching for answers and finding only deviant ones. "But I doubt he'd expect Julavese rangers. Or Caralox spearmen. And certainly not Acalian war priests." The Cypolonian listed sorts of Archaic warriors that had recently converged on Insomnia, and Tibernas realized that Kaiser had a mind to help.

"I doubt he'd expect Sojourners, Executor," Azurae suggested.

"Sojourners, yes." Kaiser grinned. "Pretty accustomed to slaying large beasts, aren't they?"

Outrage, woe, and now gratitude had been brewed so thickly in Tibernas's skull he had to lean against the horse pen.

"I didn't even think to ask you for help, because I never thought you'd consider it." Tibernas said. "The Potentate will surely put you on trial for this."

"Yes, big brother, but there's more to be gained than you think." Kaiser's cryptic words intrigued all present.

Chapter 56

Warriors from the front cycled in and out of the healer's ward in Kaiser's mansion, receiving care for their injuries. It was a good place to gather news about the goings-on outside the city walls, so Kaiser frequented the ward to absorb tidings and alleviate the wounded with conversation.

The whimpers of suffering veterans incited the Executor to softer tones, so it was easy for him to catch the voice of his captain who made his way through the bed rows.

"Executor,"—by Clayborn's humorless timbre, Kaiser could tell he had caught wind of the situation with Tibernas—"can I have a word?"

"You know you can." Kaiser arose from the side of a ranger woman whose right leg had been dressed for arrow wounds.

"Why on earth are you allowing Tibernas to leave?"

"Obviously because Dragnos is attacking his realm."

"But how will that help anything? Dragnos will not relent even if Tibernas holds him off. We're vulnerable to Septunites in the meantime, and the Hungerer will simply try again."

"No, he won't. Not if he is killed."

They dared one another to speak.

"Do you intend to march with Tibernas?" Clayborn said at last.

"Yes, we will go to Valathon."

"The Potentate has willed that we reinforce the *front, Kaiser!*" Clayborn's sudden explosion turned many bandaged heads.

"I don't appreciate your tone, Captain." Kaiser angled his black eyebrows. "We are vulnerable no matter what. But with a brief expedition to Valathon, we could sever a bloodline that has terrorized

Kasurai for far longer than Septunoth. I have to go with him, because if you haven't realized it by now, there are *two* wars to fight."

"With the Septunites representing the greater threat. We need to focus on the west!"

"We will, Clayborn. But Tibernas makes up a great part of our forces right now. Without him, we won't make a difference in the west."

"This isn't about Tibernas though, is it? It's about power, and you want more."

"Naturally."

"Dragnos himself comes to make an example of Valathon. You've found an opportunity to ambush him. With his blood on your hands, you'd be a greater candidate for his throne than his own sons."

Kaiser's look was unrepentant, so Clayborn's accusations pressed.

"Even if some nobles don't recognize your sovereignty, you'll still have the loyalty of those which honor strength of arms."

"Would that be so dreadful, Victon? With even more barbarians under my control, our push against Septunoth would be all the stronger."

"By Tethra," Clayborn breathed. "I watched as you gained control over the barbarian hordes at negotiations. But that was just the beginning. The Hungerer is just a stepping stone, isn't he? You would make yourself Lord of Kasurai. I've been so blind, you've already killed one Potentate—"

Kaiser smashed Clayborn against the wall, gripping his collar with a strength that could splinter oak.

"Open your eyes, Victon! Have you forgotten about Vendel? What about this?!" Kaiser ripped off his glove and thrust out his scarred palm. "What about the families lying in the dirt because of Dragnos's expansion?!" Kaiser struggled to contain his violence. He pointed at his palm. "*This* cannot be tolerated!"

"I cannot believe what I am hearing. I bear witness to the rise of a warlord . . ." Clayborn had not heard a word Kaiser had spoken.

"You're leaving the boundaries of my mercy, Victon," came the Executor's toxic whisper. "We need men and resources to match Septunoth. And that precious opportunity is roving through Valathon."

"And when there are no enemies left to fight, Executor? Where will your throne-seizing take you then?" Clayborn took a step to the side, away from Kaiser.

"Enough." Kaiser composed himself, frustration funneling into his golden eyes. "We are going to Valathon."

"I've restrained myself as best I could. You are unbalanced, Kaiser. As an official representative of Potentate Algus Equilion III, I hereby exercise my right to confiscate one half of Federal armies."

"You damn fool . . ."

"I'm doing what I think is right, Kaiser."

"As am I! Victon, I am no tyrant!"

"And I will ensure you don't become one." Clayborn didn't have the look of a spiteful man. He was doing what he thought was right.

"You have just broken my back," the Executor admitted to Clayborn as he turned away. "Have I really been such a pox on this nation? Do none of our struggles together compel you to reconsider?"

"You really are my friend, Kaiser. I think you know that," Clayborn said over his shoulder. "But I will defend the Apogee, even if it's from you."

***

Under a winter sun as cloudy as the future, Kaiser called his barbarian leaders together. He had to staunch his bleeding authority as half the Federal troops were being repositioned via Clayborn's edict.

"Our brother Tibernas has met with catastrophe," Kaiser began. "His homeland is invaded by Dragnos Cawn. Such is the Hungerer's hate for Tibernas that he makes the attack *in person*. Now, in the eyes of some, it is traitorous to help Tibernas at this precarious hour."

Kaiser's address went not only to his officers, but to hundreds of barbarians and loyal Federals who sensed the import. Among the throng was Tibernas, of course. But also Sidna, Caethys, and Azurae.

"I say we'd be traitors not to. And riding to save Valathon gives us the chance to face Dragnos and break his crown of vandalism forever. How many lords would die a second death just to have this chance we have?"

"Can we match the Ulcaneans, Executor?" asked one warrior. "If they mean to take Valathon, their army must be unthinkably powerful."

"It doesn't matter. We fight only as much as we have to until we can assassinate Dragnos. It's a gamble worth making, comrades. By right of conquest, we can then begin steering his overblown empire against the Septunites and end this damn war."

Kaiser's mission was laughably ambitious, but triumph would be a multiform thing. Beards were stroked and pipes were puffed until Sidna voiced her profound position.

"I'm sure as hell with you, Kaiser! I grew up in the Hungerer's flames, and I'll hang before I miss a chance to end him!"

The stubborn barbarians were not about to let a Federal woman boast more stones than them. Fear of Dragnos was something branded on all their hearts, if not their skins. But deeper than fear coursed their thirst for payback.

***

Velena wandered the ranks of the wounded in Kaiser's mansion, holding up the hem of her white robe from dragging through stray blood spills. Her hood was pulled almost over her eyes, as she wished to be inconspicuous.

She found who she was looking for in Azurae, who had fallen asleep next to Nagarei's crippled form, sharing the undersized animal skins. Velena swept aside a lock of her blonde hair and knelt, gently tapping Azurae's feet.

"Pardon, my lady. You are leader of the Sojourners, aren't you?" she asked, meeting Azurae's opening eyes.

Azurae shook away some drowsiness and sat up, piling the furs more squarely upon her sister. "What can I do for you?"

"I think I can be of some help to you. You see, we've made a bit of a discovery." Velena put a hand into her hood carefully, which soon emanated a faint bluish light. When she pulled out her hand, she was holding a tiny human form that glowed like a firefly.

"One of your faeries?" Azurae knuckled her eyes. She had seen Velena frequently healing veterans with the help of the little creatures. But the one she held now seemed different, and somehow familiar.

"Not at all actually. You recall how my faeries haven't been able to help your sister, of course?"

"Yes, because your faeries are divine creatures, correct? And Sojourners are possessed of natural magic, not divine. We are incompatible to their healing powers, you've said." Azurae recited the facts quickly, feeling hope in the air.

"We managed to find a few nature faeries like this one. City lords were keeping them illegally to tend their gardens. I was planning to release them, but I thought we might try this first."

Azurae watched the faerie skitter curiously over Velena's hand like some beautiful insect. It looked up to her with eyes like little pink agates. Then Azurae felt something, a complex flurry of sweet feelings, and remembered that young faeries communicated only through transmitted emotions. This one felt affectionate.

"I would be most grateful for your help, friend." Azurae's words were redundant, as the faerie understood her through her feelings. The creature fluttered down to Nagarei's forehead. The injured Sojourner awoke in a daze.

"Don't move, please, we're trying something," Velena told the waking woman.

Nagarei looked up with her big black eyes confusedly to feel the little creature prancing around on her brow. Soon, it knelt piously and extended its wings in an act that looked perhaps a little strenuous.

The creature seemed to draw in beads of light through its wings, soaking natural goodness up from the very air into its body, where it transferred down through her miniscule hand into her patient's skin.

Nagarei sighed as universal vitality slid through her veins and pooled at her wounds. Spots glowed through her blankets and animal skins where the magic worked the fiercest. If it was painful, it was a bright and health-giving brand of pain that the wounded Sojourner patiently endured.

When the spectacle ended, the creature loosened and fell into a fetal curl. Nagarei muttered a worried phrase in a language that Velena did not understand and reached up for the little creature. Azurae bit her fist in gladness at seeing Nagarei move more in a moment than she had in days. Sitting up, Nagarei peered closely at the little thing to see it respiring gently.

"She sleeps," said Nagarei.

"Thank the gods. Kaiser would kill me if I had harmed it," Velena breathed.

"How do you feel, Nagi?" Azurae asked. Her sister felt down to her thigh where gory bandages concealed a recent spear wound.

"Considerably better. Like ten days of healing have gone by."

"This one needs rest, it seems." Velena carefully took the faerie from Nagarei's hand and cradled it in her palms. "But there are others. I will bring them at once and heal as many Sojourners as I can."

Chapter 57

Through all the confusion on the following day, everyone sworn to the march found their strength. Armor was polished and rations were packed. Tibernas's ten-handers were arrayed on foot or horseback to disembark while the magnate himself was with Kaiser.

The two were being blessed by a variety of war priests that called the fighting strength of an entire pantheon over them. Tibernas and Kaiser wore battle regalia tailored for the greatest assassination in centuries, with the trust of their barbarian comrades resting on them in the form of tribal armlets, stone pendants, and rings.

Later, attending to final preparations, Tibernas found Norinthe curiously inspecting the barbarian commotion as saddles were cinched and horses packed. The prince had a small retinue of bodyguards with him.

"If you're not coming along, Federal, get out of here," Tibernas demanded.

"Too proud to ask for more help from the Apogee?" asked Norinthe.

"Yes."

"Well, I suppose I should thank you for dragging Kaiser and his zealots along. I've often aspired to be Executor, and it would seem there will be an opening soon."

"You think we ride to our doom? Well, you never put any faith in Archaics."

"It doesn't matter. Even if Kaiser does make it back, he'll be exiled, or even hanged. What he's doing with his Federal troops . . . oh, pardon me; his *remaining* Federal troops, is high treason. And I should think they've been lenient enough with him already."

"Men with promise deserve a little leniency. He's unpredictable, but he's trustworthy," Tibernas asserted, annoyed at prince's buttermilk tone.

"Please. That violent anarchist is as great a candidate for the gallows as any. Kaiser is no Federal."

"You're damn right he's not." Tibernas dropped the pack he had been holding and closed in. While the guards puffed up, neither Norinthe or Tibernas wavered. "Dragnos's family has molested my realm for centuries. Time and again I wrote the Federal magistrate for help. For soldiers to protect my miners, or for a little food when times were lean. I always promised to pay them back and not *once* did they send help. Kaiser comes to my aid at my darkest hour, and I hadn't even requested it."

"Septunoth is the greater evil, Tibernas. Dragnos's forces will receive justice in time. Though I doubt it will be at your hands."

"He focuses on barbarian houses. You have never known the Hungerer's wrath, Prince Norinthe. You Federals underestimate him." Tibernas turned away and mounted his horse.

"It's because you barbarians are divided that you make easy victims. If only you had joined the Apogee in our formative years, perhaps you would enjoy the same consideration he shows us."

"Perhaps he spares you because he suspects your coffers are as empty as your loins." Tibernas spurred his horse away from the aggravating exchange.

Norinthe might have retaliated, but he spotted one of the Sojourners, Velena, and a prisoner. *His* prisoner, Feo.

"I think you'll find that hellbringer is my charge, ladies. Why don't I take him off your hands?" Norinthe gestured for the chain leash Nagarei held. The hellbringer apprentice smelled bathed and balmed, and it took all the prince's will to not be outraged.

"The Executor wanted me to express his appreciation, Prince Norinthe. You've extracted valuable insight into the Septunites. Now, this hellbringer can serve another purpose," Nagarei explained

"Yes, bleeding and dying. And that honor belongs to me, doesn't it?" Norinthe clearly expected an answer from Nagarei, but the latter nodded to Velena.

"Good prince, our sessions with Feo have shown odd changes in his chrysm. Against all probability, his corrupted soul has somehow begun to absorb the divine magic I apply." She turned with conspicuous affection to the man shackled, blindfolded, and gagged. "He has the potential—"

"The potential to deceive you, light mage. He'll feign something you want to see so he can soften the security around him. And then? A thousand casualties before we can stop him. No no no, potential or not, he has a bloody price to pay." Norinthe tried for the chain, but Nagarei pulled it away.

"Apologies." Nagarei had no desire to irritate this noble. "But Executor Kaiser has assigned me as the prisoner's keeper and protector until Lady Velena's experiments are completed."

"Unacceptable. I was his captor, I will be his end. Give him to me now!"

When Nagarei moved the chain away again, Norinthe grabbed her collar. She could have attacked him, and perhaps that's what he wanted, as the prince's bodyguards were watchful and close.

But Nagarei softened and made her warm breathing heard. She fed him vulnerability from her large black eyes and pressed his fist a little lower on her chest.

"The hellbringer deserves death at your hand. You captured him. It isn't fair," she said in a lyrical accent. "Nor is it fair that my sister goes to fight while I am forced to stay here. We all have roles to play though, and I will play mine with grace."

Norinthe was not a stupid man. He was familiar with the imaginations of women who wanted something. He knew exactly the game she was playing. And yet, fighting was beginning to sound less appealing.

"If the prisoner makes any offense, I will personally deliver him to you. I would ask, until that moment, play your role, as I do. With Kaiser departing, it falls to you to defend Insomnia. Let that be your honor." Nagarei let his fist graze her chest as she released it.

He regarded her with surprise, an expression that did not suit him naturally. "Let's . . ." He started over. "Just make sure he's locked up tight. Never let his hands free. And most of all, keep him on the magic-dampening drugs. Three doses a day."

"At least. I won't suffer infernal sorcery in my custody."

"Good enough, then. Be safe, ladies." The prince walked away, hands on hips. *What a farce*, he thought. He would not be subject to a pretty woman's hypnosis. But indeed, he had no desire to fight with Nagarei anymore, and that's probably all the Sojourner wanted.

"Thank you, Nagarei." Velena smiled at her. "I didn't think the prince was capable of compromise."

"Even metal is pliable, if you get it hot enough." The Sojourner grinned back. "I owe you for healing me anyway. Just don't make any of us regret giving this sorcerer a chance. The game you're playing is a dangerous one."

"I know. But even Septunites are human. If I can help him, I want to."

***

"I can't believe you're leaving again so soon," Briston said in a tone that he hoped would make Kaiser feel guilty. "I got so much better in your time away, I wanted to show you. I can actually craft weapons with primal magic now."

The Cypolonian had been decking his horse for the ride when the young blacksmith caught up to him. The boy had been waiting to find the Executor alone.

"You're joking. You're barely sixteen," Kaiser came back.

"But it's true! Master Norving says I'm the brightest apprentice he's ever had!"

"Grumpy old Norving said that?"

"Well, not directly. But I can tell he's proud of me by the way he yells at me."

"Ha, Briston. Doubtless you'll be as fine a smith as your daddy. I can't wait to see that unfold, but I have to go where the trouble is, and there are heaps in Valathon. But this foray won't take nearly as long."

The explanation that Kaiser had hoped would assuage Briston actually seemed to hurt him. Briston watched the snow of early morning collect on Kaiser's armored shoulders.

"Look, I know you're worried, Briston," added Kaiser.

"Just go. I have to get used to this."

"Get used to what?" Kaiser frowned. But Briston took a while to reply.

"It's all right, you know? I've become stronger watching all of you. I'll carry on because I have to. I knew I'd have to see father go some day, and he did. You'll go someday too, and that's all right. I'll handle it." A rise in his face let one of his brimming tears spill off the side. "It doesn't matter how many of my friends die, I'll just keep on working. I promise I won't ever stop, Kaiser, because I want to honor what you did for me."

"Briston . . ." At the sound of his name, the boy burst. He was too embarrassed to speak any more.

Kaiser walked down to his step and wrapped his cold, armored arms around him.

"I know you're strong, son. I've seen it in all the tears you've locked away and the hard days of work you put in. And I know when you smile at me, what you really want to do is just curl up and die. That's strength, Briston, and that honors me." Kaiser pulled away again. He put his glove on the hand-shaped scar on the boy's face. "But I'm strong too. And I'll come back."

With every syllable, Briston was reminded of his father when the Septunite flames took him. Every day, Kaiser threatened to cause Briston as much sadness as hope.

"We're going to jog up north quick, knock off Dragnos's head, and ride home. All right?" Kaiser tried to stabilize the boy a bit. "Practice hard, because my armor's going to be a mess when I return."

"Nothing I can't handle." Briston wiped his eye.

***

Neither winning nor dying would be a prolonged affair, so the army packed light. Tibernas headed the procession of Federals, Sojourners, and barbarians through his southerly timberlands. The wind carried sparkling snow.

The days were long and quiet. The church-like echoes between frosted crags made sleepwalkers out of everyone. But towers were soon visible across the snowy valleys, and they were sobered by the tang of war smoke.

Established atop a huge, blunt mountain resembling a pregnancy in the earth was Castle Krale. Its towers ringed the summit like a crown. The sprawling wilderness farther down hid quarries and trading villages. It was a wild land respected by an industrious people.

In peaceful days, there was a sound here that only Tibernas could hear. It was like a million tiny bells: the rhythm of his people cutting stone.

There was a different sound today. Something horrible was happening in those evergreen heights. Smoke of an unwelcome color drifted through the canopies.

Their horses snuffled. Paused at the foot of a bridge, Tibernas realized Kaiser was waiting for him to make a decision.

"We need to keep your presence a secret, Kaiser. Any farther, and his scouts may catch wind of you," he murmured, snowflakes in his mustache.

"Then this is where we part ways. I'll go west and attack from behind," Kaiser asserted into the wind.

"I'll get my family out of the castle's south wing, which will certainly fall first. Dragnos will push hardest for my throne in the north wing. That is where I need you to be."

"The throne," Kaiser thought aloud. "That will be our bait."

Tibernas saw the ambition in his face. He knew the Executor's reasons for helping. Kaiser wanted the Hungerer's crown, to be a military emperor. He was here for gain as much as friendship.

But that suited Tibernas well enough. He needed help today, and power had sat in far crueler hands than the Cypolonian's. For now, his dear Sun Mei and the boys were waiting for him.

Tethra, let them be waiting.

"We can do this, you know. We can stop him. For good," said Kaiser.

"I won't rest until we do. You never raised a family, did you, Kaiser? No wife or children."

They never spoke of their families. Kaiser had little to contribute anyway, with his vague memories. The truth was, Kaiser didn't really know.

"No," Kaiser decided.

"Don't. Men like us have too many enemies." The magnate quietly waved for his men to begin the march across the bridge. "Gods keep you."

"And you."

He was right to get moving, Kaiser supposed. The Valathonians all spared a look over their shoulders at the allies that would share this fateful hour.

Chapter 58

Kolel had been grandfathered in as the Hungerer's siege captain at twenty and had never learned the terror of battle. For eleven years he manned the Hungerer's trebuchets and other war machines, casting stone and fire over the heads of lower-caste warriors whose annual pay couldn't equal his lobster-hide boots.

He had been watching the huge boars pull back the throwing arms of the catapults. The arms were crafted from such elastic wood that they could snap back from being curled into a full loop, allowing for magnificent throwing range. All morning he had filled the air with singing stone. The taller trebuchets whooshed dangerously higher above.

One of his scouts was groaning behind him. He turned to spy the lad stumbling from the tree line, looking like he'd been mauled by a cave bear.

"What the hell is wrong with you?" Kolel scolded, angrier more for an interruption than an assault on his soldier. "What happened?"

The spurting wound on his scalp may have impaired his speaking, because the boy could only point with a ragged arm back at the trees. A line of horsemen that did not belong to Kolel stepped into the light.

The siege captain, with no battlefield sensibility, was too stupefied to raise an alarm as the force roared in, followed by Federal infantry and barbarians. It didn't feel real until his bodyguards' blood hit him in the face.

This was the first time Caethys had ever faced Ulcaneans. They were strange men in stranger dress. Shells, bones, and scales of magical species were their armor. They roared like monsters and fought like them too. You could take off their sword arm, and they would try to bite your neck.

Every stereotype about Archaic culture was represented in them. Sidna kept close, and Caethys was glad for it. Their brutality rendered his martial tactics almost useless. Wounds didn't slow them. If they were alive, they kept fighting.

Azurae fared better. There was a formula to fighting bestial enemies that had to be felt more than calculated. She could read them like any disgruntled predator and killed them in the same way.

But she needed protection, or that's how Senlu saw it. The insect-like feline kept at her back, bowling over enemies that tried to surprise her.

Kaiser had been very specific about Azurae's role here: secure the giant boars working the siege craft. The Ulcaneans seemed to sense her objective and attempted to kill the beasts rather than let them be captured.

But Azurae was not the only Sojourner at hand. Her spear kept enemies at bay while her allies whittled down the rest. All the boars were still alive by the time the majority of the enemy was defeated.

Kaiser took stock from horseback as the siege apparatus crumbled from the blows of barbarian primal magic. The area was crowded with his warriors, most of whom never even had a chance to fight. It was best to keep moving, so he rendezvoused with Azurae, who had Senlu called to heel.

"All boars and Sojourners accounted for, Executor," she said, already in the graces of the vast animals who snuffled at her friendly aura.

"Excellent. Can you keep them calm enough on the trail?"

"Yes, but it's best if your men give us wide berth."

"Done. Let's get moving."

They just ignored him. Kolel, pride of Ulcanea, deemed unworthy of a warrior's death by his enemies. They were on the move again, leaving the wreckage of his operation bleeding and burning all around him.

A perfect reputation spoiled. He had not even shed any blood in defiance. Shame upon shame heaped upon his rounding back. Quivering fingers groped for the bejeweled blade in his scabbard. He slid it free as tears wetted his eyelashes.

Putting sword to throat, Kolel retired from an illustrious career.

***

Not far away, Tibernas dismounted and elected an entourage of ten-handers to follow him. The rest of his army awaited eagerly at the precipice of a bloody morning.

"I wish you would take more men, my lord," said a mounted lieutenant. "You have my full confidence, but there could be a thousand Ulcaneans in the south wing."

Tibernas stowed his huge mace on his horse in favor of a hunting knife. "We mustn't raise an alarm inside. I can get my family out of there more easily if I go unnoticed. You just do your part. Remember what that is?"

"Kill them all."

"Kaiser will help you push for the summit. Good luck, warrior." Tibernas let them go then and entered the mossy trench nearby. Great roots framed a cave hidden under a rock lip: the entrance to the secret warren. They entered.

They must have been the first to hike the blackness under the mountain, for none of the braziers had been lit and torches had to be passed out. Wide tunnels stretched on and on, supported by wooden arches.

It could have been a heap of trash piled in the corner, but it breathed. And through the muddied fabric and crusted blood Tibernas recognized the most faithful of his servants.

"Daelyn." Tibernas righted the man's drooping head, revealing a horrendous scrape up his face. The man had been dragged behind horses. How he escaped to the warren was anyone's guess.

"Merciful Tethra, tell me I'm not dreaming. Could it really be you, Master Tibernas?" Old Daelyn always addressed his magnate formally.

"Tell me of the south wing, old friend. Are my wife and sons there?" Tibernas did not know how many words the elder had left in him.

"Above the fourth story, that is all I know for certain."

"Can you walk, old boy? Can you wait at the entrance for us?" Tibernas was met with a slow head shake.

"Go, my lord. Save our peaceful mountain," Daelyn pleaded. Tibernas squeezed his hand and left, Daelyn's cries following him. "If the mountain falls, justice is dead! Protect it, Master Tibernas! Don't let this happen!"

The magnate ran faster than his fatigue could register. Following the old signs for the south wing, he rounded a corner and tread the incline to a hall of ladders, selecting the third.

"Time enough for battle later. Right now, we get my family and get out quicker than quick. Do we understand?" he asked his squad of ten.

Tibernas put his hunting knife in his teeth and climbed.

Above, a well-camouflaged door in the wall of a staircase swung open, creaking heavily from lack of use. The dungeon. Tibernas had little use for it in his rule, preferring leniency or outright death in his law keeping.

"What?!" erupted a man from the staircase above. An Ulcanean scout. Tibernas grabbed his foot and pulled him down to be quickly dispatched. It happened so loudly and so fast that they almost didn't hear the enemy higher up the stairs yelp and flee.

"Move, now!" Tibernas ordered, and the chase for his family was on.

***

Valathonian villages boasted good defense, but one in particular had five civilians for each soldier. The village had suffered one vanquished raid already.

The flow of villagers migrated into the woods where Kaiser's host was emerging. They were almost fired upon by suspicious archers when Caethys jogged ahead, sword sheathed.

"Is there an officer? This is Executor Kaiser's host, we've come to help!" he said, palms up. There was no mistaking the well-groomed young man for one of the bestial Ulcaneans. A Valathonian field captain shoved aside the archers to meet him.

"I'm in charge here. Fine timing on your part, son."

"How many Ulcaneans are coming?" Caethys pressed as the Federal army swelled into the town.

"Bloody more than we can handle."

"All right, take only the soldiers you need to get the villagers down the south side of the mountain." Caethys pointed back at the procession of refugees.

"Any other day I'd belt you for giving me orders, but I'll see it done."

"Good man." Caethys patted him away and joined his Federals lining up in a rocky plain where quarrying projects had been abandoned.

Across the stony meadow came a crumb of the Hungerer's army. It was difficult to tell who among the enemy were beasts and who were men, for their armor was assembled from monster parts.

But for certain they had living beasts aplenty to assist them. The furry, raptor-like longhounds swayed their vast tails while larger ones were ridden by officers.

These were the same creatures that had devoured Vendel, and Kaiser was already fuming by the time even taller brutes were insinuating themselves behind the Ulcanean warriors. They came on slow enough, so the Cypolonian took the initiative.

"I issue a challenge!" he declared. "I would gauge your leader's mettle in single combat before battle is joined! Step forward, coward!"

A man with a snail-shell helm widened his angry eyes. He used his halberd as a walking stick, waving for his warriors to hold.

Ah, barbarians, Kaiser thought to himself. *Zothre keep you proud forever.*

"Federal, I am Hugar!" the Ulcanean commander snarled through the cage of his mask. "What do you here? Go home, Federal woman! War is for men!" He beat his armored chest to the laughter of his minions.

Kaiser rubbed his chin and turned to face Sidna, whose grinding teeth could have cracked a walnut. "Sidna, what was your final score at the elite games?"

"Ninety-two, Executor."

"Ninety-two?" Kaiser had not heard her score and looked on his friend with new eyes. "Well. Would you do me a kindness?"

"Oh, I'll be kind." She slapped down the visor of her helm. It was a custom build, suited to provide maximum visibility for her one remaining eye.

Like the rest of the Federals present, she wore full plate metal armor. It was heavier than either her or Caethys were accustomed to. But then, Sidna had never been stronger than she was right now. She broke away.

"You were talking to her, right?" Kaiser pointed at his champion.

"You insult me!" Hugar roared back. "I don't kill this one. I keep her for pleasure."

"This one's for you, Mama." Sidna sent some quiet words to the sky as she produced a second broadsword and crunched across the field to meet him.

Hugar leveled his halberd, ready to meet her charge.

A stone she kicked twisted the helm on Hugar's head, skewing his vision. Sidna was able to attack at her leisure as he fought to right the helm without using his hands, which were occupied with defending.

Of course, he would rely on his strength against a smaller foe like her. That meant shoving, throttling, and hard swings. When he attempted to clothesline her with his weapon, she hooked her arm around it to keep her feet.

A chop between his neck and shoulder awarded Sidna first blood and a holler. Then came his rage, which Sidna had to navigate carefully. He managed to push her away and cycle in a pair of halberd swings.

An elite instructor had told Sidna that the only deadly part of a polearm is its head; the length of it should not be feared. She foiled his range by moving in. True enough, the shaft of the halberd struck her shoulder, but her sword landed on his hand.

Sidna knew that feeling. She had broken several of his fingers. His adrenaline would keep him painless and dangerous for a few more moments.

"Now!" Caethys said under his breath.

Hugar's broken hand could not put up enough of a defense on his right side. Sidna's sword skated up his guarding weapon to plug in between the splint mail at his hip. She cut short his yelping kneel with a knee to the face that put him on his back.

"Wait—" he implored her as she crawled on top of him and pulled off his helm. "Wait!"

It was Sidna's right as Kaiser's champion to end this life in her own way. She did not choose to be quick.

The pommel of her sword hit his head like a carpenter's hammer. It was the first of a dozen such blows that jetted blood and flecks of pink brain onto her green breastplate.

Sidna was deaf to the proud laughter of her comrades behind her. She was replacing a puzzle piece of her broken life by killing an Ulcanean officer. She imagined her brothers' hands on her working shoulders as she dismantled this tyrant's head.

"Sidna!" Caethys's warning came too late. The Ulcaneans were not sportsmanlike.

A tomahawk spiraled into her helm. She sat stunned until a pair of darts found her stomach. Sling bullets drummed over her armor as she fell.

"*Slaughter them!*" Kaiser demanded, and dragged his army into combat.

Caethys outpaced all of them, sliding in to lend his shield to Sidna's prone form. He dragged her back into the oncoming comrades who leaped them in the charge.

"Sidna, no, wake up, girl," he beckoned, just as her eye opened again, blinking away a little blood.

"Those bastards!" she growled, wrenching the tomahawk from the mercifully strong plate at her forehead. She arose, plucking the missiles from her stomach. "Come on, let's get in there, Cae!"

Before the forces became mingled, the Sojourners had a job to do. The boars were no longer docile now that violence was in the air, but they didn't have to be. The boars charged, guided by the Sojourners that volunteered to steer them.

The Eurivonean riders stampeded the hefty pigs into the enemy's center mass. It was like a landslide of hairy, squealing muscle that buried Ulcaneans.

Azurae and her troops followed, not wanting to leave her riders vulnerable when their momentum was stopped.

The horse-sized longhounds marauded Federals with talons like pickaxes. The larger ones ridden by officers could crush a helmeted man's skull with their steel fang augmentations.

As a Sojourner, Azurae had the dark honor of euthanizing creatures of disharmony. With powers of extermination arrayed in her mind, she found herself in the center of a longhound pack.

It was unclear even to Azurae if Senlu could feel fear. But the way her animal companion chittered at her side, it was obvious it could feel excitement. Its tail scales bristled enthusiastically.

Pack hunters like longhounds were always careful to wear down dangerous prey. But Azurae had quit being prey long ago. Stabbing and thrusting were too mechanical to enable the speed she needed. Azurae needed her blades to flow, and she became a dervish with her twin katar.

She did not solicit death, she only offered it. A stroke of pain met any tail or jaw extending for an attack, made easier by Senlu's harrying at their feet. Cuts accumulated over their muzzles, throats, and thighs. A mantra repeated in her mind.

By the Genephim, my body is a stone
A pillar of my teachings, with iron in my bones
By the Genephim I see with open eyes
Impervious to weakness, impervious to lies.

Chapter 59

For so large a man, Tibernas could conduct himself very quietly, and his posse followed his example. Ulcaneans stalked through the castle, taking what pleased them and breaking what didn't. They certainly resembled monsters in their strange organic armor. But if they had harmed his family, Tibernas resolved to be more monstrous than they.

It was no small pleasure leaving a handful of Ulcaneans knifed to death in the back halls, but their bulky bodies took time to hide. Tibernas was growing frantic as time slipped away. A glimpse out the window distracted him.

His ten-handers had climbed the slopes and started a monsoonal brawl against the occupying enemy. Farther up, the north wing was still contested. Arrows flew and fires burned.

His people were not giving up. The fact gave Tibernas strength enough that when his search brought him to his wife's living quarters, he did not hesitate to kick it open.

A moment's study told him many things. His wife was in a corner surrounded by men, one of which clutched a bloody nose. His sons knelt by the far wall in manacles. Tibernas tossed the knife to his eldest, who caught it.

The knife was in the belly of the nearest guard instantly. The younger son bull-rushed the knees of another. Sun Mei burst from her ring of distracted captors to prevent being taken hostage. Tibernas and his men executed a session of shanking and neck breaking that lasted fully three breaths.

"The keys, my lady." One of the magnate's men bent to resolve the manacles on Sun Mei's wrists, but her eyes followed Tibernas; something was wrong.

The youngest son was still on the ground. Freed, Sun Mei moved to find Tibernas was keeping pressure on a stomach wound that Kobon had suffered. Their oldest, Hygon, grimaced nearby.

"How bad is it?" she asked.

"Not bad enough to stop my Kobon. Right, son?" Tibernas said, taking a cloth that one of the men had ripped from the bed nearby.

"Right, father." Kobon yelped as Tibernas dressed the wound and scooped him up. They peeked out into the hallway, looking both ways.

Sun Mei, trained as a ten-hander herself, elected two small weapons with which she would escort her husband and children to the practiced escape point. The bodyguards would bring up the rear.

She glanced around the corner; when the coast was clear, she grabbed her husband's head and kissed him. "I've missed you so much."

"You've been strong for me, wife. Thank you."

At the bottom floor, Tibernas wondered if the spirit of fortune was drunk for how uneventful his return had been. But Kobon was pale, his blood flowing over his father's arms.

"Keep pressure on that, Kobon! Or you'll get weak, son."

Sun Mei had paused upon reaching the room below. When Tibernas had joined her, he too paused.

Down the hall, they were met with the huge black eyes of one of Dragnos's siege beasts. The feathered crow, but built like a lizard, paused, its bulk half-pulled through a window. Its orange forelegs clenched, bunching up the rugs in its talons as it prepared to make its move.

"Go, just go," Tibernas urged his wife as his bodyguards positioned themselves between him and the beast. The crow thing seemed to understand and made a thumping sprint, its long feathers hissing along the walls.

They ran. The ten-handers may as well have been children for how easily the beast knocked them aside. What the crow beast wanted was *real* children, and perhaps a healthy woman. It had had its fill of the unbathed soldier fare. Its desire for something prime and lean put a rapid locomotion in its fat legs.

Sun Mei and Tibernas ran almost side by side until an Ulcanean from an adjacent hallway tackled her. Tibernas, son heavy in his arms, could do nothing but turn. He met the angry eyes of his wife as she slid both daggers across the throat of the attacker on top of her.

"*Save the boys!*" She shrieked with all urgency. It was a promise Sun Mei forced him to make long ago; if he had to choose, choose the children. He ran.

Sun Mei rolled the gushing dead weight off and resumed her run. She tore a tapestry from the wall and flung it into the thing's face. It earned her precious, precious seconds as she darted for the room Tibernas entered, and Hygon, ever swift, was already waiting.

Cursing every seamstress in existence for the heavy fabric of her dress, Sun Mei hurtled through the door to the dungeon through which Tibernas had entered.

The moment she was through, Hygon kicked the lever of the guillotine he had lined up with the entrance. The heavy razor dropped, chopping halfway through the torso of the beast that just emerged. It clawed and clawed and filled the room with its hybrid scream.

"Hygon, you are a blessing on this family." Sun Mei squeezed him while Tibernas headed to the secret entrance below.

Tibernas opened the entrance and helped Kobon onto Sun Mei's back when they joined him. "Get to the forest and head to my sister's hall next to the lake. I left my two best horses at the entrance."

"Tibernas, please come back to us. We need you."

The magnate pulled his family together, stroking Hygon's hair. The eldest son stayed quiet, but spoke through the strength of his embrace.

Tibernas kissed his wife and looked to Kobon, who was looking very tired. "Kobon. Will you wait for me, son?"

The boy blinked his dilated eyes at the question, resting his chin on his mother's shoulder. "I'll wait for you, Father."

That's enough, decided a voice from Tibernas's instincts. Too much of this dulled his fighting edge. It was time to don the warrior's mask. He herded them into the entrance without further words or eye contact. Before his heart could protest, he shut the door behind them.

***

In any fighting commander's head there is a sense that develops, and it discloses how quickly one's soldiers are dying. It was easier for Kaiser this time, because the screams of the animalistic Ulcaneans were distinct from his coalition.

Too many screams from his side, he decided. The Defender's Mantle did not give strength to people, it revealed it to them. He did not want to use the Mantle's limited energy so early, but the hard truth was, Ulcaneans were the stronger warriors.

Kaiser catalyzed the blue diamond at his chest piece. It became the storm-eye of courage for any soldier serving the same cause as the Mantle's wearer. One could hear the combat quickening like a hail of metal.

Fatigue, doubt and cowardice evaporated all around Kaiser, and within him. It was time to end this. That exciting blood tickle that consumed him in the south clawed up his spine again. Once more, he was the Tireless Butcher.

Filled with hate, Kaiser crunched through their ridiculous armor like glass. Seriath fell upon Ulcanean flesh like a guillotine. He plucked a shovel out of a nearby coal cart and used it to knock aside attacks before slicing heads (or parts of them) from their owners.

Soon, the Cypolonian was the centerpiece of an Ulcanean massacre. If he could remember the recent moments, Kaiser would have remembered a call among his enemies to focus on him. And they did, poor souls.

It was over, so he checked ferocious bloodlust with ferocious reason. His men were cheering all around him, their gore-caked Executor. Their love made him laugh, and he took a theatrical bow among the mounds of dead.

"Gods, Kaiser, it's unholy how you fight." Caethys, mercifully alive, came in to be caught in a crazed hug from the Cypolonian who posed a question.

"Our count? What is our count?"

"Not good, Executor. Fully a quarter down in this engagement."

Kaiser sobered. Indeed, that wasn't good. And after the boars and the Mantle, and Sidna's inspiring victory? It was then he noticed he was holding Ulcanean weapons: one tooth-lined club and an axe made from some creature's hip bone. He dropped them.

"Where's my Seriath?"

Caethys pulled away with a smirk. It was a game among the men. Whoever returned Kaiser's blade to him received double pay for the day. The corporal slid it from an Ulcanean's head with a squishy scraping sound.

Back in its owner's hand, Seriath reflected a grimace on Kaiser's face. A scout jogged up and whispered something in Kaiser's ear. His grimace did not improve.

"We have to keep moving. Azurae?" The Sojourner appeared at Kaiser's summons. She looked perfectly unharmed, not even short of breath. "Tibernas's ten-handers will need help with the beast regiment on the eastern slopes. I'm sending a third of our forces to help, and I want you to head up beast slaying. Is that reasonable?"

"Of course, Executor. What can we expect?"

"Enemy royalty is commanding them, so I expect they are elite soldiers, to say nothing of their monsters. Mudboors, they are called. They're tall as men and use weapons, so they must be somewhat intelligent. Kill them, Tibernas's men can handle the infantry." It grated his conscience to lay this task at his lover's feet, but the truth was, she was best suited for it. Her qualifications lent themselves to his passion for her.

"And after we kill them all?"

"Remain with the defenders until Tibernas decides to attack. Dragnos is pushing for the throne room, and we'll need all our forces to deal with his honor guard."

Azurae nodded. Kaiser walked past her, quietly taking a hard squeeze of her hand that said everything he wasn't at liberty to vocalize.

***

Corphian had chosen not to fight yet. It did not interest him to waste his energies on common soldiers. Besides, the battle was being won by increments, and it was entertaining to watch. Like a murderous chess game.

He sat mounted on his rare albino longhound, watching for enemies worthy of his blade, and happened to spot the worthiest. He raised a telescope to examine who might be racing across the abandoned castle walls ahead.

Now why should Tibernas, lord of this land, be running between parapets without any guards and only a knife to defend himself? Alas, his path was across the battlefield and far too high up for Corphian's noble blade.

If he was stupid enough to make himself so vulnerable, he deserved to die like a sick rabbit.

"Boy," he called to his arms bearer, who was barely two years younger than him. He took from the servant the deadliest weapon in his arsenal: a jade flute.

He sent out a sustained note, taking care to aim it in the vicinity of Tibernas. It did not have to be precise. No small amount of sorcery allowed the instrument to convey a beam of sound that would unravel strangely upon impact.

Tibernas was confused to suddenly be enveloped in a strange warbling noise. Stranger still, it didn't seem to harm him, and it quieted as he resumed his run.

But Tibernas had been marked. The noise was on him now, and black-and-orange striped creatures took wing from near and far.

To these creatures, that noise was the most mouth-watering sensation imaginable. These wingjacks were so infamously ravenous that they vomited up previous meals so they could continue eating. For all that, they were lean and fast creatures, seven feet at the head, eight at the tips of their black ears.

Tibernas cursed himself for not being stealthier. Making it across the rampart might be the only thing that could win them this fight.

Like gargoyles, two wingjacks fluttered on either side of him. Tibernas let the first one bite down on his gauntlet; it let him get a clean shot. His hunting knife found the thing's neck, but it was too strong to die quickly.

By now the second creature was trying to latch its jaws onto him, throwing snow about as its bat wings beat to keep balance. It secured a mouthful of Tibernas's hair and pulled him back. With his arm still in the jaws of the other creature and a third wingjack diving in from above, Tibernas was seconds from being pulled apart.

An appropriate occasion for primal magic. He filled his knife with it, making it blaze like lava. He slashed it across the arm biter's eyes, popping either organ like grapes. It kicked itself off the walk while the magnate turned to plunge into the hair biter's chest.

When wingjacks were hungry, they seemed indifferent to even deadly wounds. They wanted only to guzzle blood and gnaw flesh. A foot claw raked Tibernas's chest armor, pulling him down and tearing out a handful of his dreadlocks. It was a painful convenience he was given, and he stabbed the creature through the offending foot.

An amazing collision knocked both combatants into confusion. The third wingjack had not planned out its landing and simply smashed into the delicious-sounding prey. Tibernas couldn't be sure if he was injured or not, but it didn't matter either way. He was in a grapple with a massive specimen and sent stab after stab into its gaunt, furry stomach muscles.

By the time Tibernas had dug out the thing's intestines, the wingjack with the injured foot had strode back in, its own blood streaming from its mouth.

The magnate was not so fortunate this time. His head became lodged between those powerful jaws, and the pressure they exerted on his skull was beyond unbearable. It was impossible to work his knife while his brain was in such duress. This was surely death.

Or it would have been, if one of his bodyguards had not tracked him and leaped in to strike the creature's head off with a scimitar. Tibernas's thoughts came back into focus. He wrenched the disembodied head from his own, snorting the breath stench from his nose.

His eyes focused to find one of his bodyguards from earlier had found him again. He did not look well and was missing an arm which he had haphazardly tied off.

"My lord!" the man gasped, bloodless in his pleas. "We tried to protect you, but we were overrun! Get to the tower, I beseech you! I will hold them off!"

A stream of blood fell from Tibernas's nose as he cupped the man's face.

"A true ten-hander." Tibernas stood, throwing off his dizziness.

"More of a five-hander now, aren't I?" The man laughed through a sudden spike in pain. "Go, my lord!"

Tibernas wasted no more time and sprinted down the path. Wingjacks fluttered in, finding much of Tibernas's sound curse had transmitted to his one-armed defender. The man had no chance and was pulled apart in seconds.

Chapter 60

At the cusp of a great wood, Kaiser could look down on the river and see Ulcanean ships trading spaces. Upriver, the flotsam of Tibernas's sunken navy floated around the ruins of a military dam. It was as if the magnate's defenses were nothing at all.

More distressing than the mayhem behind the ships was the mayhem they were seeding. The Hungerer's reserve infantry was being deployed, and the twisting dragon that was their formation was already slithering far up the mountain.

A cry from the woods indicated that the Ulcanean reserves had stretched up to their position. Truly, it was a massive army to be so close and still be unloading. Men in bone armor were already chugging up the slopes to have a taste of violence.

It was too soon to use the Defender's Mantle again. The honor guard protecting Dragnos would still have to be dealt with.

"We cannot win this," Caethys said, as if reading Kaiser's thoughts. "There's thousands of them. Kaiser, we're not going to make it, my friend."

"Shut up and get the shield bearers up here. We'll draw them up to the wall's defenses above." An arms bearer was called over and presented a wooden box to Kaiser. He opened it to remove Akanis's metal claws and shoved them onto his off hand. "Little victories, right? Win those little victories, Cae."

The corporal did not express much confidence in the way he wheezed through his helm, but he bowed his obeisance and did as he was told.

Sidna took it all in as Kaiser roared the army into action. It wasn't a multitude of enemies she saw coming. It was a river of evil, and it was rising to smear its wickedness over another home whose only offense was existing in the same nation.

Sidna was moderately prayerful. But it wasn't courageous Calphinas she chose to call on today. She had courage enough. Nor did she choose to call on silent Zothre.

Her words went to Kelthron, Lord of Power. It was an act simple folk deemed dangerous, for Kelthron only awarded power to the powerful, who mirrored him.

"Put power in your servant, Kelthron, make me your sword!" she whispered. "Kill through these hands!"

Federal knights with rectangular shields arrayed on the snowy hills. Allied barbarians gathered among them. Wind spirited through the lines, and it made their hands cold.

Ugly enemy soldiers came on in numbers so huge it was sickening to look upon. They fell upon the shield bearers like hungry dogs, their strangely organic weapons smashing greedily to find the meat behind the armor.

***

The Valathonians were dying at an acceptable rate, but Corphian's interest was diminishing. He stretched his back straight and took a breath of the stark winter air.

"Let's put an end to this, I'm getting tired," he voiced to his men behind him. The longhounds with riders snuffled their recognition at the mood.

"Is that wise, my lord?"

"To triumph ahead of schedule? Yes, Captain, it is wise." Corphian produced an axe whose blade was made from the diamond-hard fin of a rare sea creature. His men followed his example and followed his charge into the melee.

Not far away, Azurae emerged with the mainstay of her Sojourners. Across a field of dead, she surveyed the battle of madness. It was grotesque how the great Ulcanean mudboors had been abused and harnessed to mete out their own pain on others.

They were pig-faced, humpbacked brutes with forearms swollen and mottled to resemble swamp logs. Their massive hands could grip only the largest weapons, which they wielded with an eerie absence of sound except the quietest groans. They had been bred, tortured, and hypnotized to know nothing but battle and hibernation. Their appalling piercings and metal tags bespoke their cattle-like existence.

These things were victims as much as enemies. But Azurae did not let the injustice move her. She would be a vessel for harmony, and sometimes that required cold deeds. She coolly signed for the teams to move in.

The fighting ten-handers nearly attacked her people, for their natural armor made them resemble Ulcaneans. Captains bellowed their recognition of the Sojourners, however, and made space for them to have at the great animals that were walloping through their ranks.

Azurae felt dreamlike as she waded through the strange violence, but duty kept her efficient. She signed teams to the various mudboors that were rending the Valathonians and sought a worthy target of her own.

An ensemble of color and commotion that was the enemy commander's charge appealed to her hunger for honor. Kaiser had ordered her to kill beasts. Well, sadists like this riding officer were beast enough for her.

Corphian strode into battle proudly. His longhound Thunderfoot was a delight to ride, for she knew how to defend herself. She would not extend her neck when a simple flick of her armored tail would do. In Corphian's opinion, she was a more savvy fighter than most of his men. Certainly, she boasted more kills.

After riding down a number of ten-handers, Corphian thought it perfectly reasonable to go after the pretty, raven-haired woman that seemed to think she was his equal.

Azurae knew this was a foe to take seriously. He never lost, she could sense that in his flow. He would strike her down and forget her like he had a hundred others if she did not give him full attention. Which would be difficult, seeing as how his longhound demanded attention as well.

The longhound twirled with unexpected grace. Its heavy tail knocked Azurae's spear from her hand, but she snatched it from the air again before it could fly far. This was fortunate, because the jaws came next.

Azurae jammed the spear shaft into its mouth sideways like a bit, and its stinking spittle flecked her face. She had to abandon one hand's grip as Corphian's axe swung down, trying to sever her wrist.

That gave Thunderfoot a signal. It flicked its great neck and threw Azurae onto her side, punching the air from her lungs. But the young Sojourner did not know how to panic, so her armored shin came up in time to absorb the talons that raked over her. She pushed up and punched away another bite before twirling away.

She put a jolt of glittering electricity into her spear head as Corphian rode on again. Her weapon slammed the ground and sent up a geyser of sparks and dust that made Thunderfoot rear back. Azurae burst through the cloud of static and powdered dirt to punch the longhound's throat. Her heel came down on its forehead next, but it endured it surprisingly well. It didn't matter; she had bought herself enough time.

Azurae's next kick ripped the reins from the beast's jaws and knocked it onto its side. Corphian had leapt from the saddle to his feet. Thunderfoot, for all her magnificent fortitude, was rolling her eyes and wagging her bloody tongue, dumbstruck.

"I suppose she is getting a little old," Corphian said. He dropped a heavy strike onto the fallen beast's neck, making no effort at a quick death. The gurgle of his dying beast made him chortle. Azurae knew when she was being provoked. He looked her up and down, thirsty for any response and found none.

Until something like red shimmers skated up the weapon, feeding into Corphian's body. The ferocity of his longhound was his now, a drink of stamina and resilience to shame the sharpest drugs. To this, Azurae just shook her head.

Corphian closed in, high on predator's essence. Azurae would have been ready for any melee attack, but a flick of his offhand sent a chakram spinning toward her chest. She tilted her torso, and it scraped harmlessly across her breastplate.

She was off balance, so Corphian had time for a simple, favored combo: consecutive chops. He crashed down against her defending spear with all the commitment of a starving dog.

The attacks came harder and faster, so she broke away. He did not let up and leaped at her again. This time she managed to push off the attack and throw an elbow across his unguarded face. It didn't even slow him down. A backswing from his axe clipped her shoulder, followed by a punch that spun her back.

But when he pressed this time, her spear was ready for him. It shot forward to meet his oncoming mass and crunched into his armor. A wound, but not a deadly one. Corphian pulled out the spear and tugged her forward, taking a palm to the nose for his audacity. He swung dizzily only to be thwarted by a parry and took another stab to the crack in his armor. It nearly got him this time, but it still wasn't enough to put this mad dog down.

"Kolo! To me!" he hollered. A great head raised up from the melee behind him. A helmed mudboor shoved people out of the way to meet Corphian as quickly as possible. Azurae would have driven the spear home, but if she did not get out of the creature's way, its enormous sword would shear her in half.

She threw herself back as the mudboor's blade came on. It was the size of a small boat's sail, and its iron weight sunk two feet into the dirt where Azurae had just vacated. And over the top of it came Corphian, eager to snatch triumph at any opportunity.

Annoyed at the officer's antics, Azurae pushed him to trip over the buried blade, which was heaved back out by the giant who cycled for another swing. Azurae plucked her chrysm for a little magic, and a stream of dust and snow from the ground trailed her weapon. She shot the streamers of debris into the mudboor's face.

It was brutish, but not stupid. It did not attack wildly, it backed up and tried to clear its vision. It was all the time Azurae needed to engage a technique from Chrasmos that she had not quite mastered.

The giant whirled his head about with renewed eyes. In the corner of his vision was the falling dust of Azurae's ghostwalking steps.

For her, it was a taxing ordeal. Chrasmos could do the technique with no aid, but Azurae had a sheath of wind magic helping her achieve the proper speed. It made her breathless, but the excitement of the technique always saw her through.

The creature's calf muscles suddenly opened to an unseen blade. It took a knee only to lose another gout of hot blood to a thrust to the shoulder that made its sword arm useless. Her vast enemy was an invalid now, so Azurae disengaged the ghostwalk for a coup de grace.

But the axe of Corphian found the creature's skull first. He retrieved the weapon, the dying mudboor's essence scurrying up it to feed the commander's chrysm and body.

Azurae leaped at him, but his strength bloomed like the volume of his laughter. The might of a giant now resided in the human form of

Corphian. Azurae only realized the full scope of his new power when a shove threw her so hard she toppled a dozen fighters.

Throwing the daze from her brain, she found her feet just as Corphian found the giant's seven-foot blade. A man should not have been able to swing that piece as he did, but Azurae had little trouble avoiding the enormous attacks. Others were not so lucky, ripped through by the jagged weapon's heedless course.

***

Tibernas received a dozen confused salutes as he entered the observatory. The guards herein had expected a messenger, perhaps, but not their lord and master.

Just the same, he was here and wasted no time reaching the top story where an array of stone throwers had been kept loaded for bear for many years. They were maintained by the robed eunuch who rose from his stool in his master's presence.

"We are ready," the eunuch announced, guessing his master's intent.

Tibernas walked to the basket of one of the catapult mechanisms. Each was loaded with a clay globe filled with chemical ingots of the most combustible nature. He patted one of the globes.

"It's finally time, old man. Do it."

When one bases his life around an occasion that may never take place, no matter how atrocious, that occasion will evoke some excitement when it arrives. It was exciting enough to bring a grin to the eunuch's withered countenance.

He threw large levers at the base of each weapon and proceeded to pull a length of rope that rotated the gears in the floor. One by one, the throwing arms shuddered and snapped high. A fuse mechanism in each clay globe was plucked as it was thrown from the arm. They left orange sparks drifting behind them as they arced through the sky.

Tibernas went to the window and watched the final moments of the western timberland run out.

"Tethra. Let these ashes sow new life one day," he asked.

***

Some of the massive boulders required five men or more to push over and roll down the slope. Some only required one Cypolonian, who roared his effort to send one oblong specimen barreling down the decline.

The stones rumbled their course into the Ulcanean reserves. They bowled over no small amount of the bone-armored men, but it made little impact on their overall numbers.

A sound resembling an eagle's screech came from above. Tibernas's missiles had arrived, and they streaked toward their wide-spanning destinations calculated to cover the entire woodland.

The first missile exploded in a pillow of fire the size of a mansion. Sticky, slow-burning agents smeared over the trees while red-hot shards seeded more distant fires.

Behemoth bursts of rich flames puffed out in several locations in the snowy timberland. Whirlwinds of glowing debris washed through the forest. The screams of countless Ulcaneans went unheard in the orgy of all-consuming fire.

A second volley from Tibernas's observatory announced its own arrival in a consecutive eruption of colorful blasts that spared nothing. Fire flowed through the wilderness, making dancers of the Ulcaneans drowning in the inferno.

Kaiser's call for a retreat up the mountain was inaudible in all the noise, but his soldiers hardly had to be told. The only Federal to delay was Sidna, who deafly howled praises to Kelthron for this most thorough response to her prayer.

Chapter 61

Corphian's swings were enough to force Azurae into more caution than normal. The fight should have ended by now, but self-preservation demanded she not be too opportunistic.

The blasts on the western side of the mountain distracted Corphian. He looked away for a moment, and it was enough.

Azurae sent a fist of wind magic into the face of the enormous blade, breaking it into large panels of metal. Her fist continued into Corphian's torso wound. Something had burst inside him, and he vomited blood over Azurae's right shoulder. She threw him down to cough the blood from his injured lungs.

Corphian fainted, waking intermittently to watch the battle turn against him. The Sojourners had axed down his great beasts and the ten-handers had scraped together enough spirit to protect their remaining numbers. The Ulcanean battle flags were tipping over, and before long, the war cries gave way to the cries of the injured.

Some delirious moments must have passed, because Corphian found himself suddenly meeting Azurae's stare again.

"Death or capture?" she asked.

He regarded her curiously from his prone position. Was she really giving him a choice? Corphian had dreams far too valuable to sacrifice at the altar of honor. He held up his wrists, a response that did not seem to impress her.

"Tie him up. Tightly," she told a pair of Sojourners.

***

Ferocity had made the day go by quickly. It was dusk by the time Kaiser realized the battle had come to a standstill across most of the mountain. The summit was still held by Valathon, but Dragnos's elite army was camped just out of bowshot of its battered defenses. Scouts prowled the dark interim between camps, delivering messages or dying in the blackness to paranoid defenders.

The western timberlands were still roasting, their boughs crisping away like red and black snow. It put lead in even Kaiser's heart to think of all the human life ended in those far-reaching flames. Tibernas had truly resolved to defend his land in any and all ways. It was doubtful Dragnos had anticipated such astronomical losses.

Still, those were reserves that had burned. The elite army defending Dragnos still had the power to kill everyone on the mountain.

It wasn't often Kaiser dreaded sunrise. But tomorrow, this battle would end as one of the costliest engagements of Kaiser's career.

***

"You are no Valathonian," Tibernas was saying after wounds had been bandaged and troops debriefed. "And the battle is far from won. But if ever my home knew heroes, you are among them."

Azurae was kneeling as Sojourners watched all around her. Tibernas had left the blood on his mace for this event, as per Valathonian custom. As his captains watched, he crossed to the Sojourner and set the weapon on her shoulder.

After the mace had touched her other shoulder, he said, "For your mighty deeds, I inscribe your name in the company of Valathon's honored defenders. Stand and be known forevermore as Azurae the Protectress, friend of my house."

She stood and was gathered back to her people with smiles and slaps on the back. Tibernas however, had grim business he was eager to attend. The bloody mace still in hand, he approached the bound person of Corphian. His wounds had been left untreated, but his own fortitude kept him vigorous enough.

"I'm told Dragnos has forty sons," Tibernas started. "Has he brought any more of his heirs to my mountain?"

"I am not his heir," replied Corphian.

"Poor boy."

"One must best father in combat to inherit his throne. It is tradition."

"And none of you rich little runts have had the guts to take him on yet?" Tibernas snarled.

"We have. All of them, except me. Which is why he keeps me close, he finds me untrustworthy."

"Then Dragnos and I can agree on one thing."

"He is wise to keep me close. I meant to fight him here, on this mountain, when he is at his weakest."

"You mean to betray your father, do you?"

"He knows the rules. He must be ready at all times, and he is. Believe me, I am ready to die because even at his weakest, I cannot be certain I will defeat him. The Hungerer is king of warriors."

"What was your plan?"

"Release me and I will tell you."

It was here Corphian learned Tibernas's patience was onion-skin thin, for the magnate cracked him across the jaw as hard as he could. It was a blow that would kill most men, but Corphian indeed had a measure of his father's might in him. He was thrown to the ground and growled for the damage to his skull.

"You have no leverage with me, boy. You'll either tell me what I want to know, or I feed you your own manhood."

"There's little to tell," he answered smoothly yet meekly. Another blow like the one before might just blind him, considering the blurriness in his vision. "After he fought you, I would pounce, and finish him. I imagined Magnate Tibernas would be able to at least weaken my lord and father."

"Your plan might have just held water, if you weren't stupid enough to be captured. But I've got a Cypolonian on this mountain that will stop at nothing to kill your daddy first." That earned Tibernas a stare.

"Cypolonian? He's here? Kaiser?"

"You think the Apogee would send me troops otherwise? Feh." Tibernas booted the man's spear wound. He showed far more pain than expected. "I'll send word to your da in the morning. If releasing you isn't incentive enough to abandon his attack, you'll be first to die tomorrow."

"Shall we dress his wound, my lord?" asked one of the guards as Tibernas turned away.

"Hell no."

***

The Defender's Mantle was left in the care of the armor bearers, some of whom had enough training in holy magic to recharge its potency for what tomorrow would bring.

There would be no recharging for Kaiser, however. What sleep he did get that night came in ten- to twenty-minute catnaps in between parades of officers and messengers clamoring for his orders.

When Caethys decided night had officially become morning, the sky was still black, except for where the western fires put orange on the low-hanging clouds. It was as good a time as any to speak with Kaiser. Executor he was, but Kaiser was still his friend.

The glassy-eyed warlord did not look like anyone's friend as he hunched over a mess table where men had taken their rations earlier.

"Caethys."

"Kaiser. You're not well, my friend."

"What do you want?"

"Only to know that you have a plan for surviving tomorrow."

"Have I given evidence to the contrary?"

"Our losses have been horrifying."

"Dragnos Cawn is a horrifying man. That is why we're here."

"I recognize what you stand to gain, but—"

"We."

"Pardon?"

"What we stand to gain. I'm not hunting his crown for myself, Caethys. I'm doing this for Kasurai. The country needs soldiers, and tomorrow, all of Ulcanea's soldiers will be ours."

"A fine plan, in theory. But failure could destroy any chance we had against Septunoth."

"So, let's not fail tomorrow."

"I propose an evacuation. Tibernas knows the warrens and woods, and Dragnos is staked here. If Tibernas can be convinced to herd his people south, we could mend our losses and strike at the next opportunity."

"This is the best opportunity we'll ever have, Caethys! He's up there! Right up there, our great enemy!" Kaiser pointed near the summit of the mountain. "Our swords are a small march from his throat."

"Their swords are just as close to our throats. Kaiser, I'm concerned we will all be lost."

"No. I will not let that happen. I will kill Dragnos." Kaiser must have realized how mesmerized he sounded, because Caethys's expression loosened him up. "I want to keep us all alive, Cae. Really I do. But I am forced to ask myself, 'Is the prize worth the sacrifice?'"

Caethys was suddenly happy again to not be a man of authority. The question wasn't one he wanted to answer.

Kaiser answered it himself. "I am sad to admit that the prize is in fact worth it. The means to end the Septunite War and Dragnos's raids. Think of the generations of people we'll save. Isn't that worth it?"

The answer that would not form on Caethys's lips prevented them from opening at all. He only adopted the expression every youth puts on when the bitterness of the world is further revealed. The dying innocence put either man out of any mood to debate further.

Kaiser came forward and gripped Caethys's hand tightly. "I have always demanded everything from you, Caethys. It is not something a friend should do. But I hear you, comrade. I know these are your beloved people. Please, help me accomplish this for them."

Caethys's heart was in his answer, if not in his clammy hand. "For them, for every Kasurite, I will pay this price with you."

***

There were no proper prisons in the area, so the guards threw Corphian into a sheep pen. His armor had been stripped, and he was left barefoot in the freezing mud.

It hadn't been his plan to wait until the sun came up, but his wound was being difficult. To his detriment, the spear wound Azurae had left on him had begun closing up quickly. This was an effect of his lineage.

His fingers probed the lip of his wound. He sucked in a breath and slid them inside. He had been growling the pain of his wound since they incarcerated him, so the guards did not pay him any mind as he conducted his gruesome task.

He took another painful breath. His diaphragm nudged it to the tip of his fingers. He grunted and grasped the object, its smooth design exiting the injury without further damage.

He wiped the jade flute on his breeks. The notes he wished to perform would have to be perfect, so he was careful to clean the blood from every hole. He prepared to ignore the pain the performance would cause him and raised the flute to his lips. The song was played, undetectable to most human ears.

Tibernas rested but could take no sleep. Thoughts of his wife and his sons oppressed him. They would have made it by now. They were as safe as fate would have them.

Not far away, Azurae slept in a pack beside Senlu. Slumber rarely came difficult for her. Her thoughts trafficked at her whim and seldom got away from her: a benefit of her teachings.

But it was she who suddenly awoke with the utmost alarm. She detected hazard in the way the air vibrated on her skin. And there was a sound, wasn't there? A piping of some kind?

If there was, it was quickly beat out by a distant pounding noise. Huge wings crushing the air. They were getting closer. Senlu's sudden waking confirmed it in the way he bristled his tail.

Before she could raise any alarm, a sentry did so for her. He let out a shriek of fright as a wingjack knocked him over with a flap of his leathery folds.

Four of the animals whiffled through the camp, snuffling and blasting snow. Javelins flew for the creatures, but they would not land long enough to allow a proper throw.

Guards, completely unprepared, covered their heads as the things found the sheep pen holding Dragnos's wounded son. The sonic signature he wore made them his slave, so he climbed on the back of one creature.

"Fly, you filthy mongrel!" he yelled into its oversized ear. Words meant nothing to it, but it knew all the same to flee the gathering dangers of Tibernas's camp.

The magnate himself had thrown himself toward the event, but there was nothing he could do. The creatures and their rider were already over the perimeter.

But Corphian's mount was suddenly doubly burdened when a figure leaped from a tower of scaffolding in the moonlight. Azurae's climbing palm claws secured a hold in the wingjack's flesh and brought its flight lower.

Corphian howled like a wolf when her claws sunk into his back.

"You will return to camp with me now," she insisted close to his ear.

Corphian's mind raced. His escape was crumbling, and in moments they would crash into the snowy rocks below.

Loathe to suffer any human presence, the other wingjacks saw an offending specimen in Azurae, who did not bear Corphian's protective sonic aura. One of the flying beasts tailed them and found a mouthful of her shoulder armor. Her claws were pulled from Corphian's back, and he used the opportunity.

He threw his elbow back into Azurae's head. She had been struck four times this way before she realized her hold on the wingjack had given out, and she was plucked off by the pursuing one.

Held by its mouth, she swung her legs together to veer its flight left. The creature collided with a tree in an explosion of bark and snow. Azurae composed her trajectory and skidded some distance from the crash on her feet.

She looked skyward to watch her prey escape. He was laughing against the stars, flying straight for Dragnos's camp. She returned to the magnate, outrage straining against the chains of temperance.

"Forgive me, Lord Tibernas." She bowed her bleeding head. "I could not stop him."

"Forget it." The event seemed to hardly concern him now.

Azurae scolded herself for this. Her first night as Protectress was christened by failure.

Chapter 62

Half-nude, Corphian nevertheless carried himself with all the confidence of his station, wearing the wound under his sternum like a medal of bravery.

He was among the few sons that had the audacity to approach his father when he slept, let alone at all. The bedchamber was a dome of varnished oak that could be assembled when they made camp, and it contained every luxury the Hungerer required. The guards manning the entrance however, halted him.

"Delay me another moment, and I will have you executed," promised the progeny. He was allowed inside, for he made no empty threats.

It was dark, and the concubines lying chain leashed to the walls scented the place with their perfume. Those awake looked upon Corphian fearfully.

His father was already awake; it was obvious by the breathing Corphian could hear in the darkness. There was anger in the breathing as well, because Corphian was not kneeling.

But Corphian was more headstrong than most of his brothers. He stood.

"Father. I come with interesting news."

***

The sound of things hitting the ground the next morning resonated through the camp. Kaiser thought it was perhaps birds that were dropping from the sky. Likely inebriated by the smoke of the burned woods nearby. They struck tables and knocked over small furniture.

But when one specimen rolled into a ditch nearby, Kaiser had to investigate. It was certainly no bird. It was a slimy thing, the fetus of a great insect, large as a cat. It reeked of some preservative.

"Strange weather these Valathonians have," Sidna said nearby. She had picked up one specimen, and it dangled limply in her grasp. Her gaze shifted to the lake beyond the absent forest below. "Say, was that ship there yesterday?"

Kaiser looked to see a new ship had indeed arrived. It was barely visible through the residual smoke, but one could ascertain it was an unorthodox vessel indeed.

It was a long and narrow galleon, bearing a great rack instead of sails. It had been towed in by smaller vessels on chains. On its rack were many huge masses of gray material, like pulpy boulders the size of houses.

The vessels adjacent to it were using their catapults to throw these larval cadavers among their encampment. Kaiser raised a spyglass to his eye and examined the vessels.

"Oh no. Oh no."

"What is it?" Sidna prompted, suddenly matching Kaiser's pallid tone. He began seeking out the little insect corpses and gathering them into his arms. He found a net and began stocking them.

"Okay, Kaiser, I need directions! What am I doing now?" she demanded.

"Everyone, listen good!" Kaiser called out to all. "Gather these vile things quick as you can, and bring them to me! Spread the word! Spread the word!" He turned back to Sidna. "Bring me three horses, my friend. We need to get these things out of here." She obeyed and ran off.

Captains seemed to catch the Executor's panic. They lashed their underlings to harvest the grotesque things and brought them in droves to the horses Sidna had retrieved.

The swarm was visible over the scorched tree line when three bags were stuffed to capacity and loaded on a trio of scouting mares. The husks brimmed in the sacks, giving the light horses a heavy burden.

The Hungerer's vengeance arrived on gossamer wings. These *rippers* were large as goats, and their bodies were yellow except for their claws, which were long and black with the strength of pickaxes. They wasted no time in justifying their namesake.

They fell two or three at a time upon Federals and barbarians. With overdeveloped strength, their claws tore the armor from their victims in pieces. The scent of their dead progeny had made their swarm bloodthirsty beyond measure.

The thickest braid of flying predators came after Kaiser, who monopolized the pheromones that incited this colonial bloodlust. With no time to find a rider, he hopped the first horse and led the three of them galloping frightened out of bounds.

Abandoning camp seemed highly irresponsible but leaving these husks to mark his soldiers for annihilation seemed more so. He rode, trusting himself more than anyone else to survive an escape with this hideous cargo.

The greater part of the swarm followed Kaiser, but scores of the creatures still demanded blood from the camp dwellers.

A wave of havoc washed over the tents; soldiers were being mulched by the rippers, which did not die easily. Sidna found that they could rise up again after a good whack from her service sword. Killing one was a timely ordeal, and time marched on with more soldiers being obliterated every moment.

Caethys, in a noticeable state of calm, knelt next to Sidna. "Sidna, hold them off!" He clutched his oathkey.

She did not have to be told protect her friend and corporal, so she was too happy to crack at the large creatures that buzzed too close.

Caethys had only his own courage in this hour of pandemonium. But it would only save himself if he did not share it. He delved through the barriers of his own chrysm, harvesting untouched magic potential that he would have been too afraid to attempt in less dire instances.

Sidna saw him suddenly convulse, and a jet of blood started from his nose. Even divine magic could be harmful if forced through an unprepared vessel such as the corporal, who was drawing up bucketfuls of power he otherwise could not handle.

But an origami of his own essence angled and channeled the power where it was supposed to go: his oathkey. He held it in his left hand, where a sort of holy plasma zigzagged like wintergreen lightning from his fist. He rose and headed into a mob of his men with Sidna.

He was in agony, with the overload of magic straining the integrity of his body. It defied every lesson he had taken from light mages, but the power that crippled him was marvelous. His own soldierhood had been transformed into energy that jetted into his allies.

The young soldiers around him now shared *his* resolve and poise. Their losses dropped off as men with bolstered courage hit harder and shrugged off injuries even as their armor was ripped open.

It may have saved the camp, Caethys's effort, because the rippers could be fought off now, as their greater number followed Kaiser and his irresistible cargo.

***

Scouts injured from a night of perilous subterfuge had verified to Tibernas that the Hungerer was preparing to march not on his throne tower, but on Kaiser's camp. With his own troops already prepared, Tibernas sent word to all companies to prepare to hit the Hungerer's forces sidelong.

The magnate had hoped to pressure Dragnos between his own army and the wall defenses of his throne tower. But the Hungerer had clearly decided it was best to wipe out a pesky enemy on lower ground before mounting whatever siege he was planning. Tibernas decided he would have done the same, in reversed roles.

For now, the magnate concentrated on the horse beneath him and the soldiers behind him. The pain in his head and muscles he ignored. This would be his strongest day.

***

"Father, the Valathonians approach from the east. Let me handle them." Corphian, in his new armor, looked up to the giant that was his father.

An attendant of Dragnos leaned close to hear the throaty grunt in response. For Dragnos had not been able to speak in human words for years.

"Tibernas does not deserve to lay eyes on the Hungerer's standard," interpreted the attendant. "You have leave to attack the Valathonians." He leaned to hear more, and then added, "Bring the Green Gluttons with you."

"It would be my pleasure, Father." Corphian rode off in his glory then, a new honor heaped upon him.

Chapter 63

"Where the hell did Kaiser go?!" Sidna hollered and stopped herself. It would only sow panic. He vanished into the trees at top speed with a few hundred rippers lusting for his dismemberment. Perhaps he was dead already?

The possibility was not lost on Caethys, weary from his overpowered spell and wanting nothing more than to fall on his belly and forsake consciousness. But he was becoming as concerned as the men. They had been savaged by rippers, their commander had disappeared, and now the most elite fighting force of Ulcanea's royalty was headed down the mountain. The flags of the Hungerer himself flickered like razzing tongues above the trees.

The army was in disarray. The time to act was now. Caethys called over Sidna.

"Please, Sid. Help me." He held up his oathkey. She had been Caethys's close ally long enough to know divine magic figured highly in his strategies, so she had polished her own in support. She clasped their keys together in their hands, and she donated so much of her own power that she succumbed to a deficit of courage and vitality and knelt with a shiver in her muscles.

Caethys, revitalized, helped her to her feet and squeezed her warmly, as if to wring the fear and exhaustion out of her. "Thank you. Thank you, my friend."

When she had the faculties to stand and smile, and not before, Caethys headed to the lines where battle would be joined. Even with Sidna's generous gift of energy, the old phobias of such responsibility put a rattle in his teeth. Nevertheless, he acted.

"Hear me! We must meet this enemy as one!" His voice was as loud as his oathkey was bright. The warriors had benefited from his spells moments before and gave him his deserved attention. "Fall back, and we will form lines behind the river!"

Most of the Federals had known Caethys as a hero of Insomnia, so followed him with trustful enthusiasm. The stubborn barbarians had a predilection for Kaiser's command and didn't know why this youth was hollering orders. But they needed direction and joined the Federals on the other side of the river.

"The bridges, cut them down!" Caethys added as the Ulcanean ranks appeared at the far side of camp. Moments later, the bridges were reduced to scrap wood and floated downriver.

If the Ulcaneans wanted to meet them, they'd have to wade through chest-high water first.

"Good move, Cae," Sidna congratulated him as she took a spot at his side. She was still a bit breathless, but her mind was professionally fooling her body into forgetting its fatigue.

"Shields! Heavy shields to the front!" The corporal's order prompted a phalanx to take shape along the banks. Silvery shields reflected in the winter waters.

"Those boys are going to hit hard," Sidna was saying to Caethys of the horn-helmed enemy champions.

One of them shouted something. This prompted the hundred warriors in the line with him to react. They were powering their weapons. Orange energy burned through their axes, hammers, and swords.

Their primal magic potency did not seem to reflect the strength Caethys knew Kaiser was capable of, but it didn't matter. These men were the most dangerous human force on the mountain.

"Really hard," Sidna corrected.

There were horrible moments to endure before the honor guard would turn their blood-red fury loose on them. Caethys took the opportunity to look at Sidna. He wished he could see her face through her helm.

"Sid. You've changed so much in the last few years." Her good eye tracked him through the hole. "I'm terribly proud of you, you know."

Her gaze switched between him and the oncoming enemies.

***

The march was smooth enough, save for a few wandering scouts who were dealt with quickly. Tibernas had already decided nothing would stop him from defeating Dragnos completely.

Fate took that as a challenge. Because heralded by a stamping noise came an army unlike anything Tibernas had never seen.

A host of plant creatures with four legs. Their arms were so long that they tamped the ground ahead with their scythe-like hands.

Before the Magnate could spell out a command, Azurae had ushered in a squad of Federal volunteers.

"Allow us, Magnate," she asked of Tibernas, who made no objection. She walked down the line of her Federal students. "There is a shell called 'Doubt' over the chrysm. Beginners find holes in this shell through which they can use their magic. Masters have no shell over their chrysm at all."

The Federal troops had their swords sheathed and cupped their hands as if holding something.

"Remember our lessons. The fire is already there. You must see it, and remember that it is a part of you." These were her most promising students among the Federal troops, and they numbered less than thirty. She was charged with teaching them natural magic, but battle kept her classes sparse.

Even so, flames on the wicks of their souls took shape in their palms. Small, novice flames, but the courage that sustained them burned terribly hot.

When the Green Gluttons were a stone's throw from meeting them, the Federals were ready, and they cast their crude bolts of magic fire onto the dirt line Azurae had drawn with her spear. Splotches of sputtering flames made a barricade of weak heat.

It was nothing to the Gluttons, who took their first steps over it, primed to begin the festival of murder. But Azurae and her compatriot Meng occupied either side of the fire line and used their spears to inject their own magic into it.

The smoldering line became a tall blaze, and the first creatures had to stage their assault while being cooked from underneath. Tibernas did not trust the Federals to have the guts to fight flaming monsters and called his ten-handers forward.

The joint fire spell took more out of Azurae than she cared to admit. But having created an advantageous battle line for her allies, she was content to draw off a pair of the Gluttons to dispatch on her own. There was still elemental fire on her weapon, and she managed to fend them off long enough to recover her stamina.

The creatures shoved to be out of the fire, which burned continuously at the will of the Sojourners' magic. It was more brawl than fight, with the sizable creatures wrestling to escape harm while thrashing ten-handers apart.

Then something terrible happened. The creatures at the front seemed to find renewed strength and speed. Tibernas, having brought low one of the creatures with his mace noticed that when a droplet of his blood fell upon the creature's porous skin, it was absorbed. Green Gluttons, it would appear, flew into a rage as they gorged blood.

The Gluttons at the front flailed so fast that they could not be safely approached, so much blood had they consumed. Heavily armored Federals moved up, able to endure the strikes in their full plate. But they could not retaliate quickly enough before being bashed aside.

Tibernas called for spearmen while educated Federals cast their fire spells. Javelins and arrows flew in to deal what damage they could, but Tibernas knew that this ruinous rhythm would spell their doom.

Meng had no such concerns. Fire magic was his preferred sorcery, and in the sacred hunts back in Eurivone he had been known for his defense. The monsters he fought would sup none of his blood. He happily seared and sheared with a blade as fiery as his soul.

Tibernas was never one to stifle laughter when it was appropriate, and laughter was never more appropriate than when one is frightened. Meng's soulful martial arts filled him with mirth, so he put primal fire into his own mace, intent on making the might of Valathon known to these Eurivoneans.

Chapter 64

Caethys managed to keep the fear encapsulating his body out of his mind. He could feel the mortal threads all around him about to be severed by the storm of razors and spittle that surged forth. The Ulcaneans with their glowing weapons reached the river.

Several of them were so obscenely strong they managed to leap the width of the water and smash into the Federal shield lines. Most however slogged through the chest-high waters, their hot weapons bubbling and steaming the stream.

The beginning of the battle would be easy, Sidna knew, but cracking open her fifth skull as it tried to haul itself out of the river, it was beginning to seem tragic. Not that she let it slow her pace.

But bodies accumulated on the Federal bank, and it made a foothold for the Ulcaneans wading in. Blood drifted downstream. It began as Ulcanean, but it soon became Federal.

Caethys concentrated on venting the same morale-boosting aggression Sidna did. Fresh off her elite training, she countered and killed so wonderfully she had assembled a personal pile of corpses. Somehow, even her murderous shrieks were beautiful.

The same sight that cowed thousands of late warriors brought a weird satisfaction to Caethys. Behind the swaying rows of the honor guard came the flags of Dragnos's own caravan. They had survived long enough to find him, which meant all the blood had indeed purchased a chance at victory.

The chance was rapidly slimming. Dragnos's honor guard had delved greedily into their ranks. The Ulcaneans were fresh and supremely skilled, and these tired and demoralized Federals crumpled.

No one would have noticed the single rider from the woods in all the commotion, but the violence he brought was heralded by a mounting buzzing noise. Kaiser, with exhausted horses, rode for the honor guard through camp. In his hand, he still grasped the bait of the rippers. But not for long.

He cast the nets full of insect corpses into the crowd of enemies. It caught and tore on their pointy weapons and armor, spilling the dead creatures in the middle of their ranks. Kaiser dismounted and slapped his horse away, ready to fend off any rippers that would be attracted to the scent on him.

But the swarm was too transfixed by the concentrated aroma among the Ulcaneans. Their tearing claws had turned on their masters, who in tight confines could mount a poor defense, even with their primal magic.

Sidna let a prideful cry carry the news of the Executor's return as he raced to the river. It was not something he liked to do, wade in armor, but he had no choice. The honor guard broke off to take him, seeing his bearing as a leader.

Fortunately, there was one night in Eurivone when Kaiser had gained a brief but advantageous combat lesson. The night Azurae had taught him the fundamentals of river fighting.

The Ulcanean champions came on, and as unlearned fighters oft do in the water, held their weapons too high. Seriath found easy access to the weak points under their arms, where their chest plates could not protect.

He splashed their eyes and tripped them with underwater footwork. When too many came on at once, Kaiser disappeared under the water. His image was difficult to strike, being refracted in the snowy, flowing stream. The stabs of their swords and spears were blunted in the current, and certainly no match for his magnificent Federal armor. He kept low to the river bed and cut their ankles. When they fell, he cut their throats.

In little time he emerged again, happy to receive new breath and to be out of the knifelike coldness of the stream.

With the rippers savaging the honor guard, Caethys saw an opportunity to press the attack. After all, this was the whole reason they were here. It appeared the honor guard had moderately more success at killing these rippers, but they still suffered a perforation in their ranks from the creatures' persistent clawing.

None were more aware than Kaiser that Dragnos was nearing. Finding a berth, he made the connections in his chrysm to the Defender's Mantle and lit off the sum of its empowering energy to his troops. A shimmer came over all of them and faded as quickly, their bodies accelerated to the feeling of aligned emotions.

The armies mingled madly, and a battle spanning the entire Federal camp ensued. Weapons and shields orchestrated the final song of hundreds of lives as lifeblood poured and poured. The rippers peppered the combat with more hazard, killing on either side. With soldiers engaging one another, the rippers' numbers remained threatening.

Shoving his way to the front came Corphian on a new longhound with the last of his wingjacks above. The blast of their wings was enough to keep rippers from attacking their master.

With combat so scattered as it was, it was not difficult for Kaiser to find a path to Corphian. The Ulcanean prince smiled, mirrored on either side by the clownish, hook-toothed grins of the wingjacks perched nearby.

"It all seems rather foolish now, doesn't it?" he asked the Cypolonian.

"Gods, I do love killing nobles," Kaiser admitted quietly to himself.

If Corphian was to impede his march to the Hungerer's throat, Kaiser would gladly fight him and his pets. Nothing would stop him at this point.

That's when shapes over the melee could be seen: that of the massive Green Gluttons. They were marching through a flaming palisade.

"Hark! My Green Gluttons return with the magnate's head!" Corphian jeered, gesturing with his huge axe. "No doubt they lust for one last draught of Federal blood before it is all spilled!"

Tibernas was dead, and Kaiser was alone. No matter how much effect the Defender's Mantle had on them, he and his little army of Federals and barbarians could never resist the Hungerer's ultimate division. And now they had the added burden of these strange plant monsters.

And Azurae. She had been supporting Tibernas when they were attacked . . .

Battle cleared to make way for the disastrous arrival of these tall end-bringers. But there was a vacancy in what passed for eyes in these beasts. And the way their appendages jiggled spurred some hope in Kaiser.

Hope that was sound. The weighty Glutton heads were hauled on the ends of Sojourner spears. Indeed, Azurae, Meng, and their ilk had brought them all down, and wore copious green-yellow blood to illustrate their triumph.

Thrust into a ferocity she rarely indulged, Azurae let a scream worthy of the day's atrocities in the glow of the gate fires. None could have guessed one so invariably composed could produce such a hellish sound.

"That's my girl," Kaiser said with admiration equating her outrage.

Suddenly the fire-weakened palisade exploded. Tibernas and his ten-handers, still alive, had no more patience and crashed through. Kaiser noticed his force was a tenth of what it had been. The Green Gluttons had done their damage.

But reinforcements were something to celebrate, and the Cypolonian would do so with bloodshed. Corphian was absorbed in a tide of protective honor guard and the ten-handers that would attack him, but it was well enough for Kaiser. His prey was deeper in.

The honor guard and strange *mantis priests* launched in to try their exotic weapons on the transgressor. For all their training in the Citadel of Fangs, the honor guard could not endure Kaiser's inscrutable aggression. Each of them died in a state of confusion, their lives of martial excellence halted in a wealth of their own slopping blood.

And Tibernas wouldn't let Kaiser have all the glory. Like an iron fist, his mace made a juicy circuit through the ranks. Tibernas and Kaiser honored Archaic culture with a performance that stretched the bounds of human ability.

Chapter 65

Remembering her rivalry with the young Ulcanean officer, newly dressed in superior armor, Azurae swam her way through to Corphian. He was possessed of a greater wit than before, she could see. Electing to give up his longhound mount, he had taken to hunting Sojourners. If the bodies underneath him were any indication, he had been horribly successful.

In the broken faces at his feet, Azurae could see her myriad comrades forever silenced. He seemed to detect her sudden horror, and he smiled at her.

"Ah, good. You're the one I'm looking for." He crouched. "They cry out for 'teacher' when they die. Are you 'teacher'?"

Azurae knew what stray emotions could do to her. Still, she carefully drank from anger's chalice. It was irresistible, even for her.

"Few of your students show any promise, 'teacher.' But this one . . ." He stood, gripping a black-haired head. "He almost made me worry."

Sweet, modest Meng's sad head hung in his killer's fist. Azurae knew he wouldn't blame her for this. Meng knew the pressures his teacher endured and always volunteered to ease her burdens. She already had his spirit's forgiveness, she knew.

And that's why it hurt.

Upon becoming anointed as a Third Tier Sojourner, Azurae realized "teacher" was a bit of a misnomer. While she passed on knowledge, she learned more now than ever before. A teacher was just a student who has learned *how* to learn.

Corphian had taught her a profound lesson in grief. As a teacher, it would be irresponsible of her not to share the knowledge with him. She widened her stance and smiled back.

***

Winning the berth only feared warriors could earn, Kaiser and Tibernas found themselves before a ring of honor guard. A monstrous sound came from the center, and the honor guard parted like a gate, welcoming them to what they wanted.

Suddenly, there was nothing but empty space between Kaiser and Tibernas and the Hungerer of Ulcanea himself. Dragnos was inviting them to enter the sacred space around him that even his sons were oft forbidden to enter.

Kaiser saw a bestial approximation of Kronin in stature. Dragnos Cawn was a giant, the metal fan on his helm only adding to his height. A set of monstrous antlers protruded from his back like wings, a decoration on the animal skin cloak he suddenly threw off.

His armor was the same metal as Seriath. Pure coroneum, more than most kings would see in two lifetimes. It was fashioned into the most miraculous full plate in Kasurai, to say nothing of his weapon. In his right hand he held something that was at once a battle standard and a rune axe whose blades curved up as a two-tined spear as well.

Tibernas flared his nostrils, into which he poked a dose of his favored drug dust and tossed the bag of it to Kaiser, who could hardly refuse. He rubbed a fingerful on his teeth and gums and savored the blood buzz that followed.

"Did you get your family out, Tibernas?"

"My youngest was wounded. He will not survive."

Kaiser knew the best reply would come from Seriath. And so, his weapon adopted the sharpened light of orange primal magic. A moment of silence was followed by Tibernas's mace illuminating with the strongest primal magic Kaiser had ever known him to muster.

It made the Cypolonian proud. Injuries only make Archaics stronger, it was said. None illustrated that so well as Tibernas. For all his grief now burned at the head of his mace.

"Thank you, Kaiser," he said at last.

"Let's end this, big brother."

Dragnos's contribution was far more astonishing. He became an arcane bonfire, his full plate streaming primal magic in quantities Kaiser and Tibernas combined could not hope to match. The coroneum battle suit did its work well.

But that didn't stop them from moving in. Kaiser wished he'd had some magic left in the Mantle for this fight, but there was none. The fading enchantment would have to carry him through.

Dragnos did a strange thing then, he lowered his weapon, turning his off-hand arm to them. Their weapons came on and were stopped short by swats from his metal fist. Dragnos backed up, dragging his weapon while his hand knocked aside attacks.

He would raise his knee, and the harshest strike from Kaiser could not so much as blemish his shin guard. The rhythm of the battle was quickly deciphered.

"Go for the joints!" Tibernas roared, ducking a half-hearted punch. "The armor's too strong!"

It was a tactic Kaiser quickly adopted. But even the knees and elbows were locked up so securely that they could not be exploited. It was like fighting a vault. And Kaiser realized they were committing a grave mistake. They were fighting with no real plan.

Dragnos seemed to know this. Growing bored in his invincibility, he attacked. A punch to the shoulder dislocated Kaiser's arm. The Cypolonian scampered back, startled at the sudden agony.

Tibernas unwisely stayed engaged, but his vendetta wouldn't stand for less. While Kaiser rammed his shoulder into the dirt trying to re-socket it, Tibernas suffered a ferocious kick to the abdomen.

The Hungerer hit like a monster. Only Tibernas's battle-earned toughness kept his kidney from bursting, but he couldn't say the same for his ribs. Concern for injury was all tucked behind the curtain of his vengeance, and so he kept his focus. As did Kaiser, now, with a shoulder re-socketed and ready to try again.

***

None dared get close to the duel that played out between Azurae and Corphian. Their commitment made every stroke lethal.

Corphian hated her. She was forgiving, that was why she was trying to kill him. He was a rabid dog, and she was putting him down for his sake. Ferocity she had, but almost no hate. He knew what hate felt like, and there was none, even in her screams.

Hadn't he shown her the head of her student? Why wouldn't vengeance be her purpose now? She couldn't possibly be so ridiculously selfless. The world stepped on selfless people.

No, Corphian thought. *She's just a pretentious fool.*

Azurae caught him between thoughts. Her spear found his thigh, and she could feel the tip sink to the bone.

Apparently, he could not. Corphian simply unplugged the wound and crushed her with the blunt side of his axe. The hit threw her onto her stomach where she wanted to vomit for all the pressure her innards had suffered.

A sidelong swing was meant to cleave her head, but a push-up popped her up to let it glide under her. Azurae rose to prove to him that a spear could be effective at close range. He took a pair of hits with the shaft to the injuries she had already given him.

It won her little more than a grunt, for his retaliation came on none the slower in the form of knees that pommeled her stomach. She doubled and immediately wished she hadn't. He didn't have the position to chop, but he did meet her face with the butt of his axe.

She stumbled back, and he stumbled after, wounded yet excited by the prospect of sudden victory. She was nimble enough to evade three would-be mortal strikes, but she collided with the back of a Federal and fell.

Corphian's axe struck her guarding spear and skated down to dig into her leg. Before the pain could distract her, she rolled and scissor-kicked his legs out. He pounced to put his cold, steely fingers around her throat.

Azurae had fewer counterattacks available, for his new armor would not allow his wrists or elbows to be broken. Even so, a variety of her techniques kept unlocking the strangle he wanted desperately to complete.

She ducked under his final attempt and put him in a side chokehold with one arm. His spiked elbow found her stomach again and again. Azurae drank the punishment though, because she had one brewing for him in her other hand.

He pulled away and turned just in time to receive an electric ridge hand across the face. There was a horrible explosion of sparks and smoke and a noise so loud it rang in her ears. When her vision cleared, she saw only his back as he raced away clutching his head.

***

A ripper staked on the end of Sidna's sword was still managing to reach and tear at her shoulder armor while its counterpart succeeded in prying off a hunk of her back plate. Caethys roundhoused the creature on her back and held up his shield. Sidna obliged his gesture by smashing the ripper on her sword against it.

"This is mad, Cae!" she said as they stood back to back, her armor broken and twisted. "We've got to get out of here before we're all killed!"

"No! For the dead and the living, we have to keep fighting!"

"If you say so!" She wished her mind was as made up as it sounded. Dying wouldn't be so bad, but she'd rather die to a Septunite than these savages.

No, this was her moment of triumph against *them*. Damn the wounds whose cold blood was sticky under her broken armor. She was a punisher today, for her brothers, for Gramps and Gran, for Mama and Papa.

They were her pantheon, and their memory put power in her soul and in her oathkey. If Caethys had the time to watch, he would have noticed her necklace magnifying its glow. What he did notice as he fended off his own foes was her fighting skill.

There was a new grace in Sidna's fighting. Oh, she was a brawler forever, to be sure. But confidence had put a connectivity between her attacks. So often she used to lose momentum after landing a blow, but now she was stringing her techniques together. And all with a divine edge to her twin swords that cracked open shield and helm.

***

A crash marked Tibernas's magnificent hit against Dragnos's shoulder armor. But for all the sparks and primal electricity, it amounted to no more than retaliation. Tibernas was kicked again, but this opened Dragnos to Kaiser.

The Cypolonian seized the Hungerer's weapon arm and cranked it. Surprisingly, Dragnos took a knee. Finally, some damage, Kaiser wondered? Tibernas didn't have the patience to wonder and slammed his mace into Dragnos's head.

The Hungerer didn't so much as grunt before swinging Kaiser around to clobber Tibernas off his feet. But Kaiser would not let go. Dragnos dropped an elbow on Kaiser's shoulder, unlocking his grapple, and gave him a good knee to the chest that sent him sprawling with Tibernas.

A conspicuous growl from Kaiser demanded Tibernas's attention. The magnate took Kaiser's arm and locked the elbow. With a jab, he had fixed Kaiser's shoulder that had become dislocated a second time.

"Keep your damn guard up, Kaiser! This son of a bitch killed my boy! He killed my boy!" Tibernas turned his gaze on Dragnos. In a voice suddenly bristling with malice, Tibernas said again, *"You killed my boy!"*

The Red Rapture had taken Tibernas. The crimson rim of his eyes, the exposure of teeth, the bulging facial veins, it was obvious. A fine idea, thought Kaiser. But the Cypolonian's head was not in the right place to follow suit. Fear, overthinking, and injuries old and new all conspired to keep the adrenaline from mustering. A pity, because he would need it to keep up.

A warrior king in a blood frenzy was charging to meet him, but Dragnos looked unimpressed through his gleaming helm. Tibernas's mace swung in so fast it could only be deflected by hand twice. Dragnos raised his weapon for additional defense.

Kaiser flanked, kicking out Dragnos's legs, but the latter had excellent recovery time. The routine worked finally when Dragnos had to hold his weapon to the side for balance. Tibernas's mace collided with the side of his helm.

In that golden moment, damage was rendered on that kingly helmet, a substantial dent. Absorbing the weapon hits that followed, Dragnos pushed himself up and spun. His axe smashed between the magnate's and the Cypolonian's guard three times, shivering their marrow with every assault.

On the last rotation, the haft of Tibernas's mace failed, and the axe passed through.

Even his chest armor could not withstand the Hungerer's attack. The axe penetrated steel, skin, bone, heart. It put Tibernas where Dragnos had always wanted him: on his knees.

The eyes in Tibernas's corpse rested on Kaiser. And in them he found a much-needed strength. An icy boulder of loss scratched its way down through Kaiser's dry windpipe. But it put brimstone in his veins.

The Red Rapture had been achieved at last. Kaiser surged in, backstepping for an instant as Dragnos slashed the air before him. It threw Tibernas's blood in flecks across his face.

The same punch that might have dislocated his shoulder a third time was evaded. Kaiser seized the arm and threw the armored hulk over his own head. He landed in an explosion of powdery snow. Seriath lunged in for the eye-slot of Dragnos's helm.

Dragnos dropped his weapon to grab Seriath's blade in both armored hands. Kaiser put all his weight on the sword. It scraped through the Hungerer's metal fingers to hit something solid inside the helm. This was it, Kaiser knew. It could all end here.

Dragnos roared and trumped Kaiser's strength, removing the sword from his helm and throwing the Cypolonian aside by the arm. Like a starved wolf, Kaiser was at him again before he could retrieve his weapon. Seriath crashed to no effect against his armor until Dragnos shifted aside and punted Kaiser hard in the back.

The Cypolonian lost his sword as he flew into a collapsed house surrounded by dead Ulcaneans. Kaiser fought to rise from the burnt beams and found something of use. Dragnos reclaimed his snowy weapon and moved in to finish the job.

Only to suffer the hardest hit of the duel so far. Kaiser had found a one-man battering ram with a pyramidal point and crashed it into his opponent's chest. Dragnos staggered back and received another hit by an impatient Cypolonian.

Still, the armor remained undamaged. Not even a loosened clasp, nothing to grant Kaiser a chance at the heart inside.

He's invincible in that damn armor, Kaiser thought. With the coroneum both protecting him and amplifying his strength, the battle could only favor Dragnos in the end.

In trying to ignore the pain of his wounds, Kaiser hatched an idea and dropped the ram.

Chapter 66

A mantis priest had watched quite enough of his faithful die to Caethys and Sidna. He strode in to handle things himself. His long, curved blade, worked from some crystalline coral, promised a thousand abrasions with its jagged edge.

Before Caethys could notice him, the priest had already traded enough blows with Sidna to tear a gash through her stomach armor. It did not cut deep but stole her breath. He had claws on his off-hand fist, and he laid into her with a volley of punches.

Caethys was mortified when his claws dragged her helm from her head, thinking he had just seen her decapitated. He kicked his present foe away to help before that nightmare became reality.

Sidna knocked aside the priest's blow to allow Caethys to slice chunks of chitin from his armor. A back slash glanced off the corporal's shield while Sidna dove in for a thrust.

An honor guard wouldn't have it and tackled Sidna. He straddled her, readying to crush her bare head with his morning star. She smashed both sword pommels into his face first, and it was enough to make him roll off to try and recover his blurred sight.

The four fighters traded attacks until Sidna suffered a joint combo by both enemies who seemed adept at cooperative fighting. Her armor absorbed it all, but her knee twisted strangely and she had to fight defensively while the honor guard pressed.

The mantis priest had baited Caethys and pulled him in by his shield. Sidna saw the events before they happened.

The honor guard spared the time to attack Caethys, who was delivered stumbling nearby. The morning star crashed against the corporal's helm hard. Too hard. The spikes pulled the helm off when the honor guard withdrew, revealing the grisly damage.

Caethys was done. The blow had opened a spurting wound on the right side of his hairline. His eyes shut like theater curtains over his vision, and he retired to the snow and dirt.

Sidna expected her sudden outrage to carry her through but facing these two murderers she suddenly felt very weak. She took a stance with Caethys's prone form between her feet. If she was going to die, the least she could do was die near him.

***

Entertained by his enemy's strange decision to disarm himself, Dragnos simply raised his guard when Kaiser came on, fists beaming with primal energy. The Hungerer sensed danger and decided to take no chances.

An axe to Kaiser's shoulder warped the shape of the Defender's Mantle, but it was a hit he chose to take. He scissor-kicked the Hungerer to the ground and grappled with him.

Kaiser's glowing palm went to Dragnos's chest. The Hungerer was Kaiser's better in strength and combat. But what about will?

The coroneum at the Hungerer's chest was only strengthening him because he commanded it to. Kaiser sent his own command into the coroneum.

A duel of wills flickered the color through the metal cuirass. The Hungerer growled to feel Kaiser's soul infiltrate his sacred armor. More distressing was the heat. Kaiser wasn't seeking to weaken him, he was willing the coroneum breastplate to burn.

A hundred different exercises designed by Kronin had prepared Kaiser for this precise task. The Hungerer's will had a massive presence in the armor, but it lost ground by degrees, faster and faster.

Soon, it was a cooking primal heat that served Kaiser and burned Dragnos. The Hungerer howled through his helm as his breastplate became a stove and lit up like lava.

That a man as daunting as Dragnos could scream gave Kaiser enormous morale, but it couldn't stop him from being thrown off in the desperate wrestle. Dragnos rose to his feet, ripping the armor from his body.

His torso was a barrel of scorched muscle, seared by the impromptu furnace that Kaiser had engineered. It should have crippled him, but the Hungerer stood with all the dignity of a charred angel. What could possibly give this man the fortitude to suffer such injury?

And then Kaiser realized it. Just as his own Red Rapture was expiring, Dragnos's was just being enflamed.

***

He wasn't out yet, this Azurae knew. Corphian was as wicked an opponent as any of the slavers that blighted her past, and just as ferocious. She could feel his eyes from somewhere in the battle around her.

And she found those eyes, in a head half-blistered from her attack. His hole-toothed grin disclosed intentions as ugly as his new face.

A slipup would mean her death, but the pressure hardened Azurae's focus. She attacked, and their large weapons skimmed and thwarted.

Corphian wouldn't tire himself needlessly. He moved in to cancel out her range, but something knocked him aside. Senlu, finally finding Azurae again, bowled him over and clamped down on his arm.

Azurae's first instinct was fear for her creature. The time to end this was now, while Senlu had reinforced her. Corphian did not fear the creature in his armor, however, and used the beast as a shield. Azurae attempted a ghostwalk.

"Not this time, woman!" Corphian could see the flaw in her technique; her injured leg muscle had stunted her smoothness. He axed her guarding spear hard enough to throw her down.

Azurae knew the moment was lost.

The axe blade swung to Senlu's middle, where it opened a long cleft. Strange organs spilled from the wound basted in yellow-green hemolymph. Shock and then death loosened Senlu's bite. Corphian threw the corpse aside, having taken what he needed.

Senlu's fury was an exotic draught for the Hungerer's son indeed. Corphian marveled at his new cheetah-like nimbleness as he bounded for Azurae again.

She went on full defense. With Senlu's fighting powers surging through him, Corphian didn't leave a blink between attacks. Azurae had to use the advantage of her natural magic, but needed time, and Corphian would give none. In moments, he would achieve a hit.

So she took one willingly. She chose to take one of his weaker swings and mitigated it between her wrist armor and her chest, where the armor was thickest. She seized his arms and gained valuable moments as he struggled.

By the time Corphian freed his axe, Azurae had readied her volley. She let her spear fall and shot a fistful of lighting into his stomach, then a blast of sunlight to his eyes with a ridge hand strike.

It was her flaming palm that failed to land. Corphian had caught it somehow, and he didn't seem to care how the fire played on his steely hands.

"Was it fun?" he asked. "Your life of pretty little lies?"

He broke her hand with a practiced twist, and the flames went out. Azurae shrieked.

"You can't be just *part* warrior. You either are. Or you *aren't*."

Azurae whisked out a katar with her free hand and shot for his throat, but Senlu's reflexes were still in him. He bashed it away and grabbed her head, smashing it into his armored chest.

She hit the ground, and he stamped all his armored weight onto her stomach. Azurae groaned as her throat filled with bile.

"I've heard tales of Sojourners and your childish ideals." He stamped her stomach again. "Ideals of meekness and peace. And yet you try to be fighters? Don't you know anything?" Another stomp, and another.

Though it had been years since Azurae had tasted defeat, she had not forgotten its sting. Nor had she forgotten how to defy it. With a mouthful of blood, she weakly moved her katar to a gap in his thigh armor. The artery, she knew, was somewhere in there. Just maybe . . .

Her blade sank in. He had allowed it. But she could push it no farther. Her strength had always been in her core, which now housed bleeding internal organs.

Corphian watched as a little of his blood leaked down her impotent blade.

"Today, 'teacher,' I will teach you." His last stomp crushed the consciousness out of her, and her weapon fell away.

His underlings had gathered to watch his ministrations. Corphian pointed to Azurae's crippled form.

"Bring this one."

***

Seriath had to be reclaimed if Kaiser were to have any chance at defeating this berserker. Dragnos's breathing made a fog around his helm, and his burned muscles quivered, daring Kaiser to make a move.

Kaiser dared, darting for the sword. Dragnos smashed Kaiser off course. The only thing saving the Cypolonian from bisection was arraying his bracers against his breastplate, which cracked at the impact.

Dragnos bombarded him further, testing Kaiser's barely adequate guard. On full defense, Kaiser ducked and dodged with what remained of his waning Red Rapture.

But Dragnos could not be demoralized anymore, and Kaiser could not win by defending. He was getting no closer to Seriath.

Turning a block into an elbow against Dragnos's face cost Kaiser a slash to his side. It promised to bleed generously, but he had time to kick the broken upper half of Tibernas's mace up into his hands.

It saved Kaiser's life when the mace caught Dragnos's would-be decapitating blow. Kaiser fell to his back in the snow. The axe came down but Kaiser pulled in his legs to avoid them being severed.

He kicked up over the axe before it was pulled back out of the dirt. Finding his stance, Kaiser smashed Dragnos's belly. It availed him nothing, and the retaliatory elbow made a tooth float freely in the Cypolonian's mouth.

Spitting the bloody mess, Kaiser took another hit to the side, where he could feel a rib lurch out of place. On full defense again, Kaiser could only hope to avoid killing blows. Injuries were unavoidable.

He exposed his side, tempting a third hit. Dragnos graciously accepted, but Kaiser's block locked their weapons.

The death stroke would come if Kaiser did not make a move. The two fighters traded kicks, but only Dragnos's had any effect. The Cypolonian fell into a backward roll and succeeded in landing near Seriath. He kicked it up into his free hand.

"Father!" came the call from Corphian, who smiled through his facial burns. Both fighters looked to see what the Hungerer's son had arranged.

A line of Sojourners, on their knees and heavily wounded. They were held down by the honor guard. Azurae was among them, and Corphian brandished a large axe on the side opposite her.

"An offering of infidel blood, to commemorate your triumph over Valathon!" And with those words, Corphian held high his axe.

Off came the first Sojourner's head, an older woman with brown skin and a shaved scalp. Her death caused an outcry among the rest, who strained against the hands holding them down.

Kaiser's skin felt hotter than it ever had before, a blend of guilt and fury at seeing a broken Azurae loosing tears of woeful rage. She looked at Kaiser with pain in those beautiful turquoise eyes, and the *trust* still inside them.

The adrenaline of imminent loss only made Kaiser more afraid. He was about to lose everything on this cursed, snowy rock. Winning, surviving, it would take nothing less than the sum of Kaiser's martial wisdom.

He rolled the dice and attacked.

The final duel was a dizzying stalemate of complex maneuvers. Kaiser's mind was empty except for a sprawling equation of combat that commanded his muscles. Any more awareness would remind him that he could not win this.

Even a mad dog has the sense to die alone, his guilt told him. *You refused to die without taking thousands of good soldiers with you.*

Kaiser roared the doubt out of his head, but his fury was returned three times over by Dragnos, who put a sudden cleft into his thigh. The butt of his axe drove into Kaiser's wounded side before a back fist threw him into the snow.

Azurae had to look away. Seeing Kaiser injured was more than she could bear. But Corphian gave her more to lament when he lopped the head from another Sojourner. This time a man Azurae knew to be four years younger than she.

Kaiser's mental court-martial was still in session.

You thought you could defeat the Hungerer? What in the Holy Covenant made you think you had that sort of ability? This man has killed Anthromes in battle, you fool! You are leagues beneath him, and now you will pay for your hubris!

"*Die!*" Kaiser pleaded, throwing a hateful combination. Dragnos thwarted them with surplus enthusiasm. Unable to contain his excitement any more, he smashed the weapons from Kaiser's hands. His axe found the Cypolonian's armored shoulder. The pressure from the hit rattled Kaiser to his knees.

Another hit took Kaiser in the chest, this time breaking his chest plate, to say nothing of his injured rib bones.

Corphian beheaded a third Sojourner and cast a cruel glance at Azurae, who was next in line.

"It takes a true warrior to illuminate a false one." He admired the blood droplets on his blade as if they were jewels. He let the blood run into his palm, watched it pool.

The handful of blood went to Azurae's face then, and he smeared it as if to paint her failings on her. She growled through her teeth.

"I illuminate you, *Sojourner*."

Dragnos had his enemy's hair grasped, holding him like a poached animal. Kaiser could not breathe, could not work his muscles against the duress in his lungs. The wounds he had forgotten at his side and thigh had dripped away with his faculties. It had been difficult to move for the last bout, now it was difficult to focus his eyes.

Dragnos began a game of slowly piercing Kaiser's stomach with the pointed tip of his axe. He laughed at how he gushed like a crimson brook.

Remorseful thoughts all blended together. Kaiser felt he was in an iron pot, being stewed in his own sin . . .

Chapter 67

It had been a grim fight. And while the battle for Valathon was clear as glacier water in his mind, it was over.

Kaiser was thankful for that. The cost had been too great. And while he hadn't forgiven himself, he had the praise of that dark day's survivors. Their forgiveness must have been what kept him pushing on.

But how long had it been?

Then the absurdity dawned on him. His hair was wet, but he didn't remember having a bath. He was shaven and cleanly dressed, sitting in a cushy chair. And impossibly, his favorite drink from his Cypolonian days sweated in a crystal tumbler at his fingers. He gave it a sniff. Chilled saberwit. It even had a pinch of vanilla, to his taste.

A fireplace crackled before him in this dim, cozy room he did not recognize.

"Is it too much?" asked a voice. "I was only trying to be hospitable."

Kaiser looked over. It was Izlou, still in the body Kaiser had supplied him, reclined with his own beverage. But hadn't he lost that body to Seremet? Certainly, it hadn't been in such splendid shape. Izlou's hijacked body wore a dark vest of green satin and silver buttons with a white dress shirt underneath it. Dark green pants, tailored to fit and gleaming black boots completed his noble image. He swirled the drink, waiting for a response.

"Izlou?" Kaiser finally tried.

"Obviously."

"I thought you lost that body."

"I did."

"And . . . I don't know this place." Kaiser touched his own maroon coat.

"Of course not, I just whipped it up."

"You 'whipped it up'? What the hell does that mean?" Kaiser's questions made Izlou roll his eyes.

"All right, let me save us a hauntingly boring conversation." Izlou set his drink down and stood. He rolled up his frilly sleeve and puppeteered his hand to speak.

Disturbingly, Kaiser heard his own voice coming from Izlou's flapping fingers.

"How did the battle end?" asked Izlou's hand in Kaiser's voice.

"It's still happening, Kaiser," Izlou answered.

"Am I dead?"

"No, but you're close."

"Where am I now?"

"In a moment of mental stasis I have crafted. Desperate brains, especially injured ones, are very receptive, open to any chance at hope. I simply accepted your mind's squealing invitation."

"Where's Azurae?"

"Hurt, but alive, for the moment."

"Do I have any chance at winning?"

"Yes." Izlou put down his hand, to Kaiser's confused relief. "Now, I'm intimately aware of the brain damage you've sustained in this fight. So, I saved the most obvious question for you to ask yourself."

"What can I do to save her? To save the rest of them?" Kaiser asked, though it seemed redundant. He could feel Izlou's omnipotent gaze *inside his mind*.

Izlou stayed standing and sipped a little of the dark blue wine from the long-stemmed glass. He could indeed see Kaiser's thoughts, and they appeared so distressed that he would likely accept any answer. That was rather how Izlou wanted it.

"We've traded favors for a while now, haven't we? I think I've proven myself reliable enough, no?" asked the well-dressed mage who really wasn't there.

"I suppose." Kaiser knew Izlou was selling something.

"Even if I wasn't, you need me presently. If I don't lend you my magic, you'll die. So will Azurae. Your army will be crushed. Valathon will fall. And the Federal-Archaic alliance will likely lose enough manpower to perish under the Septunites."

Kaiser weighed his options, which might have been easier if he'd had more than one. "With your magic, I'll win?"

"My magic is severely depleted, but it'll be enough to match Dragnos. You see, every time I die, I lose a little bit more of myself. I need to restore my power, and to do that I'll require a number of small services. That will be your end of the deal." Izlou crossed the rugs with all the esteem of an emissary. "Live for a few little favors or die in agony with your friends."

Kaiser stared. He didn't like having to decide in such a state of confusion. He went over the things he knew, knowing full well Izlou could see them.

He was on the verge of dying and failing Kasurai.

Izlou was a renegade servant of the mad goddess Ixolil.

He wanted to hold Azurae again.

Kaiser decided to give voice to his doubts. "Izlou, you were sealed away by holy men. I don't know what catastrophes you caused in the past."

"And you just got thousands of Federals killed by leading them into a battle that you were never supposed to be a part of. Why would you do that, Kaiser? What do you want?" Izlou leered down over him like a judge.

"Power," Kaiser said before his thoughts could disclose it.

"And that's exactly what I'm offering. With a little nudge from me, you can end this day as lord of Ulcanea."

Izlou could see he was losing Kaiser's trust with this sort of talk. His demeanor was resembling some man named *Nytrinion*, Kaiser seemed to think. So he switched up his delivery.

"Don't think you're my only hope, Kaiser. I've vaulted between worlds and escaped danger you can't possibly understand using only my wits. If you choose to let your dreams fester in a world of burning carrion, that's fine by me, but don't you waste another moment of my time."

A painting suddenly illuminated above the fireplace. It was Azurae, standing tall with her spear on a shady autumn day. Kaiser realized then Izlou hadn't been the one to make that happen.

"I get it." Kaiser gripped Izlou's hand. "Help me kill this bastard."

Izlou smiled and held up a hand as if to snap.

"Wait." Kaiser lifted his drink and gulped it down in three huge swallows. He exhaled, savoring the illusory flavors. "All right, go ahead."

Snap.

***

Pain returned; so did the terrible gifts of sight and sound and smell.

Dragnos, his burned muscles taut, still held Kaiser by his hair, still had his axe spikes driving slowly into the Cypolonian's abdominals.

So, Kaiser pulled them out, and was dropped to his feet by an astounded Hungerer.

Not even the Red Rapture could have intoxicated Kaiser like this. Izlou's power had pervaded his physiology. Muscles and bones were frighteningly endowed. It was power, and Kaiser couldn't have resisted it if he tried.

He threw a punch. Not at Dragnos, but at the axe. The mighty weapon, as close to unbreakable as smiths could manage, bent, cracked, and exploded into pieces.

The power in Kaiser was already fading; it was a temporary gift to be sure. He had no weapon, so he made one. He tore a plate from the Defender's Mantle and crossed the torso of Dragnos with it diagonally. The wound erupted with blood.

Kaiser's clawed gauntlet punched into the sheared chest, twisted, and ripped back out with a sputtering heart locked in it.

Adrenaline alone sustained Dragnos as long as it did, long enough to fall to his knees and change his opinion of the Apogee. And long enough to see his own heart crushed in metal claws.

"*You!*" Kaiser pointed with his dripping talons.

The address went to Corphian, poised like an executioner over Azurae, who was still held down by Ulcaneans.

Dragnos fell, to the silent observation of the soldiers of either side that had decided bear witness to history. His attendant, the man who interpreted his animalistic groans, fell at his corpse and wept.

"Stand down," Kaiser demanded in the most blood-chilling tone he'd ever produced.

Corphian had pride that equaled Kaiser's fury. The son of Dragnos did not lower his axe. Only observed.

Neither noticed the quiet that had fallen over the mountain. The battle was quite done, save for the conflict of wills between Corphian who stood, and Kaiser who advanced.

The Cypolonian's eyes were the kind of gold that preceded massacre, but with green low notes that signified Izlou's presence. "I said *stand down*."

A murmur started among the Ulcaneans. The ones that spoke Civilic said things like "dead," "new magnate," and "succeed."

"Shut your mouths!" Corphian said to all around him. This woman had blemished his honor, disfigured his face, brought his strength into question. He had defeated her and would have the glory of her death.

"Last chance. Step away," Kaiser warned, crushing a dead ripper under his boot.

"I know who you are. You have no crown yet, Kaiser of Cypolon. I am Corphian, son of Dragnos Cawn, and my will—"

"Dragnos is *dead*!" Kaiser reminded him, and the primal and sorcerous authority in his words burst Corphian's armor into green flames. The son of Dragnos leaped away, swatting at his arms and torso.

Kaiser was at Azurae's side then, and those restraining her had retreated. They knew the old Law, and how quickly it worked. No one was quite sure what to do, and that included the Cypolonian.

Corphian, extinguished, with steaming shoulder plates, watched how Kaiser raised the foreign woman back on her feet. For all her injuries, she chose to stand straight, if not steady.

Izlou's presence in Kaiser faded, but a tingling on his right wrist alarmed him. A dark green brand took shape, tribal designs twisted to resemble some wispy alien creature. Izlou would have recompense for his kindness today, to be sure. Kaiser had a debt to pay.

He put his hand on Azurae's shoulder. She nodded.

Finding the most prestigious looking honor guard, Kaiser approached. The honor guard slowly removed a helm, a gesture Kaiser was grateful to see.

"Captain," said the Cypolonian. "It was a battle well fought."

"Yes."

"But it's over now, and it is time to rest. Call in all divisions and reestablish camp."

The captain absorbed the details of this regicidal stranger and made little assessment. It was a devotion to laws that had earned him his own rank. It was that same devotion that forced him to see this stranger as his superior. And *lord*.

"Yes, Magnate."

"Mingle Federal and Ulcanean healers, tend to the injured. All soldiers are to be granted equal treatment. Any attempt at sabotage, murder, treachery, or abuse between the soldiers, merits immediate execution, for either side. Do I make myself clear?"

"Perfectly."

Corphian watched. His chance had been lost. He didn't want to register in the Cypolonian's memory, not yet. Now, it was best to withdraw and play loyal. There would be another chance, but not tonight.

He turned and vanished before he could do anything else that would hinder trust from this new Magnate of Ulcanea. He would not be seen again for some time, he had already decided.

"Very good. Dismissed," Kaiser said to the captain. Everyone had carefully listened in on the transaction, unwilling to miss these historic moments. If there was contention to Kaiser's rule, it played out silently.

***

The men had formed a protective ring around Sidna. Seeing her struggle to defend the injured corporal under her had moved them to do as much.

But the skirmishes had become intermittent and finally paused altogether. Whispers among the Ulcaneans made it feel like something unspeakable had happened. They stared confusedly at the Federals now, unsure of what to do.

"What the hell is it? What's going on?" Sidna asked, throat raw from the cold.

"It's done," said one of the Federals, holding one of the frosty spears that was protecting her.

"It's done? We did it?"

"Yes, it's over."

Sidna could have fainted. Her hands seemed to, for the swords fell from them. Her knees became jelly, and she slumped to Caethys's side.

"You hear that, Cae? It's done. We got 'em." She had taken the cowl from another fallen Federal and kept him warm with it. She pulled it up to his unmoving chin. "When you're better, you're going to have a lot of ugly new faces killing Septunites along with you. And me. We'll wait for you."

Sidna didn't even know she was crying until one of her cold tears began freezing on her chin.

"You know I'll wait for you. You can bet on that."

Chapter 68

Shock had a way of passing time. Night fell quickly, and Kaiser had called a meeting of his cosmopolitan officers to the tent that had been Dragnos's hours before. When they arrived, he was surrounded by beautiful women, the last of which he was unlocking from her neck chains. The others had already been released.

"Get some food and a change of clothing. Then go to the healer's tent and help them." He dismissed them. The women had been carefully conditioned to follow orders, he reasoned. And it made him angry to see how they cowered as they left to the incoming dozen or so men of rank.

"All's as you ordered. But the men want loot, sir," said the Ulcanean captain Kaiser had spoken with before.

"Then they'll have to wait until they are among conquered enemies, Braez. We are allies as of today."

"Against whom, my lord? You cannot mean the Septunites. Dragnos had ordered their kind shall not be crossed under any circumstances."

"You were there when the rule of Dragnos expired, Captain. His order is as impotent now as mine is absolute. We have the most powerful army Kasurai has to offer, and its mettle should be tested against a worthy enemy."

"I do not question you, lord. But the men share Dragnos's sentiment toward the Septunites."

"And what sentiment is that?"

"Fear. The only thing Dragnos ever feared was black magic, and the Septunites swim in the stuff."

"Fear? That is why he didn't fight them?" Kaiser grew angry. "Dragnos knew nothing of fear!"

The captains of Ulcanea, Valathon, Federals, and other barbarians, so wary of each other, became suddenly aligned beneath their fuming lord and Executor.

"Yesterday I watched a squadron of sick fourteen-year-olds hold a line against longhounds twice their size! I knew a one-handed man who climbed a canyon wall with me beneath Insomnia to face *thousands* of Septunites! Piss on your fear!"

At that moment, even the pain from Kaiser's bandaged wounds decided to stay quiet. He was in control now and, with Seriath in his belt, knew he could exact obedience from any one of these men.

It was power. And it was his.

"It's all going to take time. But we have the element of surprise now and, with it, the opportunity to land a crippling strike against Septunoth."

"Attack our long-standing trade partners . . . ," said one officer.

"Of course, before they can attack us."

"They would never, our kindness to them has been unparalleled."

"Septunoth extracted protection money from every single province they've invaded, promising a cease-fire only until they were ready to complete the conquest. They're extorting us under the pretense of neutrality until they are strong enough to invade Ulcanea."

"They would entertain such a betrayal?"

"Genocidal demon worshipers? Yes, I should think they would, Captain." Kaiser earned a nervous chuckle from the Ulcaneans who had no doubt suppressed their own pregnant suspicions for years. "Which is why we're going to punish them. There will be a war worthy of Ulcanean strength. And I trust you, Braez, and you others, will not suffer cowardice when you bring this news to your men?"

"No, my lord."

"Nor any insubordination."

"Offenders will be executed, my lord, as per your decree." The answer came from one of the more silent Ulcanean captains, which Kaiser appreciated. He would need more than Braez's cooperation in this.

"Gird yourselves for a real conflict, gentlemen. No more of this pilfering from the weak, it's a waste of our power."

"The Ulcanean nobility will require some convincing, my lord. Likely in the Arena of Kings," Braez informed him.

"I will deal with them. Presently, I want you all to prepare for the assembly of a new expedition west." Kaiser saw his tent flap open. It was a Valathonian captain, arriving late and removing his helm.

It was Taran.

Even Kaiser's new authority softened at the sight of his old comrade. Taran gave Kaiser a knowing smile. The wily old warrior must have a story to tell. He had crossed the breadth of Kasurai from Sudel to earn a high rank serving in Tibernas's snowy kingdom. Perhaps Taran had gotten sick of the heat in the south.

There was no hiding it from the Ulcanean captains, who didn't like how Kaiser seemed to look with favor upon what had been their recent enemy. Realizing this, Kaiser recomposed himself.

"So, make ready," Kaiser said, returning the stare from Taran. "Because in the conflicts to come, you Ulcaneans will earn historic riches and glory like you've never seen . . . as my new *Siegebreakers*."

***

Everyone was paranoid in this mixing of former enemies. Federals and Ulcaneans would not stand within ten feet of one another, nor speak to each other, unless captains forced them to do so.

But after the gargantuan losses of the day on either side, violence had lost its sweetness. It was time to recognize the magnitude of the battle, and it would take more than one peaceful night.

When everyone else was huddling in or around the barracks, Sidna elected to stay awake and seat herself by Caethys's place. They were of too low standing to have a place inside the healer's tent, and the wounded were too many, so they had received their care outside.

Sidna made sure the fire next to him burned warmly, and she had no qualms about stealing enough blankets to ensure he was warm enough. She kept Caethys's oathkey necklace clutched in her grasp, releasing it only when it was time to dab sweat from his brow.

***

Azurae's responsibilities were few tonight. There were few left to which she owed them. Corphian and his troops had killed dozens of her people, so she gave her Sojourners, alive or dead, due respect before striking out for much needed isolation.

She had found where Senlu's body had fallen. Sparing a moment to caress the creature's tough but smooth forehead a final time, she produced a small knife. It was difficult with her broken hand, but from Senlu's torso she harvested a small, whitish egg sac, mercifully undamaged. If there was hope for Senlu's spirit to live on, Azurae would tend to it.

Azurae's body had never been in such disrepair. Even so, she would do the one thing she could to calm her mind when life became unbearable. She found a cold hill in the moonlight and practiced with her spear.

It wasn't an exercise of strength, but of stillness. She moved as slowly as was demanded by her bruised organs, her bleeding muscles, and her cracked bones. But if she were to die someday in this foreign land, she didn't dare miss an opportunity to dance with the universe.

She became aware that Kaiser was watching, so she made her final moves strong. He needed to see something sound. Satisfied she had showed it, she kneeled with her spear and motioned for him to join her.

"Executor."

He kneeled next to her, close enough to share body heat. "Do I look any different? As an Ulcanean lord?"

"Yes, Kaiser. You do look different."

"I have always trained to be a king of killers. But I did not realize I would kill so many good men and women. There is no road to victory, Azurae. There is only a river, and it runs as deep and as red as any found in hell."

"But *you* didn't kill them, did you? And now, with Ulcanea in your hands, we'll save so many more from being sacrificed." She chose her words carefully. This headstrong wolf that was her lover bled from the soul as much as flesh. "What is this?" she asked of the arcane mark on his forearm.

"Ah, that. Just a reminder, that I must get stronger," Kaiser said of Izlou's brand. He laughed a little. "I have to get so much stronger."

"I wonder if Tethra still says that, when innocent people die." Azurae put her forehead on his. "But we can defeat Septunoth now. Remember when we thought we couldn't? Hope is resurrected."

"I know you're right. I won't let this dark triumph stop me." He sighed. "I'm sorry. I'm just . . . very tired."

He took her bandaged hand, the very same one he had cut in Eurivone. He moved it to his lips and kissed it gently. Still, Azurae flinched at the pain. She scolded herself, as she had tried not to.

"I'm sorry. It's not that bad really," she tried.

But it was, to Kaiser at least. The Tireless Butcher tired at last, so thoroughly in fact that he could not stop his eyes from overflowing.

It was a strange sort of honor to take his head and hold it to her chest. The warlord of Kasurai had nothing left, and he had elected to collapse with her.

It was frightening, she thought. Azurae was herself nearing a breakdown and had fallen on Kaiser's shoulders in Insomnia more than once after returning from battle. Now she had to be the strong one. But why should that be such a foreign feeling?

Very well, Kaiser, she thought as she cradled his head. *On dark days, when you cannot glow for the people, I will be here, and I will glow for you.*

End of Book 1

Select Characters

Akanis (uh-KAH-niss) the Guillotine—Assassin and elder in the cult of Thel.
Algus Equilion (AL-guhs ee-QUIL-ee-ehn) —A Potentate of the Federal Apogee.
Breece (BREE-ss)—Friend of Taran.
Caethys (KAY-thiss)—A corporal in the Federal Apogee.
Dragnos Cawn (DRAG-nohs CAWN)—Infamous barbarian lord.
Kaiser (KY-zer)—Comrade to Kronin, also known as the Cypolonian (SY-po-LO-nee-enn).
Kronin (CROW-nin)—A great warrior loyal to Kasurai.
Nytrinion (ny-TRINH-ee-unn)—A Potentate of the Federal Apogee.
Purnon (PER-nun) the Hangman—Inquisitor and saboteur in the cult of Thel.
Seremet (SAER-uh-METT) the Pendulum—Spy and tracker in the cult of Thel.
Sidna (SID-na)—A Federal soldier and comrade to Caethys.
Sinra (SIN-ruh)—Sorceress and commander of Septunite forces in Kasurai.
Taran (TEHR-run)—A warrior among the Siegebreakers.
Tethra (TEH-thruh)—The Paragon of Madon. A powerful holy being protecting the human world from most demons that attempt to sneak in.
Tysis (TY-siss) the Iron Maiden—Herald and defender of the cult of Thel.
Volter (VOHL-ter) the Furnace—Enforcer and priest in the cult of Thel.
Zothre (ZOH-ther)—God of war, fire, lightning, valor, and fury. Member of the Covenant.

Select Glossary

Apogee (AP-uh-jee)—A Kasurite government that breaks from many Archaic traditions in favor of modern practices.

Archaic (ar-KAY-ick)—A "barbarian," a citizen of Kasurai unassociated with the Apogee.

Chrysm (KRIH-zum)—A part of the soul. It is what enables the use of magic.

Coroneum (kuh-ROH-nee-um)—A metal with conductive magical properties.

Evanthea (ev-AN-thee-uh)—Capital city of the Apogee.

Genephim (JENN-uh-FIMH)—Patron spirits of nature.

Kasurai (KAZ-zu-ry)—A nation known for its mighty warriors.

Madon (MAY-DON)—The common name of the world.

Potentate (POH-ten-TAYT)—Leader of the Apogee

Septunite (SEP-tu-nite)—Citizen of the nation of Septunoth (SEP-tu-NAWTH).

Sudel (Soo-DEL)—Territory in southern Kasurai.

Made in the USA
Lexington, KY
10 June 2018